"Come, come, madame. You have lost our wager and now must pay your forfeit,"

the Black Mephisto chided mockingly. His eyes darkened as they roamed over Geneviève's slender figure, coming to rest upon her heaving breasts.

Geneviève glared up at him, momentarily bereft of speech. His very nearness was overpowering her, causing her heart to hammer crazily and her senses to reel. A small pulse worked jerkily at the hollow of her throat, and his eyes fastened on the exposed spot. He reached out to caress her, his hand trailing up her body and coming to rest at her throat.

"I've a mind to see what lies beneath these boyish clothes after all."

Geneviève gasped.

"You cheat!" she cried. "You said you would hold me for ransom!"

"I said I *might*," he corrected. "I've changed my mind. I've decided you're worth far more to me than a chestful of louis d'or. Besides, I thought you wished me to ravish you."

"*Non!* I don't!"

"Don't you?" he inquired softly.

* * * * *

"Rebecca is a master storyteller in the love-and-romance genre, and her colorful historical backgrounds illuminate the pages."

Beverly Hills Courier

"One of the ten _____ ance fiction."

_____ques

Also by Rebecca Brandewyne

And Gold Was Ours
Forever My Love
Love, Cherish Me
No Gentle Love
Rose of Rapture
The Outlaw Hearts

Published by
WARNER BOOKS

Desire in Disguise

Rebecca Brandewyne

WARNER BOOKS

A Warner Communications Company

WARNER BOOKS EDITION

Cover art by Elaine Duillo

Warner Books, Inc.
666 Fifth Avenue
New York, N.Y. 10103

Ⓦ A Warner Communications Company

Printed in the United States of America

First Printing: April, 1987

10 9 8 7 6 5 4

For my special valentine,
Shane Alexander.
Welcome to the world, dear son.
With love.

The Players

Contents

Desire in Disguise

The stage was set; the props were
    placed;
The footlights flickered bright.
The audience watched with bated
    breath
The curtain rise full height.
The horns and harpsicord soon filled
The room with melody,
And then began the play all thought
Would be a tragedy.

From the wings, they entered grandly,
Those two performers of the night,
Those cloaked and mocking masquers,
Who dared change wrong to right.

First one, and then the other, came,
Both bold—and brazen, too,
To harry Madame Guillotine
And cheat her of her due.
They roused the bourgeois' wrath
With their clever deeds of dare.
The French . . . they hunted high and low.
They sought them everywhere—

Black Mephisto and Crimson Witch,
Laughed and deceived all France
And led their would-be captors
A damned elusive dance.

Each knew about the other,
So widespread was their fame,
And as their vanities were pricked,
They played a deadly game.
She seized his ship and plundered it

Of the gold that was its prize.
He, in turn, laid claim to her
And found desire in disguise.

He called her Rouge; she named him Noir.
More than this they did not know.
Even to each other,
Their true selves they dare not show.

Yet while they acted the charade,
She as smuggler, he as spy,
They discovered 'neath the pretense
Something stronger than a lie.
Love caught them in its tangled web,
As surely as a cage,
And imprisoned them with passion
That would only grow with age.

What could they do? What could they do?
They were masquers 'pon a stage,
With the bourgeois French they taunted
Still seeking them in rage.

Oh, love, oh, love, too late had come.
They must finish out the play
And know that at its curtain call,
Their hearts would slip away,
And they might as well surrender
Their heads to France's knife,
For he could not be her husband;
She could not be his wife.

But when the footlights dimmed,
The scene was bright with irony,
For beneath their masks, the actors
        smiled.
The play was farce—not tragedy!

PROLOGUE

The Overture

The High Seas, 1792

Come away with me, Rouge.

Over and over, the low, impassioned words echoed in Geneviève's mind as she gazed at the man sleeping so peacefully beside her, his naked body half covering her own, his corded legs still intertwined with hers, though even the warm, sweet afterglow of their love-making had long since faded.

Her moss-green eyes swept over him tenderly, discovering anew every dear, familiar nuance: the way his jet-black hair, with its wings of silver at the temples, caressed the nape of his neck, the ends of the queue just brushing the powerful muscles that rippled in his bronzed back; the manner in which his sensual lips curved beneath his jet-black mustache, making her long to kiss him hungrily, as she had earlier, gently at first, and then harder as his mouth became more demanding, bruising her own. His left palm still cupped one of her soft, round breasts, and she studied his long, slender fingers quietly, marveling at their strength, their sureness;

his hands were capable of killing a man brutally, as she had seen him do once, or of arousing her lingeringly, knowing those things that pleased her best.

How she loved him, this dark, elusive spy who had come into her life and stolen her heart and soul; and how very strange that it should be so, for she did not even know his name, had never even seen his handsome face, hidden beneath the black silk loo mask he wore always, even when deep in slumber.

Yet, though it might tear her apart emotionally, she was willing to give up everything she possessed—because he had asked her to do so.

Come away with me, Rouge, he had said.

Rouge. Her mouth formed a little half-smile at the thought of the name he had given her because of her fiery copper hair with its dark crimson highlights. What would he say if he knew her true one and the title that went with it? she wondered. Would it be so easy, then, for him to ask Lady Geneviève Angèle Saint-Georges Trevelyan, Countess of Blackheath, to leave her world behind for him? *Non.* She did not think so. Yet she believed he would have asked her all the same, for their lives were empty, meaningless without each other. What were rank and riches compared to that?

Oh, how fervently she wished she really were only the smuggler Rouge, the nobody. That was how Noir, as she called the mysterious spy who was her lover, knew her, though, by now, he must have suspected her background was as aristocratic as she had guessed his own must be. For, whatever else he might be, she recognized that his refined speech and manners belonged to one as highly born as she.

Oh, Noir, Noir! her heart cried out silently to his

sleeping figure in the darkness. *What a tangled web we have woven together with our deceit!*

For one wild moment, Geneviève longed to snatch away her crimson silk loo mask, which had always concealed her beautiful face from him, and reveal her true self to her lover so she would have no secrets remaining from him. But this was not possible. There were too many others whose lives depended upon her keeping her real identity unknown, and because of this, she dared not trust even Noir, the man she loved, with the knowledge of her name.

Come away with me, Rouge.

She bit her lip with anguish as she dwelled once more upon the words. If she did as Noir had asked, she would never be able to return home again. Her leaving would hurt too many: her parents, her brother, her uncle and aunt, and Justin—

Ah, Justin. Would he care if she left him? *Non,* she thought a trifle sadly, wounded by the notion. He would not miss her, would probably even feel relieved to be rid of her. He did not love her, had never loved her, though, for one all-too-fleeting moment, standing at the altar together on their wedding day, Geneviève had thought there might be a chance for them after all.

Cool, arrogant, mocking Justin, her cousin . . . her husband . . . but not the man she loved. *Non,* never that, though he might have been, had he ever stretched out his hand to her, as Noir had done. Perhaps then she would not be lying here aboard the *Black Mephisto* with the spy for whom all of France, eager to collect the reward the Assembly had offered for his capture, was searching.

Geneviève's heart lurched a little at the thought,

knowing there was a price upon her own head as well. Yet, time and again, she and Noir had evaded the French authorities, who would, with a great deal of satisfaction, have seen them both delivered up to Madame Guillotine.

It was a lonely, dangerous game the two of them played, this masquerade, and Geneviève was terribly afraid that, one way or another, it could have no happy ending.

She lay upon the narrow bunk, her lover's arm wrapped around her, and reflected on how they had come to this, two lost souls, each of them trapped in a loveless marriage, finding each other too late, too late. . . . And as always, Geneviève wondered about Noir's wife, who had no interest in him. Did she know her husband was planning to leave her? Would she care? Noir had said she would not, but Geneviève knew Justin's pride at least would be hurt by her own going, as Noir's wife's must be.

Oh, what should she do? What should she do? Geneviève asked herself silently, torn, so very torn. She did not know.

She listened to the stillness of the night, broken only by the plaintive soughing of the wind across the waters, the languid murmur of the ocean beneath the star-filled night sky, the soft whisper of the sea against the bow of the ship as the *Black Mephisto* rose and fell upon the whitecapped waves.

In a little while, Geneviève must go back to her own vessel, the *Crimson Witch*. The sloop would be sailing close behind Noir's schooner, she knew, waiting for her. Her loyal crew, though concerned about her safety, would say nothing about the long hours she had spent with her lover, for the seamen knew how matters stood between the two of them. Still, she had some time left, treasured minutes she would not let slip away, for they were all too few and far between, perilously stolen, deeply cherished.

Once more she let her eyes travel over Noir's shadowed, sleeping form, illuminated only by the hazy silver light of the moon and the stars streaming in through the window of his cabin. She felt her love for him welling up inside of her as though she were a cup running over. How could she bear to part from him, this man who had taken her so savagely yet so tenderly, turning her heart inside out and making her ache, body and soul, with longing for him? She would have nothing—*nothing!*—without him.

Geneviève stretched out one hand to touch him, to reassure herself that he was real, that he was here beside her. She could not give him up; she *would* not!

As though he had read the tumultuous thoughts chasing through her mind, the spy stirred. Instantly his eyelids flew open as, constantly wary and alert even in slumber, he realized she was awake. His smoky eyes sought her green ones reassuringly, and he tightened his grasp upon her, turning to pull her into the circle of his warm embrace.

"You do not sleep, *ma chère*," he observed, his voice low. "Are you so troubled, then?"

"*Oui, oui*," she sighed, anguished. "Oh, Noir, you ask so much of me. To abandon my husband, to forsake my family—"

"I know," he agreed quietly. "I understand how difficult it will be for us. But there is no other way, *chérie*. You know that as well as I do. If we are to make a new life for ourselves together, we must leave behind all we have ever known and begin anew. I did not say 'twould be easy—just that it was the only way.''

"*Oui*, I know.'' Geneviève spoke softly. Then she cried, "Oh, Noir, Noir! Hold me! Hold me close! Never let me go!''

"As if I ever could—or would,'' he replied, pressing her head tightly against his shoulder. "You are mine. *Mine!*'' he muttered fiercely in her ear, his lips kissing the silky strands of her hair. "Do you think I would give you up so easily?''

"*Non*. But—''

"Then shhhhh. Hush. Hush, *ma chère*. Our time together is precious. Do not waste it with words that can only hurt us both!''

So saying, he tilted her lovely, piquant face up to his, brushing her lips with his own, gently at first, for he knew there was still a little time remaining before she must return to her own ship. He would not rush her, not now, not when she was so close to being his forever.

It would not be easy for her to give up all she had ever known for him, but she would, she *must!* Noir could not live without her, could no longer bear to endure his cold, childish wife, when his heart ached with yearning for this woman he called Rouge.

If only he could tell her all he knew! She would not now be filled with such pain and guilt over their illicit relationship. But the time was not yet right, for he did not want to spoil this precious moment. Still, when she learned the truth, her wounds would heal, Noir hoped, and they would be happy together in the end.

What a jewel Rouge was, he thought, a priceless gem beyond compare, with her ruby-red hair, her emerald-green eyes, and her pearly white skin with its faint traces of summer's gold, fading now. She was a prize worth fighting for, worth dying for. He would not let her slip away.

Noir increased his hold on her possessively, feeling her respond with a rising need that matched his own. *Dieu!* How he wanted her, loved her!

His mouth moved on hers, softly, dulcetly, his tongue darting forth to trace lingeringly the tremulous, vulnerable outline of her willing, yielding lips parting eagerly beneath his own. His hands grasped the sides of her face, pulling her closer; his fingers entangled themselves in the tresses of her flaming hair, fingertips running along the velvet ribands that held her crimson mask in place. For a wild instant, he suffered an overwhelming urge to rip the concealing device from her face and to expose his own dark visage to her gaze so there would be no secrets left between them. But he did not, for they had agreed never to remove their masks in each other's presence. Too many lives hinged on Noir's keeping his true identity unknown. He could not trust even Rouge, the woman he loved, with his name, as bitterly as the fact galled him.

Still, each understood the other's caution and fear. The Assembly had very cruel, extremely persuasive means of making a prisoner talk; this way, if one of them were taken captive, the other's real identity could not be torn from the imprisoned one's lips.

Noir's heart leaped to his throat as he thought of Rouge in the vile clutches of Claude Rambouillet, the evil man who had hunted them both relentlessly and sworn to have his revenge upon them for making him look like an idiot before the entire French government, of which he'd once been a high-ranking official. Rouge had had a special grudge against the man, Noir knew, though he did not know why. He knew only that Rouge has desperately wanted Claude dead and that she had killed him herself.

Her daring, her willingness to take action that would have made any other female swoon with terror, was why Noir loved her so. Rouge was his match, his equal in every way that mattered. He would not let her go!

The pressure of his mouth upon hers grew harder, more demanding, as his passion for her swelled like a breaker rushing toward the shore. His tongue shot deeply between her lips, ravaging the satiny smoothness within, searching out every moist, hidden crevice of her mouth. How sweet she tasted, like mingled wine and honey, filling him with intoxication. Still, he made no move to rush her, knowing it took time to fulfill a woman's needs, to bring her to the peak of rapture.

Eagerly Geneviève kissed her lover back, her lips as hungry as his, her tongue intertwining passionately with his own, her teeth nibbling him as his did her. Her mouth was damp and warm with the feel of him, as though it were a wet ember, still smoldering, threatening to burst into flame once more. Then it did, growing hot with desire, her lips and tongue burning as though they were on fire, seared by his urgent kiss. Her head spun, and the pit of her belly shuddered, as though the vessel beneath her had suddenly plunged into the dark, swirling sea; and she felt as though she were drowning, drowning, being swallowed up by him as his mouth went on devouring hers, kissing her forever, it seemed, draining her very soul from her body and then pouring it back in. His lips rained fiery kisses upon her cheeks, her temples, the locks of her long, flowing hair, cascading about them both like a blazing waterfall.

"Love me, Rouge. Love me," Noir whispered huskily in her ear—and more, words of passion Geneviève only half heard, only dimly comprehended.

Her heart beat fast within her breast, hammered in her brain, making her feel dizzy and faint, as though she had drunk far too much of the rich red wine they had shared earlier. But she had not, for she knew she must always keep her wits about her. Even so, they were slipping away, her mind splintering into shards that scattered like ashes in the wind, so she could not think, could only feel, and she was helpless to prevent it. But she did not care.

She was too caught up in the churning backwash of the tide of emotions whirling up to engulf her as once more Noir's lips claimed hers and his hands roamed over her heated flesh, arousing her as only he knew how to do.

As though it had a will of its own, her body molded itself to his; her very bones melted inside of her, turning to quicksilver, so she felt as fluid as a water nymph in his arms. Her skin pressed against his, alive with sensation, tingling with electric shocks that scorched the blood in her veins and made her every nerve feel as though lightning were flashing along its length, igniting her with its intensity.

The tiny pulse at the hollow of her throat fluttered like the wings of a butterfly as Geneviève offered the slender column up to Noir, her head thrown back in exultation, the long, graceful pillar laid bare for his taking. With mingled fear and delight, she felt his mouth travel heatedly down the length of her throat, his teeth sinking gently into her flesh, one steely hand tightening possessively about the swanlike column.

"Mine. You are mine, always mine," he reiterated passionately. "I shall never let you go!"

Geneviève shivered a little at the words, feeling the power that lay coiled within him, as though he were a black jaguar, crouched and ready to spring upon her savagely, tearing her to shreds. She remembered the man he had slain once to save her life, and she marveled that those same hands that had brutally broken the French guard's neck could caress her with such tender fury.

Without her realizing they did so, her fingers crept up to entwine themselves in his shaggy black hair; her arms fastened around his neck to draw him even nearer as his lips slid down her throat to that soft, sensitive place where her nape joined her shoulder. His teeth nibbled her there, sending torrid waves of ecstasy through her body, causing her nipples to harden against his broad, furry chest.

He buried his face in the cloud of her hair, inhaling deeply the fragrant scent of lily perfume she wore always, this flower of France he had plucked from the country's heart.

His palms cupped her breasts, those twin spheres of perfection that had always so enchanted him. Like marble, they were, so pale and creamy, so translucent that Noir could trace the blue veins through which her life's blood flowed. Their rosy tips blushed even pinker as he caressed them, felt them stiffening even more excitedly into taut little peaks as his hands glided across them sensuously, moving in a languid, circular pattern that made them throb with pleasure. As though they were spinning catherine wheels that had been set alight, showers of sparks seemed to radiate from their flaring centers, filling her with anticipation and wanting. Deep in her belly, Geneviève felt a strange, warm fluttering, a maternal instinct that was gradually replaced with an even more primitive longing as Noir's fingers taunted the rigid buds, his thumbs flicking across their tops, teasing them to even greater heights.

Inexorably his mouth began to explore the valley between her breasts, branding the hollow as his own before his lips enveloped one flushed nipple, sucking it, savoring it. His teeth nipped the tiny button gently; his tongue lapped at it, swirling about it in a manner so delicious Geneviève arched against him with yearning, her hands opening wide and tensing, slipping down his back tenaciously, feeling the powerful muscles that bunched and quivered and rippled beneath his bronze skin. Her fingers tightened, dug into his flesh; her nails raked him lightly, enhancing his desire for her. The tip of her breast puckered in his mouth, strained against his lips and teeth and tongue as, on and on, he tormented her, sending her craving for him spiraling out of control, so she was like a wild thing beneath him. Like a conflagration, his mouth sizzled its way across her chest, seeking the other soft mound that blossomed beneath him as a passion flower unfurls its petals to the sun and the rain.

Deep within the dark, secret core of her womanhood, an unbearable ache came to life and began to grow, almost hurting her with its fierceness. Feverishly she clutched Noir to her, longing desperately for him to ease the stabbing pain of wanting that pierced her like a blade.

As though he sensed her urgent need, his hands swept down her belly to her hips, deliberately drifted along her legs and floated over the swells of her calves before moving upward once more and then down yet again, like a tide washing over a beach. A low, animalistic moan emanated from her throat as she writhed wantonly beneath him, spurring him on. At long last, he parted her flanks, his fingers dancing lightly, lazily, along the insides of her thighs, making them tremble.

With a sharp cry of agony, she imprisoned his tantalizing hands, and he laughed huskily with exhilaration before easily he freed them and sought the luscious, swollen folds that curved beneath the dark auburn triangle between her legs. Rhythmically he stroked the warm, wet, tremoring chasm that beckoned to him so enticingly, luring him inside, closing around his probing fingers like the sides of a quaking ravine falling inward. Again and again he thrust into her, fondled the length of her, his fingers sliding in and out of her slick, hot crevice, their rhythm matched by the age-old motion of Geneviève's hands as instinctively she reached down to grasp his hard, pulsing manhood.

Noir caught his breath jerkily at her touch, feeling the sinewy muscles in his belly and loins constrict like a thong stretched tight. Mingled pleasure and pain exploded in his groin, and he did not resist when she guided his bold sword to her waiting sheath.

The tip of his maleness found her, plunged suddenly so deeply into the moist heart of her that she gasped sharply with desire. Then, just as swiftly, he withdrew, only to plummet down into her again and then again. Over and over, he drove into her, faster and faster, until they were both panting raggedly for air. Geneviève's nails ravaged Noir's sweating shoulders, scraped little furrows of blood down his back. But he did not care. He was too caught up in the passionate response she was eliciting from him as her hips arched frantically to meet each forceful lunge of his torso against her own.

Then suddenly she stiffened and began to whimper low in her throat, glorious little moans of fulfillment, as her climax came. Almost simultaneously Noir felt himself burst like a ripe melon within her, spilling his seed. His whole body shuddered uncontrollably with overwhelming delight. He crushed her to him, burying his head in her shoulder, his cries of ecstasy mingling with her own.

Then there was no sound but the rasp of their breathing and the furious thrumming of their hearts, beating in unison against each other before gradually slowing to a steady pace.

After a time, Noir withdrew, pulling Geneviève near, cradling her head upon his shoulder and whispering those vows all lovers make.

"Well, Rouge," he murmured throatily, "will you come away with me or not?"

"*Oui*," she rejoined fervently. "*Oui, mon cher.* I will come."

Then quietly she closed her eyes, scarcely hearing his victorious sigh of satisfaction as her thoughts began to dwell once more on the curious twists of fate that had brought them to this crucial turning point in their lives.

BOOK ONE

Curtain Rising

Chapter One

Paris, France, 1746

Though she was certain she had escaped safely, the young woman lurking in the night shadows of the alley paused and glanced furtively over her shoulder to reassure herself that she was not being followed. By now, no doubt her absence had been discovered and her father's henchmen were in hot pursuit of her. How terrible it would be if they were to overtake her now—when she was so close to her goal! She must not let that happen.

Discerning from the soft glow of the flickering lamps that lined the distant street that the alley was empty save for a scrawny, stray cat, Cherise Béauville slowly exhaled a sigh of relief and leaned against a brick wall for support as she struggled to catch her breath. She had run a long way, too far for one so pale and deathly ill, and the large basket she carried was heavy besides. Still, she did not think for one moment of abandoning it, for it was the reason for her flight. If not for its precious contents, she would gladly have died at her parents' *hôtel* and spared her poor mother further heartache and shame.

But Cherise could not rest easily, knowing the two small bundles of humanity who now slept peacefully in the basket were to be left behind to the mercy of her father, Monsieur le Marquis de la Noye, Gautier Beauville. He would not even acknowledge his granddaughters, much less provide for them as he ought. Instead, he was making plans to send them to a convent, where, deprived of a family's love, they would be reared as orphans.

Cherise could not let that happen!

Her father had thought her delirious with fever as she'd lain in her bedroom, which had become virtually a prison. That was why he had not troubled to lower his voice when he'd explained his scheme to his most trusted hirelings and requested that they make inquiries about a suitable nunnery. But though her eyes had been closed and she'd been racked with chills, Cherise had heard and understood the marquis's plot. After her death, he intended to be rid of the evidence of her downfall.

Upon this realization, one thought had entered her dazed mind, and now she clung to it as a drowning person clings to a piece of driftwood: The twins must not be left with her father; they must go to Nicolas, her lover. Nicolas, whatever his faults, would take care of them, as he'd wanted to take care of her.

How happy she would have been, had not her father interfered. But Nicolas Dupré, the younger son of a younger son, though his blood was as blue and his lineage as impeccable as her own, had not been deemed good enough by the marquis to marry his only daughter.

Cherise bit her lip as she recalled her father's cruel attitude toward their love.

"Why, the man is a fortune hunter, a gambler, and a wastrel. He actually earns his living as an actor—of all things! Have you lost your mind?" Gautier had thundered when Cherise had announced her intention to wed Nicolas 'Not only will you *not* marry him, but you will never see him again, do you understand? I forbid it. Had I known this affair was afoot, I would have put a stop to it at once!" He then had turned to his wife. "I hold you responsible for this, Ophélie," he'd uttered curtly, his eyes hard. "You have once again proved inadequate for your position. *Mon Dieu*, how I curse the day I was saddled with you!"

Stricken and weeping, Ophélie Beauville had retired to her room. Cherise had not given in so easily. That night, after the household had gone to bed, she'd crept from her chamber and run away to join Nicolas.

Since she was underage, she could not marry without her father's consent. But Cherise had not cared. Young and in love, she'd given herself willingly to Nicolas, knowing she was his bride in every respect but name. She'd called herself Madame Dupré, and for a few months, they'd been happy, traveling around the countryside with Nicolas's acting company.

But then Cherise's father had discovered her whereabouts, and his henchmen had come to fetch her home. Though Cherise had fought desperately, she'd been no match for the brutish men. They'd flung her into the marquis's carriage and had driven away without even letting her bid Nicolas goodbye. From then on, she'd been a captive in the Hôtel de la Noye, unable to communicate with her lover, even to tell him what had happened.

What must he have thought when he'd returned to their room at the inn to find her missing, her things gone, and not even a note left behind? That she'd grown tired of him and the life they'd shared together? *Sainte Marie!* Surely it had not been so. *Non,* Nicolas would never have forsaken her; he must have guessed she'd been wrested from him by force.

When she'd discovered she was to bear a child, Cherise had been overjoyed, certain her father would now relent and allow her to wed Nicolas after all. But Gautier had stood firm. Cherise would remain confined to her chamber, and the marquis would continue the pretense of her illness (upon her disappearance, he had fended off inquiries about her by saying she had gone into a decline). No one would be the wiser, and the Beauville household would continue to behave as though the scandalous rumors circulating about Cherise were all so much nonsense.

As she'd waited for the birth of her child, Cherise had appeared outwardly to accept her defeat at her father's hands. But every waking moment, she'd plotted and planned, determined to escape and rejoin Nicolas. She'd done her best to befriend those who'd served as her jailers, and soon her efforts had been rewarded with scraps of information about her lover.

He'd come to Paris, to the Hôtel de la Noye. But when he'd demanded entrance to the townhouse, Gautier had icily turned him away. Undaunted, Nicolas had persisted in trying to see Cherise. But he was young and penniless, lacking the resolve and the funds to make his way in the city. Finally, realizing his suit was hopeless and having used up what little money he'd had, he'd returned to his acting company.

At long last, the twins had been born. Cherise,

who was slender, had had a difficult delivery, for her hips were too narrow to accommodate one child, let alone two. Afterward, her health had not returned, and within a few days, she'd fallen victim to childbed fever. Still, when she'd learned of the marquis's scheme for disposing of the twins, she'd called upon some inner reserve of power and courage and had managed to rise from her bed. Thinking her too sick to escape, Gautier had lessened the precautions he'd taken to secure her, and Cherise had been able to outwit the one guard still on duty outside her door.

Snippets clipped from old newspapers had kept her informed of Nicolas's whereabouts, so she'd known his acting company was providently in Paris. She had only to stay on her feet long enough to reach him.

Now, gathering the last shreds of her strength, she staggered on down the alley to the stage door of the small, out-of-the-way theater where Nicolas was playing.

She had no trouble gaining entrance, as she might have had at a larger, well-known theater. The hands and actors milling about backstage scarcely glanced at her. Painfully Cherise realized those few she knew did not recognize her, she was so changed by her illness.

As there were only three dressing rooms, it did not take her long to locate the one occupied by Nicolas. Gratefully but lovingly she set the heavy basket down and pulled aside the blankets within to gaze at the twins. She was thankful to see that they were still sleeping, their faces sweet and angelic in the candle-light. How her heart ached at the thought of parting from them! But she was failing fast, she knew, and did not have much time left with them in any event.

Reaching into the pocket of her gown, Cherise withdrew the note she had written earlier. Her handwriting was unsteady, but she knew Nicolas would be able to decipher it. Carefully she tucked the letter into the basket. Then she turned to go. How she longed to see Nicolas one last time before she died! But she dare not linger. Even now, her father's hirelings might be on their way here, and she did not want Nicolas hurt by them.

She touched the folds of her lover's cape, which lay over the back of a chair. Then she pressed the soft velvet material to her cheek, inhaling deeply the masculine scent of cologne that clung to the garment. Tears pricked her eyes for all she had known and lost.

"Goodbye, my love," Cherise whispered, her voice choked with emotion. "Goodbye."

Then blindly she made her way back to the stage door and stumbled outside into the dark alley.

Chapter Two

Paris, France, 1764

Nicolas Dupré smiled proudly and brushed a bittersweet tear from his cheek as he watched his two daughters make their curtsies to the largely male audience that had risen to its feet and was now cheering and clapping wildly with admiration and appreciation.

How beautiful the twins, Dominique and Lis-Marie, were. Each was a captivating girl with fiery red hair, moss-green eyes, and milk-white skin; but, together, the two were more than striking—they were breathtaking!

Now eighteen and as yet unwed, they had taken Paris by storm. There was not a man in the house tonight who did not aspire to be the first to taste of their innocence and to become their protector. But Nicolas was not known as *Le Renard*—the Fox—for naught, and he had no intention of seeing his daughters fall prey to the lustful rogues who patronized the theater in search of an evening's amusement or—if a woman were particularly pleasing—a more permanent affair.

Non, the twins were worth far more than that. Had it not been for their proud, arrogant, unyielding grandfather, Gautier Beauville, who had kept Nicolas and his beloved Cherise from marrying, the girls' birth would have been as "respectable" as that of any of the lords and chevaliers who thronged about the twins each night after the play had ended.

Nicolas meant to see that his daughters did not suffer for something that was no fault of their own. They would have the husbands Cherise had dreamed of for them when she'd placed the infants in his care; Nicolas was determined about that. Cherise had given her life so the girls' own lives could be all that hers had not been. Nicolas would not allow that sacrifice to be in vain.

Filled with emotion, he continued to study his daughters as they gathered the roses now being strewn at their feet upon the stage.

Ah, Cherise, he thought, *you would have been as proud of them as I am. I will make sure they have everything you ever hoped for them, I promise. I am older, wiser, and stronger these days. I will not fail you now as I did in my careless youth, this I swear.*

His eyes swept the theater, coming to rest upon two men seated in one of the best boxes. Though they seemed no different from the other cavaliers present that evening, something about them struck a favorable chord with Nicolas. Was not their manner just a trifle more respectful, their demeanor a little more humble than the rest? He recalled their politeness and decorum the few times they had managed to wedge their way through the flock of admirers who crowded the twins' dressing room each night, and he remembered, too, that the girls had not scornfully tossed aside these men's bouquets as they had all the other flowers that arrived daily.

Nicolas smiled to himself. He had taught his daughters well, he reflected. They knew, as he did, how to recognize true gems from paste copies. These men were indeed worth cultivating. They were rich enough, powerful enough, and, more important, independent enough to flout conventions and do as they pleased—without fear of social ruin. If they chose to wed two illegitimate actresses, eyebrows would be raised, but that was all. Few people cared to offend either man.

That one of them was an Englishman gave Nicolas a moment's pause, but then he shrugged. Beggars could not be choosers, and some allowances must be made, after all, if Dominique and Lis-Marie were to have husbands. As breathtaking as the twins were, there was still the stigma of their birth to overcome, no matter how much Nicolas wished it were otherwise.

Should have been otherwise, he thought angrily, silently cursing with a vengeance the now-dead Gautier Beauville, who had not left his granddaughters so much as a centime! How could the old man have been so heartless?

Nicolas had hoped that, with the passing of time, the marquis would mellow and, regretting his cruelty to the two young lovers he'd kept apart, would ask to see the product of their union. But he had not. Instead, he'd remained callously indifferent to his granddaughters and their welfare, pretending he hadn't known of their existence, though Nicolas was certain Gautier's henchmen had discovered the twins' whereabouts and reported it years ago.

Indeed, Nicolas had lived quite furtively for a

time, worried that his children would be wrested from him by force or other foul means. It was only gradually that he'd come to realize the marquis cared nothing for his granddaughters, would not have been the least bit perturbed, in fact, if they had followed their mother to the grave. Instead of filling Nicolas with relief, however, the idea had infuriated him. Though he hadn't wanted the twins to be taken from him, he'd been well aware that Gautier could have given them every luxury and advantage and sheltered them from life's hardships.

Instead, the girls had grown to womanhood with only Nicolas to support them as best he could. Now Dominique and Lis-Marie were following in his footsteps, treading the boards—and with an expertise that awed even him. They were brilliant actresses, as the cheers and applause attested. How he could have used them when he'd been a struggling young actor with a ragamuffin troupe!

Once more he glanced about the theater. It was one of the largest in Paris. Thanks to his cleverness and skill, he had come a long way from the old days, Nicolas mused. Still it was not enough for his daughters.

He sighed. He had hoped Gautier would relent before dying and would at least make some provision for Dominique and Lis-Marie in his will. But he had not.

Stubborn old bastard! Nicolas snorted contemptuously to himself. *Would that we had it all to do over, Gautier, and I were not a green youth as I was when I let you turn me away from your door! Perhaps then my beloved Cherise would still be alive and my daughters would not be working for a living.*

Again tears stung Nicolas's eyes, but, this time, they were for the past and all he had lost. If only he had not been so inexperienced and so easily cowed. The memory strengthened his resolve that Dominique and Lis-Marie should not suffer for his sins.

His eyes returned to the two men in the box. The Englishman, Lord William Trevelyan, Viscount Blackheath, was heir to the earldom of Northchurch, a very old and large estate—and one that was quite wealthy, besides. The Frenchman, Monsieur le Vicomte Port-d'Or, Edouard Saint-Georges, was heir to the county of Château-sur-Mer, also a very old, large, and rich estate.

If Dominique and Lis-Marie should be fortunate enough to marry two such men, their futures would be secure. Nicolas stroked his beard thoughtfully as he considered how best he might bring about such an unlikely occurrence.

Later that evening, to their surprise and delight, his daughters found themselves dining at one of Paris's best supper clubs, escorted by the two men who, earlier, had caught Nicolas's eye. Merrily the girls gazed at each other across the table, communicating silently in that strange manner so unique to twins, each making her preference known to her sister. Then Dominique leaned forward to address the Viscount Blackheath, while Lis-Marie concentrated her efforts on Monsieur le Vicomte Port-d'Or.

A few months later, all of Europe was scandalized by the marriages of two common actresses to two of England's and France's most eligible bachelors. Only Nicolas was not set atwitter by the notorious matches, for, after all, he thought, shrugging and grinning to himself, had he not planned it should be so?

Now he could get on with the business of acquiring his own theater and look forward to the day when, having achieved the ultimate success as an actor, he could dandle his grandchildren on his knee and buy them totally frivolous and forbidden presents, as all grandparents found joy in doing.

Ah, life was indeed grand, was it not? He must set about acquiring some children's costumes at once, Nicolas thought, and get his battered copies of Shakespeare's plays into order for the little ones who were sure to arrive in the future. They would never be actors like himself, of course, but they would have fun dressing up and putting on small, private productions for their parents.

Clapping his hands together with delight at the notion, Nicolas hurried backstage in search of Héloïse, the troupe's seamstress, his mind brimming with ideas and his heart filled with happy expectation.

Chapter Three

Château-sur-Mer, France, 1783

It was known simply as *Château-sur-Mer*—Castle-on-the-Sea—and it was aptly named, for it perched high upon a prominent cliff, not far from Brest in the west of France, overlooking the place where the waters of *La Manche*—the English Channel—mingled with those of the Bay of Biscay. The province itself was called *Finistère*—Land's End—and sometimes when Ives-Pierre Fourneaux stood upon the jagged point, he felt as though he stood upon the edge of the world.

This is what it must have been like at the beginning of time, he would think, staring down at the vast expanse of sheer crystalline rock falling away from the earth to the beach below, where the often rough and stormy waves swept in upon the sand as though to swallow it up, battering the scattered boulders that, having crumbled down from above, now protruded upward like crooked stalagmites along the wild coast.

The château itself, like the aerie upon which it sat looming over the land, was very old, having been built in the fourteenth century. Though, over the years, various more modern wings had been added here and there, creating a strange mixture of architectural styles, its antecedents as a fortress were still evident in the crenelated ramparts bordering the ancient walkways that joined the flying turrets topping each corner of the main portion of the edifice.

Here, the lords of yesteryear had stood, as Ives-Pierre did now, watching the seas beyond, for the counts of Château-sur-Mer had always been drawn by the siren's song of the ocean, and many a painting of a pirate ancestor hung in the long portrait gallery of the castle.

These men might have been less than scrupulous, but it was their courage and daring that had made possible the considerable fortune of the Saint-Georges family, to whom the château belonged and whom Ives-Pierre had served faithfully since his youth. He had been and would always be the right-hand man of Monsieur le Comte, Edouard Saint-Georges. A jack-of-all-trades, Ives-Pierre undertook any and all tasks the comte set before him, but his primary concern was the safety of the Saint-Georges family, and it was he who had trained both the comte and his children in the art of fencing.

There had been many a duel fought at the fortress during its long history, Ives-Pierre recollected, but none more entertaining, he was willing to wager, than the one that now captured his attention as, hearing a commotion from the bailey far below, he turned from his contemplation of the sea, a smile of amusement splitting his weatherbeaten face as his eyes fell upon his two seven-year-old charges.

Sunshine, bright and golden, streamed down through the branches of the green-leaved trees that towered above the open square, dappling the ancient paving blocks of the courtyard with gay patches of light and turning the copper hair of its principal occupants to fire.

Like twin flames, the two young opponents moved with supple grace upon booted feet, advancing and retreating like partners executing the intricate steps of a dance, honed silver rapiers thrusting in high carte and parrying in low tierce. Again and again, the gleaming blades clashed, metal striking metal, resounding in the slight summer breeze that rustled the branches of the old, gnarled oaks ever so gently.

"Touché," one of the costume-clad figures said with a grin, causing his mock foe to pause, frown, and stamp one dainty foot with disapproval.

"You don't have any more lines in this scene, Vachel," Geneviève Saint-Georges reprimanded her twin brother tartly. "In fact, you're supposed to die. Now you've spoiled the duel, and we shall have to begin again."

"Sorry," Vachel apologized, though it was obvious he was not in the least chastened by his sister's strictures. "But that was such a neat piece of work I couldn't help myself, Genette. I'm still not quite sure how you slipped past my guard for the hit."

"Well, you'd know if you paid more attention during our lessons with Ives-Pierre," Geneviève retorted crossly. "Don't you remember? He's shown us that tactic more than once. Now do stop wasting time, Vachel. 'Twill be dark soon. We won't be able to practice much longer, and I want the play to be perfect for Papa Nick, Maman, and Tante Dominique. You know how upset our grandfather gets when a production is not performed correctly. Now . . . where were we? *Mais, oui*. You are Tybalt, nephew of Lady Capulet, and you have just slain Mercutio and are now engaged in a battle to the death with Romeo Montague, your archenemy.''

"Oh, all right." Vachel capitulated good-naturedly. "But you must promise to show me that trick later."

"Of course. Now do let us proceed," Geneviève insisted, then turned to a third youngster, who stood silently nearby. "Watch closely, Armand," she instructed the boy, who had the role of Romeo, "for I want everything to look as real as possible, and there is something wrong with your attack in this scene."

He nodded, and once more the twins commenced their swordplay. This time, Vachel performed his part properly, and when Geneviève lunged forward for the kill, the buttoned tip of her foil appearing to stab him through the heart, he obligingly dropped his weapon and passionately clasped his hands to his breast, his face a contorted mask of pain as he staggered a few steps, then fell in a crumpled heap upon the stone paving blocks.

"Well done!" Geneviève cried, applauding enthusiastically, as quick with her praise as she had been with her admonition earlier.

"Do you really think so? Frankly I found it rather comical. Don't you believe it was just a trifle melodramatic?" a jaded voice, tinged with amusement, drawled from the edge of the square.

Geneviève pivoted to confront the intruder.

"Naturally *you* would think so, Justin." Insulted at having her directing criticized, she spoke huffily to her older cousin, who was always teasing her, since, much to her discomfiture, she invariably rose to the bait. Still, Geneviève could not bring herself to stifle her unruly tongue. "You've not one shred of thespian talent," she went on. "Tante Dominique says so. You're just angry because we wouldn't allow you to be in the play."

"Really. How ridiculous, Genette," the eighteen-year-old Justin Trevelyan replied, maddeningly unruffled, as meticulously he brushed a piece of imaginary lint from his sleeve. "As though I were interested in the charades of children. Despite what you and Maman may think, I am not without ability. I was merely trying to give you and Vachel a few pointers."

"Well, we don't need your help—so there!" Geneviève shot back, waving her rapier threateningly. "And if you interfere again, I shall tell Tante Dominique you were out here sneaking a cheroot. *Non*, 'tis no use pretending you weren't, for you still smell of smoke, and you know Tante Dominique despises cigars even more than she does snuff!"

"What a spiteful little termagant you are, Genette," Justin noted coolly, deliberately removing another thin cheroot from his jacket. He tapped one end firmly against the small, solid gold box of friction matches he took from his waistcoat, then lit the cigar and inhaled deeply. "It seems to me that instead of *Romeo and Juliet*, it would be more appropriate for you to be rehearsing *The Taming of the Shrew*."

"Oh, you—you—" Geneviève sputtered indignantly. "If you don't get out of here, I'll—I'll run you through!"

She stepped forward purposefully, her blade held at the ready. To her fury, Justin only laughed.

" 'Come, come, you wasp; i' faith, you are too angry,' " he quoted mockingly, enraging her further.

She advanced upon him until the tip of her foil pressed against his chest.

" 'If I be waspish, best beware my sting,' " she warned.

"My dear," Justin stated firmly, smiling as he gazed down at her diminutive form and casually brushed the weapon aside, "the day I can't outmatch you is the day I shall hang up my sword for good and concede your every demand. However"—he smirked, his voice smug—"as I recall, it was Petruchio who did the taming, was it not?"

"You flatter yourself, monsieur," Geneviève rejoined haughtily, tossing her head and eyeing him as though he were beneath her, "to think I would ever agree to be your Katherine."

"What makes you believe, Genette, that I would ever ask you?" her cousin inquired, raising one eyebrow as though quite astonished by the notion.

"Oh!" she exclaimed childishly, dropping her lofty pose. "You know it has been arranged these many years past that we should wed, Justin—much to my disgust," she added, grimacing.

"Perhaps, but 'twas none of my doing, I can assure you. I'm of no mind to be shackled by such a shrew. Run along now; there's a good girl. Your Romeo awaits, poor devil. Egad! I pity the man unfortunate enough to be married to the likes of you!"

With that parting remark, and still laughing, Justin turned on his heel and left the courtyard. Geneviève watched him go, sparks flashing in her eyes. The arrogant boor! How she hated him! Someday he would rue the hour he had taunted her so—and before Armand

Charbonne, too, whom she adored. *Oui*. Someday she would make Justin Trevelyan pay. She would show him she could best him—at dueling, acting, or anything else!

Twirling her blade with a flourish, she lunged at her cousin's retreating back, delivering in her mind a most satisfactory coup de grace.

BOOK TWO

The Masquers

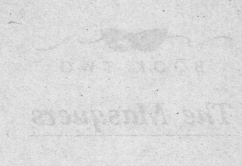

Chapter Four

Her heart beating wildly in her breast, Geneviève Saint-Georges stared at the pots of paint and powder arrayed on the dressing table before her. Then slowly she reached for a flacon of walnut stain, her hand trembling with fear.

This was real.

The thought pierced her anew with panic. Always before, it had been a pretense, an amusing pastime to while away the hours and to entertain Papa and especially Maman, who so loved the stage. But this—this was real. Today, Geneviève must give the performance of her life, and she must give it knowing that her very life depended upon how well she played her part.

Oh, if only Vachel, her twin brother, were here to help her, to rehearse her lines and help direct her movements, as he had always done in the past. But he was not. Well, thank God for it! There was a chance yet that he was still safe . . . that he had been warned in

41

time, if the letter Geneviève had managed to smuggle out of the heavily guarded townhouse had reached him. Oh, surely it had! Surely she would know in her heart if something had happened to her beloved brother.

She had always known in the past, for there was between them that strange, special bond only twins share. *Oui*. Vachel was safe. The terrible evil Claude Rambouillet had perpetrated upon the noble house of Saint-Georges had not yet harmed Geneviève's brother, though, like oozing slime, it had rendered foul all else it had touched.

What had once been the happiest of households was now a tomb of fear and despair. Outside, even now, Geneviève knew death lurked, waiting to darken forever the small light of hope that still struggled to survive within.

You will regret your denial of me, Citoyenne Saint-Georges—and bitterly, I promise you!

The words of Claude Rambouillet pounded like harsh, discordant notes in Geneviève's heart and mind, in macabre harmony to the melody of terror that reverberated like a taut lute string through her being.

The bourgeois pig!

Tears started in Geneviève's eyes, and a lump rose in her throat, threatening to choke her. Sudden fury at her helplessness welled up in her breast, and before she could stop herself, her palm swept out over the dressing table, knocking several of the glass jars and bottles to the floor, shattering them. Then, sobbing uncontrollably, she buried her face in her hands, her shoulders shaking with grief and rage at her impotence.

Claude Rambouillet had kept his promise. Geneviève's regret was bitter—very bitter indeed. Her refusal to become the mistress of the son of a common baker would cost Papa and Maman their lives. The girl knew, with certainty, that this was true.

Any day now—perhaps even today—Claude would come with his henchmen to arrest Geneviève and her parents. After a mockery of a trial, they would forfeit their heads to cruel Madame Guillotine, who, without mercy, claimed new victims hourly, as Armand Charbonne, Geneviève's childhood friend, had been claimed just yesterday afternoon. How she had wept over that!

Even if somehow, some way, the charade Maman had devised succeeded and Geneviève managed to escape from the gruesome fate that awaited her, her parents' lives must still be sacrificed.

"'Tis the only way, *ma petite*," Maman had said with a brave smile. "Three is too large a cast for this play, I'm afraid. It is written for a single performer only. To add two more actors would turn this tragedy into pathos. Alone, you have a chance at least.

"Don't you see, Genette? The charade's success depends on all appearing to go on as usual. As long as Papa and I are here, Claude may not suspect. We will say you are ill and that that is why you cannot receive him. We will buy time for you, *ma petite*, as much time as we can, precious hours—perhaps even days—that may save your life!"

"At the cost of your own! *Non!* I won't do it!" Geneviève had declared fervently. Then, more calmly, she'd offered, "I will stay and become the—the paramour of Claude Rambouillet."

"*Non*, Genette," Maman had stated softly but firmly. "Papa and I would rather die than see you fall into the clutches of that *canaille*. Besides, there is no guarantee Claude won't arrest Papa and me anyway, even if you agree to accept his disgusting proposition. There is nothing more to discuss," Maman had insisted resolutely when Geneviève again would have protested. "Papa and I have already decided. 'Tis the only way, *ma petite*."

"*Non*," Geneviève now sobbed aloud to herself in her chamber. "*Non*."

But it was as Maman had told her. There was no other way. She must go on. The stage was set, and her audience was waiting.

Forcing her red-rimmed eyes to dry, the girl bent to retrieve the broken glass upon the floor. For a moment, she gazed sorrowfully at the splintered shards, for they were symbols of what her life had become. Then, taking a deep breath, she unstoppered the flacon of walnut stain and resignedly began to pour it upon her hair, silently cursing the dark day Claude Rambouillet had determined to make her his mistress.

Before the rebellion, the son of a bourgeois merchant would never have dreamed of affronting Geneviève in such a manner, though he'd watched her in the marketplace and coveted her with a passion that eventually had become an obsession with him. Though her mother had at one time been a mere actress, Geneviève herself was an aristocrat and not for the likes of a common baker's son.

But the revolution had changed everything, turning

the French social order upside down to raise Claude and his ilk to hitherto unattainable heights. Filled with ambitions far above his station in life, he'd eagerly seized the opportunity to better himself that had been thrust so unexpectedly into his grasp; and through guile and cunning, he'd risen rapidly in the ranks of the Assembly, the French government, now run by the rabble who had overthrown France's monarchy and imprisoned her king.

He soon had discovered, however, that position and wealth were not enough. He must have Geneviève Saint-Georges as well; she would be his crowning jewel, a priceless, fiery ruby beyond compare. Although, of course, she was no longer suitable as a wife due to her changed status in life, she would, Claude had decided, make him an excellent mistress.

Though she'd quivered inwardly with fear, knowing the power he now wielded and the number of persons he'd sent to Madame Guillotine, Geneviève nevertheless had rejected Claude's overtures. How dare he insult her in such a manner—she, who was the daughter of a comte? She would rather die than consent to such an arrangement.

Claude Rambouillet reminded her of a cold, slithering reptile, and the thought of his possessing her made her physically ill.

Tall and thin to the point of being emaciated, Claude's nearly transparent skin was stretched so tightly over his skeletal frame that he appeared like a walking cadaver. His joints were all sharp angles jutting out disproportionately from his body, and his arms were so long the sleeves of the shabby coats he wore, despite his recent riches, were always too short and made him look like a scarecrow. As though this weren't enough, he disdained wigs, slicking back his own lank, dark brown hair with oil of Macassar and tying it in a stringy queue at his nape.

But it was his beady black eyes that truly had made Geneviève's flesh crawl on the day of his proposal, for they'd stared at her unblinkingly, the way a snake stares at its victim before it strikes. Geneviève had expected at any moment to see Claude's tongue dart out from between his grim lips; and when, shocked and horrified by his intentions toward her, she'd repulsed him, he'd actually hissed at her.

"You dare to deny me, Citoyenne Saint-Georges?" he'd sneered, reminding her threateningly of her fallen status in life.

"I—I must, monsieur," Geneviève had stammered, afraid. "I—I would be disgraced, ruined! You know I would be! Besides, I am engaged to be married, and have been since birth, to my cousin, Monsieur le Vicomte Blackheath, Justin Trevelyan. Indeed, had I not begged Papa for one season in Paris, I would already be wed," Geneviève had lied, for her cousin infuriated her, and she'd planned to persuade her father to allow her instead to marry Armand Charbonne, with whom she'd fallen in love.

"Betrothed to a half-English dog!" Claude had spat. "Yet that has not prevented you from encouraging the attentions of every nobleman in France who has flocked to this house to pay court to you!"

"But—but, monsieur! Such flirtations mean nothing, I assure you. Everyone knows I am to marry my cousin," Geneviève had insisted.

"And I say you shall not, Citoyenne Saint-Georges. I will give you a fortnight to reconsider your decision, after which time, you will write to *le vicomte,* breaking off your engagement. Then you will become my whore." Claude had jeered the last word with relish.

"But—but, monsieur!" Geneviève had once more protested. "I cannot! You are no gentleman even to suggest such a thing, knowing the shame it would bring to me and my family."

"You and your family will be worse than dishonored if you don't agree to accept my proposition," Claude had snarled. "For I warn you: you will regret your denial of me, Citoyenne Saint-Georges—and bitterly, I promise you!"

With that parting shot, Claude had grabbed his hat, gloves, and walking stick, and had stormed out of the townhouse, slamming the door behind him.

Since then, Geneviève and her parents had lived in perpetual fear, watched closely and constantly by Claude and his henchmen. Every day, he had come to repeat his repugnant offer, and every day, Geneviève had put him off, claiming she needed more time to think. All the while, desperately, she and her parents had tried to devise some scheme to thwart Claude's horrendous plans for them.

Three days ago, Maman had suggested the charade.

"I believe even Papa Nick would applaud my cleverness," Lis-Marie had announced when she'd outlined her plan.

Papa Nick, as his two daughters had always called him, was notorious in France for his handsome looks, his wild escapades, and his wicked temper (he was rumored to have flogged a colleague for muffing his lines). Geneviève admired him greatly and had often longed to star in one of his productions, despite his anger at the notion.

"Non!" he'd refused adamantly when once she'd ventured to propose the idea to him. "I did not work so hard to get my daughters off the stage, only to have my grandchildren return to it!"

Geneviève knew the story of her mother's past by heart, but she never tired of hearing it: how, at the age of eighteen, under Papa Nick's direction, Maman and Tante Dominique had made their debut upon a Parisian stage and had taken all of France by storm; how the cavaliers, filled with desire for and less-than-honorable intentions toward the twins whose beauty must have rivaled Helen of Troy's, had flocked to the theater night after night, hoping to be successful in their pursuit of the girls. But Papa Nick had remained unmoved. The twins were too extraordinary to throw themselves away as paramours—no matter how rich or noble their would-be protectors. In spite of their less-than-impeccable background, Papa Nick's daughters would marry— and marry well.

And so they had, Lis-Marie garnering the affection of Monsieur le Comte de Château-sur-Mer, Edouard Saint-Georges, and Dominique gaining the adoration of his visiting English friend and business partner, Lord William Trevelyan, Earl of Northchurch.

The sisters had wept disconsolately at being parted from each other. Only the thought that, despite the Channel that would separate them, they would see each other frequently had persuaded them to agree to the triumphant, scandalous matches that had set all of France and England agog.

One year later, Dominique's first and only child, a son, Justin, had been born. Eleven years after that, after Lis-Marie had long despaired of ever having any children, she had given birth to the twins, Vachel and Geneviève. Happily the two women had arranged the engagement Claude Rambouillet had taken so amiss and that now threatened the very lives of Lis-Marie and her family.

If Lis-Marie must die, then she would—as flamboyantly as she had lived. But Vachel and Geneviève must be spared.

Of Vachel, Lis-Marie knew nothing, except that he was yet safe, for Geneviève had said so. Lis-Marie understood well the bond between twins and thus had not questioned her daughter's belief that Vachel was still unharmed. But Geneviève's well-being was threatened, and Lis-Marie would not allow her to be wasted on the likes of Claude Rambouillet, any more than Papa Nick had let his own daughters become the courtesans of such men. Geneviève would *not* be Claude Rambouillet's whore—to do with as he pleased.

And so Lis-Marie had devised the charade.

When Berthe Onfroi, the milkmaid, came to deliver her shining pails of foaming white milk this morning, Geneviève would change roles with the shy, simpleminded girl. That the slow-witted Berthe only dimly comprehended her part did not trouble Lis-Marie. The milkmaid had but a walk-on performance. It was Geneviève who must not fail, Geneviève who must carry the charade to its curtain fall.

Her nerves on edge, as they'd always been before a play, Lis-Marie rapped on the door of her daughter's chamber, then turned the knob and went in.

Geneviève's eyes met her mother's worried ones briefly in the oval mirror above the dressing table. Then the girl whirled around slowly upon the chair on which she sat.

"Well, Maman," she asked softly, waiting for Lis-Marie's approval, "do I fit the part?"

Madame la Comtesse de Château-sur-Mer, Lis-Marie Beauville Saint-Georges, studied her daughter carefully for a long moment. Then, despite her anxiety, the older woman smiled gently.

"I think"—she paused and took a ragged breath—"I think, Genette, that even Papa Nick would be pleased."

Geneviève's transformation was astounding. Her long, shining, fiery copper hair had been dyed a dark, dingy brown and hung in unkempt braids tied with tattered ribbons. The pale, flawless, creamy skin she had inherited from her mother was now a nut-brown hue, as though she had lived all her life outdoors beneath the sun. The slight sloe of her almond-shaped eyes had been altered expertly with subtle kohl, making the orbs appear as wide and round as buttons, and their brilliant, moss-green color had been rendered an almost nondescript shade by the application of a greyish brown eyeshadow. The tilt of her childishly piquant nose had been changed by a dab of clay and some artistic blending of paint and powder; across her cheekbones, which now looked flat, was splayed a spattering of dusky freckles. Her generous, pouting crimson mouth had been carefully outlined to seem thin and unremarkable; her lips were tinted a dull, translucent pink.

Her figure was as changed as her face, for she had bound her full, ripe breasts, so her chest resembled Berthe's, and padded her narrow, curved hips to make them broader.

When she stood and moved across the room, it

was not with her usual flowing grace, but with an awkward, shuffling gait, her head downcast, her shoulders slumped.

Even Lis-Marie had some difficulty recognizing her beautiful daughter.

"Oh, *ma petite*, you would have made a wonderful actress. You have caught Berthe perfectly!" the older woman exclaimed.

Normally Geneviève would have been made proud by her mother's praise, but the thought of all that hung on the quality of her performance this morning dimmed her pleasure in her mother's words.

"Oh, Maman!" she cried. "Are you certain you wish me to go through with this? Oh, please, Maman, let me stay. Let me stay and become Claude Rambouillet's mistress! I don't care about my ruin! I would rather endure anything than be parted from you and Papa, and when I think of what must happen to you when all is discovered—"

"Shhhhh. Hush, Genette, hush, or I shall think you are suffering from nerves. We have been over this before. It is the only way. Now come, *ma petite*. Your audience awaits you."

When they reached the kitchen below, Berthe was already in evidence and was slipping anxiously from her much-mended garments. She gave a little start of fright upon seeing the two women, and tightly clutched her bodice to her breast. But upon perceiving it was only Madame la Comtesse and mademoiselle, she relaxed slightly.

"Hurry, Berthe," Lis-Marie directed, worriedly glancing out the window to be certain the length of the maid's stay at the townhouse was as yet unremarked upon by Claude and his henchmen.

Then, with the ease born of years of practice, she skillfully assisted her daughter into Berthe's clothes.

"Now," Lis-Marie said, stepping back to survey critically her handiwork, "go and kiss Papa goodbye, Genette. Quickly, *ma petite!* Quickly!"

Geneviève needed no further urging, knowing how crucial their timing was.

"Papa!" she called, moving awkwardly in the maid's stout, serviceable boots, which were too large and kept slipping. In order to make the shoes fit, they'd had to stuff the toes with newspaper, but this had proved only partially successful. "Papa!"

Monsieur le Comte de Château-sur-Mer, Edouard Saint-Georges, entered the kitchen rapidly upon hearing his daughter's cry. His face was etched with concern upon seeing her, and it filled with grief, as well, when Geneviève flung herself into his arms. He hugged her dearly, kissing the top of her head as though she were yet a child.

"So . . . 'tis time, Genette." He spoke at last, his voice choked with emotion.

"*Oui*, Papa."

With difficulty, Geneviève fought back the hot, bitter tears that stung her eyes. She had never seen her father look so old and tired. It was as though all the vim and vigor that had always sustained him in the past had been drained from his body, leaving him bent and broken. It was hard to believe this was the same proud, daring nobleman who had thumbed his nose at society and married Lis-Marie Beauville in the face of all opposition, the same engaging gentleman who had laughed so heartily at life's ups and downs and claimed he would come about tomorrow if luck smiled upon

him; the same wise man who had so lovingly guided his
daughter in all matters since her birth.

Now, more than ever, Geneviève hated Claude
Rambouillet, the demon who had crushed her father's
bright, just spirit and trampled it into the ground. For a
moment, she did not know if she could bring herself to
leave this man she loved so deeply. Their parting was
perhaps even harder for him than for her, she knew, for,
next to Lis-Marie, Geneviève and Vachel were the joys
of his life.

"I—I will pray for you, daughter," Edouard stated
gruffly, clutching Geneviève nearer so she would not see
the tears that blurred his eyes. Lis-Marie's breast ached
with pity as she watched her beloved husband, the man
who, so long ago, had won her hand and heart.

"And I for you, Papa," Geneviève rejoined, her
face buried against his broad, comforting chest.

"Tonight, when all are asleep, I will send Ives-
Pierre to you at the Onfroi farm," her father told her.
"Do not leave there without him, Genette, for I am
afraid for you. The times are hard," Edouard observed, "and the roads unsafe." He paused. "If, by
some chance, you should see your brother, Vachel, tell
him—" He broke off abruptly, clearing his throat. "Tell
him—"

"I know, Papa." Geneviève spared him the pain of
continuing, understanding that her father did not know
if he would ever see her or her twin again and was
bereft of words. "I will." Then, with unbearable anguish, she drew away, turning to her mother. "Maman."

Geneviève held back the tears she longed to shed
upon her mother's solace-giving breast. There was no
time now for more than a brief, parting embrace. Still,
the girl clung fiercely for an instant to Lis-Marie,

imprinting indelibly into her memory the sweet lemon verbena scent of the older woman's perfume.

For as long as Geneviève could remember, her mother had worn the fragrance. It had wafted soothingly from the delicate, lacy handkerchiefs Lis-Marie had pressed lovingly to Geneviève's forehead when, as a youngster, she'd lain ill and feverish from some childhood complaint. It had lingered reassuringly in her bedroom in the darkness, keeping shadowed monsters at bay long after her mother had bid her good night. It had wakened her gaily in the mornings, mingling with the sunlight that had streamed in from her windows as Lis-Marie had drawn back the curtains to admit the day.

"Oh, Maman," Geneviève breathed, filled with hurt. "Oh, Maman."

With great sadness and reluctance, the older woman gently pushed her daughter away.

"This is the most difficult role of your life, *ma petite*. I know you will play it brilliantly." Lis-Marie tried hard to inject a note of normalcy into her tone, as though Geneviève were but going on some pleasant outing.

Her throat taut with smothered sobs, the girl nodded bravely, attempting to smile. Then she turned to Berthe, who stood quietly in one corner, looking strange and ill at ease in Geneviève's silk dressing robe.

"I cannot tell you how much I appreciate your help, Berthe," Geneviève thanked the scared, wide-eyed maid. "You will not suffer for it, I promise you. If we are discovered, Papa and Maman will take the blame for your part."

"I—I understand, mam'selle." Berthe dropped a small curtsy.

Geneviève glanced once more at her parents, her heart swelling to bursting with the tide of love and sorrow that overwhelmed her. She would never forget them as they were now, standing there solemnly, their arms about each other tightly as they watched her depart from their lives, perhaps never to return.

"Break a leg, Genette," Lis-Marie whispered courageously the old stage adage for good luck.

"I will, Maman," Geneviève promised earnestly. "I will. I love you. I love you both so much. *Au revoir, mes pères. Au revoir.*"

Then, gathering up Berthe's empty milk pails and taking a deep breath to slow the fearful pounding of her heart, she stepped outside beneath the rising curtain of the morning sun to face Claude Rambouillet and his hirelings.

Chapter Five

Northchurch Abbey, England, 1792

Outside, the grey summer rain drizzled gently, beating a soft, soothing tattoo against the mullioned casement windows of Lord Northchurch's study. But the serene pitter-patter of the droplets had no effect upon the two men inside, one of whom was gazing idly at the rivulets trickling slowly down the fine Venetian-glass panes.

After a moment, he turned from his contemplation of the rain to the strained conversation at hand, wondering why interviews with his father were always so difficult. That he perhaps too closely resembled the older man in temperament did not occur to him. In fact, had such a suggestion been put forth, he would have been much surprised and slightly offended. He knew only that from the time he had grown able to think for himself, he had seldom agreed with his father on anything. Now was no exception.

"Well, what is to be done, my lord?" Lord Justin Trevelyan, Viscount Blackheath, asked his father somewhat impatiently in the tense silence that had fallen. "I cannot possibly marry at this point in time. You are not unaware of my position, my lord, and the responsibilities it entails. I dare not have it jeopardized, especially by a chit barely out of the schoolroom, for I've no doubt she is as silly and witless as the rest of her simpering ilk''—this last was sneered.

Lord William Trevelyan, Earl of Northchurch, lifted one satanic eyebrow and gave his son a quelling stare. It did not, however, produce any visible effect upon Lord Blackheath, who continued to regard his father coolly, as though somewhat amused by the older man's stern demeanor. Lord Northchurch grimaced sourly, but it could not be said whether this was due to his son's haughty attitude or his attire—the most casual of hunting jackets, quite inappropriate for a discussion of this importance.

"I thought, Justin, that Edouard's letter made Geneviève's circumstances perfectly clear. If she manages somehow to escape from France, she must have someplace to go. As your betrothed''—the earl stressed this word pointedly—''she quite rightfully expects you to honor the engagement arranged by your mother and your aunt, Lis-Marie.''

"Geneviève will have you and Maman to look after her," Justin dismissed his father's remarks shortly, frowning as he recalled with distaste the irritating little brat he used to tease so unmercifully and who, together with her brother, had tagged along behind him and plagued him endlessly during his summer vacations in France. "She has no need of me."

Lord Northchurch's sharp eyes did not miss the fleeting expression of discomfiture that had flitted across his son's face. Deliberately the earl shifted in his chair, removed his handkerchief from his well-tailored waistcoat, and carefully cleaned his quizzing glass. Then, as though he had suddenly spied some disgusting, obnoxious creature, he slowly raised the monocle and piercingly surveyed his son through it. After a long, uncomfortable, disconcerting minute, he abruptly dropped the eyepiece, allowing it to dangle from the cord attached to his breastpocket.

"You are unusually dense this evening, Justin," he observed with deceptive calm. "Let me attempt to clarify the situation for you. It is your mother's fondest wish in life to see you and your cousin Geneviève wed."

"Regardless of my feelings about the matter, of course," Justin droned dryly.

"But of course." The older man looked faintly surprised. "I assumed you understood that your feelings, Justin, are quite unimportant to me."

"Naturally," the viscount retorted, his voice as deceivingly pleasant as his father's. "However, it appears you, too, are inordinately slow this evening, my lord. Let me restate my position for you: I have no desire for a bride, and my current endeavors would be greatly hampered by one."

"Is that so?" Lord Northchurch questioned, his tone now slightly mocking and holding a note that had caused many to quail before him. "Then perhaps it will interest you to know Parker does not share your viewpoint. In fact, 'tis his belief that a French wife would be an enormous asset to you in many respects."

At the mention of his best friend, the younger man quirked one eyebrow upward demoniacally, in unconscious imitation of his father.

"Indeed?" he inquired frostily. "And what, pray tell, does Parker know of the matter?"

"A good deal more than you would suppose, Justin, since you are not privy to as much as you would like to think. I have it on the best authority that he is shortly to be named England's new ambassador to France."

Lord Blackheath, in the process of withdrawing his ornate snuffbox from the hunting jacket that earlier had so offended his father, paused, considering this unexpected information. Then, with an elegantly adept flick of his wrist that was the envy of every dandy in London, he sprang open the snuffbox, inhaled a pinch of snuff, and spoke again.

"I see. I had not heard, but I suspected Oldfield would be recalled after his latest idiotic blunder. The man's a fool—and no mistake. Parker is to take his place, then?"

"I thought I just said as much," the earl answered, his tone reflecting his displeasure at his son's disparaging remarks about the unfortunate Lord Oldfield.

Though the older man heartily agreed with the younger's assessment of both Lord Oldfield and the embarrassing affair that had led to his recall, it was not Justin's place to criticize his elders—something he did, much to his father's annoyance, with irritating regularity.

"Well, this is a surprise," Justin drawled, his cold, keen grey eyes narrowing slightly. "I had not realized Parker ranked so highly in political circles. I must commend him on his ability to conduct himself so discreetly."

"As do you, Justin," Lord Northchurch commented wryly. "At least . . . insofar as England is concerned."

Imperceptibly the younger man flinched, for this

last had been an unnecessary reminder that the majority of his notorious escapades were grist for the gossip mill throughout the country. The earl smiled coldly, fully aware his shot had hit home. Grimly delighted to have—for once—penetrated his son's steely armor, he continued the wary, stilted conversation.

"Have no doubt Parker was as surprised to learn of your position as you were, just now, to discover his."

"Nevertheless, my lord, I do not see what right that gives him to meddle in my affairs. There are limits, after all, to a man's friendship," Justin noted stiffly, silently determining to teach his closest companion a well-deserved lesson in manners.

"This has nothing whatsoever to do with friendship, Justin, as well you know," Lord Northchurch declared warningly. "England's welfare is at stake, and Parker has a job to accomplish, just as you do. It is my own personal opinion that he is right about this matter. I, too, believe that having Geneviève as your wife will prove an asset to you in your dealings. Besides, as I informed you previously, it is Dominique's dearest wish that you marry the girl."

"And if she turns out to be a fool?" Justin asked, his nostrils white and flared with anger.

"I am quite sure you will manage to overcome any such obstacle, Justin—and without your usual callous disregard for anyone else's feelings. In addition to you, your cousin Geneviève may now well be your mother's only surviving relative. I will not have Dominique upset by finding her niece is being made unhappy—especially at your hands. You have on too many occasions caused your mother great distress, and I do not intend to tolerate it again—most particularly in this instance, when she will suffer grief enough as it is at the probable deaths of Lis-Marie and Edouard—and perhaps Vachel, as well. I trust that, much as you may dislike the arrangement, Justin, you will take that into account, once you and Geneviève are wed.''

"And is that your final word on the subject, my lord?''

"It is.''

"I see.'' The younger man snapped his snuffbox shut with a wrathful little click, a muscle working tightly in his jaw.

"I certainly hope you do, Justin, '' Lord Northchurch asserted softly. "For I assure you that, this time, my displeasure at your highly lamentable behavior will know no bounds.''

Chapter Six

A burning desire for revenge spurred Geneviève's exhausted body onward, though her breathing was labored and the aching muscles in her tired legs whimpered piteously for respite. She had walked many long miles these past two weeks, and she had several more to travel—a daunting prospect to one whose feet had never done anything more strenuous than dance away the night at a gala ball.

How she longed to lie down and rest! But that was not possible. There was still a little daylight remaining, and she must press on. She must escape from Claude Rambouillet—the filthy *canaille!*

Damn him! Damn him to hell and back! Geneviève cursed silently as she trudged along. *If not for him . . .*

Grievous wounds that had not yet had time to heal hurt her anew at the unfinished thought. Hot tears of rage and overwhelming sorrow stung her eyes. A great, ragged sob choked her throat. Blindly Geneviève stumbled and fell, scraping her knees and palms raw on the small, sharp stones scattered here and there upon the rough dirt road over which she journeyed.

The perceptive, clear blue eyes in the leathery face of the girl's companion filled with tears at the distressing sight of his proud mistress humbled so.

Instinctively Ives-Pierre reached out to her. Then, remembering, he dropped his hands lamely at his sides. Once, there had been a time when he would have offered his mistress assistance without hesitation. But those days were no more. With a valiant little lift of her chin and a determined squaring of her shoulders—both of which gestures had tugged wrenchingly at Ives-Pierre's heart—Geneviève had put an end to the past and the old ways forever.

"I must learn to stand on my own feet, Ives-Pierre, *mon ami*," she had said resolutely when they'd begun their clandestine flight.

Still, it was hard not to help the girl who was as dear as a daughter to him, and at last Ives-Pierre bit his quivering lip and turned away, unable to bear any longer the heartrending sight of his mistress struggling painfully to rise.

It did not seem possible to Ives-Pierre that Mademoiselle Geneviève Angèle Saint-Georges, once the reigning belle of Paris, now groveled in the dirt like a common peasant.

Sacrebleu! It was not to be borne!

A fortnight ago, Geneviève had been the much-indulged only daughter of Monsieur le Comte and Madame la Comtesse de Château-sur-Mer. Now, as the shadows lengthened, the day turning slowly to dusk, the flaming sun setting the countryside ablaze, she was but one of hundreds of aristocrats fleeing for their very lives from France, their beloved homeland.

And Claude Rambouillet was to blame!

The thought twisted like a sharp knife in Geneviève's heart. Perhaps even now her parents were dead, as Armand Charbonne was dead; and where Vachel was, only God knew. Maybe he, too, had been caught and killed.

The girl shuddered at the idea and crossed herself, sending a silent prayer to heaven, beseeching Sainte Marie to watch over her father, mother, and twin brother.

Then she rose from the road and smiled tremulously at Ives-Pierre.

She was fortunate Claude had been so puffed up with his own importance that he'd paid little attention to the Saint-Georgeses' faithful servant, considering the man beneath his notice. Thus Ives-Pierre had been able to slip away without detection from the townhouse in Paris to join his mistress at the farm of Berthe's family.

Geneviève was lucky, too, that her own escape had thus far proved successful. No matter how many miles she traveled, no journey would ever seem as long to her as the one she had made from the back door of her father's *hôtel* to Monsieur Onfroi's cart, which had been waiting for her at the end of the alley. How she had managed to maintain her imitation of Berthe's slow, shuffling gait, she would never know, for her every instinct had urged her to run down the narrow lane as hard and fast as she could. Once perched on the seat beside Monsieur Onfroi, Berthe's father, who'd also been a party to their plot, Geneviève had not even dared to breathe. Not until the elderly man had driven his wagon well past the guards at the gate of the city had she finally been able to relax.

All the way to his farm, much to Monsieur Onfroi's embarrassment, for he'd been well paid for his assistance, she'd thanked him profusely for his help, and she had still been showering him with gratitude when Ives-Pierre had at last arrived to take her away.

Geneviève was grateful for her servant's presence and for his deft sword arm, as well, for though she was as skilled as any man with the rapier that hung at her side, it was not safe to be abroad in France these days. The roads were rife with thieves who would slit a man's throat for a sou, scoundrels who would take base advantage of an unprotected maid, and the vengeful bourgeoisie who would turn a decamping aristocrat over to the rabble that served as the French government these days.

For this reason, Geneviève was now disguised as a young man; dressed in old clothes given to her by one of Berthe's brothers, she spoke only when forced to, adopting the tone and speech of a slow-witted peasant.

She had a lot of time to think during those terrible, long days of silence as she and Ives-Pierre trudged furtively through the countryside, making their way carefully toward the coast and Château-sur-Mer, where they would be able to get help and, they hoped, to smuggle themselves from France to England, to Northchurch Abbey, the home of Geneviève's relatives.

She did not know whether her uncle, William, and her aunt, Dominique, had received the letter Edouard Saint-Georges had written to them, informing them of his daughter's dire circumstances and her attempt to reach them. But she did know that, should she be fortunate enough to manage to cross the English Channel, she would be expected upon reaching Northchurch Abbey to honor the betrothal her mother and aunt had arranged so long ago between herself and her cousin, Justin Trevelyan.

The prospect was not an enchanting one, coming so hard on the heels of the loss of her beloved Armand and the separation from her family.

Besides, Geneviève had not seen Justin for some years, and she recalled him with distaste as an arrogant, perpetually bored youth who, for amusement during his summer visits to France, had taken mean delight in taunting both her and Vachel.

She wondered idly if her cousin had changed much, then decided he probably had not. It did not matter. She felt dead inside and no longer cared what became of her. It was only for Papa and Maman's sake that she had agreed to leave the townhouse in Paris, though if it would have saved their lives, she would have stayed to become the wicked Claude Rambouillet's mistress. Being Justin's wife certainly could not be worse than that.

Perhaps her cousin would not want her anyway, and she would be spared the fate she believed awaited her in England. Geneviève would hope for that, for she did not think she could bear to wed Justin—and perform all the acts such a role would entail—when her heart was breaking for Armand, for her parents, and for Vachel.

At the thought, the girl recognized that there was still some spark of life within her after all, and she sought to fan it to flame, suddenly ashamed of her self-pity. Where were her courage, spirit, and backbone? The traits that had marked the proud Saint-Georges family through the centuries and sustained them during their trials? Surely, given her heritage, she should not be a creature so easily crushed!

Indeed, in the past, she had always been head-strong—or so Maman had claimed, for, from the time Geneviève had been a child, she had never been interested in the more feminine pursuits that ought to have occupied her days. Instead, she had clung like a burr to Vachel, insisting she be allowed to share his studies with Monsieur Roquefort, the tutor, his lessons in fencing and sailing with Ives-Pierre, and the rough-and-tumble games he'd played with friends. More than once, Geneviève had been found climbing a tree when she ought to have been practicing a minuet, or firing a pistol at some target when she ought to have been plying her needle at her embroidery. Maman had admonished her sternly on more than one occasion, but Papa had only laughed at her antics, saying there would be time enough later for her to become a proper young lady. He had refused to curb her stubborn vitality and zest for life, and finally Maman had thrown up her hands in resignation. Geneviève had been free then to do much as she pleased.

Only in the last few years had she grown more inclined to let down her skirts and to put up her hair, to learn how to flirt from behind her fan and to take the small, mincing steps that made her hips sway enchantingly. As her mother before her had done, Geneviève had taken Paris by storm and had claimed her place as a reigning belle. And if her impetuous manner had been thought bold and dashing by some, others had merely shrugged and remarked that the daughter of a rich and noble man such as Monsieur le Comte de Château-sur-Mer could well afford to be a trifle brazen, for she had no need to marry for position or fortune. Spiteful gossips had sourly rejoined that, sooner or later, blood would tell; after all, the girl's mother had been a common actress. But this flaw in Geneviève's bloodline had not produced any noticeable effect upon the many cavaliers who'd flocked to her side. Had she so desired, she might have had her pick of France's most eligible bachelors.

Then the world had gone mad, and now the wily, feminine arts she'd had so little time previously to employ fell one by one to the wayside as she wearily but determinedly forced one foot before the other.

Of what use were those accomplishments to her now? she wondered. She did not lack for an answer. None! Better that she had continued her practice of more masculine endeavors, for certainly they would better suit her needs upon this journey. Well, no longer would she forsake them! It had been her face and figure that had attracted Claude's hateful attentions; it would be her brains and skill that would outwit him! Somehow she would find a way to free her parents from his evil clutches and to have her revenge upon him, too. Till then, Geneviève must not allow herself to be bested and broken by the difficulties that had beset her.

Ives-Pierre's voice, whispering warningly in her ear, startled her from her reverie.

"Look sharp, mademoiselle," he hissed. "There may be trouble ahead. I mislike those trees and what they may conceal now that dusk is falling, for earlier, I spied smoke from a campfire drifting above the branches, and now 'tis gone, as though the flames were quickly extinguished."

"But, Ives-Pierre," Geneviève demurred, "we scarcely appear prosperous enough to waylay and rob. Perhaps whoever was there has simply finished an evening repast and moved on."

The servant shook his head, his eyebrows knitted with concern.

"I do not think so, mademoiselle, for I've seen no one leave the forest, and honest men would be traveling upon the road, as we ourselves are. This accursed rebellion has made cutthroats of many, and a man may lose his life for less than a crust of bread."

"*Oui*, you are right of course," Geneviève agreed with dismay, laying a wary hand upon the solid silver hilt of her tempered-steel foil. "I shall be ready, *mon ami*. Do not fear."

"*Non*, mademoiselle," Ives-Pierre protested worriedly, eyeing her slender frame and afraid for her life. "You need not fight. If it comes to that, I will protect you."

"Don't be silly, Ives-Pierre. Of course I must defend myself and assist you in any way I can," Geneviève insisted. " 'Twould be foolish to do otherwise. Besides, have you not taught me well?"

"*Oui*, but you are young yet, and there is still much you have to learn, so have care, mademoiselle. Do not join in the battle unless 'tis absolutely necessary."

"As you wish, then." She nodded, swallowing hard, her heart beginning to pound hard in her breast.

Nervously she licked her lips, watching surreptitiously for any sign of movement from the dense woods outlined in red-orange flames by the setting sun. When the attack came, she was not taken unaware.

Despite her promise to Ives-Pierre, she whipped

her razor-sharp weapon from its scabbard in a flash to engage the huge ruffian who bore down upon her, howling a bloodthirsty cry and brandishing his own sword threateningly. The thief was momentarily caught off guard, for he had not expected a struggle from the slight boy he thought Geneviève to be, and she was able to deliver a crippling blow to his shoulder before he managed to regain his senses.

He was a big man, however, and though he grunted with pain as blood gushed from the wound that had nearly severed his left arm from its socket, still, he came on, the force of his attack almost causing Geneviève to lose her grasp on her rapier.

She staggered backward before the onslaught, scrambling to retain her balance and her hold on the French grip she clutched haphazardly in her sweating fist. With an expert flick, she steadied the hilt, feeling the weighted pommel slap down firmly once more against the inside of her wrist. Metal clashed, echoing in the stillness of the setting sun, foible scraping foible as again Geneviève strove to ward off her enemy, not even aware she had not escaped unscathed from his bull-like charge. Blood welled from her injured thigh, but she did not feel the pain; all her concentration was riveted instead on parrying yet another murderous thrust.

Silently she thanked her indulgent father, who had allowed her to share Vachel's fencing lessons, overriding her mother's complaints that it was most improper.

Still, the polite bouts, governed by a strict code of etiquette, that Geneviève had fought in the past had not prepared her for anything like this. With a sinking feeling in the pit of her stomach, she realized, as the altercation wore on, that the brutal reiver had no honor and would not be bound by any of the unwritten rules adhered to by gentlemen.

Out of the corner of one eye, she looked frantically to Ives-Pierre for assistance, but he was desperately defending himself against three other men who had set upon him with blades and cudgels, and she knew she could expect no help from that quarter.

Deftly Geneviève parried another violent assault, understanding almost subconsciously that she stood no chance against this giant's barbarous strength. If she attempted to match him blow for blow, she would soon be overpowered. Her only salvation lay in her speed and cleverness, which she must put to good use before she became too weary to do so.

Quickly she retreated to gain an instant's respite, her arm aching from resisting her opponent's steel, her breath coming in short, labored gasps as she inhaled raggedly. She knew it was cowardly, but she allowed herself to be compelled even farther back until she was driven off the road toward the edge of the forest, where she turned and ran, seeking cover behind a large tree. Briefly she leaned against it for support and was able to draw a good breath at last. Revitalized, Geneviève then sprang from her hiding place, taking her foe, who had followed her, unaware.

Neatly she knocked his sword from his grasp, then lunged forward for the kill. To her horror, the oaf grabbed her foil with one hand, seeming not to feel the dreadful pain it must have caused as it sliced open his palm. The supple blade bent nearly double as they struggled for control of the weapon, until finally Geneviève was able to wrench it free. It wavered wildly in her clenched fist, slashing the man across the side of his face, narrowly missing his eye. Blood spurted from the gash, nearly blinding him as he teetered toward her, bent on seizing her and crushing her to death with his bare hands.

Rapidly Geneviève stepped back from his looming figure to regain her composure and command of her rapier. The vicious brute paused, watching her slyly, his mean little pig eyes blinking as he contemplated how best to combat the length of steel she held purposefully before her. Then, growling and chortling at the same time, as though not in full possession of his faculties, he leaned down to pick up a heavy dead branch that had fallen to the ground. Crazily he began to swing it back and forth as he approached the cringing girl. He was so intent on hitting her with the limb that he failed to notice an old, gnarled root protruding from the earth like a tentacle. When his foot made contact with the twisted strand, he tripped and fell, sprawling facedown, momentarily stunned, upon the damp moss that carpeted the woods.

Geneviève did not hesitate. Flinging away her sword, she jumped like a cat upon her disabled rival and, yanking her dagger from her belt, plunged the knife down as hard as she could into his back. Blood spewed from the place where the sharp point had struck, foaming out over her hands and spraying warm and wet and sticky upon her sobbing face. Still, not knowing if the beastly churl were dead, she withdrew the dirk and stabbed him again and then again. Then, certain he would trouble her no more, she rose shakily to her feet, managing a few unsteady steps before her knees gave way beneath her and she doubled over, retching violently on the ground.

After a time, she wiped her mouth off with the back of one hand, not recognizing until she'd done so that she was smearing herself with the dead man's blood. Upon the realization, another wave of nausea assailed her, and dizzily she forced her head down to try to stop it from spinning. Minutes later, the sickening sensation passed, and Geneviève was able to lurch again to her feet.

Reeling with shock, she wove her way blindly in the twilight toward the road, some part of her chaotic mind dimly comprehending the fact that Ives-Pierre was still embroiled in a struggle for his life with the others who had set upon them.

When she reached the edge of the forest, Geneviève saw that her servant had already dispatched one rogue to his Maker and, although evidently tiring, was continuing valiantly to counter the evil measures of the remaining two. Spying the fallen scoundrel's thick, blunt cudgel lying in the dirt, Geneviève retrieved it and, lifting it high over her head, brought it down savagely upon her nearest foe, crushing his skull. Bone splintered into spattering brain, killing him instantly.

Almost simultaneously Ives-Pierre sent three feet of shining metal spiraling into his opponent's heart. Then, clutching his injured side, he stumbled toward Geneviève, his face terrified by her appearance.

"Mademoiselle! You are hurt!" he cried, dropping his foil and hurrying to assist her.

The girl, who was limping, gazed down incredulously at her thigh, noticing for the first time the blood that had dripped slowly down her leg and was now congealing upon her breeches. Sometime during the course of the conflict, the man in the woods had dealt her a punishing blow. She'd been so concerned with saving her life that she hadn't even felt his weapon piercing her flesh. Now waves of searing pain shot through her, causing her to wobble in her tracks.

"It—it is only a scratch . . . nothing more," Geneviève rasped. "'Tis you who are the more gravely wounded. Here, lean on me, *mon ami*."

"*Non. Non.* I've had worse injuries, I assure you," Ives-Pierre asserted, but she paid him no heed.

Somehow they aided each other in reaching a large, flat-topped rock, which they sank down upon gratefully. Eyes closed, they rested in silence for a while, trying to recover from their horrendous ordeal.

At last Ives-Pierre spoke.

"Mademoiselle, I hear the gurgle of a stream somewhere in the distance. If you feel you are strong enough, we can gather our belongings and try to find it. I do not think, from the sound of it, that 'tis too far away. Soon 'twill be night and even less safe to travel. We need to make camp, wash, and tend our hurts."

"*Oui.* Let us go, then, Ives-Pierre." Geneviève's voice was tinged with exhaustion. "For I would like to cleanse this stench of death from myself."

"*Bon.* You get our things, while I search the bodies of our gruesome friends over there. They may have something of value, and the purse Monsieur le Comte gave me before I departed from the *hôtel* has grown too slim for my liking these past several days."

Briefly Geneviève was shocked by her servant's suggestion that they rifle the pockets of the corpses. But then she realized the idea was a sensible one, for the men might have any number of items that would prove useful to her and her companion.

Besides, she told herself to bolster her resolve, *that*

is exactly what they would be doing, were Ives-Pierre and I lying there!

The thought made her shiver, and once more she cursed the day Claude Rambouillet had come into her life. If not for him—and others of his ilk—she would be safe at home instead of making this desperate journey fraught with danger, skulking and hiding along the way like some hunted animal. She would not be a frightened, sixteen-year-old girl with the blood of two men on her hands. She was made for joy and laughter—not fear. And yet she was afraid, terribly afraid. She glanced at the bodies whose possessions Ives-Pierre was thoroughly examining and shuddered to think what would have become of her if not for the presence of her trusted servant. Had she been alone . . . had the men discovered she was not a young lad, but a woman . . . The notion sent chills down Geneviève's spine.

Quickly, so as not to dwell on her unpleasant thoughts, she rose and began to gather the belongings she and Ives-Pierre had tossed aside during the skirmish. Then she retrieved their weapons. Ives-Pierre dragged the corpses into the forest and carefully concealed them beneath some brush so they would not be discovered and an alarm raised.

After that, he and Geneviève made their way toward the brook that beckoned in the twilight. As the servant had surmised, the rivulet was not far, and eventually the two travelers found a quiet spot in the forest where they felt they would be safe from further attack.

Taking a few items from her knapsack, Geneviève efficiently dressed first Ives-Pierre's wound and then her own, relieved to discover neither was as severe as initially had appeared. Once this was accomplished, she looked around for some dry wood to build a small fire, while respectfully, as he had done every night during their trip when they'd been forced to sleep out in the open, Ives-Pierre fashioned a bit of privacy for the girl by tying a rope between two trees and draping a worn blanket over the line. He prepared her a bed of soft grass, moss, and pine boughs on one side of the barrier, then made his own bed on the other. Then he took from his satchel a hoard of bread and cheese, which he and Geneviève ate in silence.

After a time, as though knowing what was on her mind, Ives-Pierre cleared his throat gruffly.

"Mademoiselle Genette," he began, using her family's pet name for her, as he always did when he wished to speak of matters of the heart, "you are a young lady and not used to such hardships as we have endured during our journey. You ought to be decked out in finery and flirting at balls. But the revolution has destroyed your world—and mine, too, for I was content enough with the old ways. I am sorry for what happened today. 'Tis difficult to take a life—no matter how worthless it is—and I know it has grieved you. Still, you had no other choice, and when we were set upon, you rallied like the best of men. I am proud of you, Mademoiselle Genette."

Geneviève was touched by her servant's concern. Her throat choked with emotion, for she had not lost everything she'd ever loved, after all. Her dear friend and teacher was still with her.

"Merci." She spoke softly in the stillness that had fallen. "Merci, mon ami."

Somehow things did not seem quite so bad after that.

*   *   *

Geneviève awoke in the morning to the delicious smell of fish frying. Spurred by her hunger, she made haste to wash and dress, then joined Ives-Pierre at the riverbank.

"*Bonjour,* mademoiselle," he greeted her jovially.

"*Bonjour,* Ives-Pierre. You must have got up very early indeed to have caught all those fat fish. Mmmmm. I can't wait to taste them; I'm positively famished!"

As though by mutual consent, they did not speak of yesterday's events, but talked instead of trivial things as they ate. Then they packed their possessions, extinguished the fire, and tidied the campsite. Presently they were once more on their way.

At midday, they stopped at an inn for dinner, the search of the reivers' pockets having yielded several francs and assorted coins Ives-Pierre had tucked away in his purse, as well as a few gems Geneviève had cleverly concealed in the pouch she carried beneath her garments for safekeeping.

It was late afternoon when the girl, her every sense alert and heightened by her travails of the past few weeks, suddenly paused in her tracks, her nostrils flared as she inhaled deeply of the fresh, sweet, tangy air. She turned to her companion, a joyous smile upon her face.

"Do you smell it, Ives-Pierre?" she asked excitedly, grasping his arms tightly. "Do you smell it? 'Tis the sea! 'Tis the sea! We made it, *mon ami.* We made it! Château-sur-Mer cannot be far now. Oh, hurry, Ives-Pierre," she urged and, despite her injured leg, broke into a run. "Hurry!"

As though the salty scent of the breeze had breathed new life into them, the two travelers quickened their pace lightheartedly, and soon the slender, graceful, flying turrets of the castle belonging to the Saint-Georges family could be spied in the distance.

"Wait, mademoiselle," Ives-Pierre cautioned, laying a restraining hand upon Geneviève's arm. "We do not know if Monsieur Rambouillet has discovered your disappearance from the *hôtel*. If it is so, then no doubt he has some of his henchmen watching the château. We must proceed very carefully from here on out. 'Twould be terrrible if we were to come so far, only to be taken prisoner when we are so -2lose to escaping from France's shores."

Geneviève nodded, biting her lip anxiously at the idea that even now Claude and his hirelings might be waiting for her at Château-sur-Mer.

"Perhaps 'twould be best if we remained here in the woods until after dark, mademoiselle," Ives-Pierre suggested. "Then I can slip down to the servants' entrance to see what I may discover. That way, if I do not return, you will know something is amiss and can go on to Port-d'Or."

Although she hated the thought of being left alone at night and, worse, the notion of journeying south to Port-d'Or, her brother's estate, farther from the English Channel and the sanctuary they sought, Geneviève reluctantly agreed it was the best way. Although he might be questioned about his movements, Ives-Pierre, being a peasant, probably would not be otherwise molested or taken captive by Claude's henchmen, even if they were to observe him entering the château. Geneviève herself, however, was another matter. Ives-Pierre was right. She must stay behind.

Dusk fell. The twilight shadows lengthened, and at last darkness, like a shroud of black velvet, draped itself inexorably over the land, hiding the world beneath a soft mantle whose folds were penetrated only by the most slender shafts of moonlight. Somewhere in the distance, an owl hooted and a dog bayed mournfully at the crescent-shaped sliver in the sky.

"I'm ready to go, mademoiselle," Ives-Pierre informed Geneviève. "Are you certain you will be all right here by yourself?"

"*Oui*. You go on, Ives-Pierre. The sooner you reach the château, the sooner you will return to me."

"*Oui*. That is true," he observed. "I will hurry, mademoiselle. I promise."

"Just be careful," Geneviève admonished worriedly. "I don't want anything to happen to you, *mon ami*."

Ives-Pierre grinned, reminding her strangely of Vachel for an instant.

"Do not fret, mademoiselle. I am like your grandfather, Le Renard," the servant boasted proudly. "My papa . . . he did not raise any fools. Claude Rambouillet will have to get up pretty early in the morning to catch me!"

With that parting remark, Ives-Pierre disappeared into the silver-shot blackness, leaving Geneviève alone in the dark. Shivering a little in the cool night air, she huddled against the trunk of one of the many ancient trees that populated the forested hillside. Her eyes peered fearfully through the ebony that blanketed the woods, for she imagined every shadow to be Claude, one of his hirelings, or some other beast intent on doing her harm. The wind soughed eerily, bringing with it the sound of the breakers crashing against the wild coast beyond. The night creatures stirred, skittering through the tangled brush, and the girl glanced about uneasily.

To dispel her trepidation, Geneviève began to sing an old childhood round under her breath to herself.

"Frère Jacques, Frère Jacques. Dormez vous? Dormez vous?—" Abruptly she broke off the melody, suddenly remembering how voices—even whispers—carried so close to the sea and realizing anyone might hear and come to investigate.

She was so alarmed by the prospect that she almost started out of her skin when Ives-Pierre, whose quiet return she had not discerned, tapped her lightly on the shoulder.

"Oh!" she exclaimed, exhaling with relief upon seeing it was only her servant. "You nearly scared me to death!"

"Shhhhh." He held one finger warningly to his lips. "Your escape from the *hôtel* was discovered three days ago. Monsieur Rambouillet is here waiting for you. He and his henchmen have moved into the château."

"Moved into the château!" Geneviève cried. "Oh, this is monstrous! How dare they!" She paused for a moment, speechless with wrath at this affront. Then, grasping the full import of Claude's presence at Château-sur-Mer, she went cold with dread. "My parents," she choked out beseechingly. "What has happened to my parents, Ives-Pierre?"

He shook his head.

"I do not know. No one does. They have simply disappeared. But they are clever, and 'tis possible they, too, somehow escaped. Apparently Monsieur Rambouillet has been in an extremely foul mood ever since his arrival at the château. If Monsieur le Comte and Madame la Comtesse also slipped through this fingers..."

"*Oui*. He would indeed be most angry," Geneviève affirmed, hope lighting her eyes for the first time since leaving the townhouse in Paris. "Oh, pray God, Papa and Maman are safe!" she uttered fervently. Then anxiously she inquired, "Did they see you—Claude and his hirelings, I mean?"

"*Non*," Ives-Pierre replied. "I was very lucky. I ran into Benoit D'Arcy just outside the gate. 'Twas he who told me all that has happened. Come. We must go quickly, mademoiselle. *La Belle Fille* is still anchored in the harbor at Brest, and Benoit said she is guarded only by a few sentries Monsieur Rambouillet has hired locally. If we can round up enough of her crew, we may easily take possession of her. Mademoiselle"—Ives-Pierre's voice rose with excitement—"perhaps we may be on our way to England this very night!"

Geneviève's heart leaped at the news, even as rage once more welled within her breast.

"*La Belle Fille* is mine!" she declared fiercely, all the tiredness suddenly draining from her bones. "*Mine!* Papa gave her to me for my birthday last year. How dare Claude think he can take her from me!"

This, to Geneviève, was worse than the thought of Claude being ensconced in her home, for Château-sur-Mer was Vachel's inheritance. But *La Belle Fille* was hers—and hers alone.

A beautiful ship, *La Belle Fille* was a small, fifty-foot, gaff-rigged sloop that carried four six-pound cannons. Her rapierlike bowsprit, which was nearly as long as her sleek hull, bore enough canvas to make her even swifter than the slender schooners favored by many pirates or the fast brigantines more suitable for combat. In a good wind, with her square topsail unfurled, the speed of the nimble *La Belle Fille* sometimes exceeded eleven knots. Her hull, below the water line, was sheathed with copper to protect her from teredo worms, seaweed, barnacles, and algae, and this helped to make her even fleeter. Usually she was manned by a crew of twenty-five, but Geneviève knew the vessel could be put to sea with half that number.

"Will Benoit join us?" she asked.

"*Oui*," Ives-Pierre responded. "As will his brothers, Emile and Marc. That makes four of us. We need only eight more men, mademoiselle."

"Seven," Geneviève corrected, "for I shall captain *La Belle Fille* myself, Ives-Pierre."

"Oh, mademoiselle!" he burst out, shocked. "*Non*. I cannot allow it! You do not know the men of Brest. They are rough sailors, not fit company for a lady such as yourself. 'Tis bad enough that you must be exposed to them for the short time 'twill take to cross La Manche, though, with France turned upside down, it cannot be helped. But to think you could command them . . . why, the very idea is *très fou! Non!*" he repeated firmly. "Monsieur le Comte has entrusted you to my care. What would he say if he knew?"

"He would say I could captain the sloop as well as the next man, for did you not teach me all there is to know about sailing, Ives-Pierre?" Geneviève queried, a teasing smile beginning to play about the corners of her mouth. "Come, come, *mon ami*," she wheedled, "you know as well as I do that the old ways are gone forever. Look at me!" she demanded, her tone once more serious. "Would you have thought, a fortnight ago, that I was capable of what I have endured these past few weeks? That I could defend myself in a battle such as the one that took place just yesterday? That I could kill two men and rob them of their belongings, besides? I can do it, I tell you! I can captain *La Belle Fille*. And I will! The ship is mine!"

Doubtless, had Geneviève not recently lost almost everyone and everything she held most dear, the mad notion of commanding the vessel would never have occurred to her. But as it was, it seemed to her that *La Belle Fille* was all she had left, and thus she was determined to cling to it, whatever the cost.

Ives-Pierre shook his head, his face skeptical.

"The men . . . they will not follow you, Mademoiselle Genette," he pointed out logically. "To be captained by a mere female . . . *enfin!* They would be the laughingstocks of the seas!"

"Will *you* support me, *mon ami*?" Geneviève asked more quietly.

"Me? But of course, mademoiselle. For myself, I have no hesitation. I would follow you to the ends of the earth if necessary. I have always served the Saint-Georges family, as my father before me and his father before him. But the men of Brest . . . ?" He shrugged in typical Gallic fashion. "They are another matter altogether."

"I will make a bargain with you, Ives-Pierre," Geneviève proposed slyly. "If I can win the crew to my cause, I will command *La Belle Fille.* If not, I will bow to your authority, once on board her."

"Very well, mademoiselle," Ives-Pierre consented, knowing it was the best for which he could hope.

Geneviève had always been headstrong, no matter how often he had chastised her for wanting to do all that Vachel did and as well as he did. It was most unfortunate, the servant thought, that Monsieur le Comte, having despaired of ever having any children, had been so thankful when God had finally blessed his union with Madame la Comtesse that he had proved an overindulgent papa.

"Let us go, then," Ives-Pierre went on. "I only hope you shall not be too disappointed, Mademoiselle

Genette, when the men fail to choose you as their *capitaine*.''

When Geneviève smiled, as she always did when she was sure she had a trick or two still left up her sleeve, her companion cringed inwardly, wondering what devilment she was plotting. Still, he could not bring himself to chide her again. Whatever scheme the girl was hatching had rekindled the spark in her moss-green eyes, and not for the world would Ives-Pierre extinguish it.

Chapter Seven

Three hours later, Benoit D'Arcy arrived at the docks of Brest, at the meeting place he had arranged earlier with Ives-Pierre.

By then, the silver crescent moon had climbed high in the firmament and the stars twinkled brightly, casting a greyish white sheen over the cool, dark waves that lapped gently at the hulls of the ships and boats anchored in the harbor.

From her hiding place behind a stack of shadowed wooden barrels on the wharf, Geneviève could spy clearly the beautiful, clean lines of *La Belle Fille*, her smooth shape bobbing ever so slightly upon the waters; her tall, solitary mast, crossed with furled sails, rising proudly against the night sky; her bowsprit thrust forward like a sharp foil poised for a duel.

Of all the girl had ever owned, *La Belle Fille* was her pride and joy, and upon seeing it, her intention to captain the sloop increased its fervor. *Par Dieu!* Claude and his ilk had stripped her of everything else; they would not take her ship, nor would Geneviève relinquish her authority to another. The world she had known was irretrievably lost to her; she must make a place for herself in this new one.

She glanced down at herself, looking ruefully at the worn shirt and breeches given to her by Berthe's brother, the stout leather boots upon her feet. Perhaps never again would she wear the costly gowns and dainty slippers she had once owned. Certainly it would be a long while before she would ever again feel like dancing the night away at a ball or flirting from behind her fan with a gay cavalier.

With renewed determination and spirit, she lifted her chin and squared her small shoulders proudly, the wheels in her brain clicking furiously. If somehow she managed to escape from France, she could not leave Papa, Maman, and Vachel behind to die. She must discover their whereabouts and find some way to rescue them—especially if they had been imprisoned, for if such were the case, they might at any moment be sentenced to Madame Guillotine.

Geneviève bit her lip with anguish at the thought.

Perhaps, if she reached England, she could ask her uncle, William, or Justin for help. But her memories of Lord Northchurch were of a cold, stern, unapproachable man, and she knew he was very angry with her father, besides. On several occasions during the past year, he had warned her father that the situation in France was rapidly deteriorating and had insisted that Edouard Saint-Georges bring his family to England, where they would be safe, before it was too late. But Geneviève's father had hoped the difficulties in his beloved homeland might still be peacefully resolved, and he'd ignored his old friend's alarming predictions and offers of sanctuary. Lord Northchurch's last letter had been filled with apprehension and recrimination, and the Saint-Georges family had heard nothing more from him since. Geneviève could only assume her uncle had washed his hands of them, for surely if he'd truly been concerned about their welfare, he would have continued to write and, upon receiving their increasingly fearful responses, would have sent someone to investigate their well-being.

Non, Geneviève decided dejectedly. She could not depend on Oncle William for assistance. Why, he might still be so wroth with her father that he would refuse even to countenance her presence at Northchurch Abbey. The notion filled the girl momentarily with panic; for if such were to occur, she really would be destitute and totally alone in the world, with no place to go and no one to whom she could turn for refuge. But then she reassured herself with the idea that Tante Dominique, who loved her dearly, would never shut the door in her face, no matter how much Oncle William might fret and fume, and her trepidation lessened. Besides, despite her recollections and reservations about Lord Northchurch, Geneviève did not truly believe he was such an ogre as to cast her adrift on her own. Her silly anxiety over the idea only served to demonstrate to her how torn apart emotionally she really was and further fueled her desire to take charge of her fate. Still, there was every chance Oncle William would reject her request for aid in the search for her parents and her brother, for it would mean endangering either himself or his men, perhaps sending them to their deaths.

That left only Justin, and as Geneviève considered him, her despair grew even more abject. The cousin she remembered was a selfish, insolent youth who cared for no one and nothing but himself and could not be bothered to lift a finger unless it were sure to provide him with either profit or amusement. Neither of these was to be gained in finding Geneviève's family, so she was certain she could expect no help from that quarter.

Of course, she reflected wryly, if she married Justin, it would be his duty to assist her, and he would be forced to do so; for how would it appear if her husband allowed her father, mother, and brother to be executed? Still, even if aid were to be forthcoming from her cousin, Geneviève knew she could never be sure in her heart that the bored and imperious Justin would exhaust every possible means at his disposal in an attempt to discover her family's whereabouts, and she knew she dared not trust him. Certainly *he* would not put himself at risk, and she doubted that his supercilious attitude would convey any urgency to the men he might dispatch to France in his stead.

Non, she thought again. She had no choice but to fend for herself in the matter.

At the earlier mention of *La Belle Fille,* a tentative plan had begun to take shape in Geneviève's mind, but she knew in order to carry it out she would need to attain control of the sloop. Now, her every muscle and nerve alert, she edged nearer to her two servants whispering in the darkness.

"Did you get the men?" Ives-Pierre questioned softly as, casting a wary glance about the pier to be certain he was unobserved, Benoit furtively approached and crouched down beside them.

"*Oui,*" the younger man answered just as quietly. "Five of them have sailed for mademoiselle in the past and so are loyal to the Saint-Georges family." With a respectful touch to his cap, he acknowledged Geneviève. If he found her wearing boy's clothing strange, he made no mention of the fact, for times were hard and the world had turned topsy-turvy. "Of the remaining two, one is my cousin, Rupert, from Deauville. The last man, Thibaud, I do not know, but Fabien has vouched for him."

"*Bon*," Ives-Pierre said. "Where are they now?"

"I told them to wait with Emile and Marc at Le Perroquet Bleu. I've only to go and fetch them."

"And the guards?"

"There are three—old Gustave Mortemer and his sons. They are brutal men and not well liked in Brest. Just last week, there was trouble with Monsieur Lafitte's daughter—you know, Aurélie, the one with the pretty blond hair. So"—Benoit shrugged—"if we are forced to kill them, I do not think 'twill be any great loss. No doubt the townspeople will say we have done them a favor."

"Very well, then," Ives-Pierre replied. "Go and get the others, and meet us at the ship."

Nodding, Benoit slipped away into the darkness. After watching closely to be certain the younger man's movements had not been noticed, Ives-Pierre crept from their place of concealment, motioning for Geneviève to follow.

Making sure to remain in the shadows as much as possible, they sneaked down the docks toward *La Belle Fille*. In moments, Benoit joined them with the rest of the crew, all of whom were armed, some with pistols, others with swords. Geneviève shivered a little at the sight of them, for although she recognized some of the men, they were indeed a rough bunch, as Ives-Pierre had warned, and in the past, she had been shielded from dealing directly with any of them. Still, they had come to help her, so surely she need have no fear.

"Benoit," Ives-Pierre instructed, "take Emile and Marc and board the sloop. Act as though you merely want to have a friendly conversation with Monsieur Mortemer and his sons. Take with you that bottle of wine your cousin has so obligingly brought along with him." He frowned at Rupert, who merely smiled lopsidedly, then hiccupped.

"A fat lot of good he shall be to us," one of the men, Silvestre, remarked with disgust.

"I apologize for my cousin," Benoit stated stiffly. "He is suffering from a broken heart and thought to drown his sorrows. That is why he left Deauville. But he is a decent comrade, when sober, and a good man in a fight."

"All right, then," Ives-Pierre approved Benoit's choice. "When you have allayed the suspicions of Monsieur Mortemer and his sons, set upon them without warning. The rest of us will join you to finish the job."

Benoit inclined his head to show he understood, then he, Emile, and Marc started down the wharf toward the gangway to *La Belle Fille*.

"*Bonsoir*, Gustave," he called, slurring his words a little, as though he were as drunk as Rupert. "It is Benoit D'Arcy and his brothers, come to have some conversation with you and your sons."

From the deck of the ship, Monsieur Mortemer peered down at the pier, leaning far out over the port rail of the vessel to assure himself that no one else approached. Satisfied at last that it was just as Benoit had said, the old man indicated that the three brothers might come aboard.

The others waited below, out of sight, until finally, after a great deal of talk and laughter and the passing of the wine bottle several times, they heard the unmistakable sounds of a scuffle above.

"Now!" Ives-Pierre snapped. "Move!"

Without hesitation, Geneviève and the rest rushed up the gangway. Monsieur Mortemer and his two sons were rapidly overpowered, then thrown over the starboard side of the sloop. With loud splashes, they hit the water, yelling and cursing as they came up sputtering and gasping for air.

"Cast off! Quickly!" Ives-Pierre ordered. "Before an alarm is raised."

Hurriedly the crew scrambled to their duties, tossing aside lines, unfurling sails, and hauling up the heavy anchor. In minutes, *La Belle Fille* moved slowly from her docket in the harbor, headed toward the Bay of Biscay.

Once they were out on the open seas, Geneviève decided it was time to gain control of the ship.

"I will take command now, Ives-Pierre," she announced calmly, though the hand she laid upon the wheel he was steering trembled ever so slightly.

Though he eyed her askance, wordlessly he stepped aside.

"Here. What's this?" one of the men, Pernel, demanded curtly, observing the change. "Benoit said nothing to me about sailing under a damned female—I beg your pardon, mademoiselle. No offense intended." He doffed his cap politely.

"That's because I knew nothing about it," Benoit claimed in the sudden quiet that had fallen, glowering accusingly at Ives-Pierre, as though he had hired them all under false pretenses. "I thought Ives-Pierre was to have charge of the vessel, for he said only that we were to escort mademoiselle safely to England, then return to Brest.''

"*La Belle Fille* is mine," Geneviève insisted, "and I alone shall command her.''

"*Morbleu!*" another of the crew, Davide, swore. "I'll not sail under a female—and that's for sure! No offense intended, mademoiselle.''

"Quite right," yet another man, Olivier, put in. "Why, we should all be laughingstocks!"

"*Oui, oui,*" the rest chorused, nodding to one another in agreement.

"I never did like having a female aboard anyway," Thibaud, one of the two men unknown to Geneviève, commented unpleasantly, watching her in a manner that made her distinctly uncomfortable. " 'Tis bad luck! I say we drop the girl and her servant off in England, then elect a captain from among our own ranks. There is no hurry, surely, to return to Brest, and I, for one, would welcome a share of profits from some cargo. After all, we're risking our lives and being paid next to nothing to make this trip!"

"*Oui, oui,*" the others shouted again.

"Aren't you forgetting something?" Geneviève asked sharply, somewhat alarmed by this and fearing an imminent mutiny. She motioned to Ives-Pierre to take the wheel once more, then went on tersely. "*La Belle Fille* belongs to me. You have no right to take her anywhere without my permission. What were you planning to use her for? Fishing? That is, of course, the occupation of most of the men of Brest.'' She stared hard at Thibaud. "Or were you thinking instead of something a bit more lucrative ... like smuggling, for instance?" she suggested, her voice low. "I hear the

English pay dearly for French brandies and silks." At his guilty flush, Geneviève knew her shot had hit home.

"Well, messieurs," she addressed the crew collectively, "I'm not opposed to *La Belle Fille* carrying a cargo of contraband—as long as she is captained by me! Why, I'm as good a sailor as any of you aboard— and better than some!" She looked pointedly at the drunken Rupert, who obligingly smiled crookedly and hiccupped again.

"Mademoiselle, be reasonable," Benoit pleaded. "You cannot expect us to serve you in such a capacity. Olivier is right. We should indeed become objects of ridicule. Oh, I grant that you may know how to sail this ship—and better than some of us, too." He grimaced with disgust at his cousin. "But just knowing how to read a navigational map, chart a course, operate a sextant, reef a sail, and all the rest of it simply isn't enough. What would you do, for example, if we were attacked by pirates?"

"Why, I'd stand and fight like any man among you!"

"You?" Thibaud raised his eyebrows skeptically, then started to snigger.

The stillness of his fellows should have warned him, but it did not. Thus he was much surprised when, instead of growing angry, Geneviève actually smiled. Benoit and his two brothers, who on more than one occasion had seen the girl outmatch her twin, Vachel— who was himself no amateur with a blade—glanced at one another anxiously; and Ives-Pierre, guessing at last how Geneviève intended to win their wager, was forced to turn away so none would see the irrepressible grin that split his weatherbeaten face.

"*Oui*. Me," she declared firmly. Then, drawing the rapier at her waist, she challenged, "If there's a man among you who thinks he can best me in a duel, let him step forth. If he wins, he shall be your captain!"

"Duel?" Rupert finally roused himself from his stupor. "*Jésus!* I'll duel—hic—with you! I'll teach you, monsieur, not—hic—to steal *ma petite amie!*" he asserted, mistaking the girl's boyishly clad figure for that of his rival in Deauville.

While the rest watched in silence, astounded by this sudden display, he staggered forward, trying to yank his foil from its scabbard. After several unsuccessful attempts, he at last managed to free it, and, brandishing it wildly, he teetered toward Geneviève.

"*En garde,* monsieur." He whipped the blade about with a flourish. "For I mean—hic—to slay you where you stand."

He then lunged forward and sprawled flat on his face, much to the D'Arcys' embarrassment and the amusement of others, who howled with glee. Mirth bubbled from Geneviève's throat, too, but it did not lessen her resolve. She placed one foot upon Rupert's fallen form and glanced quizzically at the remainder of the crew.

"Anyone else?" she inquired, her lips still twitching with humor.

"*Oui,*" a voice snarled flatly, causing all laughter to cease abruptly. "Since you wish to play the part of a man, mademoiselle, *I* will gratify you with my own performance," Thibaud averred, expertly pulling his own steel from its scabbard.

"As you wish, then, monsieur." Geneviève's voice was cool and mocking, though inwardly she trembled, for she felt as though her entire scheme for rescuing her family rested on the outcome of this fight. *"En garde."*

She stepped out into the middle of the deck, where the disbelieving crew had cleared a space for them, and saluted briefly. Then she and Thibaud began to circle warily, their blades engaging lightly, slowly at first, to test each other's mettle.

From his small, rapid thrusts and parries, Geneviève recognized that Thibaud was no novice at dueling and realized she must take care if she were to be the victor. He was tall and muscular, and his arm's reach was longer than her own, compelling her to come in closer than she would have liked in order to score a touch.

Still, yesterday's battle with the reiver was fresh in her mind and gave her an added measure of confidence. After several tense moments of deft swordplay, she sent the stunned Thibaud's weapon spinning from his grasp and brought the sharp point of her rapier to rest at the base of his throat. Incredulous at the girl's victory, no one moved a muscle. The night was so still the only sounds that could be heard were the sighing of the wind in the sails and the gentle slap of the waves against the hull of the ship.

"Sacrebleu," someone cursed in a whisper, awed. "She has bested Thibaud. She is no *belle fille* but *une sorcière cramoisie."*

The crew gazed at one another uneasily at this, wondering if Geneviève was indeed a sorceress, a crimson witch, as their fellow seaman had claimed, for during the duel, her cap had come off, permitting her long, flowing red hair, which had escaped from its confining queue, to cascade down about her hips. Now the wind and spindrift whipped through the tangled locks, causing them to stream back from her piquant, hollow-cheeked face in wild disarray. Geneviève appeared like some fiery, avenging angel as she stood there in her boy's clothing upon the rolling deck, her feet spread wide apart, her sword held determinedly in her hand.

"Am I your *capitaine?*" she queried softly, ignoring the others as she pressed her blade gently into Thibaud's flesh so a drop of blood oozed forth to trickle slowly down his skin.

"*Oui*, mademoiselle," he replied, licking his lips nervously, grudging respect for her lighting his eyes.

She turned then to the rest, trying hard not to laugh at the stricken expressions upon their countenances.

"Am I your *capitaine?*" she repeated loudly.

"*Oui*, mademoiselle," they hastened to agree, superstitiously crossing themselves, afraid of and impressed by her skill with her foil, which to them had seemed born of some strange and magic power. "*Oui!*"

"*Bon*," she recognized their acceptance of her. "Then from now on, you are my men and you owe allegiance to no one but me. Deal fairly with me, and I shall do the same with you. Cross me, and you'll soon find yourself bait for the fishes," she warned, "for I am not the spawn of pirate ancestors for naught. If, in the future, *I* decide there is cargo to be carried aboard this vessel, the profits from its sale will be divided equally among us. Ives-Pierre shall serve as my first mate, Benoit my second mate, and Emile my bosun. Thibaud"—she turned to her vanquished opponent, wanting to make a friend of him—"can you handle a cannon as well as you do a rapier?"

"*Oui*, Capitaine," he affirmed, acknowledging her new status with only the slightest hesitation.

"Then you shall be in charge of the guns. Olivier has some skill as a surgeon; Silvestre will act as our cook. The rest of you may assume whatever duties you perform best. You will each be given a daily ration of food and drink, as well as a small measure of grog. But I want no drunkards aboard my ship!'' Geneviève stared scornfully at the now-snoring Rupert. ''If we were to be assaulted, an inebriated sailor would prove useless at best and, at worst, might endanger us all.

''One last thing: Though I am a woman, you have seen for yourselves that I am not defenseless. Do not ever make the mistake of thinking otherwise. Despite my appearance and my actions this night, I am a lady and will have your respect as such. Do I make myself clear?''

''*Oui*, Capitaine,'' the crew said as one.

Satisfied, Geneviève turned to Ives-Pierre.

''Helmsman, bring her hard about to starboard,'' she directed, ''and increase our speed three knots. Look lively, men! We've made good our escape from France, and I mean to set foot on England's shores before daybreak!''

Chapter Eight

The wind was brisk upon the open seas, lifting the unfurled sails and sending them billowing in the silvery darkness so they appeared like specters gliding through the night. The soughing crackle of the canvas split the greyish stillness like ghostly whispers, and the timbers of the mast and spars creaked and groaned as they strained against the breeze, adding to the eerie effect. Above, the stars shimmered like a million gleaming eyes looking down upon the earth, while below, the waves rose and fell, foaming white crests breaking gently against the sleek bow of the sloop as it sliced through the waters, traveling steadily toward the jagged coast of England in the distance.

As the hours lengthened, a cool mist began to settle over the ocean, cloaking the ship and its surroundings in a soft, hazy shroud. But, though the stars were soon obliterated, Geneviève was undaunted as she stood upon the deck of the vessel. Unerringly she guided the sloop's course, further adding to the simple seamen's suspicion that she was, in reality, a witch.

Inwardly the notion made her smile, but still, the thought had given her an idea, and she meant to put it to good use.

As the shores of France had fallen farther and farther behind until at last they'd disappeared completely, she'd mulled over her situation endlessly, trying to work out the details of the half-formed plot in her mind. It had come to her that she could not, as Geneviève Saint-Georges, readily return to her homeland, where Claude was bound to seek out and apprehend her. But, as an unknown entity . . . *oui*, she might come and go as she pleased, provided she were clever and daring. If she were careful, Claude would never suspect her true identity, and by the time he learned it, it would be too late. She would have her revenge upon him.

She smiled once more at the thought, but it was a strange, hard smile that did not quite reach her eyes, causing the sailors to glance at one another nervously again, wondering what she was thinking.

Oui, she was indeed a sorceress, a witch!—their eyes passed the message to one another silently; and, each deciding he did not want to be the one to cross her, the men returned to their duties more diligently than ever.

Turning from her contemplation of the sea, satisfied that all was in order, Geneviève spied her cap still lying upon the deck and retrieved it. Then she sought the captain's cabin she had claimed as her own.

It was not very spacious, for *La Belle Fille* was not a large ship, but what the chamber lacked in room, it more than made up for in amenities. To the right, built in along the entire wall, were a comfortable bed with a thick, colorful satin counterpane, and a pair of night tables, both of which had brass whale-oil lanterns screwed firmly to their tops. Four drawers each, with ornate brass handles that had been polished until they shone, pulled out from the tables, making the utmost use of storage space. Above the bunk and tables were more cabinets, in which were kept extra pillows, blankets, sheets, and other odds and ends. Just beneath the enclosed shelves on the wall hung a beautifully appointed tapestry that had been in Geneviève's family for generations. At the foot of the bed reposed a large, brass-bound wooden sea chest that would have contained the girl's clothes, had she had any other than what she was wearing. On the left side of the bed, anchored to the floor, stood a carefully positioned cheval mirror for dressing. On the right, also bolted to the floor, was a small washstand that bore a porcelain basin and pitcher; it was topped by an oval looking glass. Next to this sat a hammered-brass washtub that, while not very big, would easily accommodate Geneviève.

Directly ahead was an expansive bay window lined with diamond-shaped, lead-glass panes that presented a soothing view of the ocean. Below this was housed a pine bench adorned by a blue velvet cushion; its lid lifted to reveal compartments containing china, silver, and linens. The settle also served as partial seating for the narrow but heavy pine dining table arrayed before it, which was surrounded on its three remaining sides by four gracefully carved wooden chairs covered with embroidered fabric.

The left wall boasted a pine escritoire with numerous cubicles stuffed with various logbooks and papers; the top section was composed of bookshelves, which were filled to overflowing. Nearby, so it would be close at hand, was a squat map chest whose slender drawers slid out to expose several maps and navigational charts. Two leather chairs and a small occasional table completed the furniture.

A brazier for keeping warm occupied the center of the room. On the floor was a plush Turkish carpet, the legacy of one of Geneviève's pirate ancestors; at the windows hung blue silk draperies tied back with sashes.

Geneviève had inhabited the chamber on previous occasions, for she had enjoyed several outings aboard the vessel since her father had presented her with it, and the sloop's captain had always insisted she make use of his room while he bunked with the first mate. The captain's and the first mate's cabins were the only private quarters on the ship; the rest of the crew made do wherever there was room to hang a hammock.

For a moment, as she surveyed her surroundings critically, Geneviève felt a pang of wistfulness as she realized she would doubtless never again employ the vessel for her own pleasure. Instead, the sloop was to play a vital part in her plan and must be put to work as soon as possible. Then she reminded herself of all she had lost, and some of her despair lessened as she recognized that, whatever its capacity, the ship at least still belonged to her. From now on, it would be her home, for though she loved Oncle William and Tante Dominique, Northchurch Abbey belonged to them, and Geneviève had visited the residence too infrequently in the past ever to feel like more than just a guest there. Of course, if she were to marry Justin, she would become the mistress of Blackheath Hall, her cousin's manor, but Geneviève had never seen the place, so it was unknown to her. *Non.* There was only *La Belle Fille* now to call her own.

Sighing, she glanced about the cabin once more and was mortified to catch a glimpse of herself in the cheval mirror. She inhaled sharply at the sight, scarcely recognizing the disheveled woman who stared back at her. Why, no wonder her crew had thought her a witch! She looked positively wild, like someone not of this earth! Though she had done her best to clean herself up at the Onfroi farm, she saw that her hair was still streaked in places with the walnut stain she had used to color it, and the wind and spindrift had played havoc with the long strands, as well, whipping them into curls and tangles about her face like a rat's nest. Here and there upon her exposed skin were small blotches of the same dye with which she had altered her flesh tone, and dark mauve circles ringed her eyes from lack of sleep. She was covered with a layer of sweat and grime from head to toe, and the wound in her thigh had broken open during her duel with Thibaud, causing blood once more to congeal upon her leg.

Now, as she gazed at the encrusted spot, Geneviève became aware of the shards of pain and exhaustion shooting through her body, and she wanted nothing more than to lie down and rest. Still, somehow she found the strength to summon Marc D'Arcy, Benoit's youngest brother and the seaman who had been assigned to handle her personal needs. He was a shy, quiet-spoken youth, scarcely older than Geneviève herself, and because of this, the others had voted that he attend her. The girl had heartily approved their choice, for she knew the D'Arcy brothers much better than she did the rest of the men aboard the vessel and had felt Marc would pose no threat to her.

"*Oui*, Capitaine?" he said after knocking upon, then opening, the door.

"I would like to have some hot water brought for my bath, Marc," Geneviève informed him. "If there is nothing else available, tap the casks containing the drinking water. We will be able to replenish them tomorrow—*non*, today," she amended as she noticed through the window that already the sky was beginning to lighten. "Also, see if Silvestre can scrounge up something to eat. It need not be hot or fancy; some bread and cheese and a bottle of wine will do. Then have Benoit relieve Ives-Pierre at the wheel. We have traveled many long miles together these past few weeks, and I am sure Ives-Pierre is as tired as I am. Have a bath and a meal delivered to his quarters as well, and get Olivier to take a look at his wound. That is all."

"*Oui*, Capitaine." Marc nodded respectfully, then closed the door.

Gratefully Geneviève sank down upon the nearest chair and started to pull from her feet the stout leather boots that had belonged to Berthe's brother. Then she stripped off her stockings and wiggled her toes with relief. All the Onfrois, it seemed, had much larger feet than Geneviève, and she'd been forced to stuff these shoes, too, with newspaper to make them fit. Her toes had been squeezed against the crumpled wads now for days. Then she removed her shirt and breeches and thankfully unwound the length of material with which she'd bound her breasts to flatten them. Determinedly she promised herself that the first thing she would do upon reaching England would be to purchase some new garments and footwear.

At last, her bathwater having been fetched, Geneviève slipped into the hammered-brass bathtub, sighing with pleasure as the warm liquid enveloped her. She lay back against the edge of the metal enclosure, soaking her aching body until finally the water began to grow cool. Then she scrubbed herself thoroughly with a bar of strong lye soap, wrinkling her nose with distaste at the smell and the harsh feel of the cake against her scalp and skin.

Morbleu! she thought. *Before I am through I shall have sweet, perfumed soap again, too!*

After rinsing herself off, she stepped from the bathtub and toweled herself dry. Then, while studying some of the charts she'd taken from the map chest, she wolfed down the meal Marc, wishing to please her, had left carefully arranged upon the table. Geneviève reminded herself to thank him in the morning. After that, unable to fend off any longer the weariness that engulfed her, she collapsed upon the bed, not even bothering to turn down the counterpane. Feeling truly safe for the first time in many long weeks, she fell instantly into a deep, peaceful slumber.

"Land ho! Land ho!"

At the sound of the loud cry and the urgent knocking upon her cabin door, Geneviève slowly opened her eyes, wondering at first where on earth she was. The comfortable, gently rocking bunk upon which she lay felt like heaven, and she was drowsily reluctant to leave it, certain she must be dreaming, for it seemed ages since she had slept in a real bed. She licked her lips and murmured something unintelligible, closing her lids once more. Then she rolled over, groping for the covers. To her surprise, she realized there weren't any and that she was stark naked besides. This time, her eyes flew open wide as everything suddenly came flooding back to her.

"Capitaine! Capitaine! Are you in there?" Marc called from outside her door, his voice rising and somewhat distraught. "Can you hear me? Are you all right? Capitaine!"

"*Oui! Oui!*" Geneviève shouted, scrambling from the bunk and searching frantically for her clothes, afraid, since he sounded so worried, that, despite her strictest admonitions against such, Marc might open the door without her permission and spy her nudity. "I'm coming! I'm coming!"

Bon Dieu! How could she have slept so late? For just a short, sweet time, with the sound of the ocean whispering in her ear, she had thought she was safe and snug in her bed at Château-sur-Mer. How could she have forgotten Claude Rambouillet, her furtive flight from the townhouse, and all the other events that had occurred these past few weeks? Oh, where were her shirt and her breeches?

"I'm coming!" she yelled again, locating her garments at last and hastily pulling them on. With her foot jammed halfway into one boot and the other held haphazardly in her hand, she hopped to the door and opened it. "*Oui?* What is it, Marc?" she asked.

"I am sorry to disturb you, Capitaine," he apologized, uncomfortably aware of her disarray, for her shirt was only half buttoned and revealed a tantalizing glimpse of her breasts, which she had not had time to bind. "But we are just off the coast of England, and the men are awaiting your orders."

"Tell them I will join them momentarily," she directed.

"*Oui,* Capitaine."

Geneviève closed the door firmly. Then, more slowly, she finished dressing. After that, taking a silver-handled brush from atop the washstand, she started to work on her snarled tresses, hauling the bristles impatiently through her hair, yanking furiously at knots and tangles. When finally she managed to run the brush smoothly through the locks, she scraped her hair back mercilessly and carefully folded it up into a short queue at her nape. She bound the whole with a piece of twine, having lost the riband she'd previously employed for this purpose. Then she put on her cap.

Once she had completed her toilet, she took one of the navigational charts from the map chest and, with it rolled up beneath her arm, stepped out onto the deck to join the others.

Instead of dissipating, the early morning fog had deepened, obscuring the coast in the distance. A light drizzle was falling steadily, too. For a moment, Geneviève surveyed the sloop sharply to be certain all was in order. Then, climbing the ladder to the forecastle, she strode to the fore rail and silently took the spyglass Ives-Pierre handed her. She waited until the wind had shifted the mist, causing the haze to lift slightly. Then she peered through the telescope, managing just a glimpse of the crooked line of rock-strewn beach and cliffs jutting along the Cornish coast less than a league away. A smile of triumph and satisfaction curved her lips. She turned and, with Ives-Pierre following, descended the ladder to address her crew, who were assembled on the main deck.

"*Bonjour, mes hommes,*" Geneviève greeted the sailors politely. "I applaud your fine work in carrying us to England so swiftly, and I apologize for keeping you waiting this morning." She paused for an instant, then continued.

"Please,"—she motioned to them to gather around —"I want you all to take a look at this." Carefully she unrolled the map; two of the seamen took its corners in hand and stretched it upright between them so everyone could see. "We are here"—Geneviève pointed—"just off the coast of Penzance, not far from Land's End. Do you see this slight indentation here, just north of the peninsula's tip?" She indicated a place upon the chart. The men nodded, and Geneviève went on. "From the looks of the markings, I would say it is a very narrow, shallow inlet wedged within this promontory, too small for most ships to venture into, lest they prove too wide to pass through the entrance or, once inside, run aground. But *La Belle Fille* is slender, and she draws no more than eight feet of water at the most. I propose that we investigate this cove. It may prove an excellent hiding place for the vessel."

"But, Capitaine, we are safe now in England," Benoit declared, somewhat surprised. "For what purpose would we wish to conceal *La Belle Fille*?"

"I have many reasons for wanting no one save yourselves to learn I am in possession of her," Geneviève stated. "In due course, I shall explain them to you, putting forth a scheme I hope you will find to your liking. However, at the moment, I am more intent on bringing us safely to shore. I mislike the look of that sky, for it appears as though a storm is brewing. La Manche can be perilous, and it would not do at all for us to be blown off course when we are so close to achieving our goal. To your posts, men! Look sharp! Before this morning ends, we shall set foot on England's shores!"

The crew scurried to their duties, and Geneviève, once she had finished her breakfast, relieved Benoit at the helm. Ives-Pierre offered to take the wheel, but she waved him aside, insisting he rest, for she feared that the wound in his side, while not debilitating, was troubling him more than he cared to admit. He was not, after all, a young man.

"Non, mon ami. There are arduous undertakings ahead for us," she told him, "and you must regain your strength. I shall rely on you more than you know, once we reach Oncle William's estate. I only hope I shall not prove too stern a taskmaster."

"Non, never that, Capitaine," Ives-Pierre answered, smiling. "As always, I am yours to command."

"Merci," she said. *"Merci."*

Under her deft guidance, the sloop rounded the point of the Cornish peninsula, and presently the inlet Geneviève had observed upon the map came into view. It was, as she had hoped, a narrow, shallow cove, little more than a crevasse, really, for steep cliffs flanked it on either side; and she knew if she managed to maneuver the ship within, *La Belle Fille* would not be able to be seen from the open seas unless the fissure were approached dead on. Huge boulders thrust up from the waters thrashing about the inlet's mouth, which would make entry difficult and dangerous for those who might prove curious about the vessel. The ocean rushed inward here swiftly, too; its backwash, as the current was turned by the end of the cove, churned and eddied treacherously, spraying froth. No one but a fool or someone as desperate as Geneviève was would have attempted to penetrate the crevasse.

"Capitaine!" Benoit cried upon spying the fissure. "Surely you cannot mean to sail *La Belle Fille* inside there! We'll be dashed upon the rocks! We'll all be killed!''

"And I say we will not," Geneviève rejoined more calmly than she felt, for her hands were trembling upon the wheel and her heart was pounding with fear. Could she do it? *Par Dieu!* She could, and she would! "Strike the topsail," she demanded. "Reef the mainsail and the spanker, and furl the jibs. Then batten down the hatches. We're in for a rough ride. Did you hear me, sailor?" she barked sharply when Benoit failed to move. "I gave you an order, and I expect it to be carried out!"

In the end, it was Thibaud who, with a gleam of excitement and daring in his eyes, repeated Geneviève's command, prodding the petrified men to action, despite all of Benoit's pleading otherwise.

"You bloody fools!" Thibaud shouted scornfully. "Can't you see a squall's about to hit! If we don't find some sort of shelter—and soon—we're liable to be battered to pieces anyway. I'm for taking my chances with the crimson witch!"

Apparently the rest of the crew agreed, for hurriedly the sails were lowered—and none too soon, for the firmament had grown ever darker with the passing of time, and now the earlier drizzle turned suddenly to pelting rain as the skies opened up to disgorge their contents. Lightning flashed, and thunder roared, splitting the heavens, and the wind rose like a banshee howling in their ears.

Through the blinding lash of the rain that whipped her unmercifully, Geneviève stared at the narrow mouth of the inlet, praying that the charts she had studied were accurate and that the deadly boulders protruding like gaping sharks' teeth along the opening of the cove had not shifted with the passage of time, yielding to the force of the current.

Grim-faced, Ives-Pierre stood behind her, ready to steady her at the helm, should the wheel be ripped from her grasp.

"I hope you know what you are doing, Mademoiselle Genette," he remarked tersely, yelling to be heard above the gale.

Geneviève hoped so, too, for she knew she held her life—and the lives of the others—in the palms of her hands. She gripped the wheel tightly, her heart in her throat, as she steered the sloop ever forward toward the jagged rocks.

La Belle Fille rose and fell with the swell of the raging crests, her bow heaving up magnificently from the stormy waves, then plunging back down into the swirling surf. The timbers of the mast and spars creaked and groaned as they strained beneath the burden of the reefed canvas nearly torn from the riggings by each gust of wind. The crevasse and the crags drew closer and closer, seeming to grow larger and more ominous with each lunge of the sloop.

The seamen watched, stricken with terror, as slowly Geneviève began to navigate the jeopardous mouth of the fissure. Only Thibaud was not enthralled by fear. His dark head was thrown back; his teeth flashed whitely against his dark skin as he laughed with intoxication at the danger they faced.

Something in his mood caught Geneviève in its clutches, and to her horror, she felt a strange, savage thrill of exhilaration shoot through her being as she tossed her head, feeling the wind, the rain, and the spindrift tear at her hair, loosing it from its confines and sending it streaming. Her own laughter rang out clearly above the gale, sounding like something wild and wicked to the ears of her terrified crew. A streak of what in some twenty-odd years would be known as Saint Elmo's fire danced down the rigging, glowing with an eerie green light that illuminated Geneviève's mocking, sloe-eyed face. The sight of her hollow-cheeked visage caused the superstitious sailors to cross themselves and to mutter prayers to Sainte Marie to protect them from the murderous boulders and the unholy witch who was threatening to ramrod them all straight to hell. Any minute now, they expected to hear the terrible, rending noise of the ship's hull as it was bashed to splinters against the rocks.

But they waited in vain, for somehow, miraculously, the vessel slipped through the crags unscathed.

"Furl the mainsail and the spanker!" Geneviève bellowed above the roar of the wind and sea. "Quickly! Quickly, *mes hommes*, or we'll be driven against the wall!"

Even now, the dark, towering end of the long, wyndlike inlet loomed horrifyingly before them, and just when it seemed *La Belle Fille* would indeed be smashed against the solid-faced cliff, the rush of the backwash engulfed her in its grip, flinging her back toward the opening of the cove strewn with the perilous boulders.

"*Mon Dieu*," someone moaned.

Had they survived the first passage, only to be destroyed by a second?

The sloop reeled upon the whitecapped crests as Geneviève fought frantically for control of the helm, feeling the ship buck and rear beneath her feet as the backwash hurled the vessel onward. Then, without warning, uncannily, as suddenly as it had arisen, the wind died and the rain lessened to a mere trickle. Gradually the brutal pounding of the madding surf ceased, and *La Belle Fille* came slowly to rest in her hiding place, bobbing gently upon the waves.

"*Jésus*. Oh, *Jésus*."

The now-sober Rupert suddenly felt the full effects of his ghastly hangover. His face a sickly pea green, he staggered to the port rail, leaned precariously over the balustrade, and was violently ill.

Fabien fell to his knees, murmuring a silent prayer of thanks to God, while the remainder of the crew gazed at one another incredulously, scarcely daring to believe they were yet alive.

"*Merde*," Thibaud swore softly, slightly astonished. "She did it! The crimson witch actually pulled it off!" He looked at Geneviève admiringly, his respect now given freely rather than grudgingly, as it had been before. "I don't know where you learned to sail, mademoiselle, but you can be my *capitaine* anytime."

Had Geneviève not been so shaken, she would have reprimanded him sternly, for more than a flicker of interest lay deep within his dark eyes, and she would not tolerate any disrespect. She was well aware that, at any given moment, these rough men of Brest might turn on her and wreak what havoc they willed upon her person and that even Ives-Pierre would not be able to stop them. As it was, unable to summon another ounce of courage, she merely frowned.

" 'Twas a fool's gamble," she admitted honestly. "In truth, I might have killed us all."

Still quivering, she managed to pry her fingers from the wheel, unsurprised to discover they were curled like talons around the knobs and that her knuckles were as white as death. She swallowed hard, and only gradually did the terrible thudding of her heart return to normal.

At last Geneviève was able to inspect the sloop's place of concealment. It was perfect, she thought, just barely wide enough and long enough to accommodate the ship. Had *La Belle Fille* not been so small and slender, her draft so shallow, she would indeed have been caught fast at the mouth of the crevasse or run aground upon the boulders. The sheer, forbidding promontory that formed the fissure soared above them, taller than the spire-shaped mast of the vessel. Geneviève had no doubt that the sloop's riggings would not be able to be seen from the vast expanse of moor above unless one were to stand almost at the edge of the cliffs.

She closed her eyes and breathed a sigh of relief. She had done it. *Par Dieu!* She had done it!

Chapter Nine

The mist that earlier had enshrouded the seas had vanished with the coming of the rain; and now that the downpour, too, had stopped, the dark clouds that had obscured the firmament slowly gave way before the onslaught of the sun's rays struggling to break through to the earth. Though the skies were still slightly over-cast, it was evident the afternoon would be bright and warm.

The gulls rose from their resting places, where they had ridden out the storm, taking flight majestically, their white wings spread wide as they soared against the heavens. Their mournful, melodious cries rang out over the ocean, a sweet counterpoint to the sound of the breakers now rippling softly against the rocks lining the narrow strip of beach.

Fancifully Geneviève imagined the birds were welcoming her to England, and her heart lifted joyously within her. She had made it. She had escaped safely from France. She was *free!* At the recognition, tears of happiness mingled with tears of sorrow streaked her cheeks, for despite her overwhelming sense of triumph and gladness, there was, too, the sad, bitter thought of those she had left behind—Papa and Maman, who perhaps had given their lives to save her own, and Vachel, her twin, with whom she shared a special bond that would be broken only by death.

More fiercely than ever, Geneviève's determination to save her family strengthened within her, and she turned to the men who, awed by her stunning feat of daring, were silently awaiting her orders. Now, more than ever, did they believe her to be a witch, for they were convinced only a sorceress could have maneuvered *La Belle Fille* unharmed through the perilous opening of the inlet.

"Weigh anchor," Geneviève commanded. "Then lower one of the dinghies. If my calculations are correct, we are not too far from Saint Ives. I will take Ives-Pierre, Benoit, Pernel, and Davide with me. The rest of you will remain here with the sloop. Emile will be in charge during our absence. While I am gone, I expect you to inspect the ship for any damages that may have occurred during the squall and to effect any needed repairs. On no account are you to leave the vessel; and I suppose," she asserted, her voice low, a smile beginning to curve her lips, "that I need have no fear of your sailing away without me."

To her delight, Thibaud threw back his head and roared with laughter at the remark, and the strange, tense stillness that had previously filled the air was broken as, one by one, the others started to chuckle.

"Capitaine," Olivier observed dryly, "the very idea is *très fou!* How could you even consider that we might make such an attempt? You have proved your expertise as both a fencer and a sailor. I do not believe any of us will seek to challenge your authority again.''

"That is the truth!" Rupert put in, groaning. "Oh, *mes cousins,* how could you do this to me? *Sacrebleu!* I thought 'twas all just a bad dream, and now I awaken to find it is not! I am aboard a ship—when you know I suffer from *le mal de mer,''* he moaned censuringly, "and the vessel is captained by a lunatic female besides!"

"Mon Dieu!'' Benoit swore. "You shall not speak of Mademoiselle Saint-Georges so, Rupert! She has been kind enough to give you a job, which you badly needed, and to overlook your drunken attempt to run her through with your blade last evening when you mistook her for your rival in Deauville. Apologize at once, *mon cousin!''*

"Is this so?" Rupert inquired, much astonished. "But truly I do not remember....Oh, my poor head...it does ache so, and my stomach feels quite nauseated. It is the sea, of course." He glanced accusingly at Benoit once more, then turned again to Geneviève. "I do most humbly beg your pardon, Capitaine...La Folle." He grinned slyly, then winked engagingly. *"Non.* That is not quite right, is it, Capitaine Saint-Georges?" he corrected himself. "Or is it?" He shrugged and lifted his palms. "As you can see, I am not at all well."

"Rupert!" Emile burst out, mortified. "That is twice now you have insulted Mademoiselle Saint-Georges. Apologize!"

Despite her attempt to scowl at Rupert as he'd teasingly affronted her again by calling her Captain Madwoman, the girl found her mouth quirked with humor, and she could not take offense at the suggestion that she was not quite sane. Indeed, she believed she must have been crazy to steer *La Belle Fille* into the cove—especially during a storm—and she was not overly confident that she would be able to guide the sloop out once more. Besides, she needed a new identity for her plan, and perversely Geneviève rather liked the name Rupert had bestowed upon her.

"It is of no importance, Emile." She waved aside his protests. "Capitaine La Folle will serve as well as any other name, and for reasons of my own, I do not want my true one used aboard this ship again. Now, *mes hommes*, let's get busy, for we have much to accomplish in the coming weeks."

The heavy iron anchor was dropped into the water, securing the vessel's position, and one of the two dinghies was lowered overboard. After that, a rope ladder was tossed over the starboard rail, and Geneviève and her landing party descended into the small boat. This they rowed carefully through the crevasse, around one side of the cliff to the beach. Once there, they dragged the dinghy up onto the sand and covered it with some of the heather and gorse that grew thick in the region.

By chance, they discovered an old dirt track leading up the sloping terrain from the beach to the moors; evidently they were not the first to find and employ the fissure as a hiding place. Then, having no other means of transportation, they set off at a walk in the general direction of the little fishing village of Saint Ives.

As they strode along, Geneviève informed the others of the scheme she was plotting for the rescue of her family, explaining the reasons why she felt her uncle, William, and her cousin, Justin, would not be of any assistance to her and why she was therefore driven to pursue her own course of action.

"I simply must get Papa, Maman, and Vachel out

of France—if they are still alive," she declared, dismissing the expostulations of the rest. "Of course it will be dangerous. That is why, when you return to *La Belle Fille*, you must tell the others they are free to leave my service if they so desire. I want at my back only those who are loyal and unafraid! Come, come," she insisted. "Did I not best Thibaud during our duel? Did I not bring us safely into our place of concealment, past the rocks Benoit said we would be dashed upon and killed? What further proof do you need that I can do as I claim and carry out my plan?" she questioned sharply, angry and somewhat fearful that the sailors would refuse to help her after all.

"None, Mademoiselle Genette," Ives-Pierre responded soothingly. "We were merely concerned about your well-being, that is all. 'Twould not do if you were to fall into Monsieur Rambouillet's clutches when you have risked your life to escape from them—and perhaps the lives of Monsieur le Comte and Madame la Comtesse, too," he reminded her grimly. "Of course we will aid you in any way we can."

"*Oui.*" Benoit nodded, as did Davide and Pernel.

"Very well," Geneviève said, somewhat mollified. "Then, Benoit, you, Davide, and Pernel shall take these gems"—from the pouch at her waist she brought forth the stolen jewels she and Ives-Pierre had found upon the bodies of the reivers—"and sell them for the best price you can obtain. It probably will not be much, for I do not doubt that every *émigré* who has managed to reach England is parting with his possessions in much the same manner. But it should be enough to acquire the supplies we require. You will then return to *La Belle Fille* to carry out my instructions.

"Once you and the rest have finished the alterations to the sloop, I want you to find out as unobtrusively as possible whatever you can in Saint Ives and Penzance, as well. We will need information and connections if we are to dispose of our cargoes without detection, and I did not escape from the rabble who call themselves the French government, only to be taken prisoner by English dragoons!

"Ives-Pierre and I will journey on to Northchurch Abbey. Once we have discovered the lay of the land at my uncle's estate, I will send word to you."

"As you wish, Capitaine," Benoit replied. "We will do all you have asked of us, then wait until we hear from you further."

Though it had been less than a month since her flight from the townhouse in Paris, to Geneviève it had seemed like an eternity, and now, dressed in the plain but proper hat, gown, and shoes she had purchased in Saint Ives, she was surprised to find she felt distinctly uncomfortable and missed the freedom of movement her boy's clothes had provided. How easily she had adjusted to the ways of her youth, when she'd often donned such garments and demanded to be given male roles in the plays she and Vachel had performed for their parents. How strange it seemed now to revert once more to the feminine raiment and manners she had known so briefly before life in France had gone so awry.

Her countenance etched with sorrow now that she no longer needed to maintain the bold front she'd employed for the benefit of her crew, she gazed out the window of the public coach in which she and Ives-Pierre were traveling to Northchurch Abbey. There was a stark wildness about the sweep of the moors that Geneviève had always before found intriguing, but today, the savage countryside had little effect upon her. She was too engrossed in her thoughts and the mixed reception she believed she would face at her uncle's estate.

Tante Dominique, she knew, would be overjoyed to see her. But Oncle William and Justin, she was afraid, would prove another matter altogether. Oh, if only Vachel were with her! With his sly, witty remarks and his clever, though often outrageous, antics, he had always been able to coax a reluctant smile from their uncle and to give their cousin as good as he gave.

Geneviève had usually been too hesitant to engage Lord Northchurch in light banter, for, in her mind, she'd always cast him in the role of martinet and had expected him to play the part.

Justin, of course, had never failed to provoke her, causing her to lose her temper and give him the sharp edge of her tongue. On more than one occasion, she recalled with a rueful smile, she'd even threatened him with her rapier. Once, with her blade, she'd actually expertly sliced off the buttons of a new, striped waistcoat he'd been wearing and of which he'd been especially fond. Though physically uninjured, Justin had grown so angry that, for a moment, Geneviève had feared he might beat her. Only with the greatest of difficulty, she was sure, had he managed to restrain himself. No doubt, she thought, he would not view with pleasure her arrival at his parents' home. She remembered how cruel and mocking he could be when it suited him, and once more her heart sank at the idea that she would be expected to marry him.

Well, Justin had made it clear often enough in the

past that he had no desire to wed her, so perhaps he was unchanged in this resolve. Geneviève found some slight measure of comfort in the notion and prayed her cousin would not be present upon her arrival at Northchurch Abbey.

The journey to her uncle's estate, which was located on the Devon side of the River Tamar, normally a two-day trip, was tedious and took nearly twice as long, for the coach suffered a broken axle that required several hours to repair. But eventually, after numerous stops to change horses and various other assorted delays, the vehicle at last set Geneviève and Ives-Pierre down at the post nearest Northchurch Abbey. A five-mile walk followed, during which, for the first time, Geneviève was thankful she had no baggage, though at the inns at which she and Ives-Pierre had spent the night upon the road, her lack of such had caused her to be treated with a great deal of contempt until it had been learned she was an *émigrée*. After that, everyone had commiserated at her misfortune, shaking their heads sadly over her loss and offering her what small comfort they could.

Finally her uncle's estate came into view, and then Geneviève and Ives-Pierre were standing before the black wrought-iron gates of the manor.

Originally a monastery, from which it had drawn its name, Northchurch Abbey had been built during the sixteenth century. It was constructed of the finest Bath stone that, over the centuries, had mellowed to a soft cream color that shone golden in the sunlight, reflecting every nuance of light and shadow.

Quadrangular in shape, the house was three stories high, with the exceptions of the front and back portions, where over the corners of the wings, fourth stories sat like small, square buildings upon the flat roof. The center of the main part of the dwelling was also topped by a fourth floor, but instead of having a slant-sided roof like the others, this was capped by a terrace bounded on all four sides by a stone balustrade. In the middle of the square stood a tall, open, hexagonal cupola whose lead-covered dome was supported by six slim, graceful columns. Through the apertures formed by the pillars could still be seen the iron bell that had once been used to summon the monks of the abbey to prayer.

The portico leading into the manor boasted two solid oak doors with brass knockers; on either side of the entrance rose slender towers whose peaks almost but not quite soared higher than the spire that reposed upon the cupola's dome.

Long, narrow casement windows with mullioned panes of fine Venetian glass were set regularly into the house on all four sides and all stories. The panes, being *cristallo*, were made with soda and had a greyish cast, making them look like glittering diamonds when struck just so by the sun's rays.

Here and there, English ivy grew up the walls, lessening their austerity. To soften further the angularity of the manor, several tall chimneys, some round, some square, jutted up from the flat roof that, having a stone railing on either side, served as an open walkway adjoining the fourth floors.

The house itself surrounded a large courtyard filled with a gay profusion of carefully cultivated flowers and trees. Near the dwelling stood various towering old English oaks and ashes, grey poplars and black alders, and beeches and birches, whose overhanging branches provided a welcome shade. On one of the lawns was a small, cool, serene pond that had been well stocked with fish. Set on another wide expanse of green grass, a meticulously clipped hedge formed an intricate maze.

It had been some time since Geneviève had seen the place, and as, after having been admitted by the gatekeeper, she and Ives-Pierre made their way up the long, winding road leading to the manor, she was struck anew by the building's dignified elegance and grace.

When at last they stood within the portico, she took a deep breath and banged one of the brass knockers loudly. Presently the doors were opened by Kinsey, the butler.

"Lady Geneviève!" he greeted the girl, startled by the sight of her into losing his normally stiff and composed demeanor. "Is it truly you, my lady?"

"Indeed it is, Kinsey. How nice to see you again; you're looking very well." Geneviève found herself automatically making all the right responses—and in English, too—as though it were every other day she turned up without bag or baggage upon her aunt's doorstep.

"Thank you, my lady. Do come in," he urged, trying but failing to repress his excitement. "You, too, Fourneaux." He nodded politely but somewhat coolly to Ives-Pierre. Then he continued. "The countess has been anticipating your arrival ever since receipt of Monsieur le Comte's letter, and I don't mind telling you, my lady, that she will be quite relieved to learn you have reached us safely. If you'll just step this way, please, my lady, I'll send someone to fetch her immediately." He flung open the doors to the drawing room, indicating that Geneviève should enter. "Would you care for some tea, my lady, and perhaps a light repast?" he suggested.

"Oui, merci beaucoup, Kinsey."

"I shall ring for some at once, then." Needlessly he fluffed up a few pillows on the sofa before making certain Geneviève was comfortably seated. Then he turned to Ives-Pierre. "Fourneaux, if you'd care to follow me, I'll have someone direct you to a chamber in the servants' quarters."

Ives-Pierre barely suppressed a grin as he left the room, for he knew Kinsey highly disapproved of him and his easy familiarity with the Saint-Georges family. It was he, the butler felt, who had encouraged Lady Geneviève's headstrong streak and behavior in the past; and now, as he led Ives-Pierre down one of the long corridors with which the old house was riddled, Kinsey shuddered slightly to himself to think down what paths of mischief Miss Mannering, Lord Northchurch's ward and already quite a madcap young woman, might be enticed by the ne'er-do-well retainer Monsieur le Comte, for God only knew what reasons, had seen fit to employ.

The butler was relieved Miss Mannering had chosen this afternoon to join some of her companions for an alfresco luncheon, for he thought the later she was exposed to a person such as Ives-Pierre, the better; and he had no doubt that the servant would be constantly at Lady Geneviève's side. Since both Lord Northchurch's niece and his ward were the same age and of similar temperament, it was inevitable, Kinsey decided sourly, that, upon being introduced, they would soon become best of friends; and Miss Mannering would thus be treated to long hours in Ives-Pierre's company. The butler only hoped Lord Northchurch's ward would not prove to have a penchant for breeches and a foil, the accoutrements he had, much to his mortification, once discovered Lady Geneviève putting to good use during some escapade carried out with her scamp of a twin brother.

Geneviève, had she known of Kinsey's censorious musings, would have bubbled with laughter and eagerly looked forward to meeting Miss Mannering, of whose existence she was yet unaware. Since she did not know the butler's thoughts, however, there was nothing to break the tense stillness that had settled upon her, once she had been left to her own devices in the drawing room, and so she sat silently, nervously stirring her tea and scarcely nibbling at the biscuits that had been served to her by one of the maids.

She was so lost in her reverie that she started violently when the doors to the drawing room, which Kinsey had closed upon his exit, were suddenly thrown open wide to admit the Countess of Northchurch, Lady Dominique Beauville Trevelyan. The sight of her aunt, an exact duplicate of Geneviève's mother, standing there upon the threshold so overwhelmed the girl that finally the tide of emotions she had dammed up within her over the past several weeks came flooding out in an unexpected rush.

"Tante Dominique!" Geneviève cried as she rose to her feet. "Oh, Tante Dominique!"

Then, sobbing uncontrollably, she flung herself into her aunt's outstretched, loving arms.

Chapter Ten

It was a long while before Geneviève was at last able to draw away from her aunt, and Dominique did not press her, sensing the girl needed desperately to be reassured that she was loved and safe and welcome at Northchurch Abbey. When finally Geneviève had regained her composure, Dominique quickly brushed away her own tears so her niece would not see them, then smiled gently.

"So, Genette," the countess said, "you are here. Oh, *ma petite,* how very glad I am to see you! I have been so worried about all of you and so afraid something dreadful had happened! William and I both wrote many times to Edouard and Lis-Marie; and then, when we heard nothing, William sent men to France to find out what had become of you. But the men never returned, and we could only assume they were captured and killed by that rabble who have imprisoned poor King Louis the Sixteenth and Queen Marie Antoinette. Then somehow Edouard's last letter reached us, informing us of your attempt to escape. . . ." Dominique's voice trailed off as she realized, despite all her hopes to the contrary, that her twin sister had remained behind in France.

"You wrote to us?" Geneviève questioned, much startled. "Oncle William sent men? Oh, Tante Dominique! This is terrible! I'm so ashamed. I thought *mon oncle* had deserted us because he was so angry at Papa. We never received any of your letters. That *canaille*, Claude Rambouillet, must have seized them, *oui*, and the ones we wrote to you, too, though we were careful to smuggle our mail out of the *hôtel* as best we could, rather than use the post. And no doubt Oncle William's men are indeed being held prisoner, as you surmised— if they have not already been executed! Oh!" Geneviève exclaimed again. "If that is the case, things are even worse in France than I feared, for it means those who have wrested control of the government from King Louis the Sixteenth will stop at nothing to achieve their ends! Papa must have shielded me and Maman from even more than we suspected. 'Tis a miracle you even received his last letter. I can only assume it was passed on by sympathetic hands."

"*Oui*, I thought as much," Dominique agreed raggedly, trying not to weep. "So, tell me, Genette: How were my dear Lis-Marie and Edouard when last you saw them? Do you think there is any possibility that they, too, may yet manage to escape and to make their way safely to England?"

"I—I do not know, Tante Dominique," Geneviève confessed. "They were both well when I left the *hôtel*, but still, they refused to come with me, no matter how much I pleaded for them to do so. They insisted on staying behind so life at the *hôtel* would appear to go on much as usual and I could get away without Claude knowing. Then, when we reached the château, Ives-Pierre, who fled from France with me, learned from Benoit D'Arcy that all had been discovered and that Papa and Maman had disappeared. But whether they were taken captive..." Geneviève shrugged sadly. "This, I do not know. I can only hope that somehow they, too, slipped through Claude's fingers and have gone into hiding."

"*Oui*. We must pray that that is the case," Dominique stated fervently, crossing herself. Then she continued. "And Vachel? You have heard nothing of him?"

"*Non*." Geneviève shook her head. "He was away, visiting friends, when Claude's evil intentions became known to us. I smuggled a letter from the *hôtel* to my brother, warning him of what had occurred, but whether he ever received it, I do not know. However, he never returned to the *hôtel* as planned, and surely I would know in my heart if something had happened to him."

"*Oui*. So you would, Genette." Dominique brightened considerably. "As I would know if Lis-Marie were dead. Oh, Genette! Now I am certain my twin sister is still alive and well! If there is a way to reach us, I know she and Edouard will find it!"

Geneviève's heart soared at her aunt's words, and she became more determined than ever to put into action her scheme for rescuing her parents. That Oncle William, despite all her uncharitable thoughts about him previously, had already tried but failed in the attempt did not discourage her. His men, Geneviève reflected, were English—perhaps they had not even been able to speak French—and so they had been unfamiliar with the language, the customs, and the political situation in France. But her own men were French and accustomed to dealing with the many dangers that had beset the country since her king had been deposed. They would understand the importance of caution and secrecy, the need to beware of those who would denounce them to the government and cause them to forfeit their heads to Madame Guillotine.

The girl was so engrossed in her thoughts that it was some time before she became aware that her aunt was speaking to her again.

"Please forgive me, Genette," Dominique was saying. "I don't know where my manners are. Indeed, I was so overcome by emotion at your arrival that I believe I quite forgot them. No doubt you are exhausted, *ma petite,* and here I've kept you talking, for I've been so anxious. . . . Come, let me show you to your room. 'Tis the same one you have always used at Northchurch Abbey. I will see that you are made comfortable. Then I shall send someone to inform William and Justin and Kitty, too, that you are here."

"Justin is in residence?" Geneviève queried, somewhat downcast by the notion.

"*Oui.* But only temporarily, of course, for he has lived at Blackheath Hall for many years now. He had some business to discuss with William, I believe, but who knows?" Dominique shrugged and laughed a little, but Geneviève thought her aunt sounded a trifle bitter. "These days, Justin hardly tells me anything," the countess went on. "He comes and goes at odd hours, gambling and—and . . . engaging in other . . . amorous pursuits, I've no doubt. That's one of the many reasons why I'm so glad you've come, Genette." Dominique spoke impulsively as they ascended the wide, curving flight of stairs to the second floor. "I hope that as Justin's bride, you will have a steadying influence upon him. He has seemed so different of late, so—so strange and preoccupied. But I'm sure all that will change, once you and he are wed,'' the countess asserted more cheerfully, shaking off her misgivings about her son.

"He and William have gone hunting today, for the Season is quite over in London, you know, and most have retired to their estates for the summer,'' Dominique rattled on, paying no heed to how still her niece had fallen at her previous words. "Justin and William will not have foraged too far from home, however, for William suffered a riding accident last winter, and his right leg still pains him. He must walk with a cane now.

"I know they'll both be very pleased to see you, Genette, as will Kitty, William's ward. You've not met her, for until he died, Squire Mannering, her father, kept the poor child so close to home that she scarcely had any life of her own. I'm afraid''—the countess smiled ruefully—''that since her arrival at Northchurch Abbey, she's become quite a madcap, trying to make up for lost time, and I've done little to restrain her, believing that youth must have its fun and follies after all. You shall like her immensely, I promise.

"I always longed for a daughter, but after Justin was born, I couldn't have any more children, you know, so Kitty has helped to fill that void. And of course, William and I are looking forward to having you not only as our niece, but as our daughter, too, dear Genette, for it has long been my fondest wish in life, and Lis-Marie's, as well, to see you and Justin married,'' Dominique declared, giving her niece a warm, enthusiastic hug.

Geneviève, enveloped by a crush of sweet, fragrant scent, could only swallow hard and return the embrace, not wishing to cause her aunt further distress.

Though she had hoped her childhood betrothal to Justin had long been forgotten, she knew now that it had not. Her heart had sunk at her aunt's obvious pleasure in discussing the future event, and now she was cast into even deeper gloom, for she could not bring herself to utter the protests that tumbled to her lips. Not for the world would the girl hurt her aunt, who, bravely concealing her own fright and sorrow over the unknown fate of Edouard and Lis-Marie, had welcomed her so lovingly to Northchurch Abbey. How hateful she would be, Geneviève realized, to repay Tante Dominique by refusing to marry her son.

"Ah, here we are," the countess remarked as she threw open the door to Geneviève's bedroom, unaware her niece had been emotionally torn apart by their conversation just past. Dominique eyed the chamber sharply for a moment, then nodded with satisfaction. "All is in readiness, I see. *Bon.*

"Genette, this is Emeline, who shall serve as your abigail," the countess said, indicating a young maid, who curtsied to them both. "She is quite clever at arranging hair and with one's wardrobe, and she speaks a little French, besides. That is why I thought you might like to have her assist you. Perhaps she will help to ease some of the homesickness and heartache I know you must be suffering."

"*Oui.* How very like you, Tante Dominique, to think of that," Geneviève murmured, touched.

Once more she felt her aunt's kindness closing around her, effectively preventing her escape from marriage to Justin, and she sighed, deciding there was really nothing else she could do but make the best of the situation. She would be cruel and churlish to do otherwise. It was far better, Geneviève thought, to relegate that role to Justin, who might voice strenuous objections to wedding her!

With that hope in mind, she glanced about the powder-blue room, where she had always stayed the few times she'd visited the estate. Directly ahead was an elegant bed of cream-colored wood gilded with gold leaf. Its soaring canopy reached the top of the high ceiling and was draped with satin curtains, some blue, others gold; these were tied back at each Ionic pediment with gold, tasseled ropes. A cream-colored silk counterpane embroidered with soft blue and gold thread that intertwined to create beautiful, intricately detailed flowers lay upon the bed, which was surrounded by a blue silk dust ruffle. On either side were matching wood night tables with delicate, gold-handled drawers and gracefully curved cabriole legs. Upon each table was an ornate gold lamp with a glass hurricane shade. At the foot of the bed rested a bench covered with blue satin.

To one side was a dresser with compartments for storing cosmetics and other toiletries and whose top, when the center was opened, lifted to reveal a hinged mirror. Gold-filigreed trays, one filled with crystal flacons of perfume, the other bearing a gold brush, comb, and hand mirror, reposed upon the vanity. Before it sat a gorgeous Louis XV chair upholstered in blue velvet. Nearby stood a large armoire.

On the opposite wall, in front of the marble fireplace, were two chaise-longues, also done in blue velvet. Conveniently scattered here and there were small occasional tables that displayed various handpainted china vases and figurines.

The plaster ceiling boasted a crystal chandelier with several candles. Between the cream pilasters, the walls were painted a pale blue. Blue satin curtains hung at the two sets of Venetian-glass-paned French doors leading to the balcony. These had been opened to admit a refreshing breeze. A blue-and-gold Turkish carpet lay upon the floor.

It was a chamber that had been lovingly designed and furnished to appeal to a young woman, and as Geneviève gazed at it, for a moment, it was almost as though she had come home. The room appeared just as she'd left it last, and it was obvious from this that her aunt had allowed no one else to use it in Geneviève's absence. The thought that it was kept especially for her further preyed upon the girl's mind, strengthening her resolve to say nothing about not wanting to marry her cousin, Justin.

"Emeline will fetch you some bathwater"—the countess nodded to the maid—"then you shall lie down and rest, Genette, for I've no doubt these past several weeks have been a terrible strain on you, *ma petite*. How weary you must be!

"We will not dine until eight o'clock; I insist on keeping fashionable hours even in the country, so you need not rise before six. Emeline will wake you then.

"Oh, Genette! How very glad I am that you have come!" Dominique reaffirmed, her voice filled with emotion. Once more she hugged her niece. "If only Lis-Marie, Edouard, and Vachel were here, I would be the happiest woman in the world!"

Then, fearing she would give way to the tears that threatened to overwhelm her, the countess scurried from the chamber, closing the door behind her.

When her aunt had gone, Geneviève slipped gratefully into the bath Emeline, clucking over her like a mother hen, had hastened to prepare. Then, after the chattering maid had turned down the counterpane and

sheet, Geneviève slid into bed. She doubted she would
sleep, despite her exhaustion, for her thoughts were
churning too chaotically in her head. But she closed her
eyes anyway, and before she knew it, Emeline was
shaking her wide-awake.

"Mam'selle, 'tis six o'clock," the maid said.

Geneviève yawned, glancing at the little ormolu
clock that sat, ticking rhythmically, upon the mantel.
Bon cieux! She had not realized it was so late. It
seemed only a few minutes had passed since she'd lain
down to rest.

"There's a tray here, mam'selle, with some tea
and biscuits, if you're hungry," Emeline informed her.
"And Lady Northchurch will be along any moment with
some proper gowns for you, seeing as how you didn't
have any baggage and that outfit you had on when you
arrived wasn't at all the thing for dinner. Oh, mam'selle!"
The maid spoke, awed, her eyes huge and round. "Is it
true you barely escaped from France with your life?
That you crossed the English Channel in a smuggler's
small fishing boat?" she repeated the lie her new
mistress had told upon her arrival.

"Oui." Geneviève nodded, reluctantly throwing
back the covers and rising. "'Twas indeed a most
terrifying experience."

"Oh, mam'selle, I can imagine! The whole household is agog at your bravery!" Emeline confessed
artlessly as she deftly assisted her mistress into a filmy
dark peach wrapper that lay draped over the bench at
the foot of the bed.

"'Tis Miss Mannering's, mam'selle," the maid
explained at Geneviève's curious look. "I asked Rose—
that's Miss Mannering's abigail—if you might have it,
since you don't as yet have any of your own, although

I'm certain that will be remedied immediately, for Lady Northchurch has already dispatched a note to the seamstress."

"But, Emeline," Geneviève remonstrated the maid gently, "I cannot take Miss Mannering's things. She might not want to give them to me."

"Oh, she won't mind, mam'selle, I assure you. She's got a heart of gold—that one does. But the thing is—if you'll pardon a bit of gossip, mam'selle—Miss Mannering's late father, though he was worth a pretty penny, would see your nose cheese and the rats eating it before he'd part with a farthing—the old skinflint!—and Miss Mannering, before she came to us, wasn't used to wearing anything but horrid, old, dull brown and black frocks. So she doesn't have a lot of . . . well . . . sense about what colors best suit her. She *will* insist on pumpkin—and chartreuse, too—though she looks a fright in them since she's so pale, and Lady Northchurch is much too kind to tell her so straight out. Rose says your not having any clothes is a godsend, for you and Miss Mannering are about the same size, and what doesn't do at all for Miss Mannering, for she's as blond and blue-eyed as they come, will set off your vivid coloring to perfection, mam'selle. Really," Emeline stated firmly, "you shall be doing us all a favor by helping to weed out Miss Mannering's wardrobe."

Since Lady Northchurch, upon entering the chamber in time to hear the maid's last words, promptly echoed them, Geneviève could only smile ruefully and capitulate, hoping Miss Mannering would not be too angry at parting with so many garments. Indeed, from the bundles both the countess and the abigail, Rose, who had followed in her wake, were carrying, Geneviève wondered if Miss Mannering's armoire had not been virtually depleted.

"Tante Dominique!" Geneviève tried again lamely to protest. "I simply can't accept all of those!"

"Shhhhh. Of course you can, *ma petite*. It is as Emeline has said: Kitty has no notion of how to go on about clothes. See here . . . this white—like an oyster shell! And both Rose and I have suggested she choose ivory instead, for this undergown absolutely drains her of color. But observe, Genette," the countess continued, holding the dress up against Geneviève, "how it makes your skin glow and your hair appear to be aflame! *Alors!* I will hear no more about it! In no time we will have both you and Kitty looking as fine as sixpence!

"Rose"—Dominique turned to Miss Mannering's abigail—"you hang those things up in Mademoiselle Geneviève's wardrobe, while Emeline presses that gold frock and this white undergown; they will do very well for this evening. I must go to my chamber to fetch my jewel chest; I have a string of pearls that will go well with the dress. *Non*." With a wave of her hand, the countess forestalled Geneviève's further protests. "No more complaints, please, Genette, I beg of you. You are my niece after all, and besides, the pearls are part of a set that will come to you as Justin's bride anyway."

With that disconcerting remark, Dominique hurried from the room, leaving Geneviève feeling as though a whirlwind had just departed. Her head was fairly spinning from all the activity taking place around her, for the *hôtel* in Paris had been painfully still under the shroud of doom that had enveloped it, and her long days on the road with Ives-Pierre had been spent primarily in companionable silence. She had grown unused to the everyday hustle and bustle of a normal household.

To soothe her shattered nerves, she stepped outside onto the balcony, where, lost in thought, she leaned against the stone balustrade, surveying the gardens in the courtyard below. She was so absorbed in her reverie that it was some time before she realized she could hear the sounds of a conversation drifting to her ears, and she remembered that her chamber lay directly above her uncle's study.

Geneviève did not intentionally eavesdrop, but nevertheless, she couldn't seem to bring herself to budge as she recognized that the voices belonged to Lord Northchurch and Justin and that *she* was the topic of their heated discussion!

She heard her uncle mutter something unintelligible, then, very clearly, her cousin's spiteful reply floated up to her.

"Well, my lord," Justin snarled tersely to his father, "have you seen Genette yet? Have you reminded her of our betrothal—as you so decidedly reminded me? Is she indeed the impertinent, scatterbrained fool I feared, or has the incorrigible brat finally grown up and acquired some semblance of intelligence at last?"

Well, she had hoped Justin would not want to marry her, and it was plain he did not! She ought to be glad. But instead, tears of hurt and rage stung Geneviève's eyes at her cousin's hateful remarks; and she stumbled back blindly from the rail, not wanting to chance the two men seeing her, for it sounded as though they had stepped outside onto the terrace.

"Oh!" Geneviève cried softly. "How dare he? The—the . . . braying *ass!* Why, he has not changed a bit! I will kill him. I will!"

"*Non*, Genette. 'Tis I who shall have that pleasure," Dominique declared, her eyes flashing sparks and two bright spots of color high upon her cheeks. In her hands she clutched her jewel chest, and it appeared as though at any instant she would crush it, she was so wroth, for it was obvious she, too, had overheard Justin's insults. "How dare he indeed? Dear Genette, I am so sorry. I know he did not truly mean those terrible things he said. It's just that lately he has been so—so changed. Oh, Genette, though he is my son and I love him dearly, sometimes he infuriates me so badly I don't know what to do. How I wish someone would take him down a peg or two!"

She would never have a better opportunity, Geneviève realized, to inform her aunt that she did not want to marry Justin. But Dominique looked so upset and beseeching standing there in the doorway that once again the girl could not bring herself to hurt her.

Without warning, the childhood memory of another courtyard flashed into Geneviève's mind, and she saw herself as an angry seven-year-old whose wounded feelings had filled her with determination to best her cousin at dueling, acting, or anything else. She remembered how she had advanced after Justin's retreating figure and, brandishing her rapier, had delivered in her mind a perfect hit to his back. Oh, how fervently she wished now that it had not happened just in her imagination! How she wished she had actually stabbed her cousin ruthlessly, if only for the joy of seeing his dark face wiped clean of the mocking smile he'd worn upon it that day! Perhaps then he would not be so free with his mean insinuations about her now. Well, she would fix him. She would!

To the countess's surprise, Geneviève suddenly

dashed away her tears, and a sly, wicked grin stole over her face, the same unholy smile that had caused her crew to shudder and dub her a crimson witch.

"*Par Dieu*, Tante Dominique," she swore, "do not worry, for I mean to see that Justin gets the comeuppance he so richly deserves. Believe me: He shall not be so smug and arrogant, once I have done with him—the cad!"

Chapter Eleven

Geneviève stared at her reflection in the mirror, scarcely recognizing the saucy, vacuous woman, so unlike her true self, who gazed back at her, a mischievous smile of satisfaction playing about the corners of her lips. She had practiced the look for nearly twenty minutes, and now she was certain she had it down pat. How ravishingly ridiculous she appeared, she thought, exactly like the "impertinent, scatterbrained fool" Justin believed her to be.

With the eager, enthusiastic ministrations of Tante Dominique and Emeline, who were in on the plot, Geneviève had piled her long hair on top of her head so that, although it was not quite so towering a confection, it resembled the monstrous wigs of which Queen Marie Antoinette had been so fond. Long, slightly askew ringlets sprang up like corkscrews here and there from the mass and dangled haphazardly against Geneviève's neck. Emeline had powdered the bright copper locks until they were snow white, and between their howls of glee, the three conspirators had managed to pin a little gold bird's nest, complete with white bird—which they'd discovered in one of Dominique's old costume trunks—right square in the middle of Geneviève's head.

The countess had expertly painted her niece's face lightly, applying just the right shading here and there to alter subtly the girl's refined, aristocratic features. She no longer looked breathtakingly beautiful but instead was merely impishly attractive, like a sly pixie. The sloe of her eyes had been exaggerated until the orbs seemed positively catlike beneath her wickedly arched brows. The high bones of her hollow cheeks had been made even more angular and pronounced by the clever application of a touch of rouge, enhancing her spritelike appearance. Her slender, classic nose with its piquant tip had been transformed into one that was cute and snub. Her wide, generous mouth was now a tiny Cupid's bow. Despite her aunt's insistence that she choose the Gallant, Geneviève instead had defiantly affixed to her face a black patch known as the Murderous.

Pearl pendant earrings, so large they resembled bird's eggs, hung from her earlobes; a matching pearl necklace with a gold clasp just brushed her bare collarbones.

Her outer gown was all that could have been desired, for it was gold silk, a hue, Emeline had assured Geneviève, that had made Miss Mannering look all one color. On Geneviève, however, the effect was striking, for it made her skin seem like peaches and cream and brought to the surface the tiny gold flecks in her startlingly moss-green eyes. The décolletage was edged with delicate, oyster-white lace and was heart-shaped and cut very low to expose an enticing glimpse of her full, round breasts. The off-the-shoulder sleeves were skintight until they reached her elbows; there, they opened like trumpet flowers to reveal the spills of frothy oyster-white lace shot through with gold thread that formed the sleeves of her undergown. The dress nipped in at the waist, then billowed out like a bell over her small panniers to the hemline; this was scalloped, drawn up with small gold-and-white-striped bows to permit another peek at the generous ruffles of Geneviève's lacy white undergown. From beneath this peeped her gold slippers, for it had been discovered that fortuitously she and Miss Mannering wore the same size shoe, as well. A white, gold-handled fan completed her ensemble.

Now, as she pirouetted before the looking glass, then took a few mincing steps forward, Geneviève bubbled over with mirth at the sight of herself and the thought of the sweet revenge she would have on her cousin. Only when she had made a complete fool of him would she reveal her true self to him.

"Justin Duquesne Trevelyan, watch out!" she warned her reflection with a giggle of malicious merriment, waving her fan about as though it were a rapier. "For before this masquerade is over, I shall best you in more ways than one!"

"Oh, dear Genette"—Dominique laughed until tears ran down her face—"I believe you will. Truly I believe you will! Lud! I almost feel sorry for my poor, unsuspecting son!"

Justin Trevelyan, the seventh Viscount Blackheath, took inordinately special care as he dressed for dinner at

Northchurch Abbey that evening, for his father had uncomfortably impressed upon him the disagreeable consequences of his failing to make an effort to please both his mother and his cousin Geneviève, and he had no wish to suffer any of the various misfortunes that might result, should he incur the earl's wrath. Now the viscount frowned irritably at himself in the mirror over his dressing table as he tossed aside yet another ruined cravat.

Damn! What on earth was the matter with him tonight? Usually his long, dexterous fingers fairly flew when arranging the stiff creases and graceful folds of his neckerchief. With a small sigh, he turned to his valet, Wentworth, who stood nearby, holding several lengths of material draped over one arm. Justin selected another tie, pulled it somewhat impatiently around his neck, then began again the intricate details of what was known in polite circles as the Trevelyan Knot. Though it was his own invention, still, Justin could not seem to get it right, and this cravat, too, was discarded upon the floor.

This time, it was Wentworth who sighed sourly, for that was the sixth clean, starched, and pressed neckerchief that had been dealt with in so cavalier a fashion, and it was he who had taken such pains to wash and iron them. Still, he did not dare to suggest that his master allow him to fix the tie, for to do so would surely earn him one of Justin's nasty set-downs.

At last, to the viscount's satisfaction and the valet's relief, Justin's seventh attempt at tying the knot proved successful, the creases and folds of the burgundy silk cravat falling into place with perfection. Even Wentworth, who was extremely vain about his excellent skills and services, was forced to admit to himself that his lordship did indeed have a way with a neckerchief.

Justin stood, then eased himself into the well-tailored velvet dinner jacket Wentworth held out for him. The valet permitted himself a small smile as his master shrugged on the tight-fitting frock coat, for Justin did not have to pad his shoulders as so many other peers of the realm did.

"Once you have finished with your duties here, Wentworth"—the viscount spoke coolly—"you may have the rest of the evening off, for I've no doubt I shall be quite late, since 'tis Mademoiselle Geneviève's first night at Northchurch Abbey and I am sure my parents will want to see that she is properly entertained."

"Thank you, my lord," Wentworth said, pleased.

His lordship might be arrogant, but he was seldom inconsiderate, and he never left the valet sitting up waiting on him for hours on end. This was one of the reasons why Wentworth suffered Justin's temper and freaks in silence and considered himself fortunate to be employed by the viscount. Others of his ilk, Wentworth knew, were not so lucky, being overworked, underpaid, and the recipients of a great deal of additional abuse, both verbal and physical, whether well deserved or not. His master had never struck him; and though the valet was sometimes the object of a sharp, terse tongue-lashing, such was rarely given without cause, and when it was, an apology was always later forthcoming. Yes, Wentworth thought, he could do a lot worse than Lord Blackheath.

Humming under his breath to himself, the valet started to pick up the crumpled ties that littered the floor, wondering if Lady Geneviève's abigail, Emeline, was free later that evening.

* * *

If Geneviève were struck dumb by the sight of Justin, it was nothing compared to the effect she had upon him. In the process of inhaling a pinch of snuff when she and Tante Dominique made their deliberately delayed entrance into the drawing room, he inadvertently took in his nostril far too much of the special mixture and was instantly overcome by a violent fit of sneezing that soon progressed to coughing as the pulverized tobacco, which had been drawn up into his sinuses, found its way down his throat. For a moment, it appeared as though he would choke, but at last Justin managed to regain his composure, deftly downing a glass of Madeira to take away the vile taste in his mouth.

The countess, expertly summoning up all her years of acting experience, sternly quelled the peals of laughter that threatened to ring out from her lips and frowned at him with annoyance.

"Such a disagreeable habit, Justin," she remarked, "as I've told you on more than one occasion."

"The snuff or the wine, Maman?" he inquired as he dutifully stepped forward and bent to kiss her cheek.

"Both, you rogue." She tapped him playfully with her fan. "But I shall not cure you of either, I suppose. So . . ." Dominique shrugged carelessly. "*Enfin.* I wash my hands of the matter. But do make your bow to Genette so she will not think you are wholly lacking in manners. After all, she is soon to be your bride."

"But of course. It has been arranged these many years past, has it not?" Justin rejoined politely, giving no clue to his thoughts about the matter. "Ah, Cousine." He turned to Geneviève, giving her relationship to him its French pronunciation and repressing his desire to shudder slightly with distaste at the fairylike confection that confronted him, for even as a child, he had never been overly attached to elves. "Welcome to Northchurch Abbey, mademoiselle." He just brushed with his lips her outstretched hand. "France's loss is England's gain. We are indeed fortunate you reached us safely."

"*Merci*, monsieur," Geneviève said a little breathlessly, for she had not seen Justin for several years and thus had been totally unprepared for the result his appearance would have upon her.

She was devastated—absolutely and, to her, horribly devastated—for from the top of his head to the tips of his shoes, Justin Trevelyan was utterly, unbelievably handsome! This surely was not the boorish youth of her childhood memories, this man who bent his gaze upon her so coolly, appraising her as though she were a porcelain figurine he might or might not wish to purchase!

His shaggy, glossy hair was ebony, the color of a night sky without moon or stars to silver-streak its blackness, its length drawn back into a queue at his nape and carelessly bound with a grey silk riband. Beneath his unruly, demoniacally arched black brows, his keen grey eyes glittered like silver ice and were fringed with thick, spiky lashes as dark as soot. The bones above his lean, hollow cheeks were high and angular, like Geneviève's own, adding refinement and character to his sun-bronzed face. His nose was proud and aquiline, as though it had been chiseled from marble; his nostrils flared slightly above well-shaped, carnal lips that made Geneviève wonder what it would be like to be kissed by them. The cut of his jaw was square and determined, as though he were accustomed to knowing what he wanted—and to getting it, as well.

The thought furthered her agitation, for he did not appear to be a man who was easily fooled, and she was made uneasy by the fact that he might not be deceived by her masquerade. Geneviève would rather die than have Justin learn she had overheard his snide comments about her and had resorted to this silly subterfuge in order to punish him. The gold twigs that formed the bird's nest were stabbing into the top of her scalp painfully, and this heightened her dismay. She knew she would have a raging headache by the end of the evening, and she longed to tear the offending ornament from her hair before it did any further damage—either to her head or to Justin's perception of her.

How artificial and contrived she must seem, Geneviève realized, when compared to her cousin's understated elegance! And perversely, though she had wanted him to be appalled by her—and she believed he was, though he hid it well—now Geneviève wished she had not decided to make such a spectacle of herself.

The viscount was tall and, though lithe, powerfully built. His burgundy velvet, swallow-tailed frock coat, with its grey braid piping, deep cuffs, and solid silver buttons, clung snugly to his broad shoulders and muscled arms. Beneath the beautiful folds of his burgundy satin cravat, his crisp white linen shirt, with its cascade of foamy lace down the front and at his wrists, could not conceal the massiveness of his chest. This tapered to a trim waist with a firm, flat belly encased in a grey-and-burgundy-striped broadcloth waistcoat that bore the new modishly wide lapels and was adorned with solid silver buttons that matched those on his dinner jacket. The enticing outline of his narrow hips, rounded buttocks, and corded thighs was revealed by the tight cut of his grey broadcloth knee breeches (for his mother frowned on the new pantaloons made fashionable by the sans-culottes of the French Revolution), which closed at the knee with buttons like the rest. His burgundy hose displayed well-formed calves. Plain grey leather pumps with simple silver buckles were upon his feet.

He might have a dandy's care for dress, but no one would ever mistake Justin for a fop. His only jewelry were a silver signet ring and a pocket watch with a single silver fob and seal.

He was, Geneviève reflected with a touch of irritation, enough to make any woman swoon. Even now, her heart was hammering so erratically within her breast that she thought crossly that something must be wrong with it. Deliberately she forced herself to remember her recent losses and the fact that Justin, who might have eased her pain with kindness, had chosen to belittle her instead. Gradually the jerky thudding in her breast abated, and the walls Geneviève was slowly erecting around her heart inched a little higher.

"You are looking very well, Genette," her cousin told her courteously. Then he demeaned the compliment by adding, "I don't remember when I've seen such an—such an . . . interesting coiffure."

He eyed her in a way that made her uncomfortably aware of the fact that she resembled a peculiar, though not wholly unattractive, urchin, and this, coupled with her anger at him over his earlier hurtful remarks that had driven her to the impromptu charade, steeled her intent to carry it through.

"Oh, 'tis the latest thing in France, you know, to adorn one's hair in some manner," Geneviève responded airily, as though it were every day that, wearing a bird's nest, she sat down to dinner. "I think it is a charming fashion."

"Indeed?" Justin queried, lifting one eyebrow. "Then you were doubly fortunate not to have lost your head."

At this, it was all Geneviève could do to hold her tongue, but she forced herself to maintain her vacant stare, as though the true meaning of her cousin's words had escaped her.

"*Oui*," she continued with pretended earnest. "Why, a man may be murdered for a crust of bread in France these days. Only think what temptation a bird must offer!"

"What indeed!" Justin returned, swallowing hard.

"Well, *I* think it's a wonderful custom." A lovely young blond girl spoke, her hands outstretched in greeting as she hurried forward to welcome Geneviève. "I'm Kitty Mannering, Cousin Genette—oh, I do so hope I may call you such, though we aren't really related, after all. I'm Lord Northchurch's ward."

"*Oui*. Tante Dominique has told me about you. 'Tis you I have to thank for this beautiful frock I am wearing tonight and for all the other gorgeous clothes that now hang in my armoire."

"Oh, 'twas nothing, I assure you," Kitty demurred, her blue eyes somewhat shyly downcast, as though she were unsure of her reception. "For, indeed, that dress never looked half so good on me!" she confessed.

"But of course not," Geneviève noted, not being one to miss a cue and recognizing a perfect opening for assisting her aunt with Kitty's wardrobe. "For the gold of your hair must have outshone the gown, casting it into the shade."

"How sweet of you to say so." Kitty smiled, her eyes now sparkling with pleasure. "Though I suspect 'twas the other way around! Oh, isn't she pretty, Uncle

William?'' Kitty turned to the earl, who stood at her side.

"Indeed," Lord Northchurch replied, leaning heavily upon his cane as he limped forth to kiss Geneviève upon one cheek. "I would have known you anywhere, my dear, despite your somewhat unusual appearance." His keen grey eyes surveyed her piercingly for a moment, and she felt a little shiver of fright chase up her spine, for she thought she had not fooled him in the least. "How are you, Genette? Well, I trust," he continued.

"*Oui*, Oncle William. Thank you for taking me in. I shall try not to be too much of a burden to you."

"Nonsense!" the earl expostulated firmly. "You must consider Northchurch Abbey your home for as long as you wish."

"*Merci*, Oncle."

Just then Kinsey opened the doors to the drawing room.

"Dinner is served, my lord," the butler intoned solemnly.

"Well"—Lord Northchurch offered Geneviève his arm—"shall we go in, my dear?"

The evening meal was a very lively affair, for all put forth their best efforts to entertain. Conversation ranged from serious discussions to amusing anecdotes as fond memories were recalled and Geneviève and Kitty exchanged stories and gossip to become better acquainted. Both Lord Northchurch and Lord Blackheath were extremely interested in the political situation in France, about which Geneviève did her best to enlighten them, her observations so astute she earned several sharp, curious glances from both men before, after a quick, remonstrating glance from Tante Dominique, she remembered her role of the simpleton and hastily reassumed it.

After that, the viscount retreated beneath a politely cool facade, and Geneviève was able to study him surreptitiously from beneath her lashes.

How much easier things would be, she thought, if he were not so devilishly good-looking! Then perhaps she would not be so exasperatingly attracted to him, despite the fact that she strove to harden her heart against him, and she would not be, as well, so thoroughly annoyed with herself for dreaming up such childish means as a masquerade to gain her revenge upon him. How much simpler it would have been merely to have remained herself, admitted she was drawn to him, and teased him into falling in love with her. Then she could have given him the cold shoulder, after all, and had the satisfaction of watching him grovel at her feet! But, *non*, Geneviève reflected even as the idea occurred to her, Justin would never grovel. He was much too proud for that! *Non*, 'twas far more likely he would disdain her instead, especially once he learned how she had made a fool of him with her charade.

Well, even so, there was no point, surely, in allowing him to continue to think her an empty-headed chit. She was no miss just out of the schoolroom— especially after all she had lived through the past several weeks. Tomorrow, she would reveal to him the part she had played, and they could start anew. After all, she was going to marry Justin. Already her aunt had mentioned the matter, and he had not protested. So, although, from the conversation she'd overheard between him and her uncle, it seemed Justin might not relish the notion, he apparently, for reasons unknown to her, did not intend to find some means of extricating himself from their betrothal. No doubt Oncle William had had something to do with that, the girl correctly deduced.

Oh, was ever there such a tangle? It did not seem quite real that soon she would be wed to this man who, although her cousin, was almost a stranger to her and obviously had little interest in her, besides. Not that she desired him to, Geneviève hastily assured herself. Still, the idea that Justin did not want her piqued her pride and her vanity, for she had once, a lifetime ago, it seemed, been the reigning belle of Paris.

She wondered if perhaps her cousin was in love with Kitty, but after watching the two for several minutes, Geneviève concluded this was not the case. Like her relationship with Vachel, their attitudes toward each other were too much like those of brother and sister for them to be anything else, even if there was no blood bond between them. But neither—especially after overhearing his sarcastic comments about her—did Geneviève delude herself into thinking Justin loved her instead. How could he, when she hadn't even seen him for several years and it was obvious he still thought of her as a silly child? Still, if they were indeed to be wed, she would like to believe he at least respected her, and that would not be possible as long as he thought her a fool.

On the other hand, she mused, an idea slowly beginning to take shape in her mind, if he continued to believe her a brainless brat, he would not, once they were married, be encouraged to dance attendance on her and thus would leave her alone to pursue her own devices. That meant she would be free to come and go as she pleased; and Justin, assuming she whiled away her days and nights at endless routs, card parties, and various other frivolous pastimes, probably would not even bother to question her activities. It would be the perfect foil for her alias, Capitaine La Folle. Indeed, *no one* would suspect her dual role, Geneviève decided, nearly laughing out loud with sheer excitement at the notion. For Justin, if he learned of it, was bound to put an end to her fledgling scheme for rescuing her parents, since naturally he would not want his wife posing as a smuggler and traipsing about either the English or the French countryside; and certainly Geneviève could not risk being exposed to the French government by any spies it might have planted here in England. Oh, it *was* perfect! She might not win Justin's liking with her plot, but then, attracting him could never be as important as saving her parents' lives.

Her head reeled with exhilaration, and with a great deal of wicked amusement, Geneviève doubled her malicious efforts to convince her cousin she was a complete idiot.

After dinner, the ladies retired to the small salon, leaving the gentlemen alone with their port. Though Geneviève would have liked to know what the two men were discussing behind the closed dining-room doors, she realized there was quite a difference between an inadvertent eavesdropper and an intentional one, and so reluctantly she trailed along in her aunt's and Kitty's wake, listening with half an ear to the latter's amiable conversation. It was only when, a trifle breathlessly, Kitty mentioned the Black Mephisto, a purported spy, that Geneviève gave her full attention to the young blonde she had come to think of as her new cousin.

The Black Mephisto was a notorious but mysterious figure in France, for though he was infamous throughout the country, no one knew his true identity. He had been given the name the Black Mephisto because there were some who believed he was in league with the devil, as Faust's Mephistopheles had been, and because the French government always knew when he had struck, for quite insolently, as though to mock the authorities, he always left behind a black silk loo mask as his calling card.

So far, it was rumored, the Black Mephisto had managed to discover and to relay to the English, who feared war with France was imminent, numerous scraps of information regarding not only military intelligence, but other aspects of the French government, as well. Despite the Assembly's best efforts to plug its leaks, details about vital orders, strategic plans, new policies, and various other sensitive issues had all, by means unknown, somehow found their way into his hands and had been quietly conveyed to France's old enemy. In the stealthy process of uncovering and exposing this knowledge, the Black Mephisto had also, it was claimed, masterminded on at least three occasions the clever, daring escapes of several members of the French aristocracy who had been imprisoned and destined for the guillotine.

To the overthrown French nobles, he was an honored hero, and they would do anything to assist him; to the French authorities, he was an extremely dangerous adversary, and they would stop at nothing to apprehend him.

"I have heard of this man," Geneviève declared. "'Tis said the Assembly has a price on his head and has tried repeatedly to catch him—but to no avail. Always, he somehow manages to slip through the government's fingers.''

"That is because he is a master of disguise—or so I've been told," Kitty amended. "I wonder who he is.''

"In my country, it has been reported that he is a French *émigré* who, despite his escape from France, continues to work toward the restoration of the throne, like other Royalists,'' Geneviève elucidated. "Still others have said he is someone high up in the Assembly itself and a traitor to its cause.''

Kitty smiled.

"There. You see?'' She laughed delightedly. "The man is indeed adept at disguise, for here in England, 'tis claimed he is an Englishman attached to the Foreign Office.''

"Who is?'' Justin asked as he entered the small salon in time to overhear Kitty's last words.

Casually he made his way over to the silver serving tray that elegantly reposed upon a long hunting table; there, he poured himself a snifter of brandy. Then he sat down in a velvet-upholstered chair next to Geneviève.

"Why, the Black Mephisto, of course,'' Kitty answered.

"Oh, Kit,'' Justin groaned. "Let us not discuss that tiresome chap again. I swear. Was ever there such an accursed dull dog? One cannot attend even the simplest of card parties these days without being bored to death by a litany of the fellow's adventures. I tell you 'tis enough to make even the least jaded of men remain at home.''

"And you, of course, are not the least jaded of men, are you?'' Kitty shot back, pouting with irritation.

"Lud! What a pall you do cast upon us all with your perpetual ennui, Justin. Do go away and find something—anything—to entertain you, lest you put a further damper on our conversation." She turned to Geneviève. "I do not envy you him, Genette," Kitty vowed honestly, her blue eyes flashing, "for I'm certain he will prove the most wearisome of husbands."

"But then, I'm not going to marry you, am I, Kit?" Justin pointed out, provoked. "And perhaps Genette is not quite the madcap you are."

"Oh, I enjoy a soirée as well as the next person," Geneviève put in artlessly, continuing the featherbrained role she had chosen to play. "But you will not mind, will you, Justin? For you need not accompany me, I assure you."

"Well, thank God for that!" he retorted, "for I would liefer spend an evening at Cribb's Parlour."

"You shall do no such thing, Justin!" Dominique spoke up stoutly. "Why, except for our family, Genette doesn't know a soul in England. Of course you must take her about and see that she's properly introduced."

"I wouldn't dream of doing otherwise, Maman," Justin replied more evenly. "But a man must have some time to himself; certainly both you and Genette can understand that. Now I must take my leave of you, for I've some business matters that require my attention, and Father would like to see Genette in his study, besides." He turned to Geneviève. "I shall return shortly, at which time I would beg a few moments alone with you, *ma chère*."

The girl was sure the endearment was purely for her aunt's sake, but she did not demur. Instead, she merely inclined her head in agreement, wondering curiously what he wanted of her. She rose.

"If you'll excuse me, Tante Dominique, I shall go and discover what Oncle William desires of me," she said.

"*Oui*, of course. I will see you in the morning, then, *ma petite*."

"*Très bien*. Good night, Tante, Kitty." Geneviève smiled warmly at them both, then exited the small salon to make her way down one of the long, narrow corridors leading to her uncle's study.

Once she had reached the room, she rapped lightly upon the door. Then, at Lord Northchurch's low-voiced "Come," she turned the knob and went in.

"Ah, Genette." The earl glanced up from his perusal of some papers and motioned for her to be seated. "How good of you to join me so promptly."

He continued to chat about nothing in particular for a few moments as, a trifle nervously, she took a chair before his large desk. Then he cleared his throat and leaned forward deliberately, his eyes seeming to stab right through her.

"My dear," he intoned, a devilish little smile playing about the corners of his lips, "I called you here tonight to commend your most laudable performance at dinner this evening. Truly it must rank with the best of them."

"I'm—I'm sure I don't know what you mean, Oncle," Geneviève stammered, blanching. "I—I behaved just as I always do, I assure you."

"Indeed?" Lord Northchurch quirked one eyebrow in mock surprise. Then he removed his quizzing glass from the pocket of his waistcoat and, with his handkerchief, began carefully to polish it. "Geneviève," he uttered softly, his use of her full name warning her politely that he would not tolerate any games, "do you take me for a fool? No, do not bother to answer." With a wave of one hand, he curtly forestalled her reply, then went on.

"Justin, of course, never saw his mother act upon the stage, so perhaps his lamentable lack of perception is to be excused. But during my salad days—for despite what you may think, I was young once, too—I had the delightful pleasure of seeing both Dominique and Lis-Marie perform. Ah, what a pair they were, those two," the earl reminisced fondly. "Both so beautiful, so in love with life. They were breathtaking—and still are...." His voice trailed off as he remembered Dominique and Lis-Marie in their youth. Then abruptly he brought himself back to the present.

"Well, never mind that!" Lord Northchurch shook his head slightly, as though to clear it. "Now ... where was I? Oh, yes. Well, Papa Nick, the old rascal, was ever fond of Shakespeare, and thus on several occasions, I was witness to the staging of *A Midsummer Night's Dream;* my wife had a penchant for the role of Titania, the Fairy Queen, you see. But, unless I am gravely mistaken—and I never am, you know—I believe your performance as such this evening would have rivaled Dominique's own."

Slowly, as was his habit when he wished to disconcert someone, he raised his monocle, surveyed Geneviève through it piercingly, then dropped the eyepiece abruptly so it dangled from the cord attached to his breastpocket.

"Now, my dear," he stated dryly, "suppose you tell me the purpose of your enchanting little masquerade at dinner." When Geneviève did not respond, the earl permitted himself a short bark of laughter. "Come, come, Genette," he coaxed more kindly. "Surely I am not such an ogre."

Startled, she looked up to see that his keen grey eyes

were twinkling with amusement, and some of her anxiety at his words abated.

"Oh, Oncle," she confessed contritely, " 'tis true I am not normally such a—such a . . . witless sprite! But 'twas not *you* I sought to deceive; 'twas Justin!"

"But, my dear, whatever for?"

"Because I—because I . . . well, I did not mean to do so, but I was standing on my balcony, and I—I accidentally overheard you and him talking earlier this afternoon, and—and—"

"No, you need not tell me the rest," Lord Northchurch averred, again holding up one hand to silence her. "You decided that since Justin thought you were a fool, you would play the part of one."

"*Oui*, that is it," Geneviève murmured, slightly ashamed and much mortified at having been unmasked by her uncle.

"Do not look so undone, Genette," the earl chided, still smiling. "I do not care what manner of charade you choose to perpetrate upon my son; indeed, 'twill do him no harm in the least to be taken down a notch or two, and a man never fails to be intrigued by a woman who retains an air of mystery and a few surprises. *I* certainly don't intend to betray you, if that's what you are thinking."

"Do you read people's minds, Oncle?" Geneviève inquired, her own eyes starting to sparkle, for she had, in fact, been worried that he might demand she revert to her usual self.

"I have often been accused of such," Lord Northchurch reported with a small measure of satisfaction. " 'Tis a talent I have always found quite useful.

"Well, Genette," he continued, "I've no doubt from your behavior that you look upon your forthcoming marriage to my son with as little enthusiasm as he does. However, quite frankly, I do not see any other options available to you.

"No doubt both your father's and Vachel's lands have been seized by the French government, and though I was able, through our joint business ventures, to save a good deal of Edouard's funds, his fortune is not what it once was. If he manages to escape from France, he will have to work hard to restore his family to its former status.

"My dear, I don't want to be cruel, but you must face the facts, no matter how hard or unpleasant they may be," the earl insisted stoutly. "You are at this moment an *émigrée*, penniless, landless—not a combination designed to attract a man of your class. Therefore, you have three alternatives left to you: You may wed someone socially beneath you—and suffer all the consequences such a match would entail. Or you could find work, which, positions for females being what they are these days, would undoubtedly condemn you to a life of drudgery—or worse. Or, finally, you can remain here at Northchurch Abbey, where you are, of course, welcome to stay for as long as you like.

"But if you wish to have a family of your own and to rear your children in the manner to which you are accustomed to living, then you must marry Justin, despite both his and your own objections to the arrangement.

"Further," he said mysteriously, his lips twitching with wry humor, "being privy to a great deal more information than either of you, I begin to think you will do very well together, after all."

With that thoroughly bewildering and upsetting remark, Lord Northchurch dismissed her, adamantly refusing to enlighten her any further, though Geneviève pleaded for him to do so. At last, somewhat puzzled, suspicious, and deeply distressed, as well, she left the room, almost in tears. Concerned about her family, she had not previously considered any of the harsh realities with regard to herself that the earl had so astutely pointed out to her; and now, overwhelmed by dismay, she recognized the undeniable precariousness of her situation. Wedding Justin was no longer just a means of sparing her aunt's feelings; it was, for Geneviève, the only real means of securing her future.

She was so stricken by this realization that, as she shut the study door behind her and started down the hall, she failed to hear through the thick walls the muffled sounds of her uncle's amusement as he suddenly threw back his head and roared with laughter.

Chapter Twelve

The moon in the ebony night sky was at that peculiar stage when it was no longer a slender, graceful crescent, but not quite a gleaming, well-defined half-moon either. It was certainly not a lovers' moon, nor even, partially obliterated by dark clouds as it was now, was it a moon by which witches might choose to cast their spells. Still, combined with the faint light of the distant stars, the feel of the cool night breeze soughing plaintively through the gardens, and the sweet scents of the trees and flowers mingling aromatically to fill the air, it was a moon that worked its own kind of special magic.

It reminded Geneviève somehow of the secret dreams of her girlhood, fantasies she had not shared even with Vachel, when, hidden away in some place of concealment, she had retreated into her mind and become something other than what she had been as a child. She would glance down at her boyish clothes, and they would instantly be transformed into the most ravishing of court gowns. She would put away her hoydenish manners for the elegant airs practiced by ladies of quality. And, for a little while, she would dream of a night like tonight, when she walked in cool gardens beneath the light of a silvery moon, a tall, dark, handsome lover at her side.

Surreptitiously she stole a peek at Justin from beneath her lashes. If she were honest with herself, she must admit that, impossibly, he was everything she had ever fantasized about. But he was not her lover, only the man she was going to marry. How strange that it should be so. For just a moment, Geneviève wanted to reach out and touch her cousin, for he stood so close to her that she could smell the masculine scents of wine and tobacco that clung to him, the fragrant aroma of bay rum that emanated from his skin. Headily the subtle odors rose to envelop her, and suddenly she was filled with an overwhelming desire to know what it would be like if the viscount were to take her in his arms and kiss her passionately, as Armand Charbonne had kissed her once in another world so long ago and far away.

She had loved Armand, and when he'd been executed, Geneviève, her heart shattering, had believed she would never love again. But she had to admit that, despite wishing it were otherwise, just the sight of her cousin stirred her in some incomprehensible fashion that even Armand had been unable to achieve. Yet, unlike Armand, Justin had not even made any attempt to win her heart, did not even, if the truth were told, have any longing for that vital organ beating so swiftly and unevenly now in her breast. Oddly enough, here and now in the moonlit gardens, this fact hurt Geneviève worse than the viscount's nasty comments earlier that afternoon had done.

At the thought, she gave herself an angry little

mental shake. *Bon cieux!* Was she so starved for love
and affection that she would fling herself like a common
strumpet at the feet of a man who felt nothing but scorn
for her? *Non!* She must gather her wits, get rid of this
confusing, compelling attraction that pulled her toward
her cousin, and resume the ambitious, peril-ridden dual
role she had chosen to play. One false step could ruin
all her plans for rescuing her family; she must think of
them—not of Justin.

"Well, Cousin," she intoned softly, breaking the
stillness that lay heavily between them, "you said you
wished to speak with me, yet you have uttered not one
syllable since we came out into the gardens. The hour is
late, and I grow weary. Please tell me what is on your
mind so I may retire."

"Do you not know, Genette? 'Tis our wedding I
want to discuss," Justin told her, surprising her with
the solicitude of his tone.

He paused for a moment, as though clarifying in
his mind the things he wished to say to her. Then he
continued.

"Genette, you have only been recently separated
from your parents and your brother. You suffered a
harrowing escape from France, and you have just arrived in England. I fear perhaps my mother, in her
eagerness to see us bound, has given you no time in
which to collect your thoughts but is rushing you
pell-mell toward the altar. If you have no liking for this
marriage, you need not enter into it, you know. The
betrothal can be broken."

"*Oui*, I know. And, despite what you may think,
Justin, I have not made my decision lightly, " Geneviève
claimed. "I *have* considered my situation seriously and
for some length of time—ever since talking with Oncle

William, in fact. As he so sympathetically but firmly pointed out to me, I find myself, through no fault of my own, in the unenviable position of having no family or friends to speak of, with the exception of those here at Northchurch Abbey, and I am utterly destitute as well.

"Tell me, Cousin: What man wants to wed a woman whose title brings with it no lands—for mine, I'm sure, as Oncle William said, have been confiscated by the Assembly—and who will not now inherit any vast wealth either, since all is lost to me? If I do not marry you, I must find some man beneath my class, who cares not for rank or riches, or I must seek employment as a governess or a companion, lest I become a burden to your family, a—a lifelong charity case. *Non!* Do not try to deny it, Justin, for I am only too painfully aware that, right now, that is what I am.

"So . . . you see?" Geneviève shrugged in typical Gallic fashion. "I really have very little choice in the matter, and besides, I do not want to hurt Tante Dominique, who has been so kind. However, if you do not think you can bear to wed me or if there is another who holds your heart, I do not desire to force you into marriage. I know—I know there is no love between us."

Justin gazed at her speculatively for a time, slightly startled by her understanding of the difficulties she faced and the way in which she had addressed them, for he had not expected her to display such a rational thought process. Nor had he believed that Geneviève, grasping the full import of her desperate circumstances, would offer to release him from their bond. Moreover, the perceptive manner in which she had spoken to him just now did not in the least resemble her flighty conversation at dinner, and somewhat perplexed, the viscount scrutinized her more closely.

There was something almost pitiable about her, he reflected, this fanciful, mercurial creature with her unfashionably powdered hair and curiously elfin face. This evening, he had thought her pert and silly. But now, as they walked on together through the gardens, she reminded him somehow of a lost little waif, and despite himself, Justin found his previous disgust toward her slowly dissolving. He was not as unobservant as his father had remarked, and intuitively he sensed there was more to Geneviève than just the fluff and frills she outwardly displayed. The idea intrigued him, even as he pondered the reasons why he was suddenly so certain there was more to his cousin than what appeared on the surface.

At first glance, he had thought Geneviève diminutive; his mother and his aunt, he recalled, even called her *petite*. But now, standing so near to her, the viscount, somewhat surprised, recognized that his cousin was actually tall and slender, that her every movement bore a willow's grace most unlike the fidgety gestures and mincing steps she had earlier employed.

There was something not quite right here, Justin realized, but he simply could not put his finger on what it was. Like the sprite Geneviève portrayed, the intricacies of her personality eluded him, and he wondered if perhaps the depths he felt lay within her were but a trick of the moonlight after all.

"I do not find our arrangement thoroughly distasteful, Genette." Justin chose his words carefully, not wanting to distress her, as he finally spoke again. "For I'm sure you would make the right man very happy. Nor is there any special woman in my life. 'Tis merely that I have no wish for a wife. However, I would not see you throw yourself away upon some rural curate or working for a living either, and I know that is the path you will take if there is none other open to you, for I can see that you are too proud to be a charge on my parents—regardless of the fact that they do not now and would never consider you so.

"So. Let us wed as agreed. I daresay you will suit as well as any other bride." The words just seemed to slip out, insulting her, although such was not the viscount's intent, and when he realized what he'd said, he made haste to apologize. "Nay, that was ill spoken. I did not mean—"

"I know what you meant," Geneviève rejoined dryly. "Shall I get down on my knees now to thank you?" she queried sharply, once more hurt and enraged. "After all, how very gracious of you to condescend to marry me, Justin!"

"Forgive me, mademoiselle," he begged formally. " 'Twas not my deliberate goal to offend you, I assure you. I meant only that since I must take a wife, I would rather she be you than another. At least you and I, being related, need not stand on ceremony, and I know you will not cling to my sleeve, once we are wed. That is all." He was silent for a minute, then went on.

"I am used to my freedom, Genette," he explained. "My various business dealings take up a large amount of my time and often require that I be out of town for many weeks at a time, as well. If ours were a love match, my absences would prey upon your heart and mind, and soon you would grow petulant and wroth with me. You would begin to follow me about and to question me, and then our relationship would turn sour. As it is, I can promise you the protection of both my name and my estates, knowing you will expect no more of me than that.'' He shrugged, well aware of how little he truly offered. ''If you feel you can live with that, then I am content enough.''

''As I told you, Justin, I really have little choice in the matter,'' Geneviève repeated stiffly. ''It is not what I would have wished,'' she admitted, ''had my world not been turned upside down. There was another whom I dearly loved,'' she informed him, causing him to feel a sudden, brief, inexplicable prick of jealousy that startled him. ''Had he not been executed, I—I had hopes of—of . . .'' Her voice trailed away. After an instant in which to collect herself, she spoke once more, deliberately pushing the ghost of Armand from her thoughts. *''Enfin,''* she declared flatly. ''That is all in the past now; 'tis of my future I must think. I accept your proposal, such as it is, Justin. I do not ask for more, though I *would* like you to clarify my position as your bride. Am I to assume that, once we are wed, you will—you will—'' Geneviève stumbled awkwardly over her words. ''What I mean is . . . well, is this to be a marriage of convenience, then?''

''Ah, yes, I understand your dilemma now,'' the viscount asserted, somewhat amused. ''You want to know whether or not I intend to make love to you? I'm sorry, Genette, but I'm afraid I have no answer for you. Why do we not wait until we are better reacquainted and let nature take its course?'' he suggested. ''I have no desire to force myself on an unwilling maid; there are plenty of beds in England, and believe it or not, many of them are filled with women eager to satisfy me. But on the other hand, I do hope someday to have an heir.''

''And what of my needs, Justin?'' Geneviève inquired tersely, a little hurt by his easy reference to his mistresses. "Am I to pine away for lack of love because of a tragic situation beyond my control? Or is what is sauce for the gander—in this particular case—also sauce for the goose?"

"Naturally I expect you will have your cicisbei, Genette. After all, most ladies of quality do. But I trust you will remember my family's good name and keep your affairs discreet."

"But of course, Justin," she returned dryly.

"Very well, then. I will speak to Maman about the arrangements. I assume that, under the circumstances, you will want to be wed as quickly and as quietly as possible?" he inquired.

"*Oui.* There is no point, surely, in delaying our marriage. After all, we have been betrothed since childhood, and my losses are too many and too recent to warrant a large ceremony—nor would I take any pleasure in such. A small service in the chapel here at Northchurch Abbey will suffice."

"As you wish, mademoiselle. Do not look so downcast, Genette," Justin coaxed. "I am not as insensitive as you would believe. Indeed! I begin to think we shall deal very well together, after all."

"How strange," she commented, "for that is exactly what Oncle William told me. *Bonsoir,* Justin."

With a dignity that made him feel somehow lacking, she inclined her head regally. Then she departed, leaving him alone with his thoughts in the gardens that now, oddly enough, seemed suddenly quite empty and bereft without her.

* * *

They were married a fortnight later, as Geneviève had requested, very quietly in the chapel at Northchurch Abbey. Justin had secured a special license from a bishop, so they did not have to wait for the posting of the banns, much to the despair of the seamstress and her assistants, whom Dominique had hired locally to sew Geneviève's wedding gown and trousseau. The women had worked day and night to finish in time all all the well-tailored traveling ensembles and everyday dresses, the beautiful evening, ball, and court gowns, as well as the delicate, lacy corsets, pantalettes, panniers, negligees, and various other lingerie Geneviève required. That some of these garments were made over, having previously belonged to Kitty, was unimportant. Once completed, they looked brand new, and Geneviève was grateful to have them, for she knew the women could not possibly have managed to fill from scratch the numerous trunks Dominique had insisted on her having.

Geneviève herself, along with her aunt and Kitty, had journeyed to London to select additional outfits and fabrics, and hats, gloves, stockings, shoes, and reticules, too. Over the space of several days, while visiting, among other more fashionable shops, the Pantheon Bazaar, the girl had been able to slip away from her aunt and Kitty to make, as well, what she knew they would have considered several extremely odd purchases. These included an array of plain linen shirts and tight black silk pantaloons meant to be worn by a young man (these last had cost dearly, being the height of fashion); various assorted silk scarves and sashes that could be put to a number of uses; three pairs of high, flaring, black leather jackboots, on which she had gotten a real bargain, for they were no longer in style, having been ousted in favor of the newer calf-length boots; and other odds and ends. She'd also bought, in different stores and never from the same clerk twice, five black dominoes and a dozen crimson silk loo masks.

The packages containing all of these things she'd carefully and secretly stuffed inside her many smart new bandboxes, whose labels reeked of Bond Street and which Ives-Pierre, whom she'd insisted make the trip to London with them, had taken great pains to load himself on top of her uncle's well-sprung coach.

Twice since their arrival at Northchurch Abbey, Geneviève had sent her trusted servant to check on the progress of her ship and crew. Ives-Pierre had returned to report that the sloop's hiding place had yet to be discovered, that the alterations to the vessel were coming along nicely, and that the seamen had made several valuable contacts in both Saint Ives and Penzance.

"Tell Benoit and the others to concentrate their efforts in Penzance especially," Geneviève had said, "for I understand Blackheath Hall is not too far from there, and thus it will serve as the base of our operations. We shall keep our allies in Saint Ives in reserve until such time as they are needed."

"As you command, Capitaine," Ives-Pierre had rejoined, grinning. Then, more soberly, he had queried, "Are you sure you want to marry Monsieur le Vicomte, Mademoiselle Genette? You don't have to, you know. Just say the word, and I and the rest of the crew will follow you anywhere in the world."

"I know, Ives-Pierre. But . . . what kind of a life would I have then? And, worse, what kind of life would that be for my children—should I ever have any? *Non*." Geneviève had shaken her head. "I will wed Justin as agreed."

But now, standing in the tiny vestibule at the rear of the small chapel that had served the Trevelyans since Northchurch Abbey had been deeded to the family by King Charles II for assisting him in ascending to the throne of England, Geneviève was not so certain she had made the right choice.

She felt numb and dazed, as though it were all just a dream. Her arm trembled in her uncle's, and as they began the short walk down the aisle to where Justin waited, she moved as though in a trance and unaware of her surroundings. This was not the romantic wedding about which she had fantasized in her youth. Where were Papa, Maman, and Vachel? Where was Armand? Nothing was as it should have been.

Even her dress was all wrong, for it should have been the beautiful old ivory gown with Brussels lace and tiny seed pearls Maman had worn when she'd married Papa and then carefully packed away afterward. Instead, Geneviève's dress was a new, deep forest-green creation with a pale gold, ruffled undergown. Upon her head, she wore a wide-brimmed green hat covered by a gold veil. She had once again powdered her hair and lightly painted her face to disguise her true appearance. Somehow the thought made her want to weep. She did not want to be married looking like a woodland nymph! She wanted to be herself, to see, despite all her wishes to the contrary, Justin's icy grey eyes light up with pleasure and longing when they fell upon her.

Oh, this was terrible! *Terrible!* Geneviève wanted to turn and run down the aisle, to get away from the chapel as fast as she could. But almost as though he guessed her sudden, wild intention, Lord Northchurch tightened his grip upon her arm, propelling her on toward her cousin.

Then somehow she was standing between Justin and Kitty, her maid of honor, her hand tucked firmly in the groom's own. Dimly Geneviève heard the rise and fall of the priest's voice as he intoned the ancient Latin words that bound her irrevocably to the tall, dark stranger at her side. Mechanically she repeated her vows and felt her cousin slide the cold gold wedding band upon her finger. Then suddenly the viscount was lifting her veil and coolly brushing her lips with his own.

Despite herself, an odd, shocking thrill of anticipation and delight pervaded Geneviève's blood as his mouth moved on hers, lightly at first, then gradually growing fiercer and more demanding as, much to his surprise, Justin found his hold on his bride increasing. Her lips were soft, softer than he had ever dreamed, and parting sweetly beneath his own, yielding pliantly, almost welcomingly, beneath his onslaught. He inhaled deeply the fragrant lily scent that emanated from her skin and hair, and his head reeled as, without warning, a savage, unexpected stab of passion suddenly rose to clutch him in its fist, filling him with desire for her.

With difficulty, Justin broke the kiss, drawing away from Geneviève so quickly and gracelessly that he nearly poked out his eye on the netting of her veil, which he had raised and secured haphazardly over the wide brim of her hat.

"Smile, Geneviève!" he hissed in her ear to cover the awkward moment and mistaking the dazed, spell-bound look upon her face for one of stark revulsion. God! It had been only a kiss. Did she despise him that much? "For Christ's sake! You look like someone just walked over your grave!"

His harsh words penetrated Geneviève's stunned

body and brain at last, making her aware of how he was glaring at her censuringly, as though repulsed and embarrassed by her publicly wanton reaction to his kiss.

Like a puppet, mortified by her behavior, she did as he demanded, for had she not just promised to obey him? She smiled and smiled until she thought the expression would freeze upon her face as rapidly they strode down the aisle and out the chapel, Kitty and Lord Parker Wescott, Baron Hadleigh, Justin's dearest friend and best man, hard on their heels.

Once outside, seeming not to notice the taut stillness of the newlyweds, Parker began to shout and laugh uproariously, jovially breaking the silence that enveloped them. Offering his congratulations, he clapped Justin soundly on the back, claiming he had never thought he would live to see the day when his old chum would take a wife. Then he kissed Geneviève on the cheek and wished her the best, ignoring the sudden, swift scowl that darkened the groom's handsome visage at his actions.

"You'll have plenty of time with Lady Blackheath later on this evening, Justin," Parker pointed out slyly, grinning. " 'Tis my duty to be the first to kiss the bride, so keep that jealous-husband act under your hat. I've a wife of my own and no inclination to steal yours, as pretty as she is." He turned back to Geneviève. "Pay no attention to Justin's boorish manners, Lady Blackheath. 'Tis that damnable Trevelyan pride that makes him so arrogant and stiff-necked! Lud! If he ain't his old man made over, I don't know what's what!"

Geneviève merely nodded and continued to smile, scarcely even registering what was being said. It felt so strange to be addressed as Lady Blackheath that she wasn't even quite sure the baron was directing his remarks to her.

Justin, for his part, was so annoyed with his friend's observations and his own violent, inexplicable reaction to the kiss Parker had quite properly bestowed upon Geneviève that, without even thinking, he rudely snatched up his bride's arm and sternly hauled her along to the house. It was all Geneviève could do to keep up with him, and when, for the third time in as many minutes, her feet flew up from the path precariously, she pleaded breathlessly for the viscount to stop. Abruptly he came to a halt, suddenly realizing he was crushing his wife's arm in an iron grip and had caused her several times to stumble and nearly fall.

"What's the matter with you?" Geneviève asked sharply as he released her. Gingerly she rubbed the spot she was sure his fingers had bruised. "Have you lost your wits?"

"Nay. I'm sorry, Genette. 'Tis all these people milling about; they have gotten on my nerves," he lied crossly. "Egad! Where could Maman have unearthed them all on such short notice? I thought this was supposed to be a small wedding."

"It is, Justin. There's nary a soul here but our family, a few of your friends, and the household staff."

"Well, thank God you did not hold out for a large ceremony, then," he said with heartfelt relief. "You must have more brains than I suspected under that—that . . . *hat* of yours."

"Really, Justin." Geneviève frowned irritably. "There's no need to insult me, nor poor Miss Simpkins, the milliner, either. She worked very hard on this hat, I assure you." Then maliciously, having recovered sufficiently to remember her role, she added ingenuously,

"Indeed, I thought it quite plain for all the time she spent upon it!"

"Yes, well, did you have to have such a wide brim and all that netting and lace? I swear that veil nearly scratched out my eye when I kissed you!"

"But, Justin," Geneviève needled with mock sweetness, "the baron did not seem to have any trouble."

Her husband only glowered at her.

"Madame," he uttered curtly, "I take back my earlier statement. You are without a doubt lacking even a shred of common sense. Parker did not have to put up your veil to kiss you, as I did."

"*Non*, of course not, for *you* had already done that, Justin. Pray tell: What would have been the point of the baron's lowering it, only to raise it again?" Geneviève pointed out artlessly, stifling with difficulty the merriment that threatened to bubble from her throat.

"Madame"—Justin spoke through clenched teeth— "you are the most impossible— Oh, never mind! I should have known there was no talking to you, for there's no reasoning with an—with an . . . *urchin!*"

With that parting shot, the viscount turned on his heel and left her. Geneviève knew she should have been deeply angry and affronted—and she was—but still, she could not stop the silent laughter that shook her shoulders. She had bested Justin at their repartee, and, what was somehow peculiarly even more satisfying, she was certain his extreme irritation had been due not to her convoluted babble, but to the fact that Lord Hadleigh had kissed her!

The wedding reception had ended, and now, strangely,

it seemed, after its walls had shaken with so much laughter and music, the house was still. The family had withdrawn to allow the newlyweds some time alone together; the few guests had retired for the evening, and the staff had returned to their duties.

Emeline, after assisting Geneviève with the removal of her wedding gown, filling the bathtub for the girl, and carefully laying out the prettiest of her new, filmy negligees, had long since departed. Now, her face and hair devoid of any trace of paint or powder and her figure arrayed in the translucent folds of the nightgown, Geneviève waited anxiously for Justin to enter the room that adjoined his at Northchurch Abbey and into which her belongings had been moved earlier that afternoon.

Surely he would come, she thought, for had he not kissed her passionately at the altar, despite his disgusted expression afterward because she had behaved so wantonly in public? Had he not grown angry with his best friend for kissing her after the ceremony? *Alors!* So much for Justin's marriage of convenience! He was a handsome, virile man; she was an attractive woman—even if she did currently resemble a fairy queen. Had Titania not enchanted Oberon? *Oui.* Justin would come to her. Pride in his manhood would make him come, for despite what he had said about cicisbei, she knew, from his kiss at the altar and his jealous reaction to Lord Hadleigh's kissing her later, that her proud, arrogant husband would want to be the first to put his mark upon her. At last she would discover what it meant to be truly a woman.

Until today, she had not really considered this part of their marriage, assuming she would not have to deal with it right away. Now Geneviève wondered what Justin would think when he saw her, for she had realized earlier that she could scarcely go to bed with her hair pinned up and powdered and her face painted. As far as she knew, no woman did so, and she had felt that to do so herself would seem even stranger—thereby arousing Justin's suspicions—than to allow him to view her true appearance. Geneviève bit her lip nervously, pondering how best to explain the change in her, should he ask. Then, trembling a little, she decided he might not remark upon her looks if she were to stuff her fiery copper locks up inside of her lacy nightcap. This she hastily accomplished. After that, examining herself in the mirror and determining that this had indeed helped matters, some of her trepidation lessened.

Still, Geneviève continued to chew her lip, pacing about the chamber like a caged tiger. A part of her was frightened not only because of her dread with regard to her husband's reaction to her appearance, but because of her own understandable maidenly fears. Yet she could not deny that perversely she was also anticipating almost eagerly the act that would make her a woman.

What would it be like? she wondered idly.

Geneviève was not ignorant about lovemaking, for, to the French, it was as natural as breathing and not a thing of which to be ashamed. But still, she was not quite sure she would know all the right words to say and the moves to make, once the time came.

Well, she shrugged, she would just have to let her instincts be her guide. Besides, surely Justin must know and indeed be expecting that she was a virgin. No doubt, being far more experienced than she was in such matters, she thought a trifle petulantly, remembering his reference to his many mistresses, he would lead the way, letting her follow at her own pace.

Oh, why didn't he come? she asked herself fiercely, feeling wroth and stupid, as well, because her nerves were so on edge. Was she wrong? Hadn't that electrifying kiss that had left her so stunned and shaken at the altar meant anything to him after all? Hadn't his jealousy and anger over Lord Hadleigh this afternoon demonstrated that he did care for her—if only a little?

Geneviève had no answer to her questions, and finally, feeling strangely bereft, she climbed into bed. Shivering a little from the cool night breeze blowing in through the open French doors, she pulled the covers up about her, her earlier ardent expectations turning slowly to ashes as the hours passed.

Next door in his own room, Justin heard the sounds in her chamber cease and knew his wife had settled in for the evening. Still, he could not bring himself to turn the brass oval knob on the solid oak barrier that separated him from Geneviève. He remembered her initial, exciting response to him when he had kissed her at the altar, but he recalled all too clearly, as well, the stricken expression on her face afterward, as though she had regained her senses and had been appalled by the feelings he'd aroused in her. Well, to hell with her, then! He surely had no desire to force himself on an unwilling maiden—especially one who might scream and rouse his parents' entire household in the process!

Had he been at Blackheath Hall, where he was the sole master, the viscount would not even have considered this possibility, for certainly he would have dismissed his staff for the evening. It was too late now, however, to alter his mother's plans for him and Geneviève to remain at Northchurch Abbey overnight; and as, for the umpteenth time in as many long minutes, he again recollected the stirring in his loins when he had kissed his bride earlier, Justin cursed his mother with a vengeance.

Groaning, he ripped irately at the folds of the silk scarf tied in the intricate Trevelyan Knot about his throat. When at last he had managed to free it and to unbutton his collar, he settled back in his chair and poured himself another large draft of cognac. Morosely he stared at the label on the bottle. Why must it be *French* brandy? Could they not make the liquor anywhere else—the ignorant distillers?

Irrationally enraged, he dashed the snifter upon the floor, where it smashed into several large pieces, the liquid within splashing out to stain the carpet. Then he staggered over to the silver serving tray that sat upon a small table. He would drink nothing but gin from now on, he decided, good *English* gin! It was cool and clear; one could see through it. *It* held no warm surprises as the mellow amber French brandy did—as his French bride had proved to hold.

Damn her! The witch! For surely that was what she was. How else had she managed to attract him with her unfashionably powdered hair and her ridiculous ornaments and hats? Her curiously elfin face that looked at once both young and old—and so devilishly enchanting? When had it begun to seem so? he wondered glumly. How on earth had that spritelike creature gotten her hooks into him?

The viscount did not want or need a wife. His job was too delicate, too dangerous for him to become involved with a woman, to be distracted by one. Why in hell couldn't his father have seen that? Why had the earl insisted on Justin's marrying Geneviève? Was it his fault she was a penniless, homeless *émigrée*? Was it his fault that wedding him had been her only choice?

There was another man, she had said, and she had loved him . . . By God! Justin had given her his name and his protection. Despite his promises to the contrary, she owed him something in return for that, didn't she?

Unsteadily he stood and stumbled toward the door that joined his room to Geneviève. He had taken only a few steps when, in his drunken stupor, he tripped and fell, sprawling facedown upon the floor. There, he spent an extremely uncomfortable night, while Geneviève, still waiting for him in her chamber just beyond, sobbed bitterly into her pillow so he would not hear the muffled sounds of her weeping when he did not come.

BOOK THREE

Desire in Disguise

Chapter Thirteen

Blackheath Hall, England, 1792

Justin's manor house, in the south of Cornwall, was very old and not very large or beautiful when compared to the stately Northchurch Abbey. But it had a strange, savage charm all its own, and Geneviève, when she first glimpsed it through the window of the coach, felt her spirits rise for the first time in the two days following her wedding.

The manor stood upon a hill overlooking the wild sweep of the moors falling away to the jagged coastline beyond; and because this part of the countryside was almost barren of trees, save for a few ancient, twisted Cornish elms, there was naught to obscure her view of the house. From its perch, it reigned supreme, as stark and brooding as it must have been since its beginning.

Having been built during the time of King Henry VIII, Blackheath Hall was a Tudor edifice constructed in the shape of an H and made of Pentewan rock that had been hewn from the cliffs near Mevagissey at Chapel Point and brought by sea to the house that lay not far from the tip of Land's End. The stone reminded Geneviève of the color of Justin's eyes, for over the years, it had weathered to the same clear, silvery grey and was just as responsive to the effects of light and shade. The walls glistened like mist and rain now beneath the sun's rays, but Geneviève could imagine how dark and mysteriously shadowed they would grow at dusk.

The manor was a perfect jewel for the setting that held it, for it looked as though it belonged upon the heaths, lashed by the wind and the rain that often swooped down upon the vast, open terrain, bringing with them the sound of the roiling sea beyond as it crashed against the rock-strewn beach.

The house itself was imposing, forbidding in appearance. The two square, crenelated watchtowers flanking its dark, solid walnut doors rose to loom like obelisks over the land. Tiny windows called lancets, which resembled arrow slits, though they had never been employed for this purpose, were set one above the other on each floor of the twin towers.

With their diamond-shaped, Venetian-glass panes, the long, narrow casement windows that lined the front of the dwelling on all three stories seemed to peer out at Geneviève like glittering eyes behind the slits of a mask, giving her a slightly uneasy feeling, as though somehow the manor had seen right through her disguise and was secretly laughing at her.

The two wings that formed the front of the H thrust outward from the building to enclose partially the wide, flagstone courtyard that permitted carriages to drive right up to the doors. Here and there, the walls were concealed by dark strands of ivy that added to the gloom of the place. On the third floor, upon the peaks of the slant-roofed dormer windows jutting out from the steep, gabled top that covered the edifice, stone gargoyles sat, surveying their domain. Behind them, the tall, distinctive chimneys of the Tudor period broke the angularity of the main roof.

In the very center of the H, between the two towers, was a fourth story that, like the one at Northchurch Abbey, was topped by a flat terrace surrounded by a stone balustrade. It probably had been used at one time as a widow's walk, Geneviève surmised. She could almost visualize the Trevelyan women who, centuries ago, had stood at the railing, their eyes turned to the ocean in the distance as they watched for the return home of their seafaring men.

Some might have thought the house bleak, austere, and unwelcoming, for it had no dignity, no elegance, no grace. It was instead an ugly, sprawling place, awesome and powerful, like a fortress, built to withstand the brutal elements to which it was constantly exposed.

But Geneviève, gazing at it more closely as the coach rattled through the stout wrought-iron gates and up the long, winding drive, was undaunted, for oddly enough, Blackheath Hall filled her with the same kind of exhilaration that had enveloped her when she'd steered *La Belle Fille* past the perilous, rocky opening of the narrow crevasse.

"Oh, Justin, it's magnificent!" she cried, leaning forward eagerly to get a better look. "How I shall hate to give it up for Northchurch Abbey someday!"

The viscount was much startled and touched by his wife's sincerity and perception, for secretly he had feared she would despise his home, would consider it hideous and isolated, as his mistresses had done, preferring his townhouse in London and casting greedy eyes and grasping hands toward Northchurch Abbey, his inheritance. But Geneviève seemed genuinely enthralled by Blackheath Hall, as was Justin himself, and with her impulsive words, she had unknowingly struck within him a kindred chord that made him long more passionately than ever to uncover the depths of character she so carefully concealed from him.

He had yet to possess her. The morning after their wedding night, he had awakened to find himself still lying upon the carpet, and, groaning from the horrible consequences of his overindulgence in drink, he had risen stiffly and cursed himself for a fool. Geneviève was his for the taking, yet still, he could not seem to bring himself to make her his. She had been so withdrawn, so cold to him all day yesterday that at the costly inn where they'd stayed last evening, Justin had paid for two adjoining rooms, cringing at the thought of the havoc that would be wreaked if he attempted to share his wife's bed and she began screaming in such a public place. He remembered all too well the way Geneviève had shouted at him and threatened him in their youth, and he had no doubt that if she were unwilling to receive his advances, she would not hesitate to make it perfectly—and loudly—clear!

Now the viscount sighed wearily. What did it matter if his bride did not want him, if she was even now still grieving over another man, a man who had been executed, a man she'd said she'd loved . . . ? Justin could not afford to have his highly sensitive work jeopardized by a clinging wife anyway, and he could not for the life of him figure out why he had suddenly become so attracted to the woman he'd married. She persisted in powdering her hair, though courteously he'd informed her this was no longer in fashion, and the hat she was wearing today was a hideous, flowered affair that offended his eye even more than had her wedding hat with its veil of stiff lace and netting.

Well, he sighed again, at least she liked his home, which was more than he had expected of her. Justin brightened a little at the notion, and with more enthusiasm than he usually displayed, he started to point out to Geneviève the various buildings upon the grounds.

She realized, as he spoke, that he was very proud of Blackheath Hall and spared neither time nor expense in its upkeep. Hesitantly, remembering he had said he didn't want to be pestered by an inquisitive wife, she ventured to ask him about his many business dealings, and to her surprise, he replied.

"Here in Cornwall, I own several tin and kaolin mines and have interests, as well, in some fishing enterprises in Penzance. I raise both cattle and sheep on my father's estates in Devon, and I have a small farm in Cheddar Gorge, in Somerset, where cheese is made. Do you wish me to continue?" He smiled at her, amused.

"*Non.*" She shook her head. "No wonder you are so busy!"

They reached the manor at last. Justin helped Geneviève alight from the coach. Then he gave instructions for it to be unloaded and returned to Lord Northchurch, to whom it belonged. The viscount then requested that his bride wait a moment while he examined his curricle and greys, which Ferdie, his tiger, had driven down from Northchurch Abbey. The high-strung, perfectly matched set of four horses appeared to be in excellent condition, and Justin commended Ferdie on their handling.

"Thanks, guv'nor." The wizened little man beamed. "I brought 'em along real easy like. Course, hit weren't no trouble, 'is lordship's coach being so slow and all. Gor! I could 'ave run faster meself than that old thing. Hit don't begin to 'old a candle to this 'ere curricle o' yours, guv'nor. I don't know why the old gentl'man don't get 'imself a new ve'icle. 'E's got plenty o' blunt fer it, and that's the truth!"

"Yes, well, Lord Northchurch prefers to travel in comfort and with an inordinate amount of baggage, besides," Justin observed dryly. "Take the greys around to the stables, Ferdie. Wentworth"—he nodded to his valet—"you escort Fourneaux to the servants' quarters. Miss Tibbets"—he turned to Emeline—"if you will follow me and Lady Blackheath, please, I'll have someone show you to your room after you've unpacked her ladyship's trunks."

"Yes, milord." Emeline dropped a respectful curtsy.

Justin approached the doors of Blackheath Hall, but before he could knock upon them, they were opened by his butler.

"Ah, Rothfelder, there you are," the viscount noted. "Ring for two of the footmen to carry up all this baggage, will you, and inform Mrs. Fincham she's to have the suite adjoining mine prepared immediately. I've brought home a bride at last!"

Then, much to Rothfelder's astonishment, as Geneviève was standing there a trifle awkwardly, not quite sure what to do, his lordship impulsively picked his wife up and carried her over the threshold.

"Welcome to Blackheath Hall, Genette," he uttered, his voice low. "I hope you will be very happy here."

"Oh, Justin, I'm sure I shall," she replied softly. For a moment, their eyes met and locked, and a breathless little silence fell upon them. Then Rothfelder cleared his throat politely, reminding them of his presence, and the strange, disconcerting spell was broken.

Embarrassed by his unusual display of emotion, the viscount set his bride down more roughly than he had intended.

"Now that we've satisfied tradition, Genette, I trust we can get on with the business at hand," he intoned coolly.

Turning away, so he failed to notice the crushed expression she quickly masked with one of indifference, he introduced her to both Rothfelder and Mrs. Fincham, who, hearing the sounds of their arrival, had hurried to the hall to greet them.

"Mercy me," the plump, cheerful housekeeper exclaimed upon learning Geneviève's identity. "I never did think his lordship would wed, though I know he's been betrothed to you for many a long year, milady. I told him he didn't see you often enough and that if he weren't careful, you'd up and marry one of those dashing young Frenchmen who've been coming over here in droves now that that rabble in France have locked up King Louie and his poor, silly queen. But I guess I was wrong after all, and 'tis a good thing, too, for you're a pretty little creature. Lud! If I didn't know better, I'd think you were a changeling child, for there's something almost fairylike about you, milady—if you don't mind my saying so. No wonder you enchanted his lordship."

Mrs. Fincham continued to chatter brightly as she led Geneviève and Emeline up the long, curving flight of stairs to the second story; the latter both glanced about curiously, greatly impressed by their new home.

Upon reaching the landing, the housekeeper turned down a wide hall that opened onto the east wing.

"This side of the house is where the Trevelyans have always had their chambers," she explained. "The west wing is used for guests. Ah, here we are."

She selected a key from the large iron ring that dangled at her waist and, inserting it into the lock, turned the brass oval knob and flung open the door.

Involuntarily Geneviève gasped, for the room was even more beautiful than the one that had been hers at Northchurch Abbey. Unlike the gilded, cream-colored furniture and pale blue fabrics that had been a young girl's dream at Northchurch Abbey, Geneviève's suite at Blackheath Hall was obviously a woman's boudoir.

The furnishings were all extremely old and valuable, she realized, for like the house itself, most of them dated from the Tudor period. A massive, dark walnut bed with a huge canopy that almost reached the ceiling sat upon a wood dais and dominated the room. Upon the bed's flat top at each corner perched big brass urns filled with feathery plumes that had been dyed various shades of red. The canopy itself was hung with satin drapes, some crimson, others gold; these were tied back at the bedposts of the heavy headboard with gold, tasseled cords. Separate supports displayed the distinctive, melon-bulb footposts, which had been left bare so their intricate detail might be seen. A red-and-gold silk counterpane lay upon the bed, which was surrounded by a gold dust ruffle. Two plain tables, also with melon-bulb legs, flanked the bed; at its foot were two closed-sided wooden wainscot chairs.

Beside the stone fireplace was an ornate press cupboard with solid gold handles. Two newer chaise-longues, upholstered in gold velvet, and a few plain occasional tables reposed before the inviting hearth with its decorative brass screen. Opposite this stood a magnificent armoire; although from a more recent period, it, too, was made of walnut and had been constructed to resemble the rest of the furniture, as had the more modern dresser with mirror set against another wall. Before this last was a small joint stool topped by a crimson velvet cushion.

A writing table, before which sat an open-sided wainscot chair, was just to Geneviève's right. To her left, before a lovely, hand-painted screen, three antique coffers in various sizes were ranged in pleasing fashion, along with several large, satin, tasseled floor pillows of Moorish origin, some crimson, others gold.

The walls were paneled halfway up with walnut wainscoting that contrasted beautifully with the pale gold-leaf paint that finished them off. Red silk curtains hung at the French doors that opened onto the stone balcony outside. A red-and-gold Turkish carpet lay upon the hardwood floor.

A smaller, paneled dressing room, containing similar furnishings and a hammered-brass bathtub, was just beyond. Adjoining the bedroom on the opposite side was Justin's chamber.

Geneviève was thrilled, for oddly enough, it looked as though the room had been designed just for her. She knew that at night, by candlelight, the red fabrics would bring out the dark crimson highlights of her fiery copper hair; the soft golds would enhance the creaminess of her skin and the gold flecks in her green eyes. Then she remembered that Justin had yet to seek her bed and, not being interested in her after all, was unlikely to see her in her natural state, with her long tresses unbound and unpowdered and her face unpainted. So some of her happiness receded.

Still, Geneviève thought, she should be glad he'd made no effort to claim her, for it meant there was virtually no chance he would discover the dual role she played. Nevertheless, her pride and vanity had been wounded, and she could not help feeling hurt that she obviously appealed to him so little.

"What a marvelous bedroom," she said at last, forcing enthusiasm into her voice so Mrs. Fincham, who was studying her closely, would not guess her marriage to the viscount was not what it should have been.

"Yes, isn't it?" the housekeeper responded, beaming. "There's some who would not fancy it, nay, nor this house either, for it can be a gloomy place, I imagine, to those who aren't used to the moors and the way the wind and the rain can beat down upon them. But I saw right off that you weren't that kind, Lady Blackheath," Mrs. Fincham declared. "Now, if you'll step this way, please, I'll show you the suite's secret."

"Secret?" Geneviève questioned, intrigued.

"Yes, milady. Times were dangerous in the old days, and the Trevelyans were not fools. They never intended to be murdered in their beds as so many others were, so my lord's ancestor, the one who built Blackheath Hall, had small passageways hidden in both his and his lady's chambers."

She reached out and pressed a section of the paneling that covered the walls of Geneviève's dressing room. Immediately a narrow, cleverly concealed door sprang open on creaking hinges to reveal a tiny, dark exit with a winding stone staircase.

"Where does it go?" Geneviève asked excitedly

as she peered into the black void, instantly envisioning the good use to which she could put this fascinating discovery.

"Down to a long tunnel that runs under the house to several caves in the cliffs along the beach," Mrs. Fincham elucidated. "But don't you worry, Lady Blackheath. Once it's shut, the door can only be opened from the inside, so you'll be quite safe," she claimed, once more pressing the paneling, causing it to close. "No one uses the passageway nowadays anyway. I merely showed it to you in case—God forbid!—we should ever have a fire here at Blackheath Hall. I'd hate to think anyone was trapped up here when she had a means of escaping!" the kindly housekeeper confessed.

"Well, I'll leave you to get unpacked and settled in now. If you need any extra assistance, the bellrope's right over there." She indicated a stout gold cord that hung from the ceiling. "Pull once for Rothfelder, twice for me. The rest you'll learn as you go along, I'm sure. I'll have some bathwater and a light repast fetched for you. Dinner is at eight, for his lordship keeps fashionable hours even in the country, just as Lady Northchurch does." Mrs. Fincham paused, then continued.

"I hope you'll be very happy here, Lady Blackheath. If you'll pardon my saying so, 'tis high time you and his lordship were wed. 'Twill do the lad a world of good, I'm sure, for beneath all that arrogance, he's a sensitive soul."

"Thank you, Mrs. Fincham," Geneviève answered politely, carefully hiding the fact that she believed she had no influence whatsoever over her husband.

Once the housekeeper had departed, Justin stopped by to see that his wife had everything she needed. He courteously informed Geneviève that he would be downstairs in his study if she required his services for any reason, then he left her to her own devices. After he'd gone and her bathwater and a meal had been brought up, she carefully locked both doors to her bedroom so she would not be intruded upon further. Then, after ordering Emeline to start unpacking, she lit a lamp and disappeared into the dressing room to examine more closely the hidden passageway.

It was evident that, as Mrs. Fincham had told her, the exit had not been used in several years. When cautiously, after carefully propping open the door with a small marble statue, Geneviève stepped inside the dark, dirty hole, her nostrils were assaulted by a stale, musty odor, and huge clouds of dust churned up by her entrance wafted up to engulf her, causing her to sneeze so violently she nearly dropped her light. When hesitantly she began to descend the steep, narrow stairs, she saw that both the steps and the circular stone walls surrounding them were covered with giant, filmy white cobwebs that looked like delicate lace. It was clear from the size of the cobwebs that the various spiders inhabiting the passageway had been busy at their work undisturbed for some time. Grimacing, Geneviève brushed aside the gossamer creations and proceeded on down the yawning chasm.

From the pitter-patter of little feet scurrying away from her approaching figure, she knew the round, towerlike enclosure was filled with rats. But, stifling her desire to shriek, she forced herself to continue.

It seemed she walked forever, but at last a clean, tangy breath of salt-filled air told her she was reaching the bottom of the exit. The stairs here, unlike the dry, dusty steps previously, were damp from the cool sea breeze that blew in through the caves and the tunnel, and they were slick with dark green moss, besides. She had to take care not to slip and fall. She paused for a moment, listening. Somewhere in the distance she heard water dripping, and from even farther away came the sound of the ocean as its breakers swept gently over the rocky beach. The murmuring waves enticed her onward like a siren's song, and finally she stood at the gaping mouth of the tunnel Mrs. Fincham had described.

Not knowing how late it was, Geneviève reluctantly decided she must turn back for the time being, for she had no idea how long her exploration of the tunnel and the caves to which it led might take. Still, she was satisfied that the passageway would serve her needs excellently, and she resolved to inform Ives-Pierre about it as soon as possible.

Providence was fortuitously with Geneviève that evening, for during dinner, Justin received an urgent message, and after reading it, he frowned and told his wife that some problems had arisen with regard to one of his business dealings and that he must be away from Blackheath Hall for at least a fortnight, if not longer.

"I'm sorry, Genette, to leave you so soon after our marriage and when you have only just arrived here," he apologized, "but I *did* warn you how it would be, you know."

"*Oui*, I know," she answered airily, deftly concealing the sudden, sharp, odd pang of disappointment that pricked her, for she did not want him to think she was hanging on his sleeve. "Please do not bother about me, Justin. Mrs. Fincham can show me the house and instruct me on how it is run and so forth. You need not worry. I'm certain I can manage well enough without you.''

Instead of relieving the viscount's mind, as they had been intended, his bride's words served only to further his annoyance, for to him they were glaring proof of her lack of interest in him.

He might as well be on his way to perdition for all she cared, Justin reflected irritably. No doubt she was actually *glad* he had been called away, giving her a reprieve from sharing his bed. Yes, that was it! For was she not even now grinning slyly to herself—as though secretly delighted to be rid of him? The witch!

That Geneviève was smiling because she had suddenly realized his long absence would provide her with an ideal opportunity to start her plan rolling did not occur to the viscount, for he knew nothing about her scheme to rescue her parents. Therefore, he could only assume that even the idea of spending time with him— let alone the notion of developing an intimate relationship with him—was absolutely loathsome to her. He wondered how she would feel if she knew the true nature of his work, how perilous it was and that it might one day prove fatal to him. Then angrily he decided that even that knowledge would not move her. He had been mistaken; the depths of character he had thought within her were not there after all. Beneath her frivolous surface, she was just as she had appeared at first glance: empty through and through . . . empty-headed . . . empty-hearted! Any cicisbei she might attract were welcome to her!

With a measure of disgust, he abruptly threw his napkin down on his plate, then violently shoved back his chair and stood.

''You need not see me out, madame,'' Justin

snapped curtly, "for I'm certain you have more important matters to occupy your time. *Au revoir*."

Then, shouting for Wentworth, the viscount strode from the dining room, leaving Geneviève sitting there alone, feeling like an unwanted toy that had just been carelessly tossed aside.

Very well, monsieur, she determined silently, *if that is how you feel toward me, I surely shall not attempt to change your mind. To the devil with you, Justin Trevelyan, you arrogant* bâtard! *For beneath your oh-so-handsome facade, you have nothing but an extremely dense brain and a very black heart! I don't know why I ever felt drawn to you in the first place!*

With that thought to sustain her, Geneviève, too, quit the dining room, her green eyes flashing so dangerously that even Rothfelder stepped out of her path, filled with alarm at his new mistress's forbidding demeanor.

It took the girl and her trusted servant three hours to search the caves.

They waited until they were certain Justin had departed from the premises and the rest of the household had retired. Then, after she had changed into her boy's clothes, Geneviève admitted Ives-Pierre into her dressing room and sprang open the cleverly concealed door, whose hinges she had oiled earlier to prevent squeaking. Both she and her faithful companion were armed with two lanterns and an assortment of tools Ives-Pierre had filched from the storerooms. Each also carried a fat ball of twine the servant had insisted they would need if they were not to become lost. Should such a disaster occur, they would be forced to shout for help, thereby rousing the entire household—if they were even lucky enough to be heard—and the staff would learn they were prowling around the caverns.

Carefully they descended the winding stone staircase, Ives-Pierre cursing the squealing rats that scurried underfoot and the treacherous steps that gradually grew slick with slime as they neared the bottom of the passageway.

Once the two had reached the place where the long tunnel opened into the grotto, the servant hammered a short stake into the soft, wet ground, then tied the end of each ball of string to the piece of wood.

"You go that way, Madame Genette," Ives-Pierre directed. "I will go this way. Remember: If you come to a dead end, cut the twine and follow its length back to the place where you started out. Each time you begin to explore another corridor, unroll the string behind you as you go. Take this batch of sticks"—he handed her a small bundle—"and use one stake to mark each area you have searched. That way, you won't get mixed up and keep repeating your previous movements. If I'm right, these caves are a maze of catacombs. I know the echo in here makes it hard, but try to follow the sound of the sea and to walk south if you can. The opening of the caverns will lie in that direction."

"Very well," Geneviève agreed. "I will meet you back here when I have finished."

Alone with her lantern, she began her trek into the dark void of the grotto's interior, trying not to shiver, for the cold, dank air that soughed through the caves seeped into her bones, and the hushed noises of the rats and the other creatures harbored by the caverns sent chills crawling up her spine and made gooseflesh prickle her arms.

Slowly she unwound her ball of string, glad Ives-Pierre had thought of this method to prevent them from becoming lost, for after trudging along for several moments, Geneviève reached a dead end and realized she would not have been able to find her way back without the twine. The grotto was indeed a mass of twisted corridors, many of which led nowhere. Following the string, she retraced her steps, pounding a stick into the ground at the opening of each catacomb through which she'd passed. Then she started out again, choosing a different route.

Geneviève repeated this process many times, too awed by the sights she saw to allow her tiredness to force her into quitting. In the dim lantern light, brilliant stalactites glistened like icicles from the roofs of the caves; down some of the pointed shards, droplets of mist and water ran in rivulets that fell into small pools gleaming like quicksilver in the darkness. Here and there beneath the stalactites, multicolored stalagmites rose like glowing obelisks, formed by the continual dripping of calcareous liquid upon the floors of the caverns.

Once, a horde of bats was stirred up by Geneviève's entrance into a large roomlike area. With high-pitched shrieks, they flew toward her, flapping their skeletal wings furiously, their ratlike faces looking evil and menacing in the blackness. Geneviève screamed and turned to run, then realized this would only provoke the creatures into chasing her. Setting her lantern down hurriedly, she dropped to the cold earth floor and flattened herself against it until the bats had passed on.

Then, stricken by a sudden idea, she followed the

creatures, rapidly unrolling her ball of string as she went. To her delight, she found her instinct had been correct: the bats knew the route out of the grotto. Like a black cloud of smoke, they were even now winging their way across the silver-shot night sky. She glanced about with satisfaction, noting that the sea actually washed into the opening she had discovered, so a small boat could be rowed right into the caves.

Excitedly she took a piece of chalk from among her implements and began to make her way back to the tunnel, leaving a white mark on each stake she planted in the ground behind her. Ives-Pierre was already waiting for her at their starting place, and when Geneviève told him she had found a path leading to the mouth of the caverns, he quickly followed her, helping her shift the sticks and twine so both ran unobtrusively along one wall of the wyndlike corridors that snaked through the grotto. Unless one were looking for the markers, they would not now be seen. The two conspirators removed the stakes and string leading to dead ends. Then, content that they had done a good night's work, they proceeded through the tunnel to the spiral stone staircase, Geneviève relaying orders as they went.

"Tomorrow morning, I want you to go and round up the crew, Ives-Pierre," she directed. "Have them sail the sloop around Land's End and anchor it just off the coast here—not too close, for I don't want the ship to be seen, but near enough that a dinghy can easily be rowed into the cove we discovered tonight. I'll be waiting there at the mouth of the caves sometime after noon. Then we shall be on our way home, *mon ami.*"

"But, Capitaine," the servant protested, "who is to guide the vessel past the rocks at the opening of the inlet? And how will you explain your absence from Blackheath Hall, besides?''

''I have given both of the matters a great deal of thought, Ives-Pierre,'' Geneviève asserted, ''and I've come to the conclusion that, like it or not, *you* must be the one to steer *La Belle Fille* through the mouth of the crevasse. Do you think you can do it, *mon ami?*''

After a moment in which he carefully considered the difficulties he would face, her companion nodded.

''If the skies are clear and the ocean is calm, *oui*, I believe so. But that still does not solve the problem of how you are to leave Blackheath Hall—and for so long a time, Capitaine.''

''I know, but I've an answer for that, too. Like it or not, I have no other choice: I must take Emeline into my confidence and enlist her aid.''

''Oh, madame, do you think that is wise?'' Ives-Pierre queried, aghast. ''What if she talks?''

''I don't believe she will,'' Geneviève replied. ''For I shall threaten her with the idea that if she does, I shall turn her off immediately—and without a reference— and then she will be forced either to go back to Northchurch Abbey or to try to seek a position elsewhere. I don't think she wants to do that; she's infatuated with Wentworth, Justin's valet.''

''That old twit!'' Ives-Pierre cried. ''Why, he's a more pompous ass than that sorry excuse for a butler, Kinsey, whom Lord Northchurch, for reasons still unknown to me, sees fit to employ!''

''*Oui*, well, that may be true, but Emeline loves him just the same. I think we can count on her to keep silent. I shall have her inform the household that although my health is quite robust, I've nevertheless convinced myself that I have a sickly constitution, that I suffer from shattered nerves, have migraines, fall prey to the vapors, and anything else I can imagine. Physicians have been of no use to me, so when these terrible ailments afflict me, I do not want to be bothered by anyone. Instead, I shut myself up in my room and demand that I remain undisturbed, with only Emeline to attend and comfort me. Complete rest and quiet are my only salvation. What do you think, Ives-Pierre?''

The servant grinned.

"I think you are very naughty, Madame Genette, and very clever, too. You have never been sick a day in your life, but, *poof!*" He snapped his fingers. "Just like that, you will have all at Blackheath Hall convinced you are indeed ill—crazy in the head, in fact. They will sigh over your imaginary complaints, shrug their shoulders, and go on about their business. It is perfect—provided that lovesick maid can play her part properly."

"Don't worry. She will," Geneviève promised. "Just have the sloop and the crew here waiting for me tomorrow afternoon."

To Geneviève's delight, Emeline, bored with her life as an abigail, proved only too willing to take part in her mistress's plot. She would put about the false story of Geneviève's imaginary illnesses, temporarily move into Geneviève's chamber, and see that no one else got inside.

"Do not leave my room for any reason," Geneviève adjured, "lest Mrs. Fincham, who has a key, decides to look in on me."

"Nay, m'dame, I will not," Emeline promised,

her big brown eyes wide and sparkling with barely contained excitement. "I will take care of everything, so you may rescue M'sieur le Comte, M'dame la Comtesse, and your brother, M'sieur le Vicomte. Oh, just think, m'dame! Perhaps in a few days, you will be reunited with your loved ones!" the maid gushed, inclined toward the romantic.

"*Merci*, Emeline, but I do not delude myself into thinking it will be as simple and as easy as that!" Geneviève returned, somewhat amused. "I may have to make several trips across La Manche, so we must be careful not to arouse the suspicions of anyone—including Wentworth."

The maid blushed and cast down her eyes shyly.

"I understand, m'dame. Do not fear that I will breathe a word to him; for though he has paid me some attention, I can see that 'twill take me some time to prod him in the direction I wish him to go. He is very proud, like Lord Blackheath."

"Very well," Geneviève said, slightly relieved. "Have my meals and your own brought upon trays to my room; tell Mrs. Fincham it is by my command that you do not eat in the kitchen with the rest of the servants at this trying time. Say also that I have no need of buckets of bathwater, that a basin filled with enough water for a small sponge bath will suffice and should be left outside the door. If there is anything else I have forgotten, you must take care of it yourself."

"Yes, m'dame. Do not worry. I will not let you down."

"*Bon*. I should be back before Lord Blackheath, but if by some terrible chance he should return sooner than expected, he must be kept out of my chamber at all costs!"

"Yes, m'dame. I will do whatever is necessary to ensure that it is so," Emeline reassured her firmly.

"All right, then. I must go now. *Bonne chance*, Emeline."

"Good luck to you, too, m'dame," the maid responded fervently.

Satisfied that she had done all she could to maintain the secrecy of her plans, Geneviève picked up her lantern and the bundle of clothes she had gathered together earlier. Then, her heart pounding with excitement in her breast, she began her descent down the winding stone staircase in the dark passageway.

She waited forever, it seemed, at the mouth of the caves, watching the ocean as it rushed into the sheltered cove, listening to the sighing waves echoing strangely through the hollow caverns. But at last, much to her relief, for she had begun to fear that Ives-Pierre had dashed her sloop upon the rocks at the opening of *La Belle Fille*'s hiding place after all, a small dinghy appeared on the horizon. As it drew near, she recognized her servant and Thibaud.

Holding her bundle above her head so it would not get wet, she waded out into the swirling water to meet the boat as it slipped into the grotto. Then, tossing her things to Thibaud, she scrambled inside the dinghy, casting her eyes toward the high seas, where her ship and her crew were waiting.

Chapter Fourteen

Had *La Belle Fille* not belonged to her, Geneviève would not even have recognized the vessel, it had been so drastically altered.

After her escape from France, during her crossing of the English Channel, she had thought a long time about how best to disguise the sloop so it would be difficult to see at night and impossible for the French authorities, if they did observe the ship, to recognize it as *La Belle Fille*.

Originally she had considered painting the vessel black so it could come and go undetected under the cover of darkness. But then, standing at the fore rail upon the forecastle, gazing at the midnight sky and the ocean, she had realized that no night, no matter how dark, was every truly an ebony void, completely devoid of any trace of light. On good nights, the shining moon and the glittering stars filled the firmament with silver beams that streamed to the earth below, bathing it in a soft, incandescent glow. The dark green night sea, instead of absorbing them, reflected the luminescent rays, causing the frothy whitecaps of the ever-rolling waves to shimmer like quicksilver in the darkness so it appeared as though the ocean were enveloped by a greyish white sheen.

In addition, Geneviève had recognized that she and the seamen could not ever be sure they would not be caught upon the open seas during the day. Then, a solid black sloop would stick out on the horizon like a sore thumb, attracting all kinds of unwelcome attention.

Because of this, she had at first believed there was no practical way to change *La Belle Fille*'s appearance so the ship would not be seen and connected with the Saint-Georges family. Still, Geneviève had pondered the matter, unwilling to give up until she found a solution to her dilemma.

She had contemplated the way in which the surface of the deep blue waters reflecting the azure daytime sky gleamed like a mirror when caught just so by the bright sun, causing the ocean to flash silver in the distance. She had further dwelled on the manner in which the hazy mist could descend like a soft blanket to wrap the waves in an eerie shroud of whitish grey, and finally, seized by inspiration, it had come to her that this was the color *La Belle Fille* must be.

Now, as they approached the vessel, she observed with satisfaction that her instincts had been correct, for she did not even see the sloop until they were almost upon it, and then she gasped, for it looked like a ghost ship!

The hull above the water line, the mast, the rigging . . . everything had been painted pale grey. Even the canvas sails had been dyed to match. The effect was such that it rendered the vessel's figurehead all the more startling.

This was a wooden bust of a woman carefully carved to resemble Geneviève. Previously it had seemed almost lifelike. Now it appeared like a specter, for though the sailors had retained the vivid crimson shade of its long, flowing hair and the brilliant moss-green tint of its slanted eyes, they had painted the skin pale grey to match the rest of the sloop and had outlined the figurehead's mysterious orbs with a crimson mask.

The ship's name, *La Belle Fille*, had been obliterated; in its place, written boldly in black, were two words: *Crimson Witch*.

"Welcome aboard, Capitaine," Benoit greeted her as she climbed up the rope ladder he'd lowered over the rail. "It is good to have you with us again."

"'Tis good to be here," Geneviève replied, her eyes shining with delight. "I see you have carried out my orders perfectly. You and the rest of the crew are to be commended, Benoit."

"*Merci*, Capitaine. I hope you will find all to your liking."

"I'm sure I shall." Then, unable to contain her excitement any longer, she turned a little breathlessly to Emile, who was at the wheel. "Helmsman, increase our speed two knots," she ordered. "We're going home. We're going *home!*"

They weighed anchor some distance off the coast of France. Then, long after darkness had fallen, they lowered the two dinghies the vessel carried on board and rowed to the beach that lay just beyond the village of Deauville in the north of the country. Marc and Pernel had remained behind and would be joined by Emile, who would take the two small boats back to the sloop.

"Beginning on the seventh day, counting tonight as day one, return to this place for us at this time every night, Emile," Geneviève instructed. "Wait exactly one hour, then go back to the ship. On the twelfth night, if we are all not aboard, return here at this time and wait two hours. After that, the *Crimson Witch* is to set sail for England. If there are still members of the crew missing, they are to be left behind—*myself included*. I will not have the safety of all jeopardized for the sake of one. Is that clear, Emile?"

"*Oui,* Capitaine," he replied.

She looked sharply at the rest, who nodded silently, their faces grim, for they knew Geneviève had meant what she'd told them.

"*Bon,*" she said.

She tossed the lines of one dinghy to Emile, who caught them deftly and secured them to the second boat. Geneviève did not envy him having to row one and tow the other back to the sloop, which lay nearly a league off the coast of France. But she had faith that he would manage the task alone. He had to; she needed every sailor who accompanied her.

Once the two dinghies had slid away from the beach, she told Benoit and Rupert to go on to the Fontaine farm belonging to Rupert's family, where they would fetch his wagon and his stout team of dapple-grey Boulonnais draft horses. Then Geneviève and the rest set off toward the road, where they would join the two cousins.

She calculated that it would take them three days

to reach Paris, after which they would have exactly five days at the most to conclude their business in the city, leaving three additional days to return to the ship before it sailed without them—and that was cutting it very close indeed.

In order to expedite matters, she divided the crew into four groups, not counting the three men who had stayed behind on the *Crimson Witch*. With the money that remained from the sale of the reivers' gems, a vast assortment of items was to be bought; if funds ran out before the list of requirements had been met, what was still needed was to be stolen. Benoit, Rupert, and Davide were to purchase brandies, silks, and other cargo that could be smuggled into England and sold at a tidy profit. Thibaud and Fabien were to acquire guns and ammunition, as well as various other weapons. Olivier and Silvestre were in charge of medical and food supplies. Geneviève and Ives-Pierre would attempt to discover what they could regarding the whereabouts of the girl's family.

Those groups that finished their assignments early were not to wait for the others, but were to return to Deauville in Rupert's vehicle, if it were available at the time. If Benoit, Rupert, and Davide completed their business first, they would go on, leaving the rest to fend for themselves as far as transportation was concerned.

That decided, Geneviève and her followers climbed into the ponderous wooden wagon that slowly approached and drew to a halt before them. Then Rupert, who held the reins, clucked quietly to the big draft horses, and the vehicle began to roll down the rocky dirt road to Paris.

* * *

Her heart hammering rapidly in her breast, Geneviève stared up at the stern, forbidding walls of La Conciergerie that loomed over her in the darkness. Located on the north shore of the Ile de la Cité in the heart of Paris, it was an ancient castle, its construction having begun under the reign of King Philippe IV, called the Fair, at the end of the thirteenth century and having been completed in the fourteenth century. That it had taken so many years to build was not surprising, for it was a massive structure, daunting even in daylight. Now, enshrouded by night shadows, the imposing fortress appeared insurmountable, and Geneviève thought she must be out of her mind to believe she could breach the defenses of the palace.

Four stories high, the edifice was a skillful blend of red brick and buff-colored stone, its austere facade encompassing almost one entire side of the western half of the island it shared with the Sainte Chapelle. It was studded here and there with both square and circular watchtowers and capped by a black, steep-sided gabled roof rich with wrought-iron detail at its peak. Tall brick chimneys rose above the dormer windows that jutted out from the roof; each of these apertures was set directly above the muntined windows that lined the second and third stories of the building. The first floor had small, high windows and arched portals with solid wood doors.

The castle had taken its name from *le concierge*— the caretaker—the title of the royal governor in charge of it, and though it had once been the home of kings and queens, it now served as a prison. If Geneviève's parents and brother had been arrested, this was where they would be.

She crouched against the far side of the east balustrade of the Pont au Change, upon a narrow shelf that edged the stone bridge spanning the River Seine. From her position, she could spy the rectangular Tour de l'Horloge, which King Jean II, called the Good, had had constructed in 1334. The quadrangular belltower housed the first public clock of Paris, and by the dim light cast by the tall black lamps lining the bridge, she could just make out the time. It was a few minutes past midnight.

Farther on were the round twin towers that flanked the entrance to the fortress. Geneviève had no hope of getting past the guards stationed out front, so she waited until their backs were turned to her, then she crept up onto the end of the bridge, where it joined the Boulevard du Palais, the main street on the island, motioning silently for Ives-Pierre to follow.

Taking care to remain in the shadows, the two pressed themselves flat against the side of La Conciergerie, waiting for the sentries who patrolled the boulevard to resume their positions before the black wrought-iron gate, with its gold-leafed ornamentation, that led to the Sainte Chapelle adjoining the castle.

Once Geneviève was certain she would not be observed, she slipped over to one of the ancient trees that lined the street and secreted herself behind its huge, gnarled trunk. Then, after unwinding the rope she carried slung over one shoulder, she took the end bearing a stout grappling hook and tossed it up into the tree's branches, which had been carefully pruned so they could not be reached when standing on the ground. With only a slight rustling of leaves, the iron claw caught upon a limb; after tugging on the thick length of hemp to be sure the hook was secure, Geneviève started to climb. Once she was well hidden among the green boughs, Ives-Pierre joined her, and, together, they hauled up the rope.

They perched breathlessly still for a moment, listening to the sounds of the sleeping city: the low-voiced conversation and laughter of the nearby guards, the late-night revelry that drifted to their ears from a distant quarter on the Rive Gauche, the gentle lapping of the River Seine against its banks, and the whisper of the wind.

Then slowly Geneviève started to inch her way along a thick branch whose tip nearly touched the side of La Conciergerie. When she was almost at the end of the limb, she stood, grabbing another bough above to maintain her footing. When she was certain she was stable, she cautiously released her hold on the higher branch, balancing her weight on the supporting limb. She waited until another burst of merriment from the sentries split the night; then, after swinging the rope back and forth a few times to be sure it had a clear path, she heaved the end with the claw out and upward, praying it would catch on one of the spirelike stone peaks that topped the dormer windows lining the fourth story of the castle.

To her horror, the hook instead crashed with a loud thud against the roof, then slid down its steep, gabled side. The force of the downward spiraling rope, its heavy claw scraping against the fortress once or twice, almost dragged Geneviève from the tree. Swaying precariously upon her bough, Ives-Pierre's gasp sounding like a gunshot in her ears, she just managed to clutch the branch above her to keep from falling, somehow simultaneously retaining her hold on the fat strand of hemp so, instead of smashing upon the paving blocks of the boulevard, the hook, now clear of La Conciergerie, dangled a scant few inches from the ground. Her heart in her throat, Geneviève quickly regained her footing and yanked the rope up into the concealing boughs of the tree, praying that the guards had not heard the commotion.

"What was that?" one of the sentries asked sharply, starting down the street in the direction of the girl and her servant.

Not even daring to breathe, she and Ives-Pierre clung to the branches of the tree, filled with terror as they waited to be discovered. Then, as though by some miracle, a stray mongrel suddenly darted down the boulevard, whining shrilly in the silence. The pitifully thin animal paused to sniff and scratch at one of the wooden doors of the castle, then, spying the guards, ran on.

The group of men laughed.

"Look! 'Twas only a mangy cur, no doubt rummaging about for a scrap of food, Renault," another of the sentries called to the man bent on investigating the noise. "Do not waste your time chasing after it. Do you not want to hear the end of Talebot's story about the pretty Solange, eh?"

"*Oui*," Renault said and, shrugging, rejoined the others.

Slowly Geneviève and Ives-Pierre exhaled, gazing at each other silently, knowing how narrow their escape had been. Then, still quivering with fear, she rose and, trying to still the trembling of her hands, prepared once more to throw the claw upward.

"Do you want me to do it, Madame Genette?" her companion offered.

"*Non,*" she murmured, shaking her head. "I will do it."

To Geneviève's overwhelming relief, this time, the hook caught upon the stone peak topping one of the dormer windows and held fast. After glancing down the street to be certain the guards were still engrossed in Talebot's tale, she wiped her sweaty palms on her breeches, took a firmer hold upon the rope, then jumped from the limb upon which she was standing. Moments later, she was dangling against the side of the fortress. Hurriedly she began to climb, knowing how exposed she was now and that any second the sentries might see her. At last she sat, lodged awkwardly and precariously, upon the small peak of the dormer window. Pausing to catch her breath, she hauled up the thick length of hemp, wound it up and slung it over one shoulder, then started to clamber up onto the roof of La Conciergerie.

The incline was very steep, and once or twice when she nearly lost her footing, her heart leaped to her throat; if she fell, she should surely be killed. Using the short black wrought-iron ornamentation that ran along the peak of the gabled roof, she inched her way along the top of the castle, at the same time taking careful note of her surroundings. The tall, slender chimneys proved an advantage, for she could lean against them to rest without fear of discovery or of slipping and falling to the ground far below.

In her mind, she visualized the interior layout of the fortress, where she had once visited her grandfather when he'd been imprisoned briefly for some minor infraction. On the first floor, there was the Salle des Gardes, with its powerful piers that supported beautiful Gothic vaults, and the vast Salle des Gens d'Armes, which was two hundred twenty-four feet long, eighty-eight feet wide, and twenty-six feet high. This was divided by more stone piers with Gothic vaults into four aisles and had once served as the king's dining hall. It was an awesome, breathtaking chamber, for when the torches set into the shafts of the columns were lit, the flaming light seemed to travel up the great arches, making it appear as though the towering ceiling were afire. In a niche in one wall of the room was a spiral stone staircase leading to the great kitchens above, where the cooks had once prepared meals for as many as a thousand guests.

From the two halls, dimly lit corridors ran back to the cubicles used as cells. There was a large chamber with cruciform vaults where, for a price, those prisoners who could afford it could have a straw pallet on which to sleep. Nearby was a smaller room where more important captives were incarcerated. Beyond these, as well as on other floors, were tiny, dark, dank cells where various individual prisoners were kept. Housed in yet another area, even meaner than all the rest and known as the Rue de Paris, were the poor captives of the Assembly.

Outside the central jail, paved with small square blocks, was a little courtyard shaped roughly like a distorted triangle, where some of the prisoners were allowed to take the air. Here, they could sit beneath a single gnarled, leaning tree with a crooked trunk and weeping branches, which rose from one corner of what had once been a flower bed. From there, they could contemplate one of the black, spike-topped, wrought-iron gates and the high walls that held them captive. Those who wished might wash themselves and their clothes in an old stone fountain that jutted out from one short, convex side of the courtyard. Supported by bricks, the

squat fountain resembled half of a bathtub and had a
thick, curved lip. Crude and plain, it boasted no statue
or other ornament and was scarcely big enough to
accommodate all those who must use it. The buff-
colored stone of which it was built was chipped, cracked,
and green with algae.

After reaching that part of the roof that overlooked
the courtyard, Geneviève studied the enclosure carefully. The tree within was not very tall and so would be of
no use to her. But it would be possible to lower a rope
into the area so captives could climb up to the top of the
castle and, following the perilous route she herself had
taken to reach the courtyard, escape from La Conciergerie.
The prisoners would have to be young and strong, she
thought, her heart sinking slightly, for though Vachel
could flee in such a manner, her middle-aged parents
would never be able to manage it. Still, a basket they
could sit in, one at a time, might be tied to the fat
strand of hemp, and if she had help, Geneviève could
pull up the heavy burden.

All that remained, then, was to discover whether
any of her family or friends were being held captive in
the fortress and, if so, to find a guard who could be
bribed to let them out into the courtyard after dark.
Getting beyond the gates of the city itself would pose
another problem altogether.

Slowly Geneviève hooked the iron claw around a
chimney and lowered herself down the rope so she
could look into one of the mullioned windows of the
corridor that was lined on the opposite wall with cells.
The wooden doors of the few cubicles she could see
were all shut tight, their small, high, iron mesh grilles,
which admitted a tiny amount of light and air, staring
back at her like dark, sightless eyes.

She was getting ready to ascend the rope when, with a little start of anger and fear, she suddenly spied Claude Rambouillet and one of the jailors coming down the long, narrow hall. After fumbling with his ring of keys for a minute, the guard flung open one of the cell doors, motioning for the man inside to rise. Had Geneviève not known the prisoner so well, she would not even have recognized one of Vachel's closest friends, the Chevalier de la Tour-Jolie. He was so filthy and gaunt that her heart ached for him, and when Claude struck him a vicious blow, it was all she could do to keep from smashing through the window and killing the man who had torn her family apart.

With difficulty, she restrained herself, knowing that now was neither the time nor the place for such a rash action. Then, trembling with rage, she climbed back up to the top of the castle and began to retrace her steps to its eastern side.

She was halfway across the roof when, to her horror, a shadowed figure suddenly loomed out at her from behind one of the chimneys cloaked in darkness. She was so shocked by the man's presence that before she could even react, he had caught her in a strong, cruel grip and shoved her so roughly against the brick chimney that both of them slipped and almost fell.

"Don't call out, and don't try to fight me!" he snarled softly in her ear, his breath warm upon her face. "I doubt you wish to attract the attention of the sentries, and I certainly do not. Besides, if you struggle, we might both be plunged to a very unpleasant death upon the paving blocks below."

Geneviève, recognizing that this was the truth, made no effort to free herself. Instead, she glared at the tall, dark stranger who had accosted her, quite startled to discover he was disguised much as she was, for he wore a black silk loo mask, a black domino buttoned up to the throat, and tight black breeches.

His unruly, windblown hair was jet black, with solid wings of silver at the temples. She could not see his eyebrows beneath his mask, but she suspected they were as black as his shaggy locks. His eyes were the color of smoke in the darkness and seemed to glitter like diamonds when touched by the moonlight. His finely chiseled nose, outlined beneath his mask, reminded her of a hawk's beak, and his full, sensual lips curving beneath his jet-black mustache were parted to reveal even white teeth that flashed brightly against his bronze skin. Was this the infamous spy they called the Black Mephisto?

As his body pressed against her own, pinning her to the chimney, she could feel how lean and powerful he was, with strong, corded muscles that rippled sinuously in his arms and legs, sending an electric thrill of fright mingled strangely with sudden excitement through her blood.

"Let me go!" she cried, struggling against him.

"Shhhhh. Keep your voice down!" he hissed, giving her a little shake. "Do you want to bring the guards down on us?"

"*Non*. Of course not."

"Then be quiet, damn you, and tell me what you're doing up here, cavorting around like a cat. Don't you realize you might have lost your footing and been killed? What kind of games are you playing, garçon? Why, you scarcely even look old enough to shave!"

Beneath her crimson mask, Geneviève's eyes widened slightly as she realized her assailant thought her a boy. But then, dressed as she was, what else was he supposed to think?

"What I'm doing up here is none of your business, monsieur," she said sharply, keeping her voice low, "and you're hardly in a position to question me. I'm sure the government is much more interested in catching you than me, for if you are the Black Mephisto, as I suspect, the authorities have quite a pretty price on your head. No doubt they would be very interested in learning what you know about the Royalists."

The stranger smiled inscrutably, releasing his tight hold upon her but remaining near enough to grab her immediately, should she attempt to escape.

"What makes you think I'm a Royalist, garçon?" he asked coolly, refusing to confirm or deny that he was the Black Mephisto.

"I know how the members of the Assembly operate," Geneviève replied truthfully, "and though you are rumored to be one of them, your being here tonight proves you are not—unless you are now a traitor to their cause. I have heard, as well, that you are an English spy, but that, too, cannot be true."

"Oh? And why is that?" her assailant queried, a small smile of amusement still playing about the corners of his lips.

"Your French, monsieur. It is the French of France. An Englishman, no matter how fluent in the language, would have some slight accent, if only on a few words here and there. But you do not. Nor do you have the mannerisms of an Englishman," Geneviève pointed out shrewdly, recalling her husband's languid, elegant movements. This man's gestures were sure and swift. She shrugged. "You speak with your hands as well as your tongue—as all Frenchmen do."

"You're very astute and observant, garçon," the stranger remarked, "but not clever enough to be indulging in whatever mischief you are up to tonight. Go on home. You are too young to lose your head to Madame Guillotine."

"*Oui*, and I do not intend to do so. Still, it is my head to lose, after all, monsieur, and I do not need you meddling in my affairs. If you will kindly step aside, I shall be on my way, for I have tarried here overlong as it is."

To her surprise, instead of moving out of her path, her assailant placed his arms on either side of her, pressing his palms against the chimney.

"Do you have family below, inside La Conciergerie?" he inquired gently, his tone serious now and his smile gone.

Geneviève bit her lip with anguish.

"I—I do not know," she confessed. "That is one of the things I was trying to find out. But a friend of mine is inside; I saw him through one of the windows. That filthy *canaille* Claude Rambouillet was beating him!"

Tears stung her eyes at the thought, and with difficulty, she blinked the droplets away before they could fall.

"So that is why you thought you would emulate the Black Mephisto, eh? I could help, you know," the stranger offered quietly when she did not respond.

"*Non*." Geneviève shook her head reluctantly. "For in order for you to assïst me, you would have to know the names of my family and friends. I thank you, monsieur, but I—I can trust no one. *Comprenez-vous?*"

"*Oui*, garçon. *Je comprends.*"

"Then I will leave you now. *Au revoir*, monsieur."

Geneviève turned to go, and as she did so, the black velvet riband of her queue caught upon the rough brick of the chimney. She yanked her head impatiently to free the narrow band and, to her dismay, succeeded only in pulling it from her hair. Her fiery copper tresses, looking dark and crimson in the moonlight, tumbled down her back, billowing about her slender figure in the wind.

"Mon Dieu!" the masked man swore, stunned. *"Une jeune fille!"*

The Black Mephisto, for that was indeed who he was, stared at the girl before him, astounded. He had known many women in the past but never one who had risked life and limb with such daring as this young girl had.

When he had first spied her climbing the rope from the courtyard and then slinking surefootedly across the top of the building, he had been filled with admiration for her skill and courage. Now, upon learning she was a female, he was struck by a feeling even more powerful as, momentarily speechless, he went on studying her, noting the way the long strands of her hair whipped about her piquant, hollow-cheeked face; how her eyes, as dark green as the night sea in the starry blackness, slanted catlike behind the slits of her crimson mask; the manner in which her full, generous red mouth parted and her tongue darted out to moisten her lips.

Sacrebleu! She was beautiful—breathtakingly beautiful—brave, bold, and brazen, too, like no other woman he had ever known. Despite every urgent warning his mind cried out to him silently, the Black Mephisto was irresistibly drawn to her like steel to a magnet, for he sensed instinctively that she was a match for him in every way that counted. He felt suddenly as though he were looking into a mirror and seeing the other half of his soul, and inexplicably he knew somehow, some way, that he had waited all his life for this sorceress standing before him. He was so bound by the web of enchantment she wove around him that he forgot who he was, what he was doing on the roof of the castle, the sentries below, the mortal danger he and she would face if they were discovered . . . everything—but the girl herself.

"Who are you?" he questioned hoarsely. "Who are you?"

"I am known as Capitaine La Folle, commander of the *Crimson Witch*," she said softly, feeling the now highly charged atmosphere between them prick her like a sharply honed blade.

Her heart raced with excitement in her breast, for she could not mistake the glance of desire upon the Black Mephisto's face, and it, combined with their perilous situation, filled her incomprehensibly with exhilaration, as though she were rushing headlong into a tempestuous storm from which there would be no escaping.

Truly she *was* mad, she thought, made so by the wild, unexpected emotions suddenly whirling up to engulf her, making her long strangely, inexplicably, to feel this man's carnal mouth pressed against her own. . . .

"'Tis not your true name, I'll warrant," he muttered, his breath ragged. "But it suits you all the same, for you are indeed a fey creature. Still, I think I shall call you Rouge, for I have always had a fondness for red hair."

And then, as though he had read her mind, he bent his head, his lips swooping down to capture hers, imprisoning them savagely, branding them irrevocably with the hot, demanding taste of his own.

Taken unaware, Geneviève made no effort to fight him. She was too shocked and dazed by his kiss even to think, to do anything but feel. She had become a mass of quivering sensations, her flesh alive and burning with every touch of his mouth and hands, her blood like molten ore, and her nerves tingling with electric sparks. She could feel the coarse chimney catching at her hair, snarling it, and grating against her back, scraping her skin through the black domino she wore over her white linen shirt. She could feel the steep, precarious slant of the roof beneath her feet, making it seem as though the earth were tilting crazily beneath her; and she was falling, falling, spiraling down into a black void filled only with the man who held her fast, his strong embrace hurting her with its intensity. But she did not care. She was too caught up in the powerful, overwhelming emotions he aroused within her, the sleeping passion he wakened within her.

His tongue shot forth to trace the outline of her lips before forcing them to part so he might discover the soft, yielding sweetness within, plunder the innermost secrets of her mouth. As though they had a will of their own, his hands tangled themselves in her hair, drawing the tresses forward to envelop them both in a soft cascade of silken fire. His mouth slashed like a whip across her face to her temples and the satin strands intertwined with his fingers. He inhaled deeply the fragrant lily scent of her, and deep within his brain, a fleeting memory stirred, only to slip away as quickly as it had come, for it belonged to another, long ago and far away, it seemed, and she had never been like this. None of them—those many women of his past, with their seductive smiles and open arms and legs—had ever been like this, filling him so completely with desire that he could not even think, could only feel and ache with wanting.

The Black Mephisto pressed his body close against that of the girl he held, all thoughts but those of her driven from his mind by her nearness. He could feel her thighs trembling against his own as she felt his hard masculinity brush against her in a feathery caress, unmistakable evidence of the passion she was evoking in him.

His lips reclaimed hers, and his hands fumbled with the buttons of her black domino until he had freed the top two from their confines, exposing the length of her creamy throat to his hungry gaze, his searing mouth.

"Sweet. Sweet," he whispered huskily as his warm breath scorched the slender column.

Dizzily Geneviève swayed against him, feeling a smoldering ember of desire erupt into flame within her, filling her with uncontrollable yearning for him. She had been kissed before, but never like this. Even Justin, her husband, had never kissed her like this.

Justin!

Sainte Marie! What was she doing? She was a married woman, and this man was not her husband! *Sang de Christ!* She did not even know his name!

Coming to her senses at last, she began to struggle against him and, taking him by surprise, managed to wrench herself free. Then she slapped him a stunning blow across his face.

"How dare you?" she cried wrathfully, shaking with anger that this stranger had unleashed such tumultuous feelings within her that she had forgotten her husband, her family, and everything else. "You forget yourself, monsieur, as do I. I am not some common tart to be mauled upon a roof! I am Madame—I am a lady of quality!" she amended, cursing her wretched tongue, which had nearly given away her identity.

Then hurriedly, before he could recover and once more encircle her with his steely grip, Geneviève scrambled hazardously across the top of La Conciergerie.

"Rouge," the Black Mephisto called quietly, his heart in his throat as he watched her hasty, skipping progress across the gabled roof. "Rouge, come back, damn you!"

But she was gone, and he dared not follow, for fear of frightening her into making a misstep and falling. Feeling as though someone every important had just disappeared from his life, he turned away to traverse his own path across the top of the building.

It did not matter that she had fled. They would meet again, that temptress and he, the spy thought, for from what she had told him, it was obvious she believed her family was imprisoned in La Conciergerie; and, daring as she was, she would not rest until she had discovered the truth of the matter. *Oui*, she would come here again, and she would pay a late-night visit to the Temple, as well, where other captives were held, and doubtless the Place de Grève, too, where all executions took place. He had only to wait and to watch for her in those places of Paris he himself frequented on his midnight missions, and he would see her once more; he felt sure of it! Next time, he vowed, she would not elude him so easily.

Who was she? he wondered again. Something about her had seemed hauntingly familiar. Then, with a little start of surprise, he recognized that she had been the very image of the woman of his dreams, and he thought it was no wonder he had been so drawn to her! But still, that did not answer the question of her identity.

She had told him she was Capitaine La Folle and that she was the commander of the *Crimson Witch*. He almost laughed aloud at the notion. Imagine! The very idea of a woman running a ship! But then he remembered how nimbly she'd ascended her rope when she'd climbed to the roof of the fortress from the window where she'd dangled over the prisoners' courtyard, and beneath his mask, the Black Mephisto's smoky eyes narrowed. Aye, she had moved as though she were used to scaling the rigging of a vessel, as he himself was. Could it be that she had spoken truly after all? Then he recollected the moment when she had almost but not quite let her real name slip, and he knew it was not so. *Madame*, she had said. *Madame . . . ?*

With a sinking feeling in the pit of his stomach, the spy suddenly realized that the woman who had so bewitched him was married.

How ironic that it should be thus, he reflected wryly, for just for an instant when he had taken her in his arms, he had forgotten that he himself had a wife, that he was not free to pursue the enticing enchantress who had cast her magic spell upon him.

Damn! he cursed silently to himself in the darkness as he clambered over the western side of La Conciergerie and started to descend his rope to the pretty, triangular Place Dauphine below.

His wife did not love him—theirs had been an arranged match, like so many marriages of the day— and she had made it clear that she preferred to go her own way, leaving him to shift for himself. Doubtless she would not care if she discovered he had taken a mistress. After all, she did not share his bed. But would Rouge? He did not know, but he certainly intended to find out if he ever saw her again!

So thinking, the Black Mephisto dropped the short distance to the ground, then tugged on the iron hook at the end of the rope that he had first used to climb from a tree to the roof, then had pulled up behind him, reversed, and tied in a slip knot about one of the chimneys. The thick length of hemp fell away from the fortress, and he caught the strand deftly, winding it up and slinging it over his shoulder.

After that, glancing about to be certain he was unobserved, he slipped through the shadows down the Quai de l'Horloge to the Pont Neuf, which, despite its name, New Bridge, was the oldest one in Paris.

Minutes later, after rowing his small boat around the Square du Vert Galant on the far west end of the Ile de la Cité, he headed across the waters to the Rive Gauche, where his grandfather lived and would put him up safely for the night.

Chapter Fifteen

"I'm very sorry to hear you've been unwell during my absence, Genette," Justin said politely as, with a cool kiss that barely brushed her cheek, he greeted his wife as she entered the dining room at Blackheath Hall.

Then, when, after murmuring a noncommittal reply, she turned away to take her chair, he frowned with distaste, recalling Emeline's litany of Geneviève's complaints. At first the viscount had been alarmed, thinking his bride was gravely ill. But then gradually the maid had impressed upon him the fact that Geneviève's ailments were imaginary, born of her nervous, flighty disposition, and his concern had lessened.

Although she did look a trifle pale and there were mauve circles of tiredness around her eyes, it was far more likely, he now thought sourly, that his wife had hit upon this silly scheme to keep him from her bed. Well, she was welcome to remain undisturbed in her empty chamber—he certainly had no intention of intruding where he was so obviously not wanted—and if she

wished to quack herself in the process, it would doubtless do her no real harm.

The matter thus disposed of in his mind, he picked
up the bundle of *Morning Gazettes*, which had been
delivered to him from London by his secretary and now
lay beside his plate, and began to read the newspapers
in sequence, according to date.

Geneviève, sipping her tea, was slightly relieved
that Justin was paying her so little attention, for she was
afraid that if he inspected her too closely, he would
notice the telltale signs that she had not truly been abed
while he'd been gone. Beneath the pallor she'd achieved
with rice powder, her flesh had a golden, glowing hue
gained from many sunlit hours spent strolling in Les
Halles, the marketplace in Paris, listening to the grum-
blings of the merchants and the gossip of the bourgeoisie as she tried to glean any tidbit she could about her
parents and her brother. There were faint red marks on
her face and arms where the branches of the tree on the
Boulevard du Palais had scratched her, and her knees
were scraped and bruised from crawling up and down
the steep, gabled roof of La Conciergerie. Her hands
were raw and blistered from her rope climbing, and
now calluses were beginning to form upon her palms.

But it was all worth it, she mused, for already she
and her crew had made a fine start. They had rescued
the Chevalier de la Tour-Jolie and two other men.

Geneviève and Ives-Pierre had been forced to haul
them up to the top of La Conciergerie one by one in a
basket, for the knights had been too weak to ascend the
rope she had lowered into the prisoners' courtyard. But
fear that a short journey to Madame Guillotine was
imminent had propelled them across the roof and down
the rope to the tree, after which they'd dropped to the

ground and been assisted by Thibaud and Fabien into an alley, where they'd all hidden for the night. The following morning, dressed in nuns' robes, which Geneviève had borrowed from her grandfather's costume rack, they'd passed through the city gates to freedom.

After that, Geneviève had penned a taunting poem to Claude Rambouillet:

> *The Assembly hunts high; the Assembly hunts*
> *   low,*
> *And still, it can't find the Black Mephisto.*
> *Now there's another who wants to play his game.*
> *The Crimson Witch is this masquer's name.*
> *Did you think you had trouble before this morn?*
> *Claude, I'll make you wish you had never been*
> *   born.*
> *You thought you knew who freed Tour-Jolie.*
> *But now two are laughing at the bourgeoisie!*

Along with the note, which she'd paid a young boy a sou to deliver, she had enclosed a crimson mask. Oh, how she would have loved to see Claude's face when he'd received her message! Of course, he probably would have remained still about it, not wanting to look a fool. But, as a precaution against his silence, Geneviève had taken mean delight in also sending a copy to one of the radical newspapers that had sprung up all over Paris. The poem had been published that afternoon, along with a mocking caricature of Claude himself.

She and her crew had smuggled the three knights into England and given them a little money to begin a new life. Then the seamen had dropped Geneviève off at the mouth of the caves and unloaded the smuggled goods they would sell to their contacts in Penzance.

After disposing of the booty, half of which they'd bought and half of which they'd stolen, they'd sailed on around Land's End to the sloop's hiding place. That had been several days ago.

Now it did not seem possible to Geneviève that almost a fortnight had passed since she had returned to Blackheath Hall. Still, every time she thought about the events that had occurred during her furtive foray into France, she trembled with mingled fear and excitement, terrified that someone would discover her true identity and expose her. Yet perversely she was bursting to tell all who would listen the secrets she hugged to her breast like a child.

Well, some of them anyway, she amended silently to herself. She did not want anyone, least of all her husband, ever to learn about Noir, as, in her mind, she had come to call the man she suspected of being the Black Mephisto.

Though she had tried desperately to put him out of her thoughts, he still haunted her, filling her with a strange longing that would not be eased. It was almost as though he were a devil who, with a single kiss, had ensorcelled her, stealing her soul in the process. She could still taste his lips on hers, as though only a few moments had passed since he had kissed her, his mouth bruising her own, branding her as his. Her mind dwelled on him constantly, recalling his dark, handsome, masked face in every detail. At night, she dreamed about him, felt him kissing her—and more—shameful pictures that would not be banished, that made her flesh burn and her body ache with desire.

Once, Geneviève had caressed her breasts and belly with her hands, running her palms over her skin as she had imagined the spy doing, and something so vital and thrilling had burst to life within her that it had overwhelmed her with its electric intensity. As though they had been scorched, she had snatched her hands away from herself, clenching her fists by her sides, mortified by her unmentionable behavior and her passionate yearning for a man who was not her husband.

She believed she must be going mad, so thoroughly did Noir dominate her thoughts. No matter how hard she tried to fight her confusing feelings about him, she hoped fervently that she would somehow see him again, though this did not appear likely, she had to admit. Still, she felt in her bones that their paths in life were destined to cross once more, and she knew that if that happened, despite everything honorable within her, she and Noir would become lovers.

Geneviève could not let that occur; she was a married woman, and because of that, there was no future for her with anyone but Justin. For better or for worse, he was her life, as she had vowed on their wedding day. She could not throw that away for a moment's passion. But, oh, how she longed to be loved, to lay her head upon a lover's shoulder, if only for a little while, and know that he and she could face anything together.

She gazed down the long dining room to the head of the table, where her husband sat buried behind his newspapers.

Look at me, Justin, she pleaded silently. *There is more to me than meets the eye—if only you would see it.*

But he was engrossed in some article and never noticed his wife's beseeching glance.

* * *

Geneviève had never felt so bewildered and torn apart.

Like all business dealings, the course of Justin's many ventures did not run smoothly, and it seemed that scarcely any time at all had passed at Blackheath Hall before he received another urgent message that required him to leave Cornwall again. He would be out of town, he told his bride, for a month at least. She didn't know whether to cry or to feel relieved.

On the one hand, she had hoped to be able to spend some time with her husband, for it was obvious to her that, despite their promising kiss at the altar, their marriage had somehow got off to a bad start and what little relationship they'd had had been slowly deteriorating ever since. Geneviève had hoped that, given time together, they could make an attempt to set things right between them.

Justin was a handsome man; he had attracted her once and still did. It was just that she could not seem to get past his cool, arrogant facade to discover the man within. How she wished she could put off her air of superficiality and show him her real self! Surely he would take *some* interest in her if he no longer thought her a scatterbrained fool!

But this was not possible as long as she remained uncertain about the fate of her parents and her brother. If she told her husband the truth at this point, he would no doubt be furious and would refuse to allow her to continue the search for her family; and Geneviève couldn't be sure he would undertake the task himself— especially with his business affairs taking up so much of his time.

On the other hand, she was glad his work called him out of town so often, for it gave her the chance to go on with her own plans, and the success of her initial excursion into France had renewed her hope that she could get her parents and her brother out of the country alive—if they had not been executed. Although she was certain this was not the case, for surely if it had been, she would have learned of it in the streets of Paris since her father was so well known, still, her apprehension concerning her family's lives remained utmost in her mind.

Thus the situation with Justin proved a mixed blessing, and Geneviève could not help but be emotionally torn by it.

She feared it was partially her husband's lack of interest in her that had caused her to be so drawn to Noir, who still haunted her, and she was afraid that if Justin continued to ignore her, she would look elsewhere for love. Her passions ran deep and were not easily kept locked within her. She had never wanted a cold marriage of convenience, nor had she truly believed her husband would persist in such an arrangement after they were wed; that he had had deeply disappointed her.

Armand Charbonne had tenderly nurtured her childish emotions; Justin had forced her to abandon her girlish daydreams, and Noir had given her a glimpse of the woman she could be. Now she hungered to learn the full measure of that knowledge. Had her husband proved a willing teacher, Geneviève felt she could have opened her heart to him; at the very least, she would have tried. After all, he was her cousin, and she was not without feelings for him. But Justin had wounded her pride and vanity instead, hurting her and leaving her vulnerable to Noir.

Noir. She had become obsessed by him, a spy whose real name she did not even know, a man whom she did not even know if she would ever see again. Yet, over and over, her husband's carelessly spoken words— that she might take a lover if she so chose and were discreet—rang in her mind, taunting her, and the image of Noir tempted her. She was already a criminal, having broken the laws of both England and France, and if the truth were ever discovered, she would be an outcast, as well. Why not take Noir, if the chance somehow arose, when it was plain Justin did not want her? Did not every married lady of quality have her cicisbei, as her husband had casually informed her? What difference did it make if she betrayed her wedding vows? It was not as though she would be defiling a loving relationship— something she would have held sacred and pure. *Non.* She would be committing only one more illegal act, and what could that possibly matter when she had already carried out so many?

Still, something inside the girl protested, even as she felt herself weakening, acknowledging the dark void within her that yearned so desperately to be filled with love; and increasingly, as Justin's coldness toward her did not abate, her passionate fantasies and desires focused on the man she suspected was the Black Mephisto.

Chapter Sixteen

"I don't like it, Capitaine," Benoit insisted stoutly. "These are our fellow seamen you're talking about robbing, and though 'tis one thing to be a smuggler, 'tis quite another indeed to be a pirate!"

"*Oui, oui!*" Rupert put in. "Why, I barely escaped with my life from an English dragoon in Penzance when we disposed of our first cargo. I'm of no mind to be forced to walk a plank!"

Geneviève frowned at him disgustedly.

"Have you been drinking again, Rupert?" she inquired tartly. "That is an old wives' tale, as surely you would know if your ancestors had been sailors as my own were. Many a poor man was pitched overboard to serve as sharks' bait, but none, I assure you, was ever disposed of in such a pointless and time-consuming manner as being made to walk a plank. Furthermore, in this case, *we* would be the pirates, you fool! Not the other way around."

"*Oui*, Capitaine. That is true." Rupert brightened considerably at this observation.

"Besides," Geneviève went on tersely, once more addressing Benoit, "robbing your fellow seamen is certainly no worse than stealing from your fellow countrymen, and Davide reported to me that you stole every single cask of brandy you brought on board the *Crimson Witch* after our first foray into France!"

"*Oui*. It was indeed so," Benoit confessed reluctantly. "But we had run out of money, Capitaine, and cognac is especially dear to English hearts—and purses."

"Precisely," Geneviève noted dryly, "and we did indeed make quite a bundle on it. But after we divided our shares from the profits, our treasury was much depleted. We do not have enough funds remaining to purchase new goods—much less to bribe those greedy guards at La Conciergerie. We *must* find a rich ship—and attack her!"

"I agree." Thibaud spoke up. "Come, come, Benoit," he coaxed, ever fond of a fight. "France is at war—not only with herself, but with half of Europe, besides! Frenchmen are killing each other every day, and 'tis not as though our clever Capitaine La Folle has suggested we murder anyone. The crew of whatever prize we may take will be put to sea in the vessel's dinghies. That is certainly far more mercy than *we* will be shown if we are taken captive in the process, for we shall surely be clapped in irons and imprisoned in the hold!"

"All right." Benoit capitulated at last. "But we must choose our victim carefully, lest we be blown to bits. Our cannons are not very big, and we only have four of them, besides."

"Then it is decided?" Geneviève glanced at each

member of her crew. "We will select a target—a French ship only—and capture her and her cargo?"

"*Oui*, Capitaine," the men chorused as one.

"*Bon*. Fabien, take the spyglass and climb the rigging to see what you can see. If you spot anything, let me know immediately."

"*Oui*, Capitaine." He grinned, for he was as reckless as Thibaud. Then he started to clamber up the sloop's rigging.

Geneviève began to issue orders to the rest of the crew, for maneuvering the *Crimson Witch,* as well as manning the four six-pound cannons she carried, would require every hand aboard her—and then some—and the girl did not delude herself into thinking it would be easy. They would indeed have to choose their mark carefully.

Once she was certain preparations for the forthcoming battle were well under way, she retired to her cabin for a moment's respite and quiet. There, she sat down at the dining table and rested her head upon her folded arms. She was not physically tired, but mentally she felt worn out from the dual role she had chosen to play.

Justin had left Blackheath Hall two days ago; Geneviève herself had departed a day later, leaving Emeline to inform the household that her mistress was suffering another one of her "spells." There had been a terrible moment when Geneviève, already starting to descend the winding stone staircase in the passageway, had heard Mrs. Fincham knocking imperiously upon the bedroom door, demanding that she be admitted.

Hurriedly Geneviève had run back to her chamber, jammed a lacy nightcap on her head, and yanked one of her nightgowns on over her boy's clothes. Then she had hastily slipped into bed, snatching the covers up around her and instructing Emeline to open the door.

Mrs. Fincham had bustled in kindheartedly with a special draft she had sworn would make her mistress feel better in a trice. Geneviève had moaned dramatically, frowned sternly at Emeline, who had been choked with laughter, and assured the housekeeper she had tried everything and that nothing—absolutely nothing! —but lying down in a darkened room helped her aching head.

"I will drink the potion to please you, Mrs. Fincham," she had said, "but please see that I am not disturbed again."

The narrow escape had frazzled Geneviève's nerves, already stretched taut by the daily strain of maintaining her frivolous facade before Justin and her restless nights filled with shameful, erotic dreams of Noir.

Now she stood and poured herself a small shot of brandy, knowing that the course she was embarking upon this evening might damage her vessel beyond repair and possibly kill one or more of the sailors who had become her friends.

Still, there was no other way. Geneviève needed funds desperately to buy information and to bribe guards and officials alike if she were ever to save her parents and her brother.

She had thought of selling some of the jewels that had come to her as Justin's bride, but then she had realized that, despite the fact that he was often extremely bored and would not put himself forth for anyone or anything unless it were sure to amuse or to enrich him—as his business dealings did—her husband was not stupid. He could not have amassed such a considerable fortune above and beyond his inheritance if he had been. He was sure to notice if family heirlooms began to disappear, and Geneviève could not risk that. Justin had quite a nasty temper, and she felt certain he would demand—and fully expect to receive—an explanation for the loss of her gems.

Her pin money was not even worth considering, for her husband, while giving her an allowance, had instructed her merely to have the bills for the majority of her purchases sent directly to him. Geneviève was sure this was because he suspected she would otherwise capriciously gamble her way into debt, playing faro and silver loo, being empty-headed enough to throw good money after bad in the hope of recouping her losses. She was not such an idiot as that; Ives-Pierre had taught both her and Vachel how to turn a trick at cards and the foolhardiness of punting on tick, but of course, she could not tell Justin that.

She sighed. What a tangled web she had woven with her deceit! Well, there was nothing for it now but to continue the charade and hope it would all come out right in the end.

She downed her brandy, feeling much revived by the warm amber spirits, then went back up on deck to hear Fabien calling out to her excitedly.

"Sail ho! Sail ho, Capitaine!" he cried, waving at her in the darkness. Then he began to scramble down the rigging. He dropped to the deck and handed Geneviève the spyglass. "I can't be sure at this distance, but she looks like a Dutch-built flute. Still, I'm almost certain she's flying a French flag," he told her.

"A flute!" Geneviève exclaimed, smiling. "What luck!"

She knew the type of vessel. It had a round stern, a broad beam, and a flat bottom. It could neither outmaneuver nor outrun the swift sloop. Further, even an eighty-foot-long, three-hundred tonner was manned by a crew of only twelve sailors and seldom had more than ten small cannons aboard. In addition, the flute was renowned for her large cargo capacity, which was half again that of comparably sized ships with sleeker lines. If she carried a full load, there would be plenty of spoils to be divided.

"Has she seen us?"

"*Non.*" Fabien shook his head, his eyes dancing with anticipation.

"*Bon.* We will get as close to her as we can, then. After that, we will open fire."

The seamen scurried to their duties. They carted up flannel-wrapped cartridges of black powder from the tin-lined magazine in the hold, neatly stacked piles of roundshot near the cannons, where it would be readily available, and loosened the small clusters of grapeshot, with which the guns were charged, so it could be easily handled. Then they hung a line of water buckets for dousing fires and positioned axes close at hand for clearing away any wreckage that might result from the battle. After that, they wet down the canvas sails and the top deck and those below it, too, so the sloop would be less prone to go up in flames, should the *Crimson Witch* be unfortunate enough to sustain a hit.

Geneviève studied the horizon, certain the hazy silver moonlight and the slight pale mist that had settled over the dark night waters would serve to conceal the grey-painted *Crimson Witch* from the flute's telescope until the last possible moment. By then, it would be too late for the unsuspecting vessel to escape.

Presently, her heart beginning to pound with excitement, Geneviève spied the flute. She ordered Ives-

Pierre, who was at the helm, to bring the sloop around
so its starboard side faced the merchant ship. Then she
instructed the men to open the gunports and ready the
cannons.

"Double-shot the guns," she commanded grimly
to Thibaud. "I want to do as much damage as possible
with our first broadside."

Lastly, she directed Marc to run up her flag. This
was a device that had been inspired by the flag of the
infamous pirate Captain John Rackam, who, along with
his sweetheart, Anne Bonny, had terrorized the seas
until his capture in 1720. Calico Jack, as he had been
known because of the gay cotton clothing he'd often
sported, had chosen for his emblem a solid black flag
with a white skull at its center, beneath which had
reposed two white, crossed cutlasses. Geneviève had
selected for her own standard a bloodred square with a
woman's head, done in gold, centered on its field.
Beneath this were two gold, crossed rapiers.

As the *Crimson Witch* drew near to the unwary
flute, Geneviève took the wheel, having no illusions
about her ability to handle the sloop's cannons. These
were heavy cast-iron guns mounted on mobile carriages
constructed of elm, which was highly prized for its
strength, durability, and resistance to shock. While the
carriages were built to sustain powerful recoils by
means of a thick breeching rope and tackles that allowed for movement in and out of the gunports, the
system was far from perfect, and a cannon, carriage
and all, could often jump several feet into the air after
being fired. Geneviève did not intend to have any part
of her anatomy pinned and crushed by one of the guns.
Even those as small as the six-pounders aboard the

Crimson Witch could do considerable damage to a sailor not nimble enough to leap out of the way.

At last, when Geneviève thought the waiting had become almost unbearable, the light fog shifted again, and she saw that the flute was within firing range and that its captain had perceived his imminent danger. He shouted to his crew, and all hands began to scramble to the vessel's defense.

"All starboard fire!" Geneviève bellowed. "Fire!"

The *Crimson Witch* shuddered violently with the massive recoil of the guns. Then she pitched wildly upon the waves, listing dangerously to one side, her deck slanting and water washing over her main rail before Geneviève gained control of the helm and sent the ship shooting rapidly past the flute, the pungent, acrid smell of smoke burning in her nostrils. Quickly the girl hauled on the wheel, bringing the *Crimson Witch* hard about so her port side now ran parallel to her opponent's starboard side.

"All larboard fire!" Geneviève screamed hoarsely. "Fire!"

The fight was over in minutes, the flute, taken by surprise, having sustained several punishing blows before managing to get off a single shot. Grappling hooks secured the defeated ship to the side of the *Crimson Witch*. Then Geneviève and eight of her men, all of whom wore crimson silk hoods to prevent their being recognized and to strike terror into the hearts of their opponents, as well, defiantly boarded the vessel.

"Surrender, and your lives shall be spared!" Geneviève called out as she raced across the deck, stunning the flute's superstitious sailors with her bold, boyishly clothed figure and witchlike appearance, her long red hair whipped wildly by the wind, her honed silver rapier waving threateningly in her hand. ''I want only your cargo; I have no wish to see you slain!''

But the ship's seamen, once they had recovered from their shock at the sight of the girl, who seemed to them like some unworldly, avenging angel, were determined to resist the band of pirates who had set upon them. The captain and two of his men, who did not cry for quarter, were killed in the swordplay that soon followed; the others, finally conquered, were cast adrift in the vessel's dinghy.

After that, Geneviève and her crew hastily transferred what cargo they could to the *Crimson Witch*, then put as much distance as possible between themselves and the slowly sinking flute, the hull of which had been mortally hit by a cannonball during the earlier broadside engagement.

Then the *Crimson Witch* set sail for Deauville, where Geneviève would disembark and journey once more to Paris to continue the quest for her parents and her brother.

Chapter Seventeen

Monsieur le Vicomte Port-d'Or, Vachel Saint-Georges, pressed himself against one brick wall of the narrow alley that ran behind the once fashionable Place des Victoires, not far from the church of Saint Eustache, to the east, and the Palais Royal, to the west. The *place,* a circular square surrounding the symbolic statue of the Sun King, Louis XIV, which had been destroyed by the bourgeoisie just that year, was bisected by various streets, the Rue D'Abourkir and the Rue Etienne Marcel among them. Vachel had carefully traversed the former, then cut across the Rue de Louvre to the latter before making his way around the outskirts of the *place* to the alley.

Now he gazed down the dark, curving wynd to the back door of *hôtel* number 5, the townhouse of his parents. He could discern no light or movement within and felt certain in his heart that the residence was empty, but he had to make sure. He glanced about quickly to reassure himself that he was still unobserved, then slipped through the shadows to the *hôtel*. The back door was locked, but Vachel had a key, and presently he turned the knob and went in.

Immediately a stale, musty odor assailed his nostrils, and he knew his previous assumption was correct: the townhouse had not been inhabited for some time. Still, he decided to risk a hasty look around; perhaps he would discover some clue to tell him what had become of his parents and his twin sister, Geneviève.

He took a long candle and a friction match from his pocket, and soon a tiny light wavered in the blackness, illuminating faintly the inside of the *hôtel*. There was nothing of interest in the kitchen, so the vicomte moved on, examining the rooms one by one, his heart aching as he saw what looting and destruction had done to his parents' once beautiful and gracious home.

In the ceiling of the foyer was a gaping hole where the Venetian-crystal chandelier had been torn down to be carried off. Little shards of diamondlike glass still glittered upon the marble floor where a few of the light's delicate, teardrop prisms had fallen and shattered. Here and there on the pale, colored walls, brighter patches showed where priceless paintings and tapestries that had been in the Saint-Georges family for centuries had once hung. Except for a few that had apparently been smashed by the vandals, all the objets d'art were missing. The lovely, intricately patterned Sevres porcelain china off which the Saint-Georgeses had dined had been wantonly broken, and the sterling silver dinnerware had been stolen. Upholstered furniture, such as sofas, chairs, and chaise-longues, had been slashed and their stuffing scattered throughout the *hôtel*. Huge wooden furniture, such as the china cabinet and armoires, too heavy to be easily moved, had been gouged beyond repair; smaller pieces—curio stands and occasional tables mostly—had been stomped to bits. All the Turkish carpets were gone.

Vachel bent to retrieve a fragile teacup that had somehow miraculously survived the mindless ravaging and carefully placed it upon one shelf of the china cabinet. Then he laughed softly, ruefully, to himself at the useless gesture. His family, if they had managed to escape from those who had despoiled the townhouse, would never return here.

On each of the floors he searched, the damage was as extensive. Even his mother's and sister's expensive gowns had been carted away, and of course, their jewelry boxes were empty. Still, Vachel thought, if Papa and Maman had indeed had a chance to flee, as he hoped, they would have taken the gems.

He paused for a moment, reflecting. From Geneviève's letter smuggled to him by friendly hands, he knew his family had been aware of their danger, and he wondered what he would have done, had he been in their position. Geneviève, he decided, would have been his parents' first concern. No doubt they had devised some plan for her escape, remaining behind themselves to conceal the ruse. But then afterward, after Geneviève had got safely away, how would they have fled?

Vachel gazed about the attic that had once been the servants' quarters. Then, seized by sudden inspiration, he began to tug at the large dresser that stood against the wall of one of the small cubicles. There was nothing behind it, but, certain he was on the right track, he started to run almost frantically from chamber to chamber, tugging away any big piece of furniture that still sat against a wall. In his parents' room, behind his father's wardrobe, he finally found that for which he was looking: a jagged hole in the plaster. Excitedly he crawled through the opening, never even noticing when the gold chain he wore always about his neck broke and slipped to the floor.

Once on the other side of the aperture, the vicomte stood and glanced about thoughtfully, a smile of satisfaction and amusement curving his lips. He was now in *hôtel* number 4, which had once belonged to the Duc de la Feuillade, who had commissioned from Desjardins the statue of King Louis XIV that had once stood in the center of the *place*. The family who had occupied the townhouse during Vachel's time had, he recalled, been one of the first to be imprisoned by the Assembly. His parents, he surmised, had tunneled their way through the wall shared by both *hôtels* into the empty townhouse and had crawled through the aperture, just as he had. Then they'd carefully pulled his father's armoire back into place. They'd probably waited for weeks for their absence to be discovered and for the ensuing outcry to die down. After that, no doubt dressed as nondescript servants, Vachel thought with a grin as he recalled Maman's expertise with theatrical powder and paint, they'd simply walked out the back door of *hôtel* number 4. Doubtless Claude Rambouillet's henchmen had not given them a second glance, since it had been townhouse number 5 they'd been instructed to watch.

Certain now that his entire family had escaped and feeling quite relieved by the idea, Vachel started to make his way downstairs, noting absently that this *hôtel*, too, had been brutally ravaged. In the kitchen, he doused his candle and tossed away the stub that remained. Then he let himself out into the alley and disappeared into the night shadows.

*　　*　　*

Geneviève bit her lip anxiously as she stared at the townhouses that formed an arc around one side of the Place des Victoires. They were beautiful residences, cleverly joined to make one long, continuous, curving edifice constructed of cream-colored stone and topped with a dark slate roof. Arched openings with black wrought-iron balustrades were set into the second story above each door; at the peak of each arch was a carved stone bust. Above these, on a narrow shelf that extended out from the bottom of the third floor, there was another intricate railing. Set between the pilasters bounding each *hôtel* on either side on the third and fourth stories were long, narrow, mullioned casement windows. Dormer windows whose frames alternated, first arched, then square, jutted out from the roof all along the top of the building. Solid wood doors, all closed, faced the empty *place* where the statue of King Louis XIV had once stood.

Geneviève's heart caught in her throat as she studied the front door of her parents' *hôtel*. It was dangerous for her to have come here, she knew, yet she had been drawn to the Place des Victoires this evening all the same. Why? she wondered curiously. What had compelled her to come here? Surely Claude still had his hirelings watching the *place;* she might easily be taken captive. Yet she saw no one.

Well, she mused, shrugging, now that she was here, she might as well go inside. Papa and Maman would not be there; Benoit had told her they had disappeared. Still, she might find some clue to their whereabouts if she tried; it could do no harm to look.

Motioning silently for Ives-Pierre to follow, she

carefully made her way around the *place* to the alley in back.

She found the door to her parents' townhouse unlocked. Apprehensively she stepped inside, her nostrils twitching slightly at the faint, acrid odor that assailed them. Smoke. She smelled smoke, as though a candle had recently been lit within. Warily she laid one hand on the hilt of her rapier, letting her eyes adjust to the darkness, afraid to light a taper of her own.

She passed through the kitchen to the dining room, her heart turning over in her breast with sadness as her booted feet crunched upon splintered china and she saw the shapes and the shadows of the devastation Claude and his henchmen had wrought. Sheer spite, she realized, had caused them to vandalize everything with little resale value or that could not be carried away. Anger welling within her, she mentally checked off another mark on the long list of crimes for which she would someday have her vengeance upon her enemy.

As she searched the rooms of the *hôtel*, it soon became apparent that whoever had been here just moments past was now gone. Geneviève shook her head with puzzlement, wondering who it could have been. Then, just as she was about to leave her parents' chamber, she observed by the moonlight streaming in through the uncurtained window the jagged hole in the wall. As she grasped the significance of her discovery, she suddenly spied the broken gold chain lying upon the floor. She bent to retrieve it, her heart leaping with joy, for she knew now who the intruder had been. She gripped Ives-Pierre's arm tightly, tears of happiness shining in her eyes.

"That is how Papa and Maman managed to disappear." She pointed to the opening behind her father's wardrobe, which had been shifted so the aperture might be seen. "And Vachel has found their route to freedom, for look, *mon ami!*" She held out the chain excitedly, pulling her own identical one from beneath her domino. "I had these made especially for him and me. Do you see the half of the coin on each? When fitted together, they are one! Oh, Ives-Pierre! Vachel is alive! He was here! Why, I can still smell the lingering fragrance of his cologne! My brother is safe, and my parents are in hiding somewhere. We've only to find them now and to smuggle them out of the country. Vachel, now that he's sure we all escaped, will make his own way to England; I'm certain of it!"

"*Oui,* I believe you are right, Madame Genette," her companion agreed. "Come, there is nothing for us here. Let us go now to the Place de Grève and make our plans for tomorrow."

The two left the townhouse, making their way furtively down the Rue Croix des Petits Champs, beyond the Palais Royal to the west. Once they had reached the corner where the Oratoire stood, they turned east onto the Rue Sainte Honoré, following the long street that took them to Les Halles, the marketplace of Paris. From here, they continued to the Place de Grève, where the ominous Madame Guillotine had been erected in front of the Hôtel de Ville, a magnificent building that housed the apartments of most of the high-ranking officials of the Assembly.

From where she crouched in the shadows, Geneviève stared up at the guillotine, recalling its bloody history. Until the rebellion, the hideous instrument of death had not been used in France; it had been employed primarily in Scotland, England, and various other European countries to execute criminals of noble birth. But in 1789, a physician named Joseph-Ignace Guillotin of Saintes had been elected to the Assembly, and he had proved the driving force behind the passing of a law requiring all death sentences to be performed by a machine so painless decapitation would no longer be an aristocratic privilege. After the device had been satisfactorily tested on several corpses at the Hôpital Bicêtre, it had been put up in the *place*. On April 25, 1792, Louisette, as the infamous instrument had originally been called, had claimed its first victim, a common highwayman. Gradually, as the nightmarish machine had beheaded person after person, it had come to be known as *la guillotine*, a dubious honor for the "humane" physician.

Standing upon a large platform so it would be in full view of the masses who always crowded the *place* during executions, the device loomed over Geneviève in the starlit darkness, causing her heart to beat fast as she realized she might have been one of its unfortunate victims—and still might be if she were not careful. The guillotine's two thick, square, upright wooden posts were surmounted by a huge crossbeam with a hole in its center, through which a rope was drawn to pull the instrument's razorlike, death-delivering blade up to the top of the structure. The insides of the posts were grooved and had been greased, too, so the sharp, diagonally edged knife with its foreboding, downward slant could slide quickly and easily along the ruts. The silver, tempered-steel blade, which was weighted so it would fall swiftly and powerfully upon its victim's bare neck, gleamed menacingly in the moonlight. Set a little forward beneath the indented block where the helpless victim laid his or her neck was a big basket into which the severed head usually toppled.

Once the disembodied head had fallen, Geneviève

knew, the gruesome, masked executioner often grasped it by the hair and held it aloft for the throngs of watchers to see, because sometimes the victim's brain continued to function for a few seconds after the head had been decapitated, and pathetic comprehension could be seen upon the victim's face before the eyes glazed over.

Not content with this grisly evidence of shock and suffering, the Assembly had commissioned Mademoiselle Marie Grosholtz of Strasbourg, an art tutor who had, before the revolution, served the royal family, to make death masks of the guillotine's victims. These were then displayed in her mentor Dr. Curtius's famous wax exhibition in Paris, which attracted visitors from all over Europe.

Geneviève grew ill just thinking of the terrible tales she had heard about the fate of all the poor souls who had made the final, all-too-short journey from La Conciergerie, across the Pont au Change, and down the *quai* along the Rive Droit to the Place de Grève.

"We will bring the wagon up from Le Marais, Ives-Pierre," Geneviève said, "making certain the guards see us during our arrival. Tell Thibaud to plan the diversion close to Saint Jacques la Boucherie, near the church's tower, so all eyes will turn in that direction. Once the fireworks begin to go off, we must move swiftly and our timing must be perfect, or we will assuredly fail and be taken prisoner. Did Papa Nick have everything we require?"

"*Oui*, Capitaine. Once more your grandfather proved most helpful; he used both the gypsy caravan and the costumes he is lending us in one of his theatrical productions several months ago. We have only to pick the stuff up tonight."

"The old rascal!" Geneviève grinned. "I only hope the wagon looks real enough to bear close inspection and that the garments fit better than those nuns' robes did! Thank God the Chevalier de la Tour-Jolie and his two friends were too weak to stand up properly, else the sentries would surely have spied the men's boots and arrested us, for the hems of the gowns were far too short."

Ives-Pierre shrugged.

" 'Twas the best your grandfather could do, given such little notice, Madame Genette. He hasn't yet come under suspicion. In that bourgeois newspaper, he writes such an inflammatory column against his noble ancestors that it puts the hounds off the scent—but he is endangering his own life by secretly assisting us."

"*Oui*, I know, and I am grateful to him. I only wish he knew where Papa and Maman are," she uttered sadly. Then she brightened. "But perhaps Vachel will risk visiting Papa Nick before fleeing to England. Oh, come, *mon ami*. Let us hurry! Mayhap even now my beloved brother is with him!"

With hope in her heart, Geneviève began to run down the lamp-lit square toward the *quai*, Ives-Pierre hard on her heels. She thought she had been careful to remain concealed in the dark, elongated shadows, but some small movement she made attracted the attention of one of the guards who regularly patrolled the place of execution and the *hôtel*, as well. It had been the target of numerous dissidents, whose various plans to bomb it—and thus to eliminate several members of the Assembly en masse—had yet to reach fruition.

"Halt! Halt, or I'll shoot!" the sentry ordered, raising his pistol and pointing it straight at the girl.

Geneviève's heart plummeted to her toes as she

realized the man would indeed kill her. With a rapid, almost indiscernible flick of her wrist, she signaled to Íves-Pierre, whom the guard had not observed, to go on without her. Then, hands held high, she walked slowly toward the sentry who confronted her.

"*Alors*. What have we here?" the man asked, smiling triumphantly. "A young masquer? Have you been to a party, garçon? Or are you perchance a Royalist spy? We've arrested quite a number of would-be Black Mephistos here lately, you know. *Merde*. The city is practically crawling with them—the filthy swine!" He spat on the paving blocks with disgust. "Remove that foil—slowly," he warned, "and toss it over here."

Trembling a little, Geneviève did as he'd requested. The clatter of the blade upon the *place* echoed loudly in the stillness and sounded like a death knell in her ears. Still keeping one eye—and his gun, too—trained on her boyishly clothed figure, the guard knelt to retrieve her weapon.

"Well, what do you have to say for yourself, garçon? Nothing? Cat got your tongue, eh?" He laughed and shrugged. "*Voyons*. You had better come along with me to see Citoyen Rambouillet. I doubt you're the real thing—the Black Mephisto himself—this time either, but it pays to be careful. The last *cochon* I caught had a grenade in his pocket; he was planning to blow up the Hôtel de Ville. His scheme came to nothing, however; I'm afraid he met an untimely end here a few days ago." The sentry nodded his head toward the guillotine, then sliced one finger across his throat. "Young or old, the doctor's knife always gets them sooner or later. 'Twill be sooner for you, I suspect. Now get moving," he demanded, his voice hard, and waved the pistol at her threateningly.

Fear eating through her like acid, Geneviève turned and headed slowly toward the *hôtel*, knowing that any moment now she would be exposed to Claude Rambouillet and at his mercy. She glanced down the square, noticing the other sentries grouped together at the north end of the *place*, occupied with the arrival of a coach belonging to one of the members of the French government. They had not yet observed her and their fellow guard. This being the case, Geneviève wondered if she could make a break for it after all. But then, as though sensing her thoughts, her captor jammed the muzzle of his gun cruelly into her back, and with a sinking heart, she realized she dare not try to escape.

Oh, Sainte Marie, *have mercy!* she prayed fervently, and as though in answer to her prayers, the man following her was suddenly grabbed from behind without warning.

A powerful hand closed over the sentry's mouth, silencing any outcry he might have made; the other hand locked on the back of his head. Taken unaware, he was slow to respond, and by the time he had started to struggle, it was too late. The strong, suffocating fingers holding him so tightly had jerked his head too quickly and too sharply in an unnatural fashion, snapping his neck. He crumpled to the paving blocks, his face a death mask of ludicrous disbelief.

"Noir!" Geneviève whispered, stunned, for she had fully expected to see Ives-Pierre hovering over the guard's body.

The spy all of France called the Black Mephisto grinned, his teeth flashing whitely beneath his ebony mask.

"Noir? Is that your name for me, Rouge?" he inquired, amused. "I believe I rather like it. Well, don't just stand there gawking! Come on! We've got to get out of here!''

After removing her rapier from the sentry's corpse and leaving in its place a black mask taken from his pocket, the spy caught her hand and hauled her roughly down the *place*. They dropped to the *quai* below, where he thrust her unceremoniously into the small boat he had tied to a tree on the riverbank. Hurriedly he cast off the lines. Then he deftly jumped in beside her and started to row toward the Rive Gauche. The paddles, whose locks had been oiled and wrapped with leather, moved easily and noiselessly since the wood could not grate against the metal.

"Where are you taking me?" Geneviève questioned softly. "I have plans of my own to carry out, and my men are waiting for me, besides."

"You can join them in a little while," Noir told her quietly. "In the meantime, I'm escorting you to a friend's place—a theater—where you'll be safe until the furor that will surely ensue at the discovery of that guard's body dies down. My friend is an actor who writes for *La Lame*, one of the bourgeois newspapers. But 'tis only a cover. In reality, he is a Royalist, working for our cause. He goes by the name of Le Renard.''

Geneviève inhaled sharply, shocked. There was only one actor in all of Paris who was sly enough to have earned such a nickname—her grandfather! *Bon cieux!* Papa Nick must be aiding every dissident in Paris! If he were at the theater, she must somehow warn him not to give away her identity—especially to Noir, whom she still did not fully trust. Who knew what tales he might tell if ever he were captured by the Assembly, whose members were hunting him high and low. Even though he had surely saved her life, she could not risk having him learn her name; he might, under torture, reveal it to Claude.

They did not speak further, each of them knowing how sounds—even whispers—carried over water, so the stillness of their journey across the River Seine was now broken only by the soft swish of the oars as they dipped into waves, propelling the dinghy southward. Presently the two fugitives came at last to the Rive Gauche. Noir secured the small boat to another tree, which lined both riverbanks in abundance. Then he and Geneviève climbed up from the *quai* to the street a short distance above. They raced along the Rue Dauphine to another winding avenue that brought them to the Boulevard Saint Germain. Here, not far from Saint Germain des Prés, the oldest church in Paris, was Le Théâtre Dupré, Papa Nick's playhouse.

They leaned against one side of the shadowed building to catch their breath, their masked figures only blurred silhouettes in the flickering light cast by the lamps that lined the boulevard. After a while, when their rapidly pounding hearts had slowed and their breathing had returned to normal, Geneviève looked gratefully at Noir.

"Merci," she said earnestly, quietly studying the man who had haunted her dreams since coming into her world. "You saved my life."

"Oui. 'Twas indeed fortunate there were some papers in the Hôtel de Ville that I—uh—required." He patted his breastpocket, where the vital documents he had stolen now nestled securely. "But that does not explain what you were doing there—and how you came to be a prisoner of that zealous sentry."

"I told you," Geneviève reiterated, "I have plans

of my own. Do not think, just because you saved my life, that you can pry into my affairs. It was simply bad luck that the guard saw me. I was . . . excited about something and made a careless move. 'Twill not happen again, I assure you.''

"I certainly hope not. Oh, Rouge! Do you know what a dangerous game you are playing? Will you not at least let me help you? I have thought about you constantly ever since that night at La Conciergerie. 'Tis as though you have cast some spell upon me, you crimson witch. Aye, mayhap you are a sorceress indeed. . . .''

Geneviève's breath caught in her throat as he bent his head to kiss her, grasping her cheeks with his steely hands so she could not turn away.

It was wrong—all wrong, she thought frantically, torn. She had a husband to consider. Desperately she tried to picture Justin's face, but the feel of Noir's mouth upon her own caused the image of her husband slowly to blur until it faded into Noir's own dark, handsome visage, and there was no one for her but the man who was kissing her, confusing her, making everything feel so right, as though she belonged in his arms.

Guilt, stark and painful, washed over Geneviève at the shocking, traitorous notion, and she tried to free herself from Noir's iron grasp. But he was too strong for her, too determined on plundering her trembling lips that parted for him of their own accord, wanting him.

Oui. She could not deny it, could no longer go on deceiving herself when her heart knew the truth. Despite her wishing it were otherwise, she *did* desire him, this spy, this stranger whose real name she did not even

know. She wanted him to go on kissing her forever—
and more.

Bon Dieu! What was he doing to her? Why could
she not think when he took her in his arms? Why, when
he kissed her, did she become a mindless mass of
sensation who could only feel?

His mouth moved feverishly on hers, igniting her
with passion as his tongue plunged between her lips,
expertly exploring the dark, moist cavern of her
mouth, seeking out its every hidden nook and cranny.
Sweet, sweet . . .

The taste of her melted like wild honey on Noir's
tongue, maddening him with desire, and he cursed the
fact that he could not take her here and now so that, no
matter what happened in their uncertain future, he
would always have a part of her and she of him.

His mouth swept across her cheeks to her temples,
the strands of her hair. His fingers yanked impatiently
at her queue, freeing it from its confines, and her dark
copper tresses with their rich crimson highlights spilled
down about her hips, enveloping them both in a cloud of
fire.

He felt as though he were burning up with his
yearning for her as he pulled her close, his hands
roaming over her body, aching with longing. *Sacrebleu!*
How he wanted to rip off her boy's clothes to discover
the woman within, fair of face, lithe of form. She had
bound her breasts some way, he knew; he could feel the
constraining material beneath the folds of her black
domino. What would they be like, he wondered, those
twin spheres of perfection, cupped in his palms, their
nipples taut and bursting with passion?

An electric spark tingled through his loins at the
thought, causing his groin to tighten, his manhood to

harden against her thighs. Her silk breeches brushed sensuously against his as his hands traveled down to grip her buttocks, to press her body firmly against his own.

"Rouge. *Rouge!*" he whispered thickly in her ear. "What have you done to me? When I am with you I forget everything but you," he insisted, making her heart leap with joy. "I want you. God help me, but I do! Come, before I take you here upon the street. Le Renard will have a place for us."

"Oh, Noir, would that I could. But I cannot!" Geneviève wailed with anguish, coming to her senses at last. She bit her lip, her mouth twisting with sorrow. "I—I have a husband. He—he has no interest in me, but—"

"Then he is either blind or a fool!" Noir asserted harshly. Then his voice softened. "Oh, *ma chère,* what does it matter if we are doubly damned? For I, too, am married," he confessed, wrenching her soul, "and to a woman as cold and heartless as your husband! Are we to be bound by our vows, then, when we are both so miserable? Are we to throw away this happiness we have found with each other?"

"I don't know. I don't know," Geneviève repeated, bewildered and afraid for them both. "Even if we were to become lovers, as you suggest, there is no future for us when we are both already wed; surely you can see that! And I don't want to be hurt. Oh, I can't think. I can't think! Please, Noir. It is too much too soon, and too many lives depend upon us. Only look how we are standing here upon one of the main boulevards of the Rive Gauche, in plain view of anyone who might spy us!"

"*Oui.* You are right, of course." He spoke unhappily, his smoky eyes filled with bitterness and longing. "I lost my head, I'm afraid, for your very nearness overwhelms me." He paused. "At least come inside with me, Rouge, where you will be safe. I will not press you again."

"All right," she agreed, as wounded as he but not daring to tell him so, for fear he would resume his onslaught upon her senses and she would not be able to resist him.

Wordlessly they entered Le Théâtre Dupré, which belonged to Geneviève's grandfather and where she had spent so many happy hours before the rebellion.

As the stage door closed behind them, they paused to allow their eyes to adjust to the blackness within the large playhouse, for only a single candle burned backstage, and even the night, though dark, had been streaked with silver by the moon and the stars. Then they proceeded to Nicolas Dupré's small office, which lay at the side of one wing.

It was obvious that Noir had been here previously, for he knew his way about, guiding Geneviève unerringly past a backdrop that had not been raised and the ropes that dangled from the catwalks, and she made a mental note to ask her grandfather how many other Royalists he was secretly helping. She did not want herself or her crew to stumble inadvertently upon anyone who might recognize them.

At the thought of her men, she glanced about discreetly, her heart thudding jerkily as she realized they might still be around. But she saw no one, and, relieved, she decided the sailors must already have come and gone. It was, of course, entirely possible that they were downstairs, beneath the stage, where the big props were stored. But Geneviève heard no sounds to indicate this, and she breathed a little easier. She did not want Ives-Pierre, especially, to come face to face with Noir. After that night at La Conciergerie, she had been forced to make some explanation for her long absence to her companion, and though she had told him much of the truth, she had skirted the issue of Noir's kissing her. But Ives-Pierre, she feared, who had known her since childhood, had not been fooled. If he thought her honor had been sullied, he would not hesitate to avenge her. Right now, all he had were suspicions; if he were to confront Noir, however, the faithful servant would demand answers to his questions.

When Noir and Geneviève reached her grandfather's office, Noir rapped smartly upon the closed door.

"Who goes there?" a gruff but to Geneviève dearly familiar voice demanded.

"Two friends of Louis of Bourbon, Renard," Noir responded quietly.

"Then come."

Noir opened the door, and he and Geneviève entered the tiny cubicle that served as her grandfather's office.

Nicolas Dupré was a big man, and though seated, he appeared to dwarf the room he inhabited. He had been reclining in a chair drawn up to his desk, upon which a solitary lamp with a glass hurricane shade was burning steadily, illuminating the darkness. Now, removing his spectacles and tossing them aside, he leaned forward and glanced up from the script that lay open before him, which he had been reading to memorize his lines for a forthcoming production. At the sight of the two people standing in front of him, his brilliant green eyes widened, then narrowed slightly beneath his bushy grey eyebrows. Then he rose, coming around the desk to greet them, his face beaming jovially, his arms outstretched, French fashion, to Noir.

"Well, well. This *is* a surprise—"

"Capitaine Diabolique, as you may recall from our previous meetings, Renard," Noir interrupted, supplying his name almost threateningly, it seemed to Geneviève, and forestalling whatever Nicolas had been about to say.

The girl stared at both men sharply, suddenly realizing two things almost simultaneously: Noir had a ship—it must be his means of smuggling his secret communications into England—and her grandfather knew Noir's real identity. She was certain of it!

"But of course," Nicolas remarked smoothly, inclining his head, his smile fading to be replaced by a most peculiar, thoughtful expression. Absently he stroked his flaming-red beard streaked with grey. Then he raised one eyebrow speculatively. "And—"

"Capitaine La Folle, Renard," Geneviève put in hastily, warning him with a small shake of her head to say nothing to reveal her true name.

To her surprise and puzzlement, an even odder expression, as though he had suddenly perceived something unknown to both his guests, flitted across her grandfather's weathered countenance, and he grinned delightedly, motioning for them to be seated.

"Two of my favorite people—to be sure," he uttered in a voice sounding as though it were choked with laughter.

Both Noir and Geneviève frowned.

"You know Rouge, Renard?" Noir queried sharply, somewhat perplexed.

"If by Rouge, you mean . . . Capitaine La Folle," Nicolas intoned dryly, gazing at his errant granddaughter, "then, *oui*." He nodded and shrugged noncomittally. "We have done a little business together in the past, have we not, madame?"

"*Oui*, and I hope we shall do so again in the future. My men were here, then?"

"*Oui*, earlier, madame. All were saddened to learn of your capture, but a plot was already under way to effect your freedom, so perhaps 'twould be best if you went along to your rendezvous point. I presume any disruption engendered by your escape has lessened by now, so you should be safe if you are cautious. Also, I made all the arrangements you requested, and 'twould perhaps be wise if you were to inspect them. I understand there was some difficulty on the last occasion. I hope that, this time, you will find everything to your satisfaction."

"I'm sure I shall, Renard," she replied.

"Oh, in all the excitement, I almost forgot, madame," Nicolas went on, clapping one hand to his forehead. "I know you will be extremely happy to learn that . . . a very close friend of yours was here, *comprenez-vous?* There was a message: Look for me on a distant shore; there you will find the other half of your coin."

"*Merci!* Oh, Renard, *merci beaucoup!*" Geneviève exclaimed, tears of joy suddenly sparkling in her eyes, for, even though his words had been cryptic, she had grasped the fact that her grandfather had seen Vachel and that her twin brother was even now on his way to England.

"*Oui*. I thought that would please you. 'Twas too dangerous for our friend to linger here, you understand? Of the two . . . friends you are still seeking, however, I have heard nothing." Nicolas sighed sadly, his eyes closing as he sought to maintain control of his emotions. "I'm sorry. I will keep trying."

"*Merci*, Renard. I shall be on my way, then,"

Geneviève declared, some of her gladness over Vachel lessening at the realization that her parents had not yet contacted Papa Nick.

They must still be in hiding, she thought, still hopeful that they were safe. She longed to reach out and touch her grandfather reassuringly, but she did not, recognizing that Noir would be suspicious of the consoling gesture. Instead, she turned to address the tall, dark man who stood at her side.

"Noir, I mean—er—Capitaine . . . Diabolique, wasn't it?" she asked a trifle tauntingly. "Thank you for your assistance this evening. I'm sure we will meet again."

"You can count on it, Capitaine La Folle," Noir promised, his eyes dwelling on her lingeringly. "For we are not yet through, you know—you and I."

Geneviève shook her head, flushing with embarrassment that he should speak to her so before her grandfather. But then, Noir did not know Papa Nick was so closely related to her. Thank God, Justin was not likely to pay a visit to France! He would call on his grandfather, and perhaps Papa Nick, knowing his two grandchildren were now wed, would feel it his duty to inform Justin of Geneviève's escapades, though she had specifically warned her grandfather against this. Sending him an eloquent, pleading glance, she slipped silently from his office. After she had shut the door behind her, she paused for a moment, listening, as Noir's low voice reached her ears again.

"There is no need to mince words now, monsieur, since Rouge has gone," he stated coolly. "I know you are privy to her real name, and I want it. I must know who she is!"

"So that's the way the wind blows, eh?" Nicolas inquired, lifting one eyebrow. "Come now, my boy," he chided. "You are a married man. What would your wife say if she knew you had lost your heart to that red-haired minx?"

"Nothing!" Noir spat bitterly. "She has no love for me!"

"Doesn't she?" Nicolas pried, vastly amused, much to Noir's irritation

"*Non*, I tell you!" he snapped, failing to see what was so funny.

"Hmmmmm. Well, even so, my secrets are my own, and I refuse to reveal them—even to you. Run along now . . . Capitaine Diabolique! Ha, ha! What a name!" Nicolas chuckled, his sorrow lifting and his eyes twinkling once more. " 'Tis quite as fitting as Capitaine La Folle's! Well, what are you waiting for, my boy? Go on with you! I've suddenly been struck with inspiration for a new play, something along the lines of Shakespeare's *The Comedy of Errors*, I think. *Oui*. Ha, ha! 'Twill be my best work ever, I'm sure!"

Still unable to perceive the cause of Nicolas's amusement, Noir crossed the room and jerked open the door just as Geneviève, hearing his rapidly approaching footsteps, managed to sneak away and conceal herself behind the backdrop on the stage. She watched him stamp off into the candlelit blackness. Then, much to her astonishment, she observed her roguish grandfather, standing in the open doorway of his office, suddenly throw back his head and howl with laughter.

Chapter Eighteen

Northchurch Abbey, England, 1792

Katherine Mannering surveyed herself critically in the slightly tilted looking glass over her dresser, which stood elegantly against one wall of her bedroom at Northchurch Abbey. From her dainty little black cap trimmed with white lace and dangling black ribbons, which perched pertly upon her head, to her severe black dress with its stiffly starched, prim white collar and cuffs and its ruffled white pinafore, to her white stockings and her shiny black, laced shoes, she looked every inch an enchanting parlormaid. A wide smile split her lovely face, and she clapped her hands together childishly with delight.

"Oh, Rose!" she cried to her abigail. " 'Tis perfect! I'll wager that dull old Lord Frome will never recognize me in this costume—and neither will that silly, infantile Lord Bootle! Mayhap I'll finally be able to get through an entire evening without the company of either!"

The maid only sniffed.

"Lord Frome is *not* old," she pointed out logically. "Why, if he's a day over thirty-five, I should be very much surprised."

"Well, when one is just turned sixteen, thirty-five seems very old indeed," Kitty rejoined loftily. "Besides, old or not, he is certainly *dull!* And Lord Bootle, for all that he's at least eighteen, behaves as though he were scarcely out of shortpants!"

Rose merely sniffed again.

"Hmph! That's beside the point—and you know it," she insisted. " 'Tis a scandal, that's what, your going to Lady Hornsea's masquerade party . . . decked out in that—that *rig!* Daphne ought to be horsewhipped for lending it to you, and that's the truth! Gor! What Lord Northchurch will say when he sees you I shudder to think."

"Oh, pooh! Uncle William won't care," Kitty averred. "He's not nearly as stuffy as he leads everyone to believe, and he dotes on me, besides, which is more than my sour-faced, cheeseparing papa ever did—God rest his mean old soul! Uncle William will be glad to learn I'm having fun, and anyway, he doesn't like either Lord Frome or Lord Bootle. He said they both had bats in their belfries!"

"Hush now, miss! You mustn't repeat such remarks," Rose remonstrated, mortified. "I'm sure his lordship said no such thing—or if he did, he didn't mean it for your ears. Oh, please, miss. Won't you wear that pretty blue Grecian gown I laid out for you?"

"No, I won't. I'm going in what I have on, and—what's more, Rose—*you're* going to wear the Grecian outfit."

"What?" the maid exclaimed. "Why, I shall do no such thing! I don't know what deviltry you're

planning now, Miss Mannering, but I certainly shall
take no part in it, I promise you. Why, the last time I
agreed to help you with one of your madcap schemes, I
was halfway to Gretna Green before that wicked fortune
hunter who'd been pursuing you ripped off my mask
and discovered 'twas me he'd abducted instead of
you!''

"Oh, come now, Rose. You're just angry because
he did nothing more than set you down in Nottingham—
and without so much as coach fare back to London! He
was very charming, you know, even if he *was* just after
my money. Poor Sir Lucian. He never did have a
feather to fly with. I wonder what ever became of
him?''

"Lud! 'Tis more than likely he was tossed into
debtors' prison,'' the maid asserted indignantly, still
peeved by the baronet's churlish treatment of her. "At
any rate, 'tis neither here nor there. I'm not stepping
one foot into that Grecian gown, and that's that!''

"Oh, please, Rose,'' Kitty wheedled prettily. "If
you wear it—and the blue mask that goes with it—and
you fix your hair, Lord Frome and Lord Bootle are
bound to think you're me, for you're as blond as I am,
and our figures are much alike, too. 'Tis why Sir
Lucian mistook you for me. Perhaps then I can enjoy
myself for a change. I'll never attract a decent suitor as
long as those two mutton-headed dolts keep pestering
me!''

"Oh, go on with you, miss. You've more callers
than I can count.''

"Yes, but none of them is the kind of man I
want.'' Kitty sighed as though bereft. "Oh, Rose! How
I wish I could find someone handsome and exciting, a
bold, dashing young cavalier with just a hint of menace

in his demeanor for spice, who would sweep me off my feet and carry me away to his private abode!'' Hugging herself, Kitty whirled about the room.

"Stuff and nonsense, Miss Mannering!'' Rose uttered sternly. "You've been reading too many of them romance novels, that's what! I swear I don't know what Lady Northchurch would say if she knew. 'Tis one of them roguish highwaymen you've described at the very least—and no mistake! And a man like that surely wouldn't have marriage on his mind!''

"Well, 'twas just a thought after all. I doubt that I'll ever meet anyone like that anyway,'' Kitty commented, downcast, as she sank down on the stool before her dressing table. "So, if you won't put on the Grecian outfit, there's no point in my attending Lady Hornsea's masquerade party, for I'll only be harried by those two dreadfully boring clods, and I—I . . . well, I just can't bear it again!''

She gazed down at her hands folded just so in her lap and, after a minute or two, managed to conjure up a few crocodile tears, which nevertheless sparkled most convincingly beneath her lashes.

"Now, miss, you're not fooling me one bit,'' Rose stated firmly. "So you just stop that this minute.'' But, to the maid's dismay, Kitty only sobbed harder. "Here, miss, don't take on so. Please, don't cry. Oh, very well, miss!'' Rose threw up her hands in defeat. "I'll wear the Grecian gown. But if you leave me stuck with those two . . . *oafs* all evening, I'll—I'll box your ears!''

* * *

Vachel Saint-Georges started with surprise as he observed the large, ancient but well-sprung coach lumbering toward him in the moonlit darkness, rattling down the rocky dirt road winding away from Northchurch Abbey. If he were not very much mistaken, the vehicle belonged to his uncle, William. He wondered where his crusty old relative was going at this late hour, for Lord Northchurch, as his son, Justin, did, usually found soirées and other functions that required the presence of females perfectly boring. Oncle William much preferred a rousing hunt or a quiet game of faro at one of the private clubs in London, but most evenings, he remained at home.

Perhaps Justin was in residence, Vachel mused, and was escorting Geneviève to some silly affair. But, *non,* that could not be the case, for Papa Nick, when Vachel had visited him at Le Théâtre Dupré, had told him Geneviève was in Paris. Imagine! His twin sister was posing as a smuggler and was actually rescuing people from Madame Guillotine! When Vachel finally caught up with her, he would have a few choice words to deliver to that young lady—and to his cousin, as well, for letting Geneviève carry on in such a hoydenish manner! But then, apparently Justin knew nothing of his bride's furtive escapades—or so Papa Nick had claimed.

Justin's bride. Vachel nearly groaned aloud at the thought. If he lived to be a hundred years old, he would never know why his sister had wed their churlish, arrogant cousin—a real pain in the neck if Vachel had ever seen one. Surely she could have done better than that! If only she'd waited until he'd arrived in England, he would have introduced her to society and seen that she'd met some decent fellows. But, *non*, she'd had to rush into marriage with Justin instead!

Was it his cool, jaded cousin in the carriage? Vachel wondered. Surely it must be. Oncle William would not be journeying about the countryside at this hour. Suddenly seized by a malicious idea, Vachel chuckled delightedly to himself in the silver-shot blackness and reined the horse he'd acquired in Lyme Regis over to the side of the road. Then impatiently the young vicomte patted his coat pockets. Somewhere he had an old loo mask he'd worn to conceal his features from the shifty-eyed scoundrels who, for a pretty centime, had rowed him across the English Channel. Locating it at last, he pulled the green velvet device over his face. Then, still chortling, he yanked his pistols from his waist and, as his uncle's coach drew near, nudged his horse out into the center of the road.

"Stand and deliver!" Vachel cried, slightly relieved to see that it was indeed Lord Northchurch's coat of arms on the panels of the vehicle. How horribly embarrassing it would have been otherwise—robbing the wrong carriage! "Your money or your life! Here! Put that down, you fool!" He motioned sharply to the driver's escort, who was reaching for his musket. "I don't want to have to shoot you. Climb down from there now. You, too," he instructed the driver. "Wait over there in those bushes, and if you value your life, don't move a muscle or make a peep!"

Once the two men were cowering in the thick shrubbery that grew alongside the road, Vachel dismounted. Then, letting the reins trail upon the ground so his horse wouldn't run away, he ripped open the door of the coach.

Much to his surprise and mortification, the vicomte saw by the soft light glowing from the brass lanterns hanging on either side of the vehicle that it contained not his cousin, Justin, but two young women he'd never seen before. They were obviously on their way to a masquerade party, for one of them, who appeared to be a lady of quality, was clothed in a pale blue Grecian costume trimmed with gold; a blue satin loo mask covered her face. Her servant had on a maid's uniform, although Vachel didn't think it looked anything like what an abigail usually wore. He was so stunned by his error in assuming that it would be Justin he was holding up that he didn't notice the white lace loo mask in the pocket of the maid's apron.

"Who are you?" he asked in English and looked again at the coat of arms on the panels of the carriage to assure himself this was indeed his uncle's coach.

"Uh—uh—uh—" Rose stammered, then swallowed convulsively, staring with terror at the ominously gleaming black barrels of the two pistols trained straight at her heart.

"Put those guns away, you blundering idiot!" Kitty snapped indignantly. "Can't you see you're frightening Miss Mannering! There now. There now, Miss Mannering." She patted Rose's hand soothingly. "There's nothing for you to be afraid of. This ruffian isn't going to harm us. No doubt he merely wishes to rob us." She glared at Vachel censuringly. "You're a dreadful thief!" she uttered scornfully, tossing her head. "Imagine! Accosting two unprotected women!"

With amazement and disbelief at her temerity, the vicomte gazed at the abigail, who had leaned forward to issue her disparaging remarks to him and whose face was now framed by an incandescent halo cast by the flickering lantern light. Vachel's breath caught in his throat at the sight, for he thought he had never seen anyone as beautiful as she.

From the top of her head to the tips of her toes, she resembled a fragile porcelain doll. Beneath her impishly set, tiny lace cap, her hair was a mass of golden, corkscrew curls that bounced saucily whenever she moved. Her blond brows, now drawn together in a frown, arched delicately over huge, round, childlike blue eyes that flashed at him angrily from beneath thick, sooty lashes. Her little, uptilted nose was raised disdainfully, and her cheeks were flushed as pink as her rosebud lips.

Her diminutive, hourglass figure curved prettily in all the right places, as though she had been made to order. Her swanlike throat rose from full, high breasts, and her slim, nipped-in waist tapered to small, slender hips. Long, graceful hands were folded in her lap. Tiny black slippers peeked from beneath the hem of her uniform.

"You were scarcely unprotected, mademoiselle," Vachel pointed out, managing to find his tongue at last. "Your driver's escort attempted to shoot me."

"And he certainly should have!" Kitty retorted. "If I had a pistol in my purse, I would do the same!"

But truthfully she would not, she admitted silently to herself, for she thought the roguish highwayman was positively handsome! Beneath his rakishly cocked hat, his dark auburn hair was tied back in a careless queue. Emerald-green eyes that matched the color of his mask glittered devilishly in the silver starlight. His aquiline, aristocratic nose was set above a sensuous, grinning mouth that showed sparkling white teeth. His cheeks were lean and hollow; his jaw was square and thrust out with assurance.

He carried himself as though he had a chip on each broad shoulder, which, Kitty suspected, needed no padding beneath his fine brocade frock coat. His snowy white ruffled shirt and snug-fitting waistcoat displayed a muscled chest and a firm, flat belly. His tight silk breeches hugged sturdy thighs and calves. He wore high black jackboots upon his feet.

"What's your name, mademoiselle?" he questioned crossly, annoyed that the woman of his dreams had just informed him that if she had a gun, she would blow a hole through him. "You're certainly brazen for a mere abigail."

"That's because I'm not!" Kitty reported loftily. Then, remembering that, right now, she scarcely resembled her true self, she declared, "I'm—I'm, why, I'm . . . Prinda, the parlormaid, you lout! Not that it's any of your business—to be sure! Miss Mannering's abigail, Rose, took sick this morn, so I was asked to take her place tonight," Kitty rattled on falsely.

A parlormaid! Vachel groaned inwardly. His father would cut him off without a cent if he were to begin courting a parlormaid. The Saint-Georgeses were still nobility, even if they *had* recently fallen upon hard times; they did not marry servants.

"Too bad," the vicomte said at last. He would have taken wicked enjoyment in robbing Justin for a lark. But his cousin had not proved to be the vehicle's occupant, and stealing from two harmless, unknown females was another matter altogether. Still, he did not see how he could now extricate himself from the situation. Besides, he could always return the loot to his uncle. "Hand over your valuables, and be quick about it!" he ordered.

"We haven't got any," Kitty insisted stoutly, "and if you attempt to search us, we'll scream."

"Damn!" Vachel swore. Then his green eyes started to twinkle with unholy mischief. "Well, if you don't have any money or jewels, you'll have to pay a forfeit."

"What kind of forfeit?" Kitty queried suspiciously.

"A kiss, mademoiselle. One kiss. That is the price it will cost you to continue down this road."

"Oh, no, it won't!" Rose spoke up again at last, horrified. "Oh, no, it won't, you murderous rascal! Why, the very idea, charging us a kiss to pass by!"

The vicomte scowled.

"I wasn't speaking to *you*, Miss Mannering— whoever you may be!" he articulated tartly.

"I'm—I'm Lord Northchurch's ward," Rose lied, "and he shall hear of your disrespectful conduct, I assure you!"

"Well, thank God 'tisn't *you* I want to kiss, then!" Vachel shot back with spiteful glee, even though he had no doubt his uncle would be enraged by this night's prank. "Come here . . . Prinda, wasn't it?" He motioned to Kitty. "Be a good girl and give me a kiss. Then you may be on your way."

"No, don't! Don't listen to him!" Rose adjured. "He's—he's a blackguard, that's what, who means to see you ruined."

"Oh, hush!" Kitty hissed, giving her maid a sharp pinch. "Don't be such a goose! Why, he'd hardly be in a position to keep his pistols cocked and ravish me at the same time. Only think how very . . . well . . . *awkward* it would be!" she exclaimed.

"Lud! Oh, Lud! Lord Northchurch is going to skin me alive!" Rose wailed. "The very idea of you even knowing about such things—let alone mentioning them! I could just die!"

"Well, then, do so!" Vachel urged, waving one gun muzzle threateningly at the maid. "At the very least, cease that mindless prattle, for you are getting on my nerves."

This proved to be Rose's undoing. Terrified that death was imminent, she promptly swooned, toppling headfirst toward the bottom of the carriage. Before she could hit the floor, however, her body, doubled up in a V, was caught and wedged fast between the plush velvet seats. Her derriere, poking up comically in the air, looked so much like an extra cushion in the middle of the coach that it was all Kitty could do to keep from laughing. Instead, biting her tongue, she glowered at the highwayman.

"Oh! Now see what you've done!" she cried accusingly to the vicomte. "She's fainted. Oh, poor Miss Mannering. I must find her smelling salts immediately."

She began to rummage around in her reticule for her vinaigrette, but Vachel impatiently snatched the purse from her grasp and flung it to the far corner of the vehicle.

"Now, Prinda, I'll have my kiss, if you please," he demanded.

Kitty's heart beat fast as she surveyed the dashing highwayman surreptitiously. He was the epitome of her girlish, romantic fantasies. She didn't mind kissing him. In fact, she *wanted* to kiss him! This was the most exciting thing that had ever happened in her young life! She was glad Rose had fainted. Now Kitty was alone

with the highwayman! She stared into his emerald-
green eyes, mesmerized by the desire in their depths. A
thrilling little shiver chased up her spine, and after a
moment's hesitation, she edged over to the door of the
carriage, where Vachel stood outside upon the ground,
and, closing her big blue eyes, tilted her face toward his
sweetly.

Vachel swung himself up into the doorway of the
coach and bent his head to take possession of her lips.
His mouth moved on hers tenderly at first, so he
wouldn't scare her, then gradually became more demanding as tentatively she reached up to twine her arms
about his neck. How soft her lips were, yielding pliantly
beneath his own and trembling a little, as though this
were the first time she had ever kissed a man.

Maybe it was, the vicomte mused, for the maid *did*
seem very young and innocent, despite her brave spirit.
At the thought, he felt a tiny twinge of guilt, as though
he had somehow taken advantage of her, although such
was often the lot of a mere serving girl and was
expected—if not always welcomed—by most of them.

Perhaps, Vachel reflected a trifle uneasily, he ought
not to have exacted a kiss as his payment for allowing
the vehicle to pass. It really had not been fair to the
maid, although she *did* appear to be enjoying it as much
as he was.

Slowly he drew away from Kitty, his eyes lingering
on her upturned face. *Jésus!* How very enchanting she
was! The vicomte sensed instinctively that she was
everything he'd ever wanted in a woman, and he was
reluctant simply to let her disappear from his life. *Par
Dieu!* He would not let her slip through his fingers so
easily.

''I would like very much to see you again, mademoiselle, ' he whispered. "*Alors*. Although I am only a common highwayman," he lied, not wanting her to know he was a vicomte—albeit in all probability a dispossessed one, "do you think it would be possible for us to meet once more—when we may spend some time together getting to know each other? I shall not harm you, I swear."

"Well, I—I don't usually consort with criminals, sir," Kitty confessed shyly, "but I *am* grateful to you for not really hurting Miss Mannering or me—even if you *did* give us quite a fright! So I—I suppose—if you really do want to see me again, that is—you might send a note around to Northchurch Abbey. Address it in care of Miss Mannering," she added, "for then I will be sure to get it."

"Very well, then. Till we meet again, Prinda, *au revoir,* my sweet angel. Dream of me," Vachel said.

Then, as marvelingly Kitty touched her fingers to her lips, certain they must somehow be changed, the vicomte mounted his horse and rode off into the darkness. It was only after he'd disappeared that she realized she did not even know his name. It must be an impressive one, she thought, for he had surely been the most dashing of cavaliers, not too young, not too old, in fact, just right for her!

Though, unbeknown to Kitty, Vachel himself was just sixteen, the same age as she, he was a very bright, daring, and resourceful young man, and he felt and acted a good deal older than his years. He had been forced by the revolution to grow up quickly. The stubble of a man's beard already graced his cheeks, and no one, during his furtive flight from France, had believed him less than twenty-one. Further, because as a child he had spent so many long hours studying with Ives-Pierre, the vicomte was a master swordsman and sailor, in addition to being quite adept at languages, history, mathematics, and a number of other things he had learned from his tutor, Monsieur Roquefort. Vachel's father, Edouard Saint-Georges, believed in a man's being well rounded and was inclined to look the other way where lights o' love were concerned. Still, he certainly would not countenance his only son's becoming seriously involved with a parlormaid, the vicomte thought with a groan.

Nevertheless, he decided firmly, having Prinda would be worth losing his inheritance—that is, if he still had one coming to him. For a moment, he had almost forgotten that no doubt both his and his father's estates had been confiscated by the Assembly. Right now, Vachel was nothing but a penniless French *émigré* with an empty title.

Instead of depressing him, however, the notion elated him. Doubtless here in England, he would be looked upon as a fortune hunter; matchmaking mamas would therefore consider him unsuitable as a prospective husband for their daughters. As distasteful as the idea was, Vachel realized he might actually even be forced to go to work to support himself. As a man of trade, he would be scorned by his own social class. Who could blame him, then, if he chose to run off with that parlormaid who had so enthralled him?

As his horse cantered along, the vicomte determined that he dared not show his face at Northchurch Abbey now, for both Miss Mannering and Prinda were sure to recognize him. Miss Mannering was bound to inform his uncle that, posing as a highwayman, he had been parading about the countryside, and Vachel had no great desire to be the object of one of Lord Northchurch's unpleasant lectures regarding suitable conduct for a member of the ruling class. Further, if Prinda learned he was a vicomte, she might think he was merely trifling with her, and she might refuse to permit his courtship of her.

He would go on to Blackheath Hall instead, Vachel decided, and put a stop to his sister's reckless escapades before she managed to get herself captured and executed. Imagine their grandfather's not only permitting her activities, but actually approving of them! Sometimes Vachel thought Papa Nick didn't have an ounce of sense. Why, the old man wouldn't even have told him Geneviève's secret, had she not agreed beforehand that he was to be trusted with the knowledge of her furtive forays into France.

The vicomte groaned. Geneviève had always been headstrong. No doubt the wretched girl, instead of listening to his strictures, would attempt to make him a part of her plot!

Grimly he spurred his horse forward, trying to think how best he might persuade his sister to cease her dangerous masquerade as Capitaine La Folle, the Crimson Witch.

Chapter Nineteen

At precisely two o'clock in the afternoon, near the belltower of Saint Jacques la Boucherie, not far from the Place de Grève, Thibaud and Fabien began to set off the fireworks they had acquired earlier that week. In broad daylight, the glittering spectacle the rockets normally presented was reduced to bright flashes, but their din was as frightening as though the entire area were being raked by a barrage of cannons. The fireworks spiraled off in all directions, some of them falling onto the *place* and exploding like bombshells.

As Geneviève had foreseen, the crowd that had gathered in the square to watch the executions of three aristocrats panicked and started to stampede from the *place*, people mindlessly running this way and that and trampling one another in their haste to escape. The guards could do nothing to control the throng, and by yelling for order and firing warning shots into the air, they only added to the general pandemonium.

Geneviève, perched upon the seat of the brightly

painted gypsy caravan belonging to her grandfather, bit her lip as the wagon, pushed and pummeled by the masses, swayed precariously on its high wheels, threatening to topple over. Rupert's big Boulonnais draft horses whinnied loudly, white-eyed with fear, and it was all the girl could do to maintain her hold upon the reins. One of the animals reared, pawing the air and nearly yanking the shaft from the caravan. Rupert, spying what was occurring, ran to the horse's head, grabbed hold of the harness, and hauled the animal back down to the ground.

Meanwhile, Ives-Pierre and Benoit, seeing that the sentries had turned their attention from the tumbril that held the three condemned prisoners to the mass of people racing wildly about the square, sneaked up to the cart and rapidly freed its terrified occupants. In all the cacophony and confusion, no one noticed the two men hustling the shackled captives across the square to the gypsy wagon. Unceremoniously Ives-Pierre propelled the bewildered nobles up the short flight of steps leading to the inside of the caravan. Then Benoit slammed the door shut and motioned for Geneviève to drive on. Rupert released his hold on the snorting horses and scrambled up beside her on the seat. Geneviève slapped the reins down hard upon the animals' backs, and they leaped forward at her command.

Inside the wagon, Ives-Pierre and the rest were tossed about haphazardly as the caravan lurched down the street toward Le Marais, its high wheels clattering noisily over the cobblestones. Ives-Pierre swore savagely under his breath as he lost his balance and sprawled upon the floor of the vehicle. With difficulty, he righted himself and bent once more to his task of picking the locks that fastened the shackles on the wrists and ankles of the frightened prisoners. Once he had the iron bonds undone, he threw them into a burlap bag in one corner of the wagon and stuffed some old props—jugglers' devices mostly—on top to conceal them. Then he raised the lid of one of the benches that lined the sides of the caravan and removed some garish costumes. He flung them toward the mute, cowering aristocrats, who, numbed by their petrifying ordeal, still had not grasped the fact that Geneviève and her men were helping them to escape.

"Get into those clothes," Ives-Pierre ordered harshly, "and be quick about it! We don't have much time! Well, what are you waiting for? Move!"

Hope and understanding at last lighting their eyes, the freed captives, an elderly gentleman, a middle-aged female, and a younger woman, started to pull on the garments that had been handed to them. Ives-Pierre jammed wigs and hats on their heads, for their hair had been shorn to bare their napes for the guillotine. Then he informed them that if anyone asked, they were to say they were gypsies and part of a traveling medicine show. He gave them forged papers to display if they were indeed questioned, then he spoke again grimly.

"I'm sure I don't need to warn you that if you cannot deceive the guard at the city gates, we shall all feel France's sharp knife at our necks!"

At Ives-Pierre's words, the elderly gentleman, once a duke of the realm, drew himself up proudly, seeming to regain some of his former vigor.

"Have no fear on our account, monsieur," he stated quietly, his eyes now clear and unafraid. "We shall not disappoint you, I assure you. My daughter by marriage and my granddaughter"—he indicated the two women—"have yet to fail me in a crisis. I do not expect that they will do so now."

"*Non,* we shall not," the older woman, a marquise, affirmed.

Ives-Pierre's expression softened.

"*Bon,*" he uttered, his voice low. "Do not despair, madame," he went on more kindly. "If all goes well, you shall be reunited with your husband this night."

"But—but he is still in La Conciergerie," the marquise protested.

"*Oui,*" Ives-Pierrre agreed. "But there are ways of getting him out. Trust me. The Crimson Witch and her band know what they are about."

"So that is who you are!" the granddaughter exclaimed, her eyes round with awe. "Even in La Conciergerie, we have heard rumors of this brave woman who risks her life to save others. *C'est très courageux! C'est magnifique!*"

"*Oui*". Ives-Pierre nodded, then lasped into silence.

The gypsy wagon rumbled past Le Marais and the *place* where La Bastille, destroyed by the bourgeoisie during the rebellion, had once stood. Then finally the caravan reached the city gates. Here, Geneviève leaned forward to accost the sentry boldly, her legs spread apart brazenly, her colorful skirts hiked up to provide more than just a glimpse of her shapely limbs. She rested her elbows on her vulgarly sprawling knees.

"You there! Sergent!" she called, her eyes traveling over the guard's stiff form suggestively. She licked her lips. "Let us pass. The Place de Grève has been bombed, and the crowd has run wild. I'm afraid 'twas all too much for my poor husband. He is old, and his health is not robust, *comprenez-vous?* I must take him into the country, where the air is fresh and he will be able to breathe properly.''

"Eh? Is that so?'' the sentry inquired politely, but he was suspicious all the same, and he knew his duty, besides. "Let me see your papers,'' he demanded.

Geneviève shrugged.

"*Certainement*, Sergent,'' she replied carelessly, handing him her forged documents. "Search the wagon if you must! But be quick about it, for I fear my poor husband is not long for this world, and I would like him to die in peace. Though he is old and not much use to a lusty *jeune fille* like myself, he has been kind to me, you understand? 'Tis the least I can do to make sure his last hours are happy ones.''

"*Assurement*, madame,'' the guard said, smirking ribaldly at the thought that the girl was not satisfied by her decrepit spouse. No wonder she had such a roving eye! The sergent almost felt sorry for her poor husband, who no doubt had been cuckolded many times over. "Everything appears to be in order, madame,'' he said, returning her papers. "I will just look inside the wagon to be certain. . . .''

He opened the door and glanced cursorily at the caravan's occupants, noting the elderly duke, who, having overheard the conversation outside and being astute enough to play the part assigned to him, was leaning against one wall of the wagon, gasping raggedly for breath and clutching one hand to his chest.

"My *pauvre* daughter Hélène,'' Ives-Pierre mumbled to himself. "I should never have given her to such an old man, who is like to die and be of no further use to us. *Zut!* He cannot even fill up the medicine bottles properly; he broke four of them this morning, not caring that they cost a pretty centime. Do not fear,

Babette," he rattled on, now addressing the duke's granddaughter as though she were his own daughter. "For you, I will find a young husband, one who is strong and virile like a bull, eh? And who will be able to help us with our medicine show—not like your sister's worthless old husband, who cannot even give her the grandson for which I yearn."

Disgusted and deciding he had heard quite enough, the sentry closed the door with a bang and, to her relief, directed Geneviève to drive on.

"I am sorry, monseigneur," Ives-Pierre uttered quietly to the duke, "if I have offended you, but 'twas necessary to deceive the guard."

"*Oui*, I know. Think nothing of it." His grace waved away the servant's apologies. "I have been more grossly insulted by that rabble in La Conciergerie—and they, *mon ami*, were not attempting to save my life."

Reminded again of the peril they all faced, the wagon's occupants once more fell still, the silence broken only by the sound of the caravan's high wheels as it bounced on down the road away from Paris.

Once the *Crimson Witch* had sailed from where she'd been anchored just off the coast of Deauville, Geneviève deposited the duke and his family, including his son, who had been rescued from La Conciergerie, safely in Portsmouth on the southern shore of England. Then she turned the sloop westward to traverse the English Channel.

The black night sky stretched above her endlessly, its far horizon meeting the deep, fathomless sea in a shadowed swirl of light and darkness that made it seem as though the silver moon and the stars were sweeping across the firmament to fall into the ocean. A fine, sheer, pale grey haze had settled over the waters, and the minute droplets of mist mingled refreshingly with the spindrift sprayed up from the churning whitecaps as the ship sliced through the foamy waves, traveling steadily onward.

The air was cool and growing colder, and Geneviève, standing at the wheel of the vessel, shivered a little, realizing summer was almost over, that already the breeze that caressed her skin carried the chill of autumn. Soon the leaves on the trees would begin to turn to gold and flame, and the countryside, after the harvest had ended, would fall silent as it awaited winter's coming.

Geneviève sighed at the thought, for it meant her activities would become all the more difficult. Autumn marked the start of the Season in London, and she felt sure Justin would insist on closing Blackheath Hall and taking up residence in his townhouse in the city. Perhaps then he would not be so preoccupied by his business affairs and would begin to notice his wife's existence and would note the peculiar manner in which her imaginary illnesses always coincided with his trips out of town. Further, Geneviève was certain her chamber at Justin's townhouse would contain no secret passageway, making it harder for her to sneak away unseen.

Well, she would think of something, she determined. Perhaps she could move her base of operations to Brighton, for she knew the road leading from London to the popular seaside resort could be covered in four hours if one possessed a fast vehicle and a swift team of horses. Surely Justin would not begrudge her a phaeton or a curricle and a matched set of purebloods like his greys.

"Capitaine La Folle"—Pernel climbed down from the rigging to interrupt her musings—"take a look over there, please." He handed her the spyglass through which he'd been peering and pointed to the southwest. "A moment ago, I could have sworn I saw a ship—a schooner, I thought—not a league away. 'Twas as though she were . . . well . . . *following* us, Capitaine. I became alarmed, but then suddenly she just seemed to vanish." He shook his head as though to clear it. "Perhaps 'twas just a shadow, after all: the mist, the moon reflecting upon the waves . . . who knows?" He shrugged, frowning. "Still . . . is that not how the *Crimson Witch* would appear to another vessel in the darkness?"

"*Oui*," Geneviève muttered uneasily, her eyes narrowing beneath her crimson mask as she, too, began to feel a sense of disquiet. "Was she flying a flag, Pernel?"

"*Non*. That was the strangest thing of all, Capitaine."

The girl could see nothing in the distance, but still, an odd chill of premonition tingled down her spine, and abruptly she collapsed the telescope.

"Gather the men, Pernel," she ordered softly. "Tell them to prepare for battle. I mislike the idea of being chased by a phantom—particularly one that displays no colors from her mast. It may be that she is a pirate ship, intent on stealing our cargo. On the other hand, she may be a French naval vessel that has learned our identity and is bent on capturing us.

"I know 'tis hard on them and that it limits their range, but instruct Thibaud to double-shot our cannons again. I do not want our ghost to have the advantage, and if she is indeed a schooner, as you suspect, she's probably manned by pirates and carrying eight cannons and four swivel guns, besides. Doubtless she is having as much difficulty spying us as we are her, and if she is indeed after us, she may not know we have seen her. If we are able to draw near enough to her before she realizes we have turned the tables, a double-shot broadside will prove effective.

"*Peste!*" Geneviève cursed. "I wish we could outrun her, but no doubt she is as fleet as the *Crimson Witch* and her draft even more shallow, so we dare not attempt to hide along the coast either." She bit her lip. "*Non*. We shall have to fight; there is no other way."

Thus decided, Geneviève shifted course, bringing the sloop about so it would slowly circle around until it was behind the phantom ship. She hoped the vessel's captain, taken unaware, would not suspect the *Crimson Witch*'s maneuver until it was too late.

Quietly the men opened the gunports and, with the stores they had taken from the tin-lined magazine and the shot rack, loaded the cannons with both cannonballs and chain-shot. This last was a small iron missile especially designed to destroy sails, spars, and rigging. It consisted of three iron chain links with a hollow, cuplike device suspended from each end. When fired, it would whip about wildly in flight, like a mace, wreaking havoc upon the enemy.

The moon had risen higher over the waters, and the earlier gentle wind had strengthened, causing the light fog to lift a little and the sails to flog. Geneviève listened to the sound of the rippling canvas and the slap of the waves against the bow of the sloop as she gazed out over the ocean intently, searching for some sign of the elusive ship that should now be somewhere ahead of them in the distance.

There! There it was!

As Pernel had said, the vessel seemed to shimmer
for a moment upon the sea and then disappear, but
Geneviève knew it was only a trick of the gleaming
moon and starlight. Like the *Crimson Witch,* the schooner had been painted a silvery grey and her sails dyed to
match.

Smiling grimly to herself in the blackness, Geneviève
silently saluted the unknown ship's captain for his
cleverness. Then she pivoted on her heel to begin
issuing commands to her crew.

Presently the *Crimson Witch* came within firing
range of the schooner. Swiftly, seeing that the enemy
vessel had spied the sloop at last, Geneviève bade her
men back the topsail. Then she turned the wheel so her
ship was in a position to rake the other vessel's stern
with a broadside. She waited only until the schooner
had run up its flag, a square field of black upon which
reposed a white, grinning devil's head and a white arm
poised to strike with the rapier clutched in its fist,
before she gave the order to fire.

The cannons boomed, belching fire and ammunition and filling the air with the pungent, acrid smell of
gunpowder. Shot spewed across the water, tearing gaping holes in the schooner's canvas and poop deck. But
despite Geneviève's best efforts, this ship had not been
taken totally by surprise, as the flute had been, and
immediately two of the opposing vessel's swivel guns
bombarded the *Crimson Witch* with a barrage of shells.

Geneviève prayed none of her men had been hit as
she sent the sloop, still reeling from the massive recoil
of its cannons, shooting past the schooner. She hauled
on the helm, wheeling her ship about so she could bring
the port side around to her enemy's stern, for she dared

not risk being broadsided by the row of cannons that lined either side of her foe's vessel.

Barefoot for better traction and to avoid sparks from static electricity, which could ignite the gunpowder, half the men in her crew hastily reloaded the starboard guns, pushing charges into the bores and ramming them home, then jamming stiff wires down the vents to pierce the flannel-wrapped powder cartridges, preparing them to be primed and fired. The rest of the crew discharged the larboard guns. To Geneviève's dismay, one of the flintlocks misfired, and Thibaud was forced to hold a slow-burning match to the cannon to set it off. But the shot was good, for it shattered the lower shaft of the schooner's mizzenmast, causing it to topple, its spanker in shreds and flapping uselessly in the wind as the canvas fluttered to the deck.

Quickly Geneviève brought the sloop about again, but this time, her opponent was prepared for the maneuver, and as the *Crimson Witch* drew away, the other ship fired its port cannons, blasting a jagged hole in the sloop's quarterdeck. The oak planks cracked and splintered, sending debris flying in all directions. Instinctively Geneviève held up one arm before her eyes to protect them from the wooden shards. As a horrified shriek sounded from below deck, she cringed and wondered anxiously who had been wounded—or killed.

"All starboard fire!" she screamed. "Fire!"

Then she left the helm to stagger across the slanting deck, where Silvestre was attempting to douse the tongues of flame licking their way up the mast. Her eyes watering and her throat burning from the smoke, Geneviève hauled water buckets to help him put out the fire. Then she stumbled back to the wheel, hearing

Fabien yelling for Marc, who was acting as "powder monkey," sealing the cartridges in leather "salt boxes" and carrying them from the magazine to the gunners.

To her relief, Geneviève saw that the last broadside had crippled the schooner, which was listing badly. Its crewmen were even now raising its boarding nets to prevent it from being overtaken. Hurriedly she steered the sloop alongside and ordered her men to secure the vessel with grappling hooks to the *Crimson Witch*.

Both ships' cannons continued to pummel each other unmercifully, riddling each other's hulls. The schooner's swivel guns went on firing, and Geneviève knew they must be put out of commission before her sailors could even attempt to board the enemy vessel. Grabbing a basketful of grenades, she scrambled up the rigging and inched her way out onto the yardarm, from where she lobbed several of the small bombs onto the deck of the schooner and down one of its hatches. Her aim was deadly, and she could hear the exploding grenades hit their mark. At last her seamen, after jerking on their crimson hoods to conceal their faces, were able to slice through their opponent's boarding nets to lay claim to the ship.

Viciously swords and hand-to-hand combat were engaged. The clash of steel rang out over the water as men lunged and parried, metal scraping upon metal as blades clanged together, sometimes locking at their hilts, in a desperate battle for survival. Wooden cudgels knocked against the handles of sharply honed axes and even broken barrel staves and stout chunks of the shattered mast that had been hastily grabbed for defense. Hoarsely Geneviève urged on her crewmen, who fought like demons at her side. In their crimson hoods, they looked like gruesome executioners to their terror-stricken foes.

"Surrender!" Geneviève cried over the din to her enemies. "Surrender, and your lives shall be spared!"

But whether her voice had even penetrated the noise and confusion, she could not tell.

The frantic conflict continued to rage as men clambered over the wreckage that littered the deck and skirted the fires that blazed heatedly here and there. The crackling flames filled the air with smoke, making it difficult to see and breathe. Soot and embers of charred wood carried aloft by the breeze flew about, burning like hot needles when they touched exposed skin. Geneviève jumped over a fallen spar, then paused to wipe the sweat and grime from her eyes.

In that instant, one of those strange lulls that sometimes occurs during a battle fell upon the devastated ship; and to her utter horror, in the tense, peculiar stillness that now blanketed the night, Geneviève heard someone shout:

"Rouge! *Mon Dieu!* Rouge!"

Filled with shock and disbelief, she glanced up to see Noir running toward her, slashing his way through her men, his rapier dripping with blood, his face a murderous mask of wrath and incredulity.

Geneviève was so stunned by the sight of him that she failed to hear the ominous creaking of a burning timber above her as it splintered away from the main mast, then began to drop to the deck below. There was a ghastly minute in which she comprehended the fact that she had mistakenly attacked Noir's ship. Then, puzzled, she saw his terrible anger fade to be replaced by a sudden, chilling dread. He shouted a warning to her, but it was too late. The heavy, tumbling yardarm was already crashing down upon her, its end jamming against her back, knocking the wind from her and sending her reeling. She tried valiantly but could not keep her balance. She stumbled to her knees, then crumpled facedown upon the violently heaving deck, where she rolled across the oak planks, striking her head against a wooden cask. For a moment, she struggled to rise, but her eyes refused to focus properly, and after a brief interlude of bewilderment and disorientation, a black haze whirled up to engulf her, and her world seemed slowly to spin away into nothingness.

Chapter Twenty

A steady clunking sound wakened Geneviève at last. As the noise penetrated her consciousness, she gradually glided back to reality, her eyes fluttering open to stare fixedly at the ceiling above the bed where she lay. She wondered what was making the dull thumps. After a time, her brain started to function once more, and she realized it was the pump in the bilge. Then bits and pieces of the night's events came flooding back to her. Of course! The *Crimson Witch* had taken several shots in her hull. Instead of letting the ship sink, an irreplaceable loss, the men were working to keep the vessel afloat just long enough to reach England's shores, where they could effect repairs.

Abruptly Geneviève tossed back the covers, sat up, and looked around, wincing at the sudden pain in her head as she moved it. Gingerly she felt the right side of her forehead, grimacing as her fingers discerned a tender, swollen lump. No doubt she had a nasty cut and a bruise there, as well, she thought. At least she was in her own cabin. Her men must have carried her here, she decided.

Swaying a little on her feet, she stood. She must go up on deck and find out what had happened. Still a trifle dazed, she reached for her boots and then sat back down on the edge of the bed to pull them on. Inwardly she groaned. *Sacrebleu!* What a dreadful thing she had done, attacking Noir's ship. What must he have thought when he saw her? And—worse—what had become of him?

Just then Olivier knocked and, at her low-voiced "Come," entered her quarters.

"So. You're once again among the living," the surgeon observed dryly. "Well, I did not think a little bump on the head would keep you down for long."

"Non," Geneviève agreed. Then she asked, "What is going on, Olivier? What happened after I was knocked unconscious?"

"Well, Capitaine Diabolique, the commander of the *Black Mephisto*—the schooner—went racing across the deck like a madman when he saw you fall. Thibaud thought he meant to murder you, so he whacked him real hard on the back of the head with a cudgel. When Capitaine Diabolique went down, Thibaud grabbed him about the neck and held a knife to his throat, threatening to slay him if he didn't call off his men. Fortunately Capitaine Diabolique was still conscious, so that put an end to all the resistance right away—which was a good thing, too, I might add, for we were grossly outnumbered and would surely have all been killed sooner or later.

"Anyway, we loaded Capitaine Diabolique's crew in their dinghies and cast them adrift. But there were so many of them that we were afraid they'd come back, for they didn't like abandoning their vessel at all, so we kept Capitaine Diabolique as a hostage. Then we ransacked the ship. We salvaged what cargo we could— plus a chestful of louis d'or we found in the captain's cabin. I never saw so much gold in my life! At any rate, after that, we returned to the *Crimson Witch*, bringing the booty and Capitaine Diabolique with us. 'Twas just as well, too, for I'll be damned if his crew didn't row themselves back to the *Black Mephisto*. They're less than a league behind us, pumping like mad to empty their bilge and keep the schooner afloat, so I don't think we need worry about them at the moment. Still, there's no telling what they might do. I believe they're all crazy myself, for if the *Black Mephisto* makes it to shore, I shall be very much surprised!

"Capitaine Diabolique is tied up in the hold. We figured, after we saw the name of his vessel, that he was the spy the Assembly's been hunting. He was wearing a black mask, too, so it all seemed to fit, and if that's the case, he's worth a pretty centime."

"*Oui*." Geneviève nodded. "Still, we'll not hand him over to the French authorities, Olivier. He's a Royalist, like ourselves, and I'll not inform on those who aid our cause."

"We thought you'd see it that way, Capitaine," the surgeon confessed, "so he hasn't been harmed. But what the devil are we to do with him? That's what I'd like to know. We've got to get rid of him one way or another."

"Bring him to my cabin for now," Geneviève directed. "I want to question him. Then we'll determine how best to dispose of him. Perhaps we can ransom him back to his crew. If his men are loyal to him—and, from what you've told me, it seems that they are—they will no doubt be willing to bargain for his safe return.''

''That's an idea. *Très bien,* Capitaine. I will have him brought to your quarters, then,'' the surgeon replied, starting toward the door.

''*Bon.* Oh, one more thing, Olivier,'' she called, causing him to pause, one hand on the doorknob, ''you and the others keep your hoods on around . . . Capitaine Diabolique. I don't want him to be able to recognize any of us again.''

The surgeon inclined his head.

''A wise precaution, Capitaine. We've already done that. Capitaine Diabolique has seen none of us, nor has he heard us speak any names. If he is ever captured by those less benevolent than ourselves, he will know nothing of the *Crimson Witch* and her crew.''

''*Bon,*'' Geneviève repeated softly.

Then, after the surgeon had departed, she turned to her looking glass and began to prepare herself to face Noir, the man whose ship she had just wantonly attacked and nearly destroyed, the man who had haunted her dreams since coming into her life, the man to whom she feared she was losing her heart and soul.

Chapter Twenty-one

"What are you about, Rouge?" Noir asked after two of Geneviève's men had escorted him to her cabin. "Sinking my ship? Murdering my crew? *Par Dieu!* If you had not been struck by that yardarm, I would have given you the beating you so richly deserve! As it is, I see that you suffered no ill effects, after all," he observed acidly. "I should have guessed as much, for you are like a cat with nine lives; you always land on your feet."

"But of course," Geneviève uttered softly. "If one does not play the game to win, what is the point in playing at all? Come, come, Noir. Things are not as black as you paint them. Your vessel is still afloat—I admit I don't know how—but the *Black Mephisto* sails not a league behind us, ably manned by your crewmen, who were merely cast adrift in dinghies and who returned the moment we had disembarked. I am no murderess. I would not even have attacked you, had you not been following the *Crimson Witch*, and even then, had I known 'twas you, I would not have given the order to fire.''

"I thought you were a pirate vessel," Noir confessed less harshly, "for you flew no colors at your mast, and I wished to meet the commander of a phantom ship so closely resembling my own, for you were like a shadow, a reflection upon the waves....*Enfin!*" He shrugged. '' 'Twas my own folly that I did not suspect sooner that you had spied us and circled around to come up on our stern. Then, when I saw the flag you had run up at last and your figurehead, as well, and I realized it was your own *Crimson Witch* I had been chasing—that you really were a ship's commander, as you'd once said—'twas too late. You had already fired upon us.''

"*I* thought *your* vessel was manned by pirates," Geneviève asserted, "for you weren't showing any colors either, and then when you did, it looked like you had run up a damned *joli rouge!*''

For the first time since entering her quarters, Noir grinned, his teeth flashing whitely beneath his black mask, which, curiously enough, no one had removed, even though his hands were bound and he could not have prevented anyone from untying it. For a moment, Geneviève was sorely tempted to rip the mask from his face herself so she could gaze without hindrance upon the dark, sun-bronzed visage of the man with whom she feared she was falling in love. But then she realized this would scarcely be fair, for she had no intention of taking off her own crimson mask, and she thrust the idea aside.

Silently she studied him, wondering again who he truly was and why he attracted her so, driving all thoughts of Justin from her mind. Noir's face—at least what she could see of it—was no more handsome than her husband's, nor was his powerful physique any better molded than Justin's lithe, muscular form. Yet there was something about Noir, something vibrant and alive that cool, reserved Justin, with his haughty disdain and arrogant, aloof manner, lacked. Noir was daring and exciting; he exuded a savage charisma, an animal magnetism, an earthy passion that Justin did not. Geneviève could not imagine her well-tailored husband standing upon the deck of a violently rolling ship, his hair windblown and damp with spindrift; his clothes in careless disorder, torn, grimy, and drenched with sweat; a bloody rapier clenched in one fist as he battled his enemies and shouted commands to his men. Justin, Geneviève realized sadly, had no lust for life; he was like a cold, hard glacier, sharp-edged and quietly menacing. Noir was a blazing wildfire, mercurial and unpredictable—and therefore all the more dangerous and deadly. She recognized that Noir appealed to something in her that was primitive and coarse, a mad, wild, wanton desire to sail headlong into a storm, to conquer the elements, to feel the thrill of knowing she alone was mistress of her fate. *Oui*, Noir unleashed her dark side, for it matched his own.

Noir wondered what Geneviève was thinking as she surveyed him so thoughtfully, a slight frown marring her features. Was she even now realizing, as he had some time ago, that their destiny together was inevitable, that they were meant for each other, body and soul? He would show her that, now, if he could only loosen the bonds about his wrists.

Soundlessly in the chair in which he sat, his arms behind his back, he worked at the ropes that constrained him. The rough hemp had been tightly tied, nearly cutting off his circulation, and it chafed his wrists. But, as the time passed, he continued to twist his hands about, his fingers pulling where they could at the cord. Ah! There had been a little give then, had there not?

So she would not discern his subtle movements, Noir went on gazing lazily at Geneviève, responding now and then to the questions she put to him in an attempt to elicit information from him. She was frustrated, he knew, by the way he effectively evaded her queries with noncomittal replies, giving nothing away. He smiled at her shrewdness, her intelligence—for she *was* clever—and had he been any less astute, he would have been like wet clay in her skillful hands, his entire life's history revealed layer upon layer to take shape in her mind. He could almost hear her brain whirling like a potter's wheel, trying to form an image from the bits and pieces with which he tantalized her. Why couldn't she see how much alike they were? That she turned aside his own inquiries as adeptly as he did hers?

The knot that secured the rope imprisoning Noir's wrists gave a little more, loosening considerably, and, encouraged, he concentrated even harder on undoing it, his hands jerking impatiently at the cord, his fingers stretching and curling as they tugged on the knot. Sweat beaded his brow, but Geneviève didn't notice, she was so intent on her interrogation of him.

Damn the witch! Did she not recognize how she tormented him, strutting before him with her hair unbound and snarled from the wind, her figure plainly outlined in her boy's clothes? Clearly she did not bother to disguise herself when aboard her sloop, for she wore no black domino now, and he could tell that she had dispensed with the binding about her breasts, as well. The twin globes strained against the fine white linen fabric of her shirt, which was open at the throat to reveal a tempting glimpse of her fragile collarbones gold-dusted by the sun. The slenderness of her waist was accented by a broad red silk sash with trailing ends. Her tight black silk breeches clung enticingly to her round buttocks and her long, shapely legs that disappeared into her high black jackboots. Only the crimson mask covering her face allowed her to retain her air of mystery.

It galled Noir no end to watch her parade before him, spitting out the questions he refused to answer or turned aside with queries of his own. She had teased him with her emerald eyes and ruby lips that had always hinted at so much more than she had ever given him. She had permitted him a taste or two of her mouth, then denied him the feast for which he hungered. She had attacked his ship—and had probably sunk it and murdered his crew, too, despite her assurances to the contrary. She had so haunted his dreams that he could barely bring himself to look upon his cold, childish wife, who alternately infuriated him and bored him with her silly chatter and her flighty disposition.

Once, for one brief moment, though theirs had been an arranged marriage, he had believed there was a chance for them together, after all; that there was more to his wife than met the eye. But somehow, beginning with their wedding night, everything had gone miserably awry, and their relationship had slowly but surely deteriorated with the passing of time. Now they went their separate ways, scarcely even seeing each other, though Noir was forced to admit this was primarily because he was seldom in residence. Perhaps he was to blame for the state of his marriage. He could have tried harder, he knew, to woo and win his wife. He had even told himself that he *would* try.

But since Rouge had so unexpectedly come into his life and cast her spell of enchantment upon him, he had desired no woman but her. That she wanted him, too, he had no doubt. With every fiber of his being, he had felt her yearning for him when he'd taken her in his arms. If not for her misplaced loyalty to her boorish husband, she would already be his. She had led him an exciting chase, but now it had ended. She would not escape from him again, he vowed silently. Tonight, she would be his.

With a grim little smile of triumph, Noir felt the knot tying the rope about his wrists unravel at last. Quickly he caught the cord before it could fall to the floor, exposing the fact that he was no longer held captive.

"Tell me the truth, damn you! Or I *will* turn you over to the Assembly for the price on your head!" Geneviève threatened when he still refused to give straight answers to her questions.

At that, Noir stood, towering over her startled figure in the soft glow of the lamplight like a demon risen up from hell.

"*Sang de Christ!*" she cried, stricken. "You are free!"

"*Oui,*" he agreed smugly, "and now I think the time for talking has past. You have jabbered like a magpie for well over an hour—and learned little or nothing for your trouble, Rouge, for as much I would like to do so, I dare not trust you, any more than you can afford to trust me. We both know the Assembly has too many convincing—albeit unpleasant—means of making its prisoners speak. *Alors.* We are at an impasse, *non?* Still, that does not mean we cannot be friends—or even . . . lovers," he murmured, his breath warm upon her face as he caught her in his embrace.

"I have told you before that that is impossible," Geneviève insisted stiffly, refusing to yield to the lips that kissed her hair so gently, though she found them most persuasive.

"And I tell you now that it is not. You will be mine this night—before I leave this cabin—I swear it!"

"Non!" she spat, wrenching herself from his grasp before he could wreak any further havoc upon her senses. "I think you forget, monsieur, that this is *my* ship! I have only to call my men, *n'est-ce pas?* And once more you will find yourself tossed in the hold, chained hand and foot—if I so choose!"

"And what will you do with me, then, eh?" he asked, growing angry. "Turn me over to the Assembly for the reward—as you threatened to do earlier?"

"Non." Geneviève shook her head. "I spoke in anger then. I am not so cruel. I mean only to ransom you back to your men. They seemed a loyal sort, and there were things left behind on your vessel—casks of brandy and wine, some bolts of silk and satin. The ship was sinking; we dared not linger, *comprenez-vous?* No doubt your crew will part with the rest in exchange for your safe return, and I must have money, you understand? To bribe the guards at La Conciergerie and to buy cargoes and supplies. My men must eat and have coins to jingle in their pockets, or they may seek another *capitaine* who has more profits to divide."

"I see," Noir said. Then he laughed shortly, wickedly arching one brow. *"Morbleu!* That's rich! So . . . I'm to be sold for a few bottles of liquor and some scraps of cloth, eh? *Non.* I don't think so, madame." He started to walk toward her purposefully, his jaw set with determination. "I think it is you who shall pay—and now!"

"Stay back!" Geneviève hissed, yanking her rapier from its scabbard at her waist. "I'll run you through. I do not wish to hurt you, Noir, but I will defend myself if necessary."

"I did not think you would not, Rouge," he uttered softly. Then, before she realized what he was about, he snatched a foil down from the crossed pair that hung beneath an old shield on one wall of the cabin. "*En garde.*" He saluted her, smiling devilishly. "We shall see whether you fight as well as you boast!"

They were mad, Geneviève thought, both of them. It was crazy to duel with each other—and in such close quarters, besides. One of them was bound to be hurt, perhaps even killed! Her heart lurched a little as she pictured Noir lying in a pool of blood on her cabin floor, and she wished she had never issued her challenge to him.

"This is ridiculous," she noted coolly. "I shall not fight you. I will call my men and have you returned to the hold until such time as your ransom is paid."

"Coward," Noir accused, his voice low and filled with scorn.

Geneviève drew herself up stiffly. She could not let his insult pass unheeded, and he knew it. If she did, he would have no respect for her, and neither would her men if they somehow discovered what had occurred. Her pride and honor demanded satisfaction for the offensive remark. She tossed her head haughtily.

"Very well, monsieur. Since you have made it impossible for me to withdraw from our engagement in good conscience, I will duel with you," she said. "But

I promise you: I am no amateur with a blade. You will not find it so easy to best me!''

"Words, madame, mere words," Noir rejoined, his tone full of meaning. " 'Tis all I ever get from you." He paused. Then he taunted sardonically, "I am a man of action myself."

Geneviève flushed brightly, knowing he did not refer to their forthcoming swordplay, but to the kisses he had claimed from her and the way in which, with dialogue, she had forestalled any further assaults upon her senses.

"En garde!" she snapped curtly. "Let us have action, then! Prepare yourself, monsieur, for when I am done with you, you shall be fit only to be fed to the fish!"

"Since you are sure of yourself, madame, would you care to hazard a small wager on the outcome of our battle?" he asked, an amused smile now twitching at the corners of his lips.

"What kind of a wager?" Geneviève queried suspiciously.

"Only this: If you win, you may do with me what you will, and I will make no further attempts to escape."

"And if I lose?"

"Turnabout is fair play, don't you agree?"

Geneviève gasped with outrage, for the expression on his face when he had outlined his proposition had left her no doubt as to what he would do with her, should he prove to be the victor. Inadvertently her eyes strayed to her bed, causing him to chuckle low in his throat. Angry and mortified, she wrenched her gaze away, blushing crimson, for once more Noir had read her thoughts.

"What? No answer?" he inquired when she did

not respond. Then he shrugged. "It is as I guessed," he mocked. "You are afraid."

"*Non!* I am not!" she declared, swallowing hard. "I agree to your terms, monsieur, however unsporting I may think them!"

"Ah, but then, you do not truly know what I may choose to do with you, Rouge, do you? *Tsk, tsk!* What a vain, wicked mind you have! Can it be that you believed I would ... ravish you? For shame! I had decided only to ransom you, as you would me. No doubt in return for you, your crew would be willing to part with my chestful of louis d'or, which I'm certain they confiscated from my cabin aboard the *Black Mephisto*. 'Twill prove a great loss to me otherwise, for I confess I have need of the gold."

"O-o-oh!" Geneviève sputtered indignantly, affronted.

"Well, of course, if you insist, I will be only too happy to ... have my way with you instead," Noir continued, his eyes glinting with merriment and desire. "In fact, nothing would please me more!"

With that, he began to circle her warily, his blade held at the ready. His quick, sure steps, his form and stance, the way he grasped the rapier, its weighted pommel straight and laid flat against his wrist ... all these things let her know he was no novice with a foil. Geneviève knew she would have to be very clever and careful if she wished to be the victor at the end of their confrontation.

Facing him, she moved as he did, like a tiger stalking its prey, her countenance, beneath her crimson mask, consciously immobile now, giving away none of her thoughts, for she knew how easily he had read them previously and that he would do so again, using them against her.

Tentatively their blades engaged, metal striking lightly against metal, resounding in the cabin, breaking the suddenly tense, quiet atmosphere that had arisen. Momentarily the two opponents drew back, watching each other intently through the slits of their masks. Then the rapiers scraped together once more, this time more forcefully, though, still, Geneviève and Noir tested each other's skill and mettle, each smiling grimly with satisfaction at encountering a worthy foe. After that, as though by unspoken agreement, the battle began in earnest, each determined to conquer—although not to slay—the other. Geneviève shuddered a little at the thought of what the duel would have been like, had each intended to kill the other, for even now, it was a dangerous game they played, both of them dancing upon booted feet, thrusting in high carte and parrying in low tierce.

The murderous clash of their finely honed, tempered steel echoed through the cabin as Geneviève and Noir alternately advanced and retreated, their respect and admiration for each other growing with each graceful, deadly lunge, each swift, brutal counterattack.

Geneviève's brow and upper lip were beaded with sweat; she could feel it hot and sticky beneath her mask, clinging to her lashes, momentarily blinding her. She slashed her blade back and forth wildly, causing Noir to step back, giving her an instant's respite, during which, with her sleeve, she wiped her eyes. Then she licked her dry lips, studying her opponent surreptitiously.

Noir smiled, a hateful, mocking grin that somehow reminded her oddly of Justin and that day so many years ago in the courtyard at Château-sur-Mer. Now, as she had been then, she was filled with wrath. How she wanted to wipe the arrogant smirk from Noir's face, as she had longed to see it banished from Justin's! But her imagination could not help her now; she had only her wits and daring to assist her.

Once more her weapon engaged her foe's own, and the fight resumed. She was at a disadvantage, Geneviève knew, for Noir's reach was longer than hers, and she did not have much space in which to maneuver properly, to put to good use her nimbleness. Time and again, she found her way blocked by a wall or a piece of furniture, and once, she accidentally kicked over the brazier in the middle of the room, scattering chunks of coal across the floor. Fortunately the small brass pan had not been lit, for its upheaval would doubtless have started a fire. She had no sooner recovered from that mishap than she narrowly missed smashing one of the glass-paned brass lanterns that burned brightly on the tables, illuminating the cabin.

Noir paused, lifting one eyebrow.

"Are you intent on consigning us to perdition, Rouge?" he asked teasingly. "If so, I can think of a better way to set us ablaze."

A murderous scowl darkened Geneviève's countenance, and in response, she lashed out at him violently with her foil. Noir, however, was prepared for her assault, and deftly defended himself, compelling her back once more.

Geneviève was tiring fast; her breath came in labored gasps, and she realized she could not hang on much longer. If she did not win the battle—and quickly— she would soon be lost. Desperately she lunged forward yet again, putting all her remaining strength into her attack. It was then that she recognized how expertly

Noir had dueled with her, carefully restraining himself so she would not know the full measure of his power or aptitude. Now, deliberately, he advanced upon her, his steel whipping at her mercilessly, the muscles in his arms and legs rippling as he employed his entire force against her. She was helpless against him, and she knew it. Skillfully he sliced the sleeves of her shirt to ribbons—yet without once touching her skin. Then, with a little cry of triumph, he artfully cut off a strand of her long, unbound hair. With his free hand, Noir caught the fiery lock as it flew through the air, while simultaneously he propelled Geneviève back, so she tripped over her open sea chest. As, with a wail of dismay, she stumbled and fell into the coffer, he knocked her rapier from her grasp and sent the blade spinning across the room. Then victoriously he tossed aside his own weapon. After that, dropping the tress he held into his pocket, Noir bent over Geneviève, his fingers locked on either side of the chest, imprisoning her. Her arms flailing, she scrambled about, attempting to rise. But her efforts proved fruitless, and, highly conscious of her humiliating defeat and her ridiculous position, she glared up at him indignantly, momentarily speechless.

To her utter fury, Noir had the unmitigated gall to laugh. The sound echoed devilishly in her ears, mocking her, and at last she found her tongue and cursed him in a most unladylike manner, hurling at him every epithet she had ever heard her crew use when provoked. Noir only went on chuckling with malicious glee, spurring her anger to the boiling point.

"Such profanity," he chided, his tone filled with mirth. " 'Tis quite obvious you have spent far too much time with your pack of sailors. So how much worse can a single spy be? Come, come, madame. Arise. You

have lost our wager and now must pay your forfeit.''
His eyes darkened as they roamed over her slender
figure appraisingly, coming to rest upon her heaving
breasts. He reached out to caress her, his hand trailing
up her body and coming to rest at her throat. ''I've a
mind to see what lies beneath these boy's clothes, after
all.''

Geneviève gasped.

''You cheat!'' she expostulated. ''You said you
would hold me for ransom!''

''I said I *might*,'' he corrected. ''I've changed my
mind. I've decided you're worth far more to me than a
chestful of louis d'or. Besides, I thought you wished me
to ravish you.''

''*Non!* I don't!''

''Don't you?'' he inquired softly. Then, ''What a
liar you are, Rouge. Don't you think I can feel how
your heart is pounding? You want me just as much as I
want you.''

''*Non!* I don't!'' she repeated, but she knew it was
not true.

Noir was right. His very nearness was overpowering
her, causing her heart to hammer crazily in her breast
and her senses to reel. A small pulse worked jerkily at
the hollow of her throat, and his eyes fastened on the
exposed spot, disconcerting her even further.

''Let me up!'' she demanded.

''Are you going to keep your bargain?'' he
questioned.

''*Non!*''

''Then I'm afraid I must deal with you in the same
manner as I do all those who renege on their promises
to me,'' he declared.

Before Geneviève became aware of what he intended, he grabbed her tightly and, snatching one of her long silk scarves from the sea chest, began to bind her wrists.

"Stop it! Stop it!" she cried, struggling against him furiously. "Just what do you think you're doing?"

"Collecting . . . my . . . bet," he ground out through clenched teeth as she managed to free one hand and deliver a ringing slap to his ear.

Irately he caught hold of her again and, pinioning her arms above her head, started once more to wrap the sash about her wrists. Though Geneviève fought him tooth and nail, twisting and thrashing about wildly, all she accomplished was to bury herself deeper in the bundle of garments inside the coffer, which was now in total disarray. Clothes had scattered this way and that during her writhing attempt to loose herself from Noir's clutches. Some had tangled about her limbs; some were hanging over the sides of the sea chest, and still others lay strewn upon the floor. But Geneviève paid no heed to the disorder she was creating, for Noir, having finished tying her wrists, had yanked off her boots and stockings and pulled another long silk scarf from the coffer. He was now busy knotting the sash about one of her ankles. Defiantly she kicked out at him, aiming for his groin, but apparently he was wise to such feminine means of offense and quickly eluded her blow.

"What a little hellcat you are," he observed, "all fangs and claws. 'Tis growing quite obvious to me that you desperately need someone to teach you some manners!"

"And I suppose you think *you're* the one to do so!" she shot back tartly, glowering at him and longing fiercely to box his ears once more.

"But of course, Rouge," he returned easily. "I would scarcely be wasting my time otherwise."

"Oh! Just wait until I get my hands on you," she threatened, her eyes narrowing dangerously and flashing sparks.

But Noir merely laughed again, his gaze raking her impudently.

"I think that should have been *my* line, Rouge," he pointed out slyly, "for, indeed, I do not know if I *can* wait to get my hands on you! 'Tis plain enough to see that you have sorely provoked me in more ways than one."

To her mortification, she inadvertently glanced at his breeches and saw that this was the truth. She flushed scarlet with embarrassment, and, biting her lip, she prayed fervently for the lid of the sea chest to come crashing down upon her to hide her stricken face. It did no such thing, but as the thought occurred to her, she was suddenly seized by another idea, and, stretching up awkwardly with her bound wrists, she strained to reach the hinged brass hasp that hung down from the top of the coffer. If only she could get hold of the lock, she could use the lid as a weapon, banging it down upon Noir's head. She extended her fingers as far up as possible, swearing silently to herself as they just brushed the bottom edge of the hasp. Only an inch or two more and she would have had it! There was no time to try again, however, for Noir had finished with her ankles, and without warning, he suddenly hauled her from the sea chest and slung her over his shoulder.

"Put me down!" Geneviève shrieked, pummeling his back with her fists and damning the scarves that bound her, making her struggles all the more futile. "Put me down, curse you!"

Noir acceded to her demand, tossing her upon the bed. Before Geneviève could roll away from him and rise, however, he flung himself upon her. Taking the trailing end of the scarf wrapped around her wrists, he knotted it securely about one of the brass knobs on the cabinets above the bed. Then he grabbed her legs and spread them wide, and, catching hold of the sashes he'd tied around each ankle, he secured them to two of the brass handles on the drawers under either side of the bed. Seething with rage and the beginnings of real apprehension, as well, Geneviève once more swore at him soundly, but to no avail.

"Rouge," he stated with false sadness, shaking his head, "I truly hate to do this, but I'm afraid you leave me no other choice, for if you continue to screech like a banshee, your crew will surely come to investigate."

With that, he stuffed a handkerchief in her mouth, abruptly cutting off her yelps of fury and indignation. Then he got up, strode across the cabin, and shot home the bolt on the door. After that, he picked up Geneviève's dagger, which lay upon her desk, and started to swagger toward her purposefully, smiling with obvious enjoyment and seeming not to notice the sudden alarm in her eyes.

"Now, Rouge, you shall see what happens to women who promise me much with their veiled eyes and parted lips but who, in reality, mean only to tease me!"

Frantically she strained against the bonds that held her sprawled fast upon the bed, but though she thrashed and twisted and writhed, she could not free herself. With her tongue, she attempted to push the handkerchief from her mouth, but the wadded cloth was wedged tight between her lips and would not be budged. She screamed and screamed, but the only sound that emanated from her throat was a muffled sob that turned to gagging as she nearly choked on the handkerchief.

" 'Twill do you no good to try to fight me in an effort to escape," Noir informed her needlessly, "for this time, I have made certain you will not tempt me and then disappear, as you have on previous occasions!"

Geneviève was truly frightened now, for she was utterly helpless to prevent whatever he intended; and though he had haunted her dreams, crept into her heart and soul, and saved her life, too, she realized she really knew nothing about him at all. Who was he? A dangerous, hunted spy whose real name she did not even know. Why, he might be a vicious murderer, a perverted fiend, mentally unbalanced . . . anything! A thousand horrid thoughts chased through her mind, increasing her terror as he straddled her body, the knife in his hand.

Seeing the fear and horror in her eyes, Noir took pity on her at last.

"Rest easy, Rouge," he murmured. "I do not mean to hurt you. Quite the opposite, in fact."

But despite his reassurances, she could not keep her flesh from cringing as, with the blade he wielded, he began to cut off her garments. Soon, though with her limited abilities she had done her best to thwart him, she lay stark naked beneath him, bathed in the soft, incandescent glow of the lantern light.

Noir inhaled sharply at the sight of her, for she was even more beautiful than he had imagined, her satiny skin like the twining of pearls and gold, the color of rich cream where her clothes had shielded her from the sun, like sweet wild honey where the rays of the sky's yellow orb had kissed her. Her swanlike throat sloped down to full, high breasts that rose and fell rapidly with each shallow, ragged breath she took, all too aware of his passion-darkened eyes and how they ravaged her. Her twin spheres were blue-veined, like marble, crested with rosy nipples, taut now from the caress of the cool night air, touched by the sea, that filtered into the cabin. Her slender waist and gently curving belly met narrow hips and long, firm, graceful legs. Her parted thighs trembled a little, revealing a tantalizing glimpse of the folds of her womanhood hidden beneath a forest of dark auburn curls.

How Noir wanted her! Even now, his breath came in harsh, quick rasps; he could hear his blood roaring in his ears, feel his heart thudding in his chest and his loins tightening with aching desire. She was everything he'd ever dreamed—and more. . . .

"I want you, Rouge," he muttered, his voice low and thick, like warm syrup melting in her ears, "and I shall have you now—tonight! *Non*," he answered the unspoken challenge in her eyes. " 'Twill not be rape; I have never stooped so low and will not now. You'll see. I won't have to take you by force, for by the time I am through, you will want me as much as I want you. I promise you, you shall be willing in my arms."

Geneviève gasped softly and quivered slightly as her gaze locked upon his own, for she could not mistake his expression, the hunger for her that was evident in his eyes; and she knew now that he *did* mean to torture her, although not in the cruel, horrible manner she had previously wildly imagined. *Non,* this would be sweet torment, although she had no doubt it would prove just as devastating to her as the other would have been, for Noir had tossed the dagger away, and now he held another long silk scarf he had taken from the sea chest. From the look on his face, Geneviève could guess what he intended to do with the sash, and moments later, when she felt its cool smooth texture trail lightly across her flesh, she knew her mortified assumption had been correct.

She closed her eyes and reddened with shame as she felt her body leap wantonly to life in response to the length of material that slid slowly, inexorably, over her skin, taunting her with its feathery touch. Gently he flicked the scarf down one side of her face, brushing her eyelids, her temples, her mouth.

Ah, her mouth, Noir thought, his hot, smoky eyes lingering upon it.

It was too full and generous to be truly beautiful in the classical sense, but it lured him all the same. How he longed to kiss those scarlet, bee-stung lips! But he did not, for that would require his removing the handkerchief that kept her silent, and he had no doubt that, at this juncture, she would surely scream for assistance. From the noises he heard through the walls of the cabin, he was certain her crew was working hard to keep the *Crimson Witch* afloat. But that did not mean the seamen would not reply to a call for aid from their *capitaine. Non,* he realized with regret. He could not kiss her—not yet.

Deliberately he drew the sash down the length of her neck, remaining at the place where her pulse throbbed erratically at the hollow of her throat. Though Geneviève did her best to turn away, her bonds held her fast, and she had no choice but to suffer the havoc he wreaked upon her body and senses. She moaned a little, as though begging him to cease, but the wadded cloth between her lips distorted the small cry so that, even to her ears, it sounded like a groan of pleasure. Once more she blushed, stricken, knowing Noir would think she was actually enjoying the erotic things he was doing to her—and, God help her, she was! What a terrible truth to have to face!

Her flesh felt as though it were on fire, burning up from the heat of her wrath and embarrassment, her humiliation and desire. *Oui*, desire. She could not deny that. Her blood was singing in her ears; her heart was beating far too quickly, and her traitorous body was pervaded by an overwhelming languor, as though every ounce of her strength and resistance were being drained from her limbs, leaving her pliant and yielding and filled with yearning. She felt like a rag doll, limp and boneless, his to do with as he willed, to take as he pleased, and he would. Oh, he would! And she would be powerless to stop him!

With the end of the scarf, Noir had found that sensitive place where her nape joined her shoulder, and now relentlessly he teased the vulnerable spot. Sharp electric sparks of anticipation and longing tingled through Geneviève's veins, scorching her with their vibrant intensity. Involuntarily she shivered and again tried to wriggle away, but there was no escape for her, and with his low laughter, Noir mocked her futile attempts to flee.

With exquisite finesse, he pulled the scarf down along the valley between her breasts to explore the soft mounds that heaved with anger and disgrace at being so easily conquered. Geneviève bit down hard upon the handkerchief that kept her silent, hoping the pain of her teeth grating against the wadded cloth and her tongue would drive from her mind all thoughts of his terribly persuasive onslaught upon her. Determinedly she forced herself to lie still beneath him, willed herself to show no emotion, no reaction as the length of silk danced across her nipples. But it was no use. Despite herself, the twin peaks contracted, stiffening like two soldiers standing at attention, awaiting the instructions of their commander. Circles of delight radiated from their centers, shooting through Geneviève's body like spinning pinwheels that had been set aflame.

She felt her back arch uncontrollably, her breasts thrusting eagerly against the sash, as though they had a will all their own. On and on, he stroked them with his delicate instrument of torture until Geneviève believed she would go mad with wanting.

Her green eyes flew open pleadingly; crystal tears streamed from their corners. But Noir did not see the salty droplets that pooled beneath her mask, then trickled out slowly to be lost in the strands of her fiery copper hair. He was too caught up in the task he had undertaken and his own rapidly spiraling passion.

With irrepressible fascination, Geneviève felt her gaze drawn like steel to a magnet to the scarf he plied so seductively against her. The sight of it filled her with an insane desire to laugh, for appropriately the silk device was an intricate design of crimson and black, the colors running together and intertwining like lovers.

Had he chosen it specifically because of that fact? she wondered wildly. No doubt he had, for like an actor, he was a man of many moods and faces, and he selected his props with care. The sash would have suited his sense of the ironic. *Rouge et Noir* . . . There was a game called that, she thought crazily, a game of chance as hazardous as the one they played. . . .

The fabric drifted down, floating across her belly, where her muscles bunched and fluttered in response, as though seeking to hold the scarf at bay, to keep it from sliding even lower. But presently Geneviève felt it gliding provocatively over the dark auburn curls that nestled between her thighs, and she wanted to scream as her taut nerves stretched like a thong to the breaking point from the delicious waves of agony and ecstasy that coursed through her being. An unbearable ache of desire, piercing and sharp-edged, stabbed through her, knifing up from the deep core of her secret place. Without even realizing she did so, she writhed suggestively upon the bed, as though seeking some kind of ease-ment, but there was none to be had as Noir went on tormenting her, driving her passion to rapturous heights.

Tantalizingly he inched the material down along the insides of her flanks, making her shudder with desire. Desperately she tried to shrink away, to close her thighs against his encroachment, but, bound as she was, she was helpless to deny him, and, ashamed of her wantonness, she knew she did not truly wish to halt his assault upon her anyway. She wanted him to make love with her, this man who was touching her so intimately, as no other man—even her husband—had ever touched her, filling her with anguished longing. Her earlier rage had faded; even her sense of disgrace was curiously tempered by the fact that though Noir had mocked her for her refusing him, he had sought, too, to give her pleasure, taunting her, it was true, but wordlessly, tenderly, showing her what they might share together, as well. Now she wanted to know the full measure of her womanhood.

Gently the sash flitted down her legs, then retraced its path. Then abruptly, as though he had sensed her readiness to receive him, Noir threw away the length of silk and removed the handkerchief from her mouth. Geneviève would have spoken then, but he silenced her with a kiss, his lips claiming hers possessively, as though they had every right to do so.

Slowly, lingeringly, his tongue outlined her alluring mouth, feeling it tremble vulnerably beneath the pressure of his hard, demanding lips, lips that gave as much as they took and went on kissing her forever, it seemed, until at last she was kissing him back, straining feverishly against the bonds that held her captive and prevented her from reaching out to caress him, as she so suddenly yearned to do. Urgently his tongue compelled her mouth to open, shot deeply between her parted lips to pillage the sweetness within. Savagely, like a reiver, he ravaged the dark, moist inner recesses of her mouth, leaving no crevice unexplored.

Geneviève's head reeled with exquisite sensations: the sharp, masculine taste of him—brandy mingled with tobacco—though dimly she realized she had never seen him drink or smoke; the feel of him against her, his sun-bronzed chest matted with dark fur pressing into her soft, heaving breasts. When had he unbuttoned his shirt? She didn't know; she didn't care. She was too caught up in the rising passion he was evoking in her as he continued to devour her hungrily, his teeth grazing her lips, his tongue darting enticingly in and out of her mouth, his mustache tickling her.

Time and again, her lips met his own; her tongue intertwined with his until she was panting for breath and purring low in her throat, like a cat, with pleasure and expectation. His heated mouth slashed across her face like a hot poker, branding her as his. He rained searing kisses on her cheeks, her eyelids, her temples, the strands of her long, flowing hair, until she felt as though she were being showered by a spray of sparks that burned her everywhere, leaving her wild and breathless—and greedily longing for more.

He buried his masked face in her tresses and blew gently in her ear, his breath warm against her skin, making her shiver with delight. He muttered thickly into the curved shell, words of love and sex describing the things he wanted to do to her, *would*, in fact, do to her, things that made her flush scarlet yet perversely filled her with eager excitement, making her blood pound and her heart race. She knew she ought to have been deeply shocked by the things he said, and she was, a little. But his words aroused her on some primitive level, and a long-suppressed sensuality rushed to take control of her, ruthlessly sweeping aside her maidenly trepidation.

This was what her wedding night should have been like, she thought dully in some dark corner of her mind. It should have been Justin who took her so! But Justin did not want her, had never wanted her, and his very image receded into nothingness before Noir's bold, deliberate onslaught against her senses. She had never known anyone like him—her mysterious, masked lover— yet she knew him not at all. It didn't matter. Nothing mattered anymore but Noir himself and the things he was doing to her, things that made her feel dizzy and lethargic as she sprawled beneath him, as though she were drunk or dying; but Geneviève had never felt more alive.

Violently Noir's fingers burrowed through her hair as he crushed her to him once more and his lips swooped down to cover her own. Fervently Geneviève returned his kisses, then flung back her head in exultation as his mouth coursed hotly down the length of her slender throat laid bare for his taking. She felt his tongue probe the small pulse that fluttered so quickly and unevenly there, then slowly trace the outline of her collarbones, delicate and fragile beneath her skin. His teeth nipped her shoulders lightly, finding those sensitive places at the base of her nape and stimulating them so her whole body shuddered with glorious euphoria. Giddily she felt her nipples harden like buds bursting into flower as his callused palms slid across them ever so tenderly, as tantalizingly as the silk scarf had done.

With a sharp, ragged gasp, he cupped the voluptuous globes of perfection, his hands closing over them ardently, melting them, molding them to fit his palms. Endlessly, it seemed, his fingers fondled the twin spheres, teasing their stiff peaks to even greater heights; his thumbs flicked the rigid little buttons, causing torrid waves of delight to ripple through Geneviève's being in all directions.

She was like quicksilver in his hands, dissolving beneath him, her body melding itself to his. Soft, low whimpers emanated from her throat as she arched against him; it did not even occur to her that she was free now to cry out, to call to her crew for aid. She did not want to be rescued. She wanted to go on being deliciously tortured by him forever.

Noir's lips pressed tiny kisses around the rosy aureola of one breast, then imprisoned her nipple, his teeth holding it fast while his tongue just lapped the tip in a feathery caress so thrilling it sent tingles down Geneviève's spine. Slowly he took the entire crest into his mouth, sucking it, his tongue swirling about its center in a manner that made her shiver uncontrollably with intoxication. Then leisurely his lips sizzled across the hollow of her chest to the other full, ripe mound that beckoned to him like a siren, and he pleasured it as expertly and thoroughly as he had its mate.

Gradually Noir's head and hands slid lower, his fingers tightening on Geneviève's slim waist, his tongue investigating her navel, his mustache brushing against her skin. She felt his palms close around her hips; his lips trailed down her abdomen, seeking the downy pelt that twined between her thighs.

"*Non,*" she whispered, her eyes flying open with shock. "*Non!*"

"Hush, Rouge," he murmured huskily. "Hush!"

And then he was touching her so intimately she thought she would die of shame. As she had earlier, she tried to shut her legs against him, but the scarves he had tied around her ankles and to the bed restrained her still. She was powerless to stop him—and soon she did not want to, for sensations such as she had never known before blossomed to life within her as, with one hand, he found the swollen folds of her womanhood and began rhythmically to stroke the deep, mellifluous cleft hidden beneath the triangle of dark auburn curls. She could feel her warm, wet desire for him upon the insides of her flanks as he explored her, his fingers dipping into her, his thumb manipulating her tiny, secret button that would send her passion soaring beyond all limits of endurance. The intense, frantic ache that had seized her previously was momentarily stilled, but presently an even stronger stimulus rose to clutch her in its grasp, and with wild abandon, Geneviève arched against his hand, instinctively knowing there was something more she sought and needed.

She gasped as he pressed his mouth to her, tasting the musky essence of her that flowed over his laving tongue like the sweetest of ambrosias. She closed her eyes, bit her lip, and clenched her fists together tightly above her head, her nerves suddenly raw and screaming desperately for release. Her thighs quivered, and deep within the dark, damp cavern of her being, molten ore burst into flame, blazing more and more forcefully until she thought she would surely be ignited by the conflagration. Without warning, a million shimmering stars exploded within her, white-hot, blinding. The earth fell away, and all that remained was heaven, so sheer and beautiful that it left her breathless.

Melodiously Geneviève cried out with fulfillment; on her face was an expression so rapt Noir caught his breath sharply, not knowing if he could continue to maintain the iron check on himself that he'd kept deliberately but with such difficulty.

"Oh, Noir! What have you done to me?" Geneviève wailed softly. "What have you done? It's not fair. It's just not fair that I should want you so when you can never truly belong to me."

"All is fair in love, Rouge," he told her quietly. "And I *do* love you, you know. *Dieu,* how I love you! More than life itself! I would give up everything I have for you. But if you do not wish to be mine, tell me now, and I will leave and never see you again, I swear."

"*Non!* I could not bear it! I know I could not!" Geneviève breathed. "Not after tonight. Take me. Oh, take me now, Noir!" she begged. "My heart cannot hold all the love I have for you."

He closed his eyes tightly for a moment, his heart leaping at her words even as his mind echoed her anguish, for he, too, knew, they were not free to utter the vows that would make them one.

I shall find a way for us, he thought. Par Dieu, *but I shall!*

Then he grabbed the dagger he had tossed aside earlier and swiftly cut the bonds that held Geneviève fast. After that, he cast away his clothes and eased himself upon her, kissing her passionately, his loins taut with excitement and desire.

Desperately, as though she feared he would somehow disappear, Geneviève clung to him, her hands clutching him and caressing him everywhere, as though to make up for the time earlier when she'd been unable to touch him at all. Her fingers tangled themselves in his shaggy black hair, drawing him near, then slid down his neck to grip his back tightly as the tip of his hard masculinity pressed against her womanhood. Instinctively, a trace of her maidenly fears returning, she tensed as he plunged down into the warm, inviting pool of her, his smoky eyes opening wide with shock as they encountered the evidence of her virginity.

It could not be! Noir reflected in some distant part of his brain. She was a married woman. The two notions conflicted, confused him. Still, he could not deny what he felt. Ah, *Jésus!* She should have told him! He would have been more gentle with her.

But it was too late now to draw back. His desire for her was too intense, overwhelming him, driving all thoughts but possessing her from his mind. Sharply, powerfully, he thrust into her, swallowing her cries of pain with his mouth as the fragile membrane tore, was ripped away by his assault.

" 'Twill not hurt long," he muttered reassuringly against her lips, "but, damn it, Rouge! You should have told me!"

"I did not think it mattered," she whispered. Then she uttered fiercely, "But I'm glad you were the first!"

His heart sang with joy at her words, and the pressure of his strong embrace increased as he clasped her to him more closely. He lay buried within her for a while, accustoming her to the feel of him inside her. Then gradually he began to move in a rhythm as old as time. Over and over, he plummeted into the slick, hot core of her, his hands beneath her buttocks, lifting her in rapturous harmony to the melody he played. Geneviève's whole body shook with tiny tremors of ecstasy that started at the apex of her being and spread like fiery, red-hot lava through her veins, licking flames setting her ablaze. A low moan of surrender issued hoarsely from her throat as the raw, heated sensations grew so searing she thought she could bear no more. Her hands tensed, fingers spread wide. Then wantonly she dug her nails into Noir's smooth, broad back, spurring him on, feeling his corded muscles bunch and ripple beneath her palms as he gyrated down into her, his hips grinding forcefully against her own.

With wild abandon, she arched against him violently of her own accord, some primitive part of her taking control of her body and mind. She was like a savage, untamed cat beneath him, all teeth and claws. Her nails raked little furrows down his back; her teeth nipped his shoulder. But the pain she caused was mingled with a pleasure so extreme Noir merely cried out raspingly, his voice grating harshly in her ear, his panting breath matching the pace of her own, his heart thudding in frenzied counterpoint to hers as he ripped the lid from her powder keg and ignited the fuse.

She exploded like a sun going nova, blindingly, burning with a glorious incandescence. She felt as though pieces of herself were being whipped through the galaxy and beyond, her world colliding with Noir's own and sending them both spinning through the universe, spiraling into a dark, hot void that was empty of all save them. His body stiffened against hers; a sighing shudder racked him uncontrollably as his own release came, and, groaning with delight, he burst within her, spilling his seed.

It did not seem possible to Geneviève that they yet breathed (but they did, albeit raggedly), that their hearts still beat (though they did, far too quickly). She lay still beneath him, listening quietly to the mingled sounds of their gasps and the thrumming of their hearts, knowing now, with certainty, that there would never be another man for her but this one. Her deep, abiding love for him deluged her like a riptide, engulfing her with its madding, whitecapped waves as she basked in the warm afterglow of their lovemaking.

They were indeed like the sand and the sea, she thought, one boundless and alone without the other.

Silently Noir withdrew, pulling her into the circle of his arms as he stared down at her, his fathomless eyes taking in the wild tangle of her dark crimson hair, her eyelashes like sooty smudges beneath her mask, her scarlet lips bruised and swollen from his kisses. The sharp, musky scent of their lovemaking emanated from their flesh, mingling headily with the fragrant perfume of lilies that was hers alone, that yet intoxicated him. Sweat glistened on her velvet skin, marking her as his, now and forever. He would never let her go; somehow he would find a way for them. He could not live without her.

"What manner of man is your husband?" he asked, his voice low and incredulous as his gaze swept down to the traces of blood upon her thighs. "That you were yet a virgin . . . *Sang de Christ!* The man is either blind or a fool!"

"He is neither," Geneviève said. She shrugged.

" 'Tis as I told you before: He simply has no interest in me.''

"He is *très fou*, then, a selfish, insensitive clod who does not deserve you. Ah, *ma chère*, you were meant for me, and you know it. When will I see you again?''

"I—I do not know." She bit her lip with anguish. "Whenever I can safely get away, then I will come to you. I will find you, wherever you are, somehow, some way. Till then, I will count the hours, my love.''

"As will I, *ma chère*. As will I.''

"Your ship... you will return to it now?" she questioned hesitantly, hoping it would not be so.

But it was.

"I must. You know I must, that you would do the same.''

"*Oui*." She nodded, then fell silent once more, her heart aching at their parting.

"You must say I escaped," he stated, then pointed out, "for I do not think your crew will be too happy over losing their share of my ransom.''

He kissed her deeply, tenderly, then reluctantly rose and dressed. Moments later, the cabin was empty save for the silvery shimmer of the moon and starlight that streamed in through the window, intertwining with the soft golden glow of the lanterns. Geneviève closed her eyes as she heard the gentle splash that told her Noir had slipped over the side of the *Crimson Witch* and was swimming toward his own vessel.

"Godspeed, my love," she breathed. *'Au revoir.''*

She would have liked to linger in the sheets, to hug his love for her close to herself, to fall asleep inhaling the masculine essence of him that remained behind, as though a part of him were with her still. But

Geneviève knew this was not possible. She must see to her ship and her crew.

Slowly she got up from the bed, sponged herself off with some water in the pitcher on her washstand, and donned her clothes. Then she called for Ives-Pierre.

"Capitaine Diabolique has escaped," she informed him, once he had entered her quarters. "Tell the rest of the men they may divide among themselves my share of the chestful of louis d'or to replace the profits from the ransom goods that have been lost as a result."

Wordlessly Ives-Pierre gazed about the disarranged room. Then his eyes fell upon the bed.

"*Sacrebleu!*" he swore, realizing instantly what had occurred. "You are mad, quite mad! What will the others say when they discover the truth?"

"I do not care," Geneviève rejoined coolly. "I am the commander of this sloop, after all, and my life is my own. I need answer to no one," she warned, forestalling any further strictures he might have made. "Give them the money, for this night, I have received a treasure far more precious than gold."

BOOK FOUR

'Neath the Pretense

Chapter Twenty-two

Paris, France, 1792

Claude Rambouillet was so angry he couldn't see straight as he glared at the missive he held in his hand, the insulting, threatening letter that had been delivered to him at the Hôtel de Ville a few days ago by a young lad who hadn't been aware of its contents. Red-faced with ire, Claude gnashed his teeth and tore his stringy hair as he read again the mocking, sarcastic note. That it had been sent to him was bad enough. But the insult had been made even more unendurable because the poem had been published that same day by one of the radical newspapers that had sprung up all over the city. It taunted him:

> *Condemned, they were, to France's sharp knife,*
> *But* un duc, *his granddaughter, and his son's wife*
> *Were brave and daring and quick to see*
> *Their rescue lay with a bold gypsy.*
> *While fireworks blazed from a nearby church,*
> *A painted caravan* un sergent *did search.*

Like a fool, he believed a witch's lies,
For no crimson mask concealed her eyes,
And though a guard spied her on your hotel square,
The Black Mephisto left him lying there.
Claude, I'm still laughing, howling with glee.
You brainless twit, you'll never catch me!
Like a ghost, I'll haunt you till your dying breath.
'Twill be my foil that causes your death!

Enclosed with the missive had been a crimson silk loo mask.

Suddenly banging his fist down violently upon his desk, causing the other two men in the room to jump nervously, Claude swore aloud, cursing his aides.

"You stupid *cochons!*" he shouted, glowering at them. "Because of your incompetence, I am made to look a fool time and again—first by this spy, the Black Mephisto, and now by this . . . Crimson Witch, whoever that may be!"

" 'Tis obviously a woman, citoyen," one of the men, Citoyen Doré, pointed out logically in an attempt to soothe his master. "The way in which the letter is worded tells us that."

"Duuuuuh," Claude drawled scornfully, giving the aide a disgusted glance. "*Merde!* I am surrounded by imbeciles! 'Tis little wonder I cannot apprehend these two . . . *masquers!* who dare to play games with me; and, what is even worse, now it appears they have banded together against me!"

He recalled only too well the dead sentry whose body had been discovered some nights ago, lying in the Place de Grève before the Hôtel de Ville. It was now obvious that the guard had captured the Crimson Witch and, while escorting her to the authorities, had been murdered by the Black Mephisto. Indeed, a black silk loo mask had been found lying by the man's corpse.

Impatiently Claude drummed his fingers upon his desk, thinking furiously. What woman would be clever and brazen enough to be pulling off such coups? It must be someone with a personal grudge against him, he mused, for why else would he be singled out of all the members of the Assembly as the recipient of these dreadful, taunting poems? He frowned. He could think of a number of females he had disgraced and dishonored in the past by coercing them into his bed, but the majority of these had been sentenced to Madame Guillotine, and those who were still alive were not intelligent or courageous enough to be plotting these crimes against him—much less carrying them out with such success.

But there was one he had offended who had managed to flee from his arm's long, vindictive reach. His eyes narrowed at the thought, and silently he cursed her. She had been very young and frightened, but she had defied him nevertheless, and, outwitting both him and his henchmen, she had escaped from him. He had yet to find her, though he had searched the city ceaselessly, leaving no stone unturned.

He scowled once more at his aides.

"Citoyen Doré," he intoned, his voice harsh, his words clipped, "you will find an artist immediately who is capable of constructing a portrait of this Crimson Witch, based on that unfit dullard Sergent Guilbert's description of her, the whore! The man was absolutely besotted by her and has been removed from his post, of course. He is now in prison, awaiting trial, so that is where you will find him. Though the bitch doubtless disguised her appearance in some fashion, I want the picture copied and distributed to every *garde* and *gendarme* in Paris.

"Citoyen Neuveville"—Claude directed his attention to the second man—"you will go at once to La Conciergerie and bring here to my office Citoyen Edouard Saint-Georges and his wife. They were taken prisoner some weeks ago, and for reasons of my own, I have had them kept in isolation. They are guarded by two of my most trusted men, so you will need a writ for their release." Claude hastily scribbled some instructions on a piece of paper, signed his name with a flourish, and handed the note to his aide. "This will authorize the sentries to remand the two prisoners into your custody temporarily. I warn you that 'twill mean your neck if they somehow manage to escape during the transfer. That is all."

After the two men had departed, Claude leaned back in his chair, nibbling thoughtfully on the tip of his quill pen.

Was his speculation correct? he wondered. Was Geneviève Saint-Georges the Crimson Witch?

He did not know, but he certainly intended to find out. Shrewdly he would allow himself to be played the fool a little while longer as he carefully made his plans. Then, when he was ready, he would spring his trap, and the Crimson Witch would not elude him again. Perhaps he would even catch the Black Mephisto, as well, since it was apparent the two were now working—if not together—at least in cooperation with each other.

Just who is that damned spy? Claude asked himself silently, but he had no answer to his question.

Obviously the man was a master of disguise. Claude decided he would have all the actors in the city interrogated again. Perhaps, this time, he would discover some clue to the Black Mephisto's identity.

Chapter Twenty-three

The man all of France called the Black Mephisto stood shivering before the washstand in his cabin aboard his schooner. He was dripping wet and chilled to the bone from his midnight dip in the English Channel. Thank God his ship had been less than half a league behind the *Crimson Witch*! Otherwise, he thought, he would surely have frozen to death in the cold water. He was a very strong swimmer, but after a few minutes in the sea, his limbs had begun to feel like lead, and he'd been hampered, besides, by the fact that he'd been forced to hang on to his boots with one hand. He ought to have left them behind, he reflected, but they had been expensive and were one of his favorite pairs, and he'd hated to abandon them. Fortunately his crewmen had heard him yelling and had temporarily weighed anchor and lowered a rope ladder so he could climb aboard his vessel.

Now he removed the black mask from his face and gazed at himself in the mirror. Christ! He looked a sight! He must remember never to go swimming with Rouge, for the ocean had made a complete mess of his carefully contrived disguise. The grey mixture he had used to dye the neat, remarkable—and therefore memorable—silver wings at his temples had streaked, puddling beneath his mask and running in rivulets down the sides of his cheeks. The black kohl with which he'd narrowly outlined his eyes and the subtle tint of grey paint with which he'd shadowed his lids, both of which devices he employed to make the icy silver orbs appear dark, smoky, and opaque, had smudged as well, leaving jagged-edged ebony circles beneath his lower lashes and ashlike creases beneath his brows. One end of his false jet-black mustache had come unglued, and, wincing slightly, he peeled the rest of it away and tossed it aside.

Then rapidly he stripped off his sodden garments and stepped into a large wooden bathtub lined with copper and filled with steaming-hot water. He sighed gratefully as the liquid enveloped him. As the small fire his cabin boy had lit earlier heated the room, the chill began to seep from his bones to be replaced by a welcome warmth. He closed his eyes and leaned back against the edge of the tub wearily.

It had been a long night but one Noir would not have traded for anything in the world. Rouge was his. At long last, she was his, and she had come to his arms willingly in the end, sharing his lovemaking with an abandon he would not have believed possible and giving her heart trustingly into his keeping.

Now, in the quiet of his cabin, he reviewed the evening's events, recalling his profound shock when he'd learned she was a virgin. He had been so stunned by the discovery and so swept away by the fury of their passion that, afterward, he'd scarcely paid any heed to her explanation of why her maidenhead had still been intact, although she was a married woman. But now, suddenly, Noir was struck by an incredibly ludicrous thought. At first he dismissed it as being a wildly improbable notion not even worth considering. Yet he could not put it from his mind, and the more he dwelled upon the idea, the more convinced he became that he had, by one of those supremely ironic twists of fate, stumbled upon the highly unlikely but undeniable truth.

His and Rouge's lives were like a puzzle; yet now that he was certain he had figured it out, he saw how perfectly all the odd pieces fell into place. Mentally he checked off the list of items in his head: His had been an arranged marriage, as had hers. Noir had no interest in his wife; Rouge's husband had none in her. Noir's wife was French, as was Rouge. Every time Noir went out of town on one of his assigned missions, his wife took to her bed, complaining of an assorted array of imaginary illnesses and allowing no one to enter her chamber to ascertain whether she was truly in it. Rouge, he presumed, must use some such ruse on her husband in order that she might spend long periods of time away from home undetected. Finally—and most damning of all in Noir's eyes—he had never sought his wife's bed, and Rouge's husband had never sought hers. Noir's thoughtful gaze narrowed abruptly with suspicion. There were simply too many similarities in their lives for it to be coincidence alone.

Noir suddenly clapped himself on the forehead, smiling peculiarly to himself and wondering how he could ever have been so imperceptive, so thoroughly and expertly duped. Some spy he was! A blind fool, he had called Rouge's husband. Well, he was indeed, for Noir was now absolutely certain in his heart that the man could be none other than Lord Justin Duquesne Trevelyan, Earl of Blackheath, alias Capitaine Diabolique, commander of the *Black Mephisto*—in fact, himself!

If he were not grossly mistaken—and, like his father, he seldom was—he had just made love to his own extremely beautiful, clever, enchanting, and quite deceitful bride, Lady Geneviève Angèle Saint-Georges Trevelyan, Countess of Blackheath!

Geneviève hurried through the winding catacombs of the caves leading to the tunnel and the hidden passageway to her bedroom at Blackheath Hall, her candle flickering in the cool, salty sea breeze that filtered into the caverns.

How many days had she been gone from the manor? she wondered, for in all the excitement, she had lost count. Well over a fortnight, she was sure. She wondered if her absence had been discovered, for she had never been away so long before. Biting her lip nervously, she prayed that it had not. She hoped, too, that Justin had not returned home unexpectedly, for he surely would have demanded entrance to her chamber and found it empty. *Morbleu!* What would he say if he learned she had been cavorting around both the English and the French countrysides, posing as a smuggler? She shivered at the thought. He would be so angry that perhaps he would beat her! There would be nothing she could do, however, to stop him, for the law permitted—and indeed approved of—a man chastising his errant wife in such a manner, provided he used a stick no larger than his thumb to accomplish his purpose.

Preoccupied and worried, she scurried on, wondering if the *Crimson Witch* had managed to make it to her place of concealment. The sloop had been leaking badly when Geneviève and her crew had reached England's shores, but emptying the hold of its cargo had helped greatly. Well, there was no use fretting about it. One way or another, her sailors would manage to effect the necessary repairs. Ives-Pierre would see to that, then he would report back to her at Blackheath Hall. Geneviève's only regret was that with the vessel temporarily out of commission, she would be unable to see Noir anytime soon.

She sighed. Perhaps it was just as well. She needed time to collect her thoughts and to ponder seriously the course on which she had embarked. Her parents' and Vachel's lives might depend on her, and she could allow nothing to jeopardize their safety, no matter how much she might love the man who had taken her virginity with such tenderness and passion. Besides, if she kept pretending she were ill, sooner or later, someone—kindhearted Mrs. Fincham, no doubt—was bound to send for a doctor and discover her ruse. Emeline could not keep people away forever.

Geneviève had almost reached the tunnel when a sudden noise jarred her from her musings. What was that? She paused, listening intently. Why, it sounded as though someone were coming through the grotto. Quickly, her instinct for self-preservation guiding her movements, the girl peered about for a place of concealment.

There! On tiptoe, she raced to press herself against a wall of the cave, hiding herself behind a large rock that jutted out near the mouth of one of the wynds. Then she blew out her candle and waited, her heart thumping jerkily in her breast.

Presently a tall, dark man carrying a lantern came into view. Geneviève's heart leaped to her throat. For an instant, she thought it was Noir and that he had followed her. But then, to her horror, she realized it was Justin. *Sainte Marie!* When had *he* got home? And, more important, what on earth was he doing down here, sneaking through the catacombs like a thief? *Bon cieux!* Was it possible Justin, too, was a smuggler?

Geneviève's moss-green eyes narrowed thoughtfully at the idea. It would explain so much—his odd comings and goings, his "business" affairs that required such a great deal of his time and interest. *Oui,* it would be just like him to turn a tidy profit on illegal goods, for he had never cared what chances he took, as long as he made money or amused himself. No doubt as a smuggler he did both.

He looked so strange in the lantern light; it was as though Geneviève had never really seen him before, had never really noticed how hard and dangerous, how downright . . . wolfish he could appear. He did not look like a man one would want to cross right now; and, shuddering, she shrank back against the damp stone wall covered with moss, praying he would not spy her, for she was suddenly quite certain she did not want to explain to him what she was doing in the grotto.

When she was sure he had passed on, she once more lit her candle and made her way tentatively down the tunnel, half rushing, for she knew she needed to reach her bedroom immediately, yet half dragging her feet, for fear of overtaking her husband in the shadowed darkness. She was breathless with apprehension, her heart pounding like a hammer on an anvil when she finally ascended the spiral staircase leading to her dressing room and tapped gently on the secret panel.

"Emeline," she called softly. "It's me, Madame la Comtesse. Let me in! Quickly!"

"Oh, m'dame!" the maid exclaimed quietly as she opened the hidden door, one hand held anxiously to her breast. "You were gone so long I began to worry about you! Mrs. Fincham has been up here all week, demanding to be admitted, and, worse still, just minutes ago, his lordship arrived home unexpectedly. He is even now in his chamber."

"So I feared. Hurry now. Fetch me a nightcap and a negligee, and turn down my bed. Hurry!" Geneviève urged, frantic that any moment Justin would enter her room.

Rapidly she stripped off her boy's clothes, wound her hair up on top of her head, and jammed on the nightcap. Then she struggled into the negligee, hastening over to her dressing table as she did so. There, she grabbed a powder puff and dusted her face, throat, and chest until they were so white she really did look sick. After that, she jumped into bed and yanked the covers up.

She was not a minute too soon, for a few seconds later, Justin abruptly flung open the door that connected their chambers and strode into her room.

Improvising magnificently, Geneviève grabbed a handkerchief that lay upon her night table and coughed violently into the lacy square. Then, the filmy linen still pressed to her face to conceal her unpainted features, she sniffed loudly and greeted her husband.

"Hello, Justin. When did you get back?" she uttered with a low moan, as though in great pain.

"Shortly after breakfast." He glanced pointedly at the uneaten tray of food that sat at the foot of her bed. "I hear that, during my absence, you've been ill again, Genette. I'm afraid perhaps our Cornish climate does not agree with you. Were you not hungry this morning?"

"*Non*. I—I had difficulty sleeping last night and did not get much rest. I—I found I had no appetite," she lied, for, in truth, she was absolutely famished. "Mayhap I will be able to eat a bit of broth and some fruit at lunch. . . ." Her voice trailed off weakly as again she coughed dramatically into the handkerchief, hoping he would take the hint and leave.

He had a strange expression on his face, and she did not care in the least for the peculiar manner in which he was staring at her, his pale grey eyes glittering oddly as they raked her, almost as though he knew what she looked like naked. *Sang de Christ!* Was it possible he could somehow tell she was no longer a virgin, that she had spent a very long night making passionate, exquisite love? She cringed visibly at the guilty thought, clutching the bedclothes to her breast protectively, as though she feared he intended suddenly to rip off her garments and to accuse her of adultery.

But of course, he did nothing of the sort. Instead, his gaze took in the dark mauve circles under her eyes and the artificially contrived pallor of her skin. Then, without warning, the corners of his mouth quirked upward in a curious little half-smile that only furthered her uneasiness. After that, he made another solicitous remark about her poor health, then turned on his heel and left her.

Once he had closed the door behind him, Geneviève breathed a sigh of relief and fell upon the tray of food like a woman starving. She would not have been so filled with relief, however, had she been aware that Justin had, with a great deal of amusement and satisfaction, observed a single long strand of copper hair with crimson highlights peeking from beneath the edge of her lacy nightcap.

Chapter Twenty-four

Geneviève knew she must get out of the house or go crazy, she was so filled with guilt and alarm. Incredibly Justin had changed; oh, gradually, to be sure—it hadn't happened overnight, of course. Nevertheless, he had definitely changed. At first she had fancied it was all in her head, that because she had played him false—and in more ways than one—she had allowed her justifiable fears and her vivid imagination to run away with her. But now she was certain it was not so.

For over a fortnight now, he had been so pleasant to her that she could scarcely credit it. He had talked to her—really *talked* to her—as though she were one of the most intelligent and capable females of his acquaintance, though she had continued her ruse of being a featherbrained idiot. He had paid her every sort of courtesy and attention, from offering her the morning newspaper to sharing a snifter of brandy with her in the evenings. He had even informed her that he had his business affairs well in hand now, and he had intimated that he thought they should begin spending more time together getting to know each other.

"After all," he'd told her, "a man does not live forever, and I would like to know that all I've worked so hard for will be passed on to my children."

Children! Plural. More than one. That meant he not only wished to stop living like a monk, but that he intended to share her bed indefinitely! This morning, he had actually kissed her at the breakfast table, a long, lingering kiss that, despite herself, had played havoc with her senses, like the kiss he had given her on their wedding day at the altar, like the kisses Noir had so urgently bestowed upon her that night aboard the *Crimson Witch*!

Soon, perhaps even tonight, Justin would come to her chamber, demanding his rights, and he would discover her terrible secret: that she was no longer a virgin! *Cher Dieu!* What would he do to her then, when he learned she had already given herself to another man? Geneviève shuddered to think, for although he had indeed said she could have her cicisbei if she were discreet, she did not truly believe he would take lightly such a slur upon his manhood. He was a proud, arrogant man; a pair of horns would not rest ignored upon his head. Why, he might even be so angry he would divorce her. He sat in the House of Lords; he could appeal to Parliament for a legal dissolution of their marriage. Oh, just think of the scandal that would result if he did! She would never be able to show her face in England again, and perhaps then Noir would hear of her disgrace and be so appalled by the notoriety attached to her that *he* would not want her either!

Zut! What a mess she had made with her foolish charade, her childish attempts to best her husband. She ought to have told him the truth immediately, after that first night at Northchurch Abbey, and begged his pardon. Now it was too late. The damage had been done, and she had no choice but to proceed on the path she had chosen.

Attired in her riding habit, carefully selected for its bizarre appearance, she started toward the stables, her powdered hair topped by an enormous hat adorned with several sharp-tipped pheasant feathers, one of which narrowly missed puncturing Justin's eardrum as she passed him on her way out the door.

"My dear," he intoned, his eyes sweeping disbelievingly over her figure, "I do not mind these ridiculous outfits of yours; truly I do not. But those—those monstrous creations you call hats, *ma chère*, really, yes, I'm very much afraid they must go. I vow I have just barely escaped injury—possibly even death—on too many occasions to consider myself safe when you are wearing one."

"I'm sorry, Justin," Geneviève said hastily. "But they are the latest fashion, I assure you, and I simply do not see how I can part with a single one."

"Of course." He nodded. "I understand. They are necessary props, I suppose. Very well. Have a pleasant ride."

He gazed at her strangely, as though he would have liked to say something further, but at last he merely shrugged and went on.

Mounted upon her chestnut hackney, Sans Souci, the mare Justin had bought for her shortly after their wedding, Geneviève was halfway across the moors before she thought to wonder at her husband's peculiar choice of words with regard to her hats. *Props*, he called them. How very odd. A tiny shiver of trepidation chased up her spine at the realization. Was it somehow possible he had finally penetrated her disguise? *Non.* Surely not. Surely he would have taken her to task over the matter if he had.

At last, determinedly, Geneviève shoved the notion from her mind. It was a beautiful autumn day; the leaves on the trees had turned to gold and flame, and she was not going to waste it. She might not have many more of them before Justin insisted on taking up residence in his London townhouse for the Season. Lightly she spurred Sans Souci forward, removed her ridiculous hat, and tossed her head with joy as she felt the wind whip exhilaratingly through her hair. For today at least, she would be like the name she had given her horse, without care. Wildly she cantered over the gorse-strewn heath, expertly skirting the spiny shrubs.

She could hear the sound of the sea breaking against the rocks lining the coast in the distance and the shrill, mournful cries of the gulls that soared against the mellow sun-streaked sky. How she loved the ocean. She thought she could be happy just sailing upon it forever, stopping when she chose to see the world. There must be hundreds of fascinating ports where the *Crimson Witch* might call. If Justin ever discovered her perfidy and decided to divorce her, would it be so terrible a life if Noir were at her side? *Non.* It would be wonderful!

Abruptly Geneviève reined her mare to a halt, roused from her reverie by the sight of a man, astride a bay gelding, riding toward her. For a moment, she was startled, thinking he meant her some harm, for she had far outdistanced the groom who accompanied her and was now totally alone on the common. Then suddenly she recognized the man upon the horse. Her heart leaped with stunned disbelief and incredible gladness, and, laughing and shouting at the same time, she began to gallop headlong toward him. Once she had reached him, she yanked Sans Souci to a sliding stop and dismounted before the mare had come to a complete halt. Yelling at her joyfully, the man mimicked her impatient actions, leaving his gelding to prance skittishly at his rough treatment of it. Then, tears of happiness streaming down her cheeks, Geneviève flung herself into his outstretched, loving arms.

"Vachel! Oh, Vachel!" she cried. "*Mon Dieu!* Is it truly you, my dear, beloved twin? Is it truly you?"

"None other. Oh, Genette. Genette! How I have missed you!"

He hugged her so tightly she feared she would break, but she didn't care. He was real. He was alive. He was here. That was all that mattered. She felt as though a very important part of her had been missing and was suddenly once more in place. It was a strange feeling, being a twin.

"Come," she said finally, drawing away to look at him. "Let me take you up to the manor. I've married Justin, you know."

"I know. Papa Nick told me. *Jésus*, Genette," Vachel groaned. "What did you go and do a crazy thing like that for? Justin was always a real pain in the neck, and I doubt that he has changed much over the years."

"How strange that you should say that," Geneviève mused, "for that is why I went riding today, to get away from him because he *has* changed—but only recently. Come, let us walk together, then—if you do not wish to go to the house—for I have so much to tell you, and I want to know, too, how you managed to escape from France and to make your way safely to England.''

Vachel agreed, and, leading their horses behind them, they strode leisurely over the moors, recounting to each other the events of their lives from the time of their parting to the moment of their reunion. After that, thinking of their parents, whose fate was still unknown, they fell silent. Then at last Vachel spoke again.

''I tell you, Genette,'' he uttered, his tone censuring, '' 'tis a good thing I'm here, for it appears I arrived just in time to prevent you from making a complete muddle of your affairs. I'm sure I don't know what Ives-Pierre was thinking of, actually abetting you in such a plot. I shall certainly speak to him about it later! What a mess you have made already, wedding Justin, chasing about as a smuggler and then running into this spy chap and going off your head over him. I say, *ma chère:* it won't do, it won't do at all, you know. Why, you don't know anything at all about the fellow, not even his name! He might be a real bounder, for all you know. Spies have no scruples whatsoever—they can't afford to have them—and it's as plain as a pikestaff that this Noir of yours certainly has none . . . seducing a married woman indeed! Why, the very idea is monstrous!'' he huffed indignantly, sure the man had taken gross advantage of Geneviève's innocence.

''Oh, Vachel, it all sounds so dreadful when you put it that way,'' she stated tremulously, ''but it's not, I tell you! It's not like that at all! I love him, and he loves me. I'm certain of it!''

''*Oui*, well, that may be,'' he went on more gently, ''but surely you can see there's no future in it, Genette. If there's one thing the Trevelyans have in common, 'tis their damnable stiff necks and pride, and I

can assure you Justin will never agree to drag his
family's good name through the mud by petitioning for
a divorce. *Non*, you're stuck with the arrogant boor
now—whether you like it or not, Genette. Besides,
sang de Christ! Think of our own family, *ma soeur!* The
Saint-Georgeses don't wash their dirty linen in public
any more than the Trevelyans do! It just isn't done,
Genette.''

''*Oui*, I know,'' she sighed. ''What I don't know is
what I'm to do. I won't give Noir up; I'm determined
about that.''

''Then you ought to tell Justin the whole of it and
try to make some sort of civilized arrangement. Still,
there's no getting around it: there's bound to be a
scandal one way or another,'' Vachel told her gravely.
''Damn it, Genette! Whatever possessed you to insti-
gate such an outrageous plan?''

''Well, you're a fine one to talk!'' Geneviève
retorted hotly. ''Especially considering all the foolish
pranks you've played in the past! I was only trying to
help Papa and Maman!''

''Come now, Genette,'' he chided. ''That's doing
it a shade too brown, isn't it? You might have laid your
cards on the table with Oncle William, after all, and
requested his assistance, as well as Justin's. Either one
could have issued orders to your crew about making
further inquiries in Paris, bribing the sentries at La
Conciergerie, and so forth, while *you* remained safe at
home.

''*Non*.'' He shook his head. ''It just won't do, *ma
chère*. You always were a headstrong little termagant,
and the real truth of the matter is that you thought you'd
give Justin a dose of his own medicine. Well, look what
you've got for your pains! Whatever else Justin may be,

he's not a fool, and no doubt he *is* suspicious of you. Why else the sudden change in his behavior? He's trying to lull you into a false sense of security so you'll lower your guard. That's when he'll strike, and then you really *will* be in a fix! Personally I wouldn't blame him if he decided to spank your pretty *derrière*!''

''Well, I never thought I'd live to see the day when you'd take Justin's part against me!'' Geneviève sniffed. ''And when I think of the risks I took to try to save you . . . Oh! I don't know why I even wasted my time! Certainly Papa and Maman will not prove so ungrateful! *Non*. There's no use arguing with me, Vachel.'' With a wave of one hand, she forestalled anything further he might have said. ''My mind is made up. I intend to continue searching for them, and if you don't wish to assist me, well . . . you may as well return to Northchurch Abbey. I'm certain Oncle Wiliam and especially Tante Dominique were overjoyed to see you. No doubt they wondered why you didn't stay with them longer, for you might have sent word to me of your arrival instead of coming here in person, especially when you had no inclination to see Justin anyway. I would have come posthaste to Northchurch Abbey, as well you know.''

Vachel had the good grace to flush guiltily, jamming his hands into his pockets like a mischievous child who has just been caught stealing cookies from a jar.

''Well, the—er—truth is, Genette, that I—er—didn't actually see Oncle William and Tante Dominique. In fact, I doubt if they even know I'm here in England.''

''What do you mean . . . you didn't see them?'' Geneviève queried, much startled. ''You went first to Northchurch Abbey, didn't you?'' When Vachel didn't respond, her brows flew together with sudden comprehension. "Oh, what have you done, you wicked man? How dare you stand there, chastising me, when 'tis clear *you*, too, have pulled another one of your infamous stunts? No wonder Oncle William and Tante Dominique didn't inform me of your arrival—and here I thought you merely wanted to surprise me! Well, out with it, *mon frère*! What terrible trick have you turned this time?"

Vachel grinned sheepishly, his green eyes glinting with merriment.

"Well, I really *was* on my way to Northchurch Abbey to report to Oncle William, but halfway down the road, I saw his coach coming toward me. You know what an ancient monstrosity it is; one could recognize it anywhere! And since it was so late, I knew he couldn't be inside, for what would he have been doing out at that hour when he positively abhors routs and parties and such, and Tante Dominique has practically to twist his arm to get him to accompany her to any social function?

"Well, at any rate, I decided Justin must be within, and I thought it would be a grand lark to pretend to be a highwayman and hold him up. I was only going to take that silver pocket watch of his; you know how he prizes it! And I would have returned it later. But, the upshot was, after I'd shouted at the vehicle to stop, sent the driver and his escort, at gunpoint, to cower in the bushes, and ripped open the door, I discovered the carriage was occupied by two females I'd never seen before.

"One of the women turned out to be Oncle William's ward, a Miss Mannering, she said her name was, a real prude if I ever saw one and no fun at all, believe me! But the other one, Prinda, the parlormaid, was a priceless gem, and since I could hardly rob them, I demanded that she give me a kiss before they continued on their way. Well, Miss Mannering, the nincompoop, got a bee in her bonnet—probably because I didn't want to kiss her, too—and she said she intended to tell Oncle William all, and then she fainted.

"Of course, I didn't dare to show my face at Northchurch Abbey after that, for I don't mind telling you, Genette, I was of no mind to be the recipient of one of Oncle William's nasty dressing-downs, which is surely what I would have got!"

"And most assuredly what you deserved," Geneviève asserted. "Imagine! Frightening poor Kitty half to death— and when she is not in the least disagreeable, besides, but is the kindest, sweetest, most lovely person. I vow I don't know what is going to become of you, *mon cher,* if you don't cease these irresponsible pranks of yours."

"Well, you needn't talk, Genette!" Vachel returned loftily. "For *I'm* not in half the pickle *you* are!"

"*Oui,* that's true," Geneviève agreed glumly. "*Dieu!* What a fine kettle of fish we have fried! Well, don't just stand there. Try to think of what we can do, for I swear if you don't help me, I'll—I'll never speak to you again!"

"As bad as that, huh?" Vachel raised one eyebrow inquisitively. "Oh, all right. I admit I don't mind in the least misleading Justin, but, damn it, Genette, you're not to play any of your accursed witch's tricks on me!"

"*Non.* I won't. But . . . what is to be done? We simply *must* get Papa and Maman out of France!"

"*Oui,* and that I can do." Vachel spoke grimly. "And *without* your assistance, Genette. I'll take command of the *Crimson Witch,* go back to France, and see what I can learn. Indeed, I did not know Papa and

Maman were still there, or I would never have left. I fully expected to find all three of you here in England. You, *ma chère,* will remain here, to continue, if you so choose, this silly charade you're enacting for poor Justin's benefit.''

"I will not! The sloop is mine, and I alone am her *capitaine*!" Geneviève insisted, firmly overriding her brother's suggestion. "*Alors.* 'Twill be better if *you* stay here! You can oversee the investing of our profits from the cargoes, for you know I have not your head for business, *mon frère,* and besides, bankers do not wish to deal with a female. Oncle William has managed to save some of papa's fortune. We must do what we can to restore the rest."

"*Oui.*" Vachel nodded. "Papa Nick, when I saw him before leaving Paris, gave me the same assignment. Did he tell you anything about what he was doing in France, Genette?"

"*Non.*"

"Well, unbeknown to the authorities, he has been systematically removing the remaining contents of Château-sur-Mer and Port-d'Or—things Claude and his henchmen didn't carry off or destroy. Papa Nick has actually laid his hands on several valuable paintings and other objets d'art that were stored up in the attics of both estates. I guess Claude didn't think to look there when he ransacked the places. Anyway, Papa Nick has been crating them up and shipping them—labeled as props and costumes—over here to England, to a theater in London he bought some months ago. I believe what I shall do, then, since you're so opposed to my commanding your precious ship, is to go to London after I've settled myself here and have met your crew and so forth. I'll unpack the boxes and try to find out what their contents will bring on the open market. I'll also need to work out some kind of arrangements with Ives-Pierre about transferring our profits to the city, but I can take care of that later. By the time we finally locate Papa and Maman, we might have enough money to purchase a couple of manor houses here in England, for I do not think any of us shall ever return to France to live again—at least not the way things stand right now."

"*Oui*, that is true," Geneviève conceded. "All right. 'Tis settled, then. You see what you can do as far as our finances go, and I'll do what I can to find Papa and Maman and get them safely out of France. I don't know why you didn't tell me this about Papa Nick immediately, Vachel. *Morbleu!* He should have told me himself, but of course, I have had little opportunity to speak with him. If he's managed to save some of our belongings, he can certainly obtain other goods in France, and I can smuggle them into England, along with my own cargoes, and turn a tidy profit."

"I'm sorry, Genette," Vachel said. "I know I should have told you about Papa Nick sooner, but you have set my head spinning with the stories of your exploits and that damned spy fellow! I only hope you know what you are doing, *ma soeur*, for I shouldn't at all like to be in your shoes when Justin, as he surely will, finally discovers what you have been doing!"

Chapter Twenty-five

Justin Trevelyan gazed with some annoyance at the missive from his father that lay upon his desk, and silently he cursed all well-meaning but interfering servants. It seemed that during his absence from Blackheath Hall, kindly Mrs. Fincham had grown quite alarmed about Geneviève's keeping to her chamber and the list of her complaints dutifully enumerated to the housekeeper by Emeline, the abigail. Having been told that to send for the physician was pointless, since Geneviève would not see him, Mrs. Fincham had at last taken it upon herself to write to Lady Northchurch regarding Geneviève's poor health and curious behavior. The countess would have set forth immediately for Blackheath Hall, had not her husband prevented her from doing so, insisting that had Geneviève required either her aunt's presence or her assistance, she would surely have requested it herself.

"Depend upon it," Lord Northchurch had declared acidly, "this is somehow a part of Genette's plan to best Justin—and do not tell me you know nothing about it, my dear Dominique, for I have already heard the truth from Genette herself! Did you think I would not recognize your facial artistry for Titania, the Fairy Queen, my dear? Really, Dominique! I may not have approved of your acting, but I have never scorned your considerable talent and ability. I can quite understand that you and Genette both were thoroughly provoked by your son, and I do not care in the least that you sought to teach him a well-deserved lesson. Be at ease. I shall not give the game away. However, I do think it would be best if you would allow me to ascertain from Justin myself the true state of affairs at Blackheath Hall. Because he is our only child and you love him dearly, you are far too lenient with him, Dominique. He will fob you off with one of his noncommittal replies, and with that, you will have to be content. I, on the other hand, shall be relentless in my pursuit of the veracity of the matter!''

Justin sighed. As his father had surmised, he knew he would be unable to satisfy Lord Northchurch with a vague response. But how on earth was he to explain the incredibly tangled situation at Blackheath Hall—especially in a letter? There was no way for him to do so, he determined at last. He would have to journey to Northchurch Abbey to deliver his explanation in person.

Thus resolved, he instructed his errant bride to pack her trunks for a visit to Devon to spend several days with his parents. This information Geneviève secretly relayed in a note to her twin brother, who had taken up residence at a nearby inn, the Horn and Hound, in Penzance. He had, after a great deal of thought, decided he could best help his sister by keeping his presence in

England unknown. That way, at least one of them would be free to come and go at will, without having to answer to anyone. Besides, he wanted at all costs to avoid having his uncle learn who had held up Miss Mannering in the coach.

The fact that Justin intended a sojourn at Northchurch Abbey suited Vachel completely, despite the slight risk he would run of being spied in the vicinity and recognized, for it would give him a chance to see Prinda again. She had been constantly on his mind, and he had determined that for him to become involved with a parlormaid was certainly no worse than Geneviève's falling in love with a notorious and thoroughly unscrupulous spy!

So thinking, he informed his sister that he would set out for Devon at once and would stay at an inn in Tavistock, near Northchurch Abbey, where he would be close at hand if she needed him.

Ives-Pierre, the twins agreed, would be left behind in Cornwall as their liaison to Geneviève's crew. That way, his movements, too, would be unhampered, and he could continue his progress reports on the repairs currently being effected upon the *Crimson Witch*.

The Earl of Northchurch leaned back in the chair behind his desk in his study at Northchurch Abbey. His eyebrows were drawn together thoughtfully, but a little smile of amusement hovered at the corners of his lips as he removed his monocle from the breastpocket of his waistcoat and, with his handkerchief, began to clean the eyepiece. Off and on during this process, he held the quizzing glass up to the light streaming in from the windows to be certain he was getting all the smudges. Then finally he poked the monocle back into his pocket and turned to his son.

"Well," he intoned dryly, "I'm sure I don't need to tell you, Justin, how utterly fascinating—if a trifle fantastic—I find this incredible story you have just related to me. Nay, hold your tongue." He held up one hand warningly. "I'm not saying I don't believe you. In fact, I think in all probability what you have told me—remarkable as it may sound—is indeed the truth. I fear I am all too well acquainted with my niece and her headstrong behavior to put anything, even posing as a infamous smuggler, past her.

"I know for a fact that Edouard purchased her a ship—a sloop, by the way—for her birthday last year. 'Twas christened *La Belle Fille*, as I recall. I surmise that, before leaving France, Genette—ever an intelligent and enterprising young woman, I have always thought—somehow managed to take both possession and command of the vessel, aided, no doubt, by Ives-Pierre Fourneaux. She must have acquired a crew, perhaps in Brest, to man it for her, changed both its name and appearance, and put it to work for her. Doubtless she sailed it to England, rather than arriving in a small fishing boat, as she informed us.

"Upon learning that my own attempts to discover the whereabouts of Edouard, Lis-Marie, and Vachel had failed, and no doubt thinking she could not turn to you for assistance, she decided to take matters into her own hands. Overhearing your snide comments about her that day on the terrace—oh, yes, she heard them all right, as did your mother, I might add—she persuaded Dominique to help her with the masquerade she perpetrated at dinner that evening and has subsequently continued to employ, both to teach you a lesson and to conceal her true appearance. I'm quite certain your mother, however, knows nothing about Genette's other, more dangerous role, for I simply cannot see Dominique condoning *that*, even if she does on too many occasions indulgently turn a blind eye to less serious caprices.

"Yes, I'm afraid the pieces do indeed all fit together very nicely, as you said, Justin." The earl shook his head. "I'm naturally relieved, of course, as I'm sure your mother will be, to discover there is nothing wrong with Genette's health. However, I do not see how my niece can be allowed to continue her—er—admirable, although quite hazardous, activities. I think you must confront her at once, Justin, and tell her you know the whole."

"Yes, so I had thought. But, the truth of the matter is, Father"—Justin's form of address was a loving appeal that demonstrated to Lord Northchurch the extent of agitation beneath his son's composed facade—"I hesitate to do so, because . . . well . . . damn it! I know I didn't want to marry her, but—but . . . well, the truth is, I've fallen in love with her, Father, and I can't bear the thought of losing her now! I'm afraid that if I tell her I know all, she'll be so angry she'll despise me! She loves me as Noir; I know she does! But I fear she has no feelings whatsoever for Justin Trevelyan, her husband," he declared bitterly. "She'll think I've known about her charade all along and played her for a fool—as she has me! And if I tell I *didn't* know, then she'll accuse me of cheating on her—even if 'twas *she* with whom I was unfaithful. You know how women are about such things—and how irrational they can be, besides.

"Oh, I freely admit I was wrong there, that I

ought never even to have looked at another woman after marrying Genette, but . . . well . . . everything just seemed to go completely awry from the start of our marriage, and—and—Oh, I know it's no use making excuses for myself. Genette will hate me—I know she will!—and rightly so. Doubtless she'll deny everything, and I won't have one shred of evidence to force her to admit the truth so we can straighten out this mess between us. Then she'll simply cut me off on both fronts, and I'll never learn the veracity of the matter—or win her love either!''

''Yes, I do see your point,'' Lord Northchurch said, feeling almost sorry for his proud, arrogant son. ''Well, I admit I hoped Genette would bring you down a peg a two, Justin, but I never dreamed your comeuppance would produce such a long, hard fall. You've no one but yourself to blame, of course. Still, I believe you have learned your lesson, and, from what you have told me, I know you wish to put matters right between the two of you. What is to be done, then?''

''I have a plan,'' the viscount announced. ''I don't know that you'll approve of it, my lord, for it entails allowing Genette to continue her ruse and the risks she is running. But I just don't see any other way out of this dreadful maze.

''I mean, first of all, to find out if she truly *is* Rouge, although I think there can be little doubt on that score—especially when I consider Papa Nick's thoroughly reprehensible behavior that night in France! The old rascal! He must have put two and two together then and there—and kept both Genette and me in the dark for a lark! No wonder he found the situation so amusing! Just wait until next I see him! He will not find me so funny then, I'll wager! A comedy of errors indeed!

"At any rate, I'm going to remain at Blackheath Hall for a while, even though the Season in London has already started. I'll inform Genette that I've been called out of town again and that we'll have to delay taking up residence at my townhouse in the city. I'll pretend to leave Cornwall, but in reality, I will be at the Horn and Hound inn, in Penzance.

"If Genette really is Rouge," he went on, "she'll take advantage of my absence to make another foray into France, for by then, the repairs on her ship ought to have been completed. I intend to arrange for Parker to impersonate me as the Black Mephisto. She'll expect her path to cross his somehow, as they have in the past, and naturally I want him to get a good look at her face to be certain it truly is Rouge. Parker, who is aware of my—er—interest in her, has sent me a sketch of the Crimson Witch, which someone has distributed to all the guards and *gendarmes* in Paris. How the authorities obtained it, I don't know. I'm afraid it bears a close enough resemblance to Rouge's true likeness that Parker will be able to recognize her without any difficulty— even though she'll be masked. In addition, I want to be sure I don't arouse Genette's suspicions with regard to myself, which is a real—although remote, I think— possibility if Noir doesn't appear and she finds out *I* was home all the time, too!

"Then, while she's in France, I'll return unexpectedly to Blackheath Hall. Emeline, Genette's abigail, who must be in on the plot, shan't keep *me* out of my wife's room, I assure you," Justin insisted with the assurance of a man who knew his rights. "I shall ascertain just whether or not Genette is truly inside and ill, as she has claimed. If she's not there, then I'll know for certain that she and Rouge are one and the same; and, playing the part of her enraged spouse, I shall demand a complete explanation upon her return. That will put her—instead of me—on the defensive. Then I believe that, after turning the tables on her, so to speak, I can demand that she give up this man Noir, telling her I have come to care for her and refuse to let her go.

"In the meantime, to make this fact seem entirely plausible to her, I have begun to alter drastically my behavior toward her so she will gradually come to learn that I *do* love her. That way, if all goes right, I need never reveal the real truth to her—or can do so at some later date when she has come to love me as Justin as well as Noir."

The earl nodded thoughtfully, his eyes gleaming with appreciation and an odd little half-smile once more curving his lips.

"I admit there have been times in the past, Justin, when I have quite despaired of you," he confessed, "but I see you are not lacking in intelligence, compassion, or emotion, after all. 'Tis a most ingenious scheme, if I do say so myself. The only thing I cannot like is Genette's continued exposure to the authorities in France. You and Parker must take great care to ensure that she does not fall into their hands."

The viscount's mouth tightened grimly at the thought.

"We will, Father, I assure you. We will. In the meanwhile, I will leave no stone unturned in an effort to locate and rescue—if they are still alive—Uncle Edouard and Aunt Lis-Marie and Vachel, too. Had I not been so selfish and churlish from the start, so callous and inconsiderate of Genette's feelings, she would never have been driven to this rash plan. If only she had felt she could trust me, could confide in me, none of this would have happened. I will make it all up to her, I swear!''

"I'm sure you will," Lord Northchurch replied. "In the meantime, however, I believe 'twould be best if your conjectures and plans remained our secret, Justin. I know you do not wish Genette to learn of the matter until you are absolutely sure of your facts, and I certainly have no desire for your mother to be worried about either you or her niece.

"Good Lord!" the earl concluded, shaking his head again. "What a complete tangle! Well, that is what comes of having too many actors on one stage! I am sure I do not know why your grandfather couldn't have chosen a less damnably dissembling profession! No doubt, before it's all over, that young scamp Vachel will show up in disguise, too!"

Chapter Twenty-six

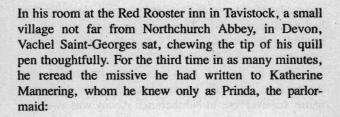

In his room at the Red Rooster inn in Tavistock, a small village not far from Northchurch Abbey, in Devon, Vachel Saint-Georges sat, chewing the tip of his quill pen thoughtfully. For the third time in as many minutes, he reread the missive he had written to Katherine Mannering, whom he knew only as Prinda, the parlor-maid:

September 12, 1792

Dear Prinda,

> *I am sorry I have not got in touch with you previously, but, as you may have guessed, the life of a highwayman is fraught with many hazards, and, due to various difficulties, I have been forced to lie low for a while. However, I have now returned to Devon and would like very much to see you again, provided, of course, that you are still willing. I have thought about you*

*endlessly since the night of our first meeting and
assure you my intentions toward you are strictly
honorable. If you can and still want to, please
come to the big oak tree by the road where I
held up the coach. I will be waiting there for
you tonight at midnight. If you cannot come, leave
a letter for me at the base of the tree. If you do
not appear and there is no note either, I will
understand that you don't care to see me again,
and I will trouble you no more.*

Yours, etc.,

Frowning, Vachel crossed out the words *held up*
and replaced them with the word *stopped*, deciding that
had a better ring to it. There was no point, after all, in
reminding Prinda that he had halted the vehicle with the
apparent aim of robbing it.

Then he paused, wondering how he should sign
the missive. After all, he could scarcely reveal his true
name, for everyone at Northchurch Abbey was aware of
his identity, and Prinda was sure to know who he really
was. No doubt then she would think he was merely bent
on trifling with her for a bit of sport, and perhaps she
would not come.

At last, after a great deal of consideration, Vachel
ended the letter by boldly scrawling *The French Cow*
near the bottom of the page. He thought this was rather
clever, for *vachel*, in French, meant "little cow," but
Prinda would not know that, and he could tell her it was
his nickname—because he had once been a cowherder
or some other such nonsense—for many criminals were
called by similar, descriptive monikers; Farmer Frye,
Sykes the Smith, and so forth.

Prinda knew he was French, of course, for like Geneviève, he spoke English with an accent and had referred to her as *mademoiselle* besides. But England was teeming with *émigrés,* so that did not matter.

Finally finished and humming to himself under his breath, Vachel tucked the paper into an envelope and sealed it. Then he carefully addressed it to Miss Prinda, parlormaid, in care of Miss Mannering, Northchurch Abbey, Devon. After that, he went downstairs and paid a young lad a shilling to deliver the note.

Katherine Mannering hugged herself tightly and giddily whirled about her room at Northchurch Abbey. She was absolutely, positively, head over heels in love! She was sure of it! Oh, what a simply marvelous, enchanting, glorious feeling! Last night had been the most wonderful, thrilling night of her life! For the highwayman she knew only as the French Cow—a thoroughly horrid nickname for a man so very handsome and dashing, she thought—had come back into her world and had stolen away her heart!

She had thought about him endlessly after their first meeting, and when his missive had been delivered to her yesterday, Kitty had been so eager to read it that her hands had fairly trembled as she'd torn open the envelope to unfold the letter inside. Then, all day long, she'd been filled with such anticipation and excitement that she'd scarcely been able to contain herself. She'd felt as though she were going to burst if she didn't share her secret with someone. But wisely she'd held her tongue.

Then, long after the household had fallen asleep,

she'd carefully dressed and crept quietly down the backstairs to sneak out into the night. She'd run so fast down the road leading away from Northchurch Abbey that she'd arrived at the big oak tree exhausted and gasping for breath. But it hadn't mattered, for there, her bold highwayman had been waiting, as promised!

Now, as though in a trance, Kitty closed her blue eyes and, singing softly to herself, danced a few graceful steps across the floor, smiling wistfully as she remembered the way in which Cowper, as she'd decided to call him, had clutched her to him and kissed her so thoroughly and passionately. She blushed as she recalled her own ardent response, but still, she could not stop the quick, erratic beating of her heart. She had never before met a man like him; he was everything she'd ever dreamed of in her wildest, most romantic fantasies.

Suddenly Kitty remembered how, when she'd described her ideal man to her maid, Rose had snorted and said he sounded like a highwayman. Oh, how right she had been! Kitty thought. And that very night, as though fate had intended it should be so, Cowper had held up Lord Northchurch's coach. Truly they had been destined for each other, she reflected happily.

After a time, however, Kitty's youthful, effervescent buoyancy faded to be replaced by a terrible feeling of despondency as she considered her position. What would Uncle William and Aunt Dominique say if they knew she had fallen in love with a roguish highwayman? They would be furious, she knew, and without a doubt, Uncle William would forbid her ever to see Cowper again. That, Kitty knew with certainty, she could not bear.

Suddenly struck by inspiration, she hurried from

her chamber and down the stairs to Lord Northchurch's
study. Hesitantly, glancing about to be sure she was
unobserved, she pressed her ear to the door. Earlier,
Uncle William and Justin had been closeted within, but
now it seemed the room was empty. Kitty opened the
door just a crack and peeked in to make certain this was
so. Then she slipped inside and carefully began to rifle
through the contents of the earl's huge desk. At last she
found the document she sought—a copy of her father's
last will and testament—and she sat down to scan its
contents.

Her heart sank. It was just as she feared: Before
she came of age she was not allowed to marry without
Uncle William's permission. If she did, she would
forfeit the bulk of her inheritance. Even when she had
attained the age of consent, if Uncle William didn't
approve of her choice, he had the right to continue her
trust fund and, as its administrator, to withhold the
principal of her not inconsiderable fortune.

How monstrous! It just wasn't fair, Kitty thought
angrily, that her father had been such a pinch-penny that
she'd had to do without all her life and that now, having
fallen in love with Cowper, she would have to relinquish all the money the skinflint squire had saved and
would be forced to go on scrimping to make ends meet!
Her only consolation was that Cowper, believing her to
be Prinda, the parlormaid, knew nothing at all about her
inheritance and thus could never be accused of being a
fortune hunter.

Well, Kitty's chin flew up squarely, if she must
give up all her money for Cowper, then she would!
That was simply all there was to it. Determinedly she
thrust the will back into Lord Northchurch's desk, then
hastened from the study before she was discovered.

After a minute, feeling she needed to talk with someone about her momentous decision, she went upstairs and knocked upon Geneviève's door.

"Come in. Oh, Kitty, I was just wondering where you were," Geneviève said as she glanced up from the materials she was examining. "I was choosing some fabrics for some new hats and gowns, and I found some colors I thought would look lovely on you. Come and see."

But Kitty was not interested in clothes, for she knew that even the garments she now possessed would be entirely unsuitable for life with a highwayman, and with all the passionate longing and urgency of youth, she had flatly made up her mind to wed Cowper if he would have her.

"May I speak to you a moment, Cousin Genette? In privacy?" Kitty inclined her head subtly toward Emeline.

"But of course," Geneviève replied, slightly surprised, as she motioned for the maid to leave them alone together. Once Emeline had departed, she asked, "Now, what can I do for you?"

"Well, first you must swear you will never breathe to a single soul a word of what I'm about to reveal to you. Do you promise?"

"*Oui*, of course," Geneviève answered, mystified and intrigued.

"Very well, then." Kitty nodded. Then, her voice almost a wail, she exclaimed without warning, "Oh, Genette! I've—I've fallen in love!"

"In love!" Geneviève cried, delighted and missing the peculiar, haunted expression upon Kitty's face. "Oh, how wonderful! With whom? Is he anyone I know?"

"No," Kitty rejoined, shaking her head, her eyes suddenly downcast with sorrow. Then she went on dully. "That's the whole trouble. He isn't a person anyone would know. He's—he's . . . well . . . he's quite . . . common," she explained, unable to bring herself to tell even Geneviève that Cowper was the highwayman who had held up Lord Northchurch's coach. "And now I—I don't know what to do. I don't want to hurt Uncle William and Aunt Dominique, for they've been so kind to me. But I won't give Cowper up either!" she declared, lifting her head, her eyes flashing defiantly. "I—I know he isn't at all the sort of man one marries, but—but—" She broke off abruptly, biting her lip.

"But you love him all the same," Geneviève finished quietly, distressed for her friend. "Oh, Kitty! Have you—have you thought at all that this man, this . . . Cowper, did you say? What an odd name, to be sure! What I mean is . . . well, I do so hate to suggest this, *mon amie*, but has it occurred to you that he may simply be . . . well . . . after your money? You've a considerable inheritance, you know."

"Yes, I know," Kitty agreed, tears now starting in her eyes. "But that's just it, Genette. He doesn't know anything about my fortune. He thinks I'm merely a— He thinks I'm just as common as he is," she amended, suddenly realizing that to confess that Cowper thought her a parlormaid might reveal his identity, for the whole household had learned from Rose the details of the hold-up the night of Lady Hornsea's masquerade party.

Geneviève frowned, unsure of what she should say next. Now she wished fervently that Kitty had not chosen her as a confidante, for, considering her own involvement with someone as unsuitable as Noir, she felt she was hardly in a position to offer advice. She sighed.

"Frankly, Kitty, I don't know what to tell you," she admitted at last. "It would be easy for me to insist you must follow your heart rather than the dictates of your conscience. But I—I know from experience that that sometimes causes just as much pain as letting go of the man you love. You must think things over very carefully before you decide upon the course to pursue."

"Yes, I know, and I—I suspect I really wasn't wanting advice. I guess I just wanted to tell someone my secret, that's all. Well, thanks for listening anyway, Genette. I was so depressed. But I feel better now. If you ever need a friend, just let me know."

For one awful, tempting moment, an explanation of Geneviève's own miserable predicament hovered on her lips. But resolutely she dammed the words that threatened to come flooding out. Kitty could not help her, and there was no point in burdening the girl when she had problems of her own. *Non.* Geneviève must keep silent about her own secret love, the notorious spy who had enthralled her heart and soul.

Chapter Twenty-seven

"I tell you 'tis a trap!" Vachel burst out, scowling at his sister. "Genette, I *saw* him! Justin has checked into the Horn and Hound, in Penzance, and 'twas only by the merest chance that he did not notice me, as well, for you know I've been hiding in the place ever since we left Devon and returned to Cornwall! I tell you 'tis a trap!" he repeated insistently.

"But—but why would Justin do such a thing?" Geneviève questioned sharply, her nerves on edge. "He's—he's been so . . . different of late, so—so . . . caring! Why, 'tis almost as though he is falling in love with me! Why, then, would he seek to deceive me by telling me he was going out of town on business and then taking quarters at an inn in Penzance instead? It doesn't make sense."

"*Mon Dieu, ma soeur!*" Vachel cried, exasperated. "Think! 'Tis just as I said. He meant to lull you into a false sense of security, and now he has. Oh, he's clever, all right. I never claimed he wasn't. He's laid his trap well, and now he means to spring it shut! Despite what you may think, he's grown *suspicious*—not solicitous— of your imaginary illnesses and how they always coincide so mysteriously with his own absences. I tell you if you take the *Crimson Witch* to France this week, Justin will return unexpectedly to Blackheath Hall and discover you are not in your chamber. Then the game will be up indeed, Genette, for he will not rest until he pries the truth from you! You can count on that!''

Silently Geneviève mulled over her brother's words. Then, without warning, her eyes flew open wide as a terrible notion suddenly occurred to her.

"Oh, Vachel!" she exclaimed, stricken. "If what you say is true and Justin *does* suspect that my various complaints and my keeping to my room, as well, are just excuses to cover my disappearances from the manor, do you think he has—he has somehow *found out* about the Crimson Witch and the fact that I have been masquerading as Capitaine La Folle?''

Vachel shrugged and shook his head.

"I don't know, Genette. I don't see *how* he could have learned of it, but anything's possible, I suppose. Perhaps, despite your warning him against such, Papa Nick, believing it was in your best interests, wrote Justin a letter anyway, informing him of your escapades. Perhaps Justin has been to France himself and has somehow become aware of your activities. You don't really know where he goes on these business trips of his, do you? *Merde!* He speaks French like a Frenchman, Genette! You know he does. He could have gone to France, overheard a conversation about you, read one of those poems of yours that have been published in those radical newspapers, or even have spied you there himself by some damned mischance. Hell! I don't know. It could be anything. I've told you repeatedly he's not a fool. In fact, how you have managed to deceive him this long is a mystery to me."

"Well, we dare leave nothing to chance, then," Geneviève declared firmly, her eyes narrowing so intently that her twin could almost hear the wheels clicking furiously in her brain. "We must assume that, in some manner unknown to us, Justin *has* discovered my dual role and is planning to catch me. Therefore, we must mislead him yet again. *Oui.* That is the best way. Thank God you decided to return to Cornwall with me to make all the financial arrangements with Ives-Pierre before going on to London! The boxes at Papa Nick's theater can wait! *You* must pretend to be me, Vachel, and travel to France in my stead, while I remain at home. For Justin must learn the Crimson Witch has struck again— and at a time when he knows it was absolutely impossible for me to have been in France."

"*Jésus*, Genette," Vachel cursed. "And just what am I supposed to say to this damned Noir fellow if *he* shows up? *'Allo* there. I'm not really Rouge, so keep your paws to yourself!'? Surely you can't imagine I'll fool *him! Sacrebleu!* You've made love with the chap, Genette! He's bound to know I'm not you, for I'm not about to even so much as kiss him, and I mean it! *Sang de Christ!* That *is* carrying things a bit too far!"

"Don't be silly, *mon frère*," Geneviève chided, glowering at him. "Of course I don't intend for you to suffer anything of an amorous nature. You may not even see him, for always our paths have crossed by chance. But if you do, I'm sure you can handle the matter. Simply tell him you're sick and must return to your ship as quickly as possible. He won't press any unwelcome attentions on you then, I assure you, for though he may be an unscrupulous spy, as you have claimed, he is a gentleman and not without honor.

"*Alors*," she went on, glancing briefly about the windswept common to be certain they were still unobserved. "I shall return to Blackheath Hall now to inform Ives-Pierre of our plans. The *Crimson Witch* will pick you up there"—she pointed toward the sea in the distance—"by that large boulder. Ives-Pierre will let you know when. *Bonne chance, mon frère*," she said, hugging him close. Then she mounted her mare, Sans Souci, spurred the horse forward, and, grinning, called back over her shoulder, "Oh, and, Vachel, be sure to get a long red wig!" before she galloped toward the manor, the sound of her laughter borne away by the wind.

Geneviève, in collusion with Emeline, had perpetrated her usual charade upon the household. But this time, after she had locked the door to her chamber, she carefully made up her face as always, powdered her pinned-up hair, and dressed in her nightcap and negligee. Then, after artfully arranging an assortment of tins of pastilles and bottles of tonic (with which women of the day were known to quack themselves) on her night table, she climbed into bed. A novel to pass the time lay open before her, and she soon became absorbed in the story, managing to read several chapters before there reached her ears the distinct sounds of Justin arriving home "unexpectedly."

Quickly, her mouth dry and her heart beating nervously, Geneviève slammed the book shut and shoved it into the drawer of her night table. Then she settled back among the pillows and closed her eyes, as though prostrate with a migraine. Emeline, playing her part to perfection, dragged a chair up to the bed and sat, a basin of cool, cologne-scented water in her lap, a damp lacy handkerchief in her hand. Geneviève began to moan, and Emeline pressed the fragrant cloth to her mistress's temples to soothe her.

It was this skillfully enacted tableau that met Justin's astonished eyes as, without warning, he deliberately pounded on, then, with his key, unlocked the connecting door leading from his room to Geneviève's. With a bang, he flung the door open and strode purposefully into the chamber.

At the sight of his bride in her bed, he abruptly drew up short, his mouth gaping ludicrously with disbelief.

"Nay, it can't be!" he muttered.

"What did you say, Justin?' Geneviève inquired weakly, pretending to try to rise and failing. "Please. Do not make any more loud noises. As you can see, I have been afflicted with another one of my dreadful headaches, and I simply must have quiet. Is your business over with so quickly, then? I thought you were to be gone at least a fortnight."

"Yes, I was, but things were not as pressing as I feared," Justin lied, managing rapidly to cover his surprise, "so I decided to come back early. Mrs. Fincham reported to me that you were ill again, so I thought I would pay you a visit and see how you were doing. Why on earth was that door locked, Genette?"

"So I wouldn't be disturbed, naturally," she returned coolly. "I told you: I cannot tolerate any disruptions when I am stricken so. Now, if there's nothing else, please do go away, Justin. I'm glad you're home, but I really must have my rest.''

Thoroughly confused now and angry, too, the viscount turned on his heel and departed, wondering how he could have made such a drastic error in assembling the pieces of the puzzle that had plagued him. Then his eyes narrowed as suddenly he realized he could not yet be sure—until he heard from his friend Lord Hadleigh— that the picture *was* wrong. Justin smiled grimly to himself at the thought. If the Crimson Witch were not at this very moment in France, then he would know why!

Geneviève, assuming that something along these lines was even now chasing through her husband's brain, waited until she was certain he had gone downstairs to his study. Then, reconstructing in her mind the expression on his dark visage when he had thrown open the door and spied her lying there in her bed, she buried her face in the pillows and pulled the covers up over her head, as well, to muffle her triumphant peals of laughter.

Lord Parker Wescott, Baron Hadleigh, had never felt more like a fool in his life as he crouched beneath the end of the Pont au Change on the Ile de la Cité side, watching La Conciergerie. Damn Justin Trevelyan! Parker was an ambassador, not a spy, and he didn't relish his mission tonight—or the remainder of the week either, if he should fail to spot his quarry this late evening. Christ! The things a man would do for his best friend!

Despite the chill of the autumn wind blowing across the River Seine, the black mask that concealed Parker's features was positively stifling, and he was sure he didn't know how Justin could breathe when wearing it. Moreover, the unaccustomed black wig, with its carefully dyed wings of silver at the temples, which covered the baron's blond hair, was making his scalp itch intolerably, and he was certain that at any moment, he would sneeze, because the false black mustache glued above his upper lip was tickling his nose. Parker shivered, drawing his black domino more closely about him and assuring himself that he would write to the Foreign Office tomorrow to inform them that, without a doubt, Justin deserved a medal for spending so many long hours in this horribly uncomfortable disguise. But then, the baron thought irritably, no doubt Justin was used to it, for his mother, Lady Northchurch, had once been an actress. That was why Justin had been selected for this particular job.

Impatiently Parker glanced up at the public clock in the rectangular Tour de l'Horloge of La Conciergerie. By the light of the moon, he could see that it was just after midnight. He would wait a few more minutes, he decided. Then he would make his way to the Place de Grève. After that, if this Rouge woman, as his friend called her, still hadn't shown up, he would go home.

Imagine Justin believing the Crimson Witch was his wife! Personally the baron thought his old chum must have gone completely over the edge. Spying did that to a man sometimes, sprang the cuckoo right out of his clock! Yes, it was ludicrous in the extreme, Parker determined, to think Lady Blackheath, that delightfully pretty but silly young female Justin married, had brains enough to carry out the daring schemes this Rouge woman had managed to pull off.

There! Someone had moved in the shadows then; the baron was sure of it! Suddenly wary and totally alert, he studied the Quai aux Fleurs that arced around the northeast side of the island, where La Cathedrale Notre Dame was located. Yes, there was definitely someone slipping down the street there. Parker prayed it was the Crimson Witch, for then he could get this charade over with and return home to his wife, Nell, who, he knew, would never dream of pulling a stunt such as Justin had accused his own bride of performing.

The baron waited until he had got a good look at the shadowed figure and recognized that it was indeed a woman in boy's clothes, though he never would guessed this, had it not been for his friend's description of her. Then he called out to her softly in his best French.

"Rouge, it's me, Noir. I'm over here."

With a start, Vachel glance about surreptitiously, finally spotting the form crouched beneath the end of the Pont au Change. Carefully adjusting his wig to be sure it was on straight and that its queue, folded into a thick club at the nape of his neck, had not come undone, he moved slowly toward the masked man, fancying that he had got Geneviève's walk down rather well.

"Noir," he whispered huskily in his sister's throaty, dulcet tones. "Oh, Noir, is it really you?"

"*Oui, ma chère*," Parker replied, his eyes taking in sharply the woman's masked face. It was Rouge all right, for she too closely resembled the sketch the French authorities had distributed about Paris to be anyone else. Coughing a little to lend credence to his next words, he continued quietly. "But I pray you: Do not come too near, for I have a touch of *la grippe*, and I don't want you to catch it. I have waited many long nights, hoping to see you again, for I did not know if you made it safely to shore."

"*Oui*, I did," Vachel answered, relieved that he would not have to get too close to the man, "and the sloop has now been repaired, as I hope your schooner has been."

"*Oui*, all is well. When shall I see you again, *chérie*? We must arrange for a meeting place, you know. 'Tis no good anymore—leaving things to chance like this, *n'est-ce pas?*"

"*Non*. But still, I can never be sure when I may get away. I must think of my husband, you understand? And now I must go, for I dare not linger any longer. My men are waiting for me, and we have much to do this night. *Au revoir, mon cher.*"

Then, deciding he had said quite enough, Vachel blew the baron a kiss and disappeared into the darkness.

Chapter Twenty-eight

Incredibly there had been another daring escape from La Conciergerie. It was impossible, Claude Rambouillet thought, filled with wrath at his impotence in the matter, yet somehow it was true—and the woman known as the Crimson Witch was once more responsible, for he had received still another hateful missive poking fun at his ineptness! It was enough to make him tear his hair out by the roots! This time, the taunting letter had read:

> *The Chevalier de Grasse and his chère amie,*
> *Last night across La Manche in a ship did flee*
> *To England's shores with a Crimson Witch,*
> *Whose plan went off without a single hitch.*
> *Hang that picture of her on your wall,*
> *So you'll know whom to blame for your*
>   *downfall.*
> *Claude, you're a fool, and that's no lie!*
> *An idiot like you deserves to die.*

But Madame Guillotine, with her sharp knife,
Won't be the one to take your life.
That's my goal; I mean to see it through.
One of these nights, I'll put an end to you!

Like the others, this poem had been published by one of the radical newspapers in Paris.

Claude was so enraged he feared he would have a stroke; the blood was pounding in his head, and his temples were throbbing horribly. But, even worse, he was beginning to feel the slightest bit afraid, as well, for this was the second time his life had been threatened; and since he could not catch her, he was starting uneasily to think that perhaps the Crimson Witch really might be able to carry out her proposed scheme and kill him, after all. He had doubled his guard, but even so, the woman had time and again managed to elude every sentry and *gendarme* in the city. Why should the next occasion prove to be any different?

Well, it must, that was all, for Claude's superiors were growing as impatient and angry with him as he was with his own subordinates. He could almost feel Madame Guillotine's blade at the back of his neck!

Oh, he just knew, despite her stupid parents' insistent statements to the contrary, that Geneviève Saint-Georges was behind all this. She had somehow escaped from her parents' *hôtel* in Paris, made her way to Brest, and decamped to England in her sloop, *La Belle Fille*, which she and a gang of men had wrested from Gustave Mortemer and his two sons, who had been guarding the vessel. *Oui*. That was what must have happened, for Claude had searched all of Paris for her, and then all of France, but she had never been found. Even the sketch the artist had drawn from Sergent Guilbert's description had resembled her. *Oui.* It *was* Geneviève, smuggling herself into the country to commit her crimes and then sailing away to England afterward. That was why she could not be located. *Enfin!* It all fit together too well to be otherwise.

What luck that one of his most trusted henchmen had intercepted a note from Geneviève's parents to Citoyenne Lis-Marie Saint-Georges's father, Citoyen Nicolas Dupré, begging him, although he was without a doubt a loyal supporter of the Assembly, to aid them in fleeing from France! Claude had taken them captive immediately; but, feeling they would prove useful to him in finding Geneviève and making her his mistress, he had kept them in isolation and had yet to have them bound over for trial. Now he must think of a way to let the bitch know her parents were his prisoners. Then he would use them as bait to apprehend her.

But first, he would interrogate them again. They were too stubborn. There must be something they had not told him, some clue he could employ in his search for the woman who had dared to defy him and who now sought to make him a fool and a dead man.

Monsieur le Comte de Château-sur-Mer, Edouard Saint-Georges, and his wife, Madame la Comtesse, Lis-Marie, though they had both been starved and savagely beaten in their solitary cell at La Conciergerie, refused to quail beneath Claude's stern, fanatical eye and evil, menacing demeanor. They could tell him nothing more, they reiterated, refusing to respond further to his brutal demands for information.

Despite their weakness from hunger and their painful cuts and bruises, they made a careful survey of his office, noting the placement of its two doors and various windows, and the comings and goings of both the uniformed sentries and the plainclothed hirelings who reported to him. Unbeknown to Claude, Edouard and Lis-Marie were even now planning their escape from him. They were both fairly certain he was not done with them yet. *Oui*. He would have them brought again to his office, and then they would carry out their desperate plot to overcome him and flee.

Chapter Twenty-nine

It just couldn't be! Justin thought wildly as he stared at the missive that had been sent to him by Lord Hadleigh. There must be some mistake! Rouge—Geneviève—couldn't possibly have been in France as Parker had informed him. She had been here in her chamber at Blackheath Hall for the past fortnight. Justin was certain of that, for he'd had the first mate of the *Black Mephisto*, Hilary Sherbourne, stationed at the end of the tunnel in the caves to ensure that Geneviève didn't leave the house by means of the secret passageway in her room; he'd positioned his tiger, Ferdie, in the stables to make certain her mare remained in its stall; he'd ordered Wentworth, his valet, to keep an eye on her door, and Justin himself had visited Geneviève every day to ascertain that she was still in her room. There was simply no way she could have gone anywhere without his knowing about it.

Yet Parker had seen Rouge—the baron had made it clear in his letter that it *had* been she—and from the clipping he had snipped from one of the radical newspapers in Paris and enclosed with his note, it was obvious the Crimson Witch had indeed stuck again.

But it simply could not be! Justin had been so positive that Geneviève and Rouge were one and the same. Still, she could not have been in two places at once. There was no other explanation except that he had been mistaken. How could he have been so wrong? he wondered, deeply shocked. He thought he must be going mad. He was passionately in love with Rouge, and now, much to his consternation and despair, it appeared she was not, after all, his deceptive bride.

Justin's heart sank horribly at the notion, and he had a queasy feeling at the pit of his stomach. What would his father say when he learned of this new development? The viscount shuddered to think, knowing Lord Northchurch would demand and fully expect that he put an end immediately to his affair with Rouge and return home to Geneviève, his wife. But how could he give up Rouge, the other half of his heart and soul, for Geneviève? Justin knew he could not. God help him, he *would* not!

Geneviève was so confused she didn't know what to do. Justin had been so kind and caring toward her these past several weeks that she had been sure he was falling in love with her. The idea had torn her apart inside, for she had seen all too clearly that, surprisingly enough, beneath his cool, arrogant facade lay a man whom she believed she could learn to love in return; and, attempting to thrust all thoughts of Noir from her mind, she had

begun to respond to the overtures from her husband that
bore all the marks of a courtship.

Now, just as suddenly as the viscount had started
to allow her to believe there might be hope for them
together, after all, he had withdrawn into his hard,
impenetrable shell, making her wonder if she had imagined the entire episode, if it had been simply wishful
thinking on her part, born of her guilt over her relationship with Noir.

Justin had finally suggested closing Blackheath
Hall and taking up residence in his townhouse, which
was located in Berkeley Square, in the fashionable
Mayfair district of London; and it seemed that ever
since they had arrived in the city, he'd had no interest
whatsoever in Geneviève. She did not know he was as
emotionally torn as she was, that the profound shock he
had received upon realizing she could not possibly be
masquerading as Rouge had temporarily left him at a
loss.

Justin's pride and conscience demanded he honor
his wedding vows, but his reckless heart and soul
longed to be free to claim the woman of his dreams.
When he had believed her to be his bride, the conflict
had resolved itself beautifully. Now he once more sat
squarely upon the horns of a dilemma, forced to weigh
the consequences of choosing his mistress over his
wife.

His mind told him it was not logical, but still, his
heart kept hoping and insisting the two *were* one and
the same, that somehow, some way, Geneviève had
pulled off the impossible—a trait of the Crimson Witch
if there ever was one—that she *had* managed to be in
two places at once. But how? How could she have done
it? the viscount asked himself repeatedly. She must

have sent someone to France in her stead. That was the only satisfactory explanation. But whom? Outside of his family, she knew no one in England. She might have taken Kitty into her confidence, he supposed, but Kitty looked nothing like her and, even in disguise, would not have fooled Parker, he thought.

Nevertheless, the notion that Geneviève *was* Rouge nagged incessantly at Justin, for he felt certain he was overlooking some obvious, important piece that would clarify the puzzle. Still, he could not for the life of him figure out what it was, and the more he thought about it, the more withdrawn he became, unwittingly driving away the bride he sought to win as himself rather than as Noir.

As the days passed and her husband showed no intention of resuming his previous interest in her, Geneviève began again to be haunted by dreams of her mysterious, dark lover and to long for him increasingly, to yearn to feel his lips upon her own once more and his arms about her tightly. She wondered if he had recovered from *la grippe* and if he had suspected it had not really been she he had seen that night at the Pont au Change. Geneviève wished she knew who he was, where he was, and whether he missed her. Finally she determined that at the next opportunity, she would sail to France and hope their paths would cross once more; for it was evident from what Vachel had told her that Noir now watched for and waited at those places in Paris where she was most likely to be.

Fortuitously her bedroom at Justin's townhouse was a rear chamber with a window overlooking the alley below. She had instructed Ives-Pierre, when next he visited the *Crimson Witch*, to bring her back a long rope ladder so she could make good her escape without anyone in the household learning of it.

Now she sighed, feeling as though she had lost all sense of reality, that she was an actress in a play with interminably long acts and numerous changes of scene. She wished fervently that the curtain would fall, signaling the end of the charade, but something told her this was not about to occur anytime soon, that this lull in her life was but an intermission and that the climax had yet to come.

At last she finished clasping on her jewelry and examined her reflection in the mirror over her dressing table. Though she looked a trifle pale and worn from her troubled, sleepless nights, she could find no other fault with her appearance. Her coppery locks had been powdered, swept up into a sophisticated style known as the Quesaco, and adorned by several large plumes, some green, others gold. She had painted her face lightly, artfully, and affixed there, as well, a black patch known as the Roguish. Her gown was of green Italian taffeta, the low décolletage ruffled with gold lace and square-cut to allow a tantalizing peek at her full, round breasts. The puffed sleeves of the dress were wide-set upon her shoulders and ended at her elbows, where they met the edges of her long gold gloves. The frock billowed out over her small panniers, emphasizing her slender waist, from where the dress was cut away in an inverted V to the hemline to expose her ruffled gold undergown. From beneath, her gold slippers studded with emeralds shone. A matched set of emerald earrings, necklace, and bracelet; and a green reticule and a gold fan completed her ensemble.

Shortly after she had gathered up her accessories and wrap, Justin appeared in her chamber, eyeing with a great deal of misgiving the huge bunch of feathers pinned in her tresses.

"My dear," he drawled dryly, "I beg you will not assault me with those plumes. Must you truly have had your hair dressed in the Quesaco fashion? But of course. Let me guess. 'Tis all the rage, is it not? And naturally your role requires that you be all the crack."

"Naturally," Geneviève rejoined coolly, for she did not like at all the odd way in which he was looking at her or his peculiar choice of words with regard to her position in society.

Despite her attempts to pay him no heed, he quite unnerved her, and she wished he would go out of town again and leave her alone. She had come to the conclusion that his previous advances toward her had been as Vachel had claimed: for the sole purpose of lulling her into a false sense of security. His subsequent coldness, she felt, was due to his failure to entrap her.

The idea frightened her a little, for she shuddered to think how contemptuously Justin would have treated her, had he discovered the truth. Thank God her brother had spied him at the Horn and Hound that day and they had been able to lay their own plans accordingly. Otherwise, Justin would surely have uncovered the whole.

How she had ever thought she could learn to love him, Geneviève could not fathom. It was now obvious to her that he cared nothing at all for her but was merely bent on ensuring that she did not make a fool out of him in some way. That he would be very angry if she left him, she did not doubt. But she now felt sure, too, that it would be only his damnable pride she would injure, and that, she thought, could not signify when her heart was so painfully at stake in this hazardous game they played.

"Are you ready to go?" Geneviève inquired dully, wishing fervently that Lord Hadleigh had not returned home to England on leave and that his wife, Nell, had not invited her and Justin to accompany them to Almack's this evening.

"Whenever you are," the viscount replied, glancing at his pocket watch. "Indeed, the coach has been waiting for us for the past fifteen minutes."

They descended the stairs together, and a short time later, they had turned onto King Street, where Almack's was located. It was not far from White's club, with its notorious bow window, and Brook's and Boodles's clubs, all of which were just around the corner on Saint James's Street, upon which no decent female would be seen—or so Justin informed his errant bride as they made polite, stilted conversation to pass the time in the vehicle.

It was on the tip of Geneviève's tongue to retort tartly that she had committed far worse crimes than parading down an avenue lined with gentlemen's establishments, but resolutely she bit back her words, knowing that to utter them would assuredly prove her undoing.

When at last they came to a stop, Justin helped her alight from the carriage, and Geneviève had her first glimpse of one of the most famous and exclusive clubs in London.

Almack's, an offshoot of its strictly male counterpart on Pall Mall, had been founded by a group of ladies under the direction of Mrs. Fitzroy and Lady Pembroke. The price of subscription was modest—only ten guineas. But Geneviève, after learning that until later in the evening, nothing stronger than orgeat and tea was served, along with a light supper and spice cakes, felt that, in light of this, the cost could scarcely have been higher. Although there was a card room, the stakes played for were quite low, for dancing was the primary diversion for those who came to see and be seen. These included numerous unattached females just out of the schoolroom, who hoped to catch husbands there, and for this reason, Almack's was often referred to as the Marriage Mart.

Geneviève, although she was not unaware how difficult it was to obtain vouchers for the club from its sternly correct patronesses, wished Lady Hadleigh had invited her and Justin to an evening at the Lyceum Theatre on the Strand instead. Nevertheless, after greeting both the Wescotts, who were waiting for her and Justin in the lobby, she obediently stood up with her husband for the opening minuet. After that, there followed several more dances, for which she had various partners, one of whom was naturally Lord Hadleigh. She thought the baron looked at her most peculiarly, but as his behavior toward her was all that could be wished, Geneviève decided she must have imagined his expression, after all. She felt slightly relieved, however, when after the country dance had ended, he offered to fetch her a glass of ratafia from the refreshment room. This, she gratefully accepted, observing on her program that she had wisely promised the next dance to no one. Glad of the breather, she sat down upon one of the chairs that lined the walls.

There, she fell into conversation with a lively set of young bucks and ladies who were discussing a forthcoming card party and the merits of various games that were sure to be played. One of the gentlemen courteously included Geneviève in the dialogue by asking which of the pastimes was her favorite, and without thinking, she heard herself reply softly:

"*Rouge et Noir.*"

Since Red and Black was a popular card game, no one present, with the exception of Geneviève's husband, placed any special significance upon her words. But Justin himself, who had come to claim his wife for the next dance and who had arrived in time to hear her response, was so startled he quite forgot why he had sought her out. Instead of leading her out onto the floor, as he had intended, he stood there staring down at her, his eyes glinting strangely and narrowed in thought, a wolfish little half-smile curving his lips.

For a moment, Justin studied quietly the emerald earring he held in one hand, thinking how like the color of Rouge's eyes it was—and Geneviève's, as well. Then after tapping on the door that adjoined his chamber with his bride's, he turned the brass oval knob and went in.

He drew up with a start at the sight that met his eyes, for Geneviève was seated before her dressing table and was obviously preparing for bed. She had unpinned her long hair, which now tumbled down about her hips, and it occurred to him suddenly that this was the first time when not in disguise that he had ever seen it unbound. Before he had come in, she had been brushing the locks, and part of the side she had completed was now devoid of powder. It glowed with a fiery copper sheen in the lamplight, and the viscount felt surer than ever that those dark, crimson-highlighted tresses belonged to the woman he called Rouge.

She was wearing a filmy orange negligee that left little to the imagination and caused his loins to tighten with sudden keen desire as his eyes raked the body he was almost certain had lain sprawled beneath him with such wild abandon aboard the *Crimson Witch*. Justin caught his breath sharply at the thought and, with difficulty, dragged his gaze back to her face, from which she had yet to remove her makeup.

Still, with her hair undone, she did not look nearly as pixieish as she normally appeared, and he could now perceive that the planes and angles of her countenance were identical to Rouge's.

They *were* one and the same. They simply must be! The viscount did not know how Geneviève had managed to deceive him, but he was now more positive than ever that somehow she had. He must find a way to unmask her, he thought, before she drove him crazy with wanting, for it was sheer torment to remember what she had been like in bed that night on board the *Crimson Witch* and to restrain himself from touching her now, for fear of . . . what? She was his wife; he had every right to take her. He need not hold himself in check at all.

"What—what do you want, Justin?" Geneviève asked a trifle apprehensively, for she had not missed the hungry expression on his dark visage.

Laying down her silver-handled brush, she rose and pulled on her wrapper, clutching its edges together tightly at her throat, as though the flimsy robe might offer some protection from him.

"You dropped your earring in the hall." He tossed it casually upon her dressing table. " 'Tis very valuable, Genette. You ought to be more careful with your possessions, as I am with mine. I never lose anything,

you know,'' he uttered softly, his voice low and filled
with meaning.

He knows! Geneviève thought guiltily, frightened.
Somehow he knows about Noir and me!

Don't be a fool! a small but sensible voice inside
of her snapped. *How could he? 'Tis a trick. He's trying
to ensnare you again, taking shots in the dark to see
whether they'll find their marks. Get hold of yourself,
Geneviève! Don't let him rattle you, lest you blurt out
things you'll be sorry for later.*

She took a deep breath and turned away so she
would no longer have to face him.

''Thank you,'' she said, glad to hear her voice
sounded entirely normal. She retrieved the earring and
placed it in her jewelry chest. ''I missed it earlier. I was
going to tell you about it in the morning if one of the
servants hadn't found it by then, for I was sure I was
still wearing it when we returned home. Is there''—to
her dismay her voice faltered slightly—''is there something else, Justin?'' she queried nervously when he did
not leave the room.

To her distress, he came up behind her and placed
his hands on her shoulders, filling her with trepidation
as, after a moment, he began to run his fingers through
her unbound tresses.

''I've never seen your hair down before,'' he
murmured huskily in her ear. ''You must wear it that
way more often. Its color, too, is most striking. Why do
you persist in powdering it—especially when 'tis no
longer the fashion?''

''I—I have always done so,'' Geneviève lied.
''The queen—Marie Antoinette, I mean—often did so,
and 'twas the custom in France before the rebellion.''

''I see,'' he breathed, burying his face in the

locks, inhaling deeply the fragrant lily scent that emanated from the silky strands.

Lilies . . . *fleurs de lis*. Ah, yes. Now he had it. *That* was the smell that had prompted the fleeting connection his brain had almost but not quite made between his bride and Rouge that night upon the roof of La Conciergerie. Gently he pressed his mouth to her hair, lightly kissing the satin cascade. Then he turned her around to face him.

Geneviève, her body so tense with anxiety beneath his grasp that she felt as though she would shatter, suddenly could bear no more. Curtly she jerked away from him.

"Please, Justin!" Her voice was brittle. "I'm— I'm afraid you were right; I should never have let Emeline dress my hair in the Quesaco. It has given me the most excruciating headache! So, if there's nothing else . . ."

"Oh, but there is, Genette," he insisted quietly but determinedly. "You see, I am weary of living like a monk, and I mean to put our marriage on a proper footing at last. You have no objections to that, surely. After all, you did agree, did you not, to give me an heir if I so chose?"

"*O-o-oui,*" she stuttered, "but—but I did not realize . . . I mean . . . must it be tonight, Justin? Truly I—I do not feel at all well," Geneviève declared, frantic.

Dieu! She had never dreamed he would want to make love with her after all this time—and she dare not let him touch her! He would surely know, if he took her, that she was no longer a virgin, and God only knew what he would do to her then. Certainly he would force the truth of the matter from her. Afterward, without a doubt, he would forbid her to see Noir again, for had he not just informed her that he never lost any of his possessions? And that was what she was to him, she knew.

"Are you denying me, Genette?" the viscount questioned softly, his tone silkily deceiving. Roughly, without warning, so she had no chance to flee, his hand suddenly shot out and grabbed her by the wrist. Then he snatched her to him, pressing her to his chest, where he could feel her heart pounding violently against his own. "I do not have to take no for an answer, you know," he told her. "You are mine. I can claim you so whenever I choose."

"Will you rape me, then, my lord?" she asked stiffly. "For that is what it shall be, I promise you!"

"Do you think so? Ah, but you would not fight for long, Genette, I swear, for I am far stronger than you, and once I had subdued you, I might take my neckerchief like this"—slowly he drew his silk cravat, which was unknotted, from beneath his collar and trailed it lingeringly over her wrists—"and tie you to the bed. Then I would be free to do with you as I pleased, things beyond your wildest imaginings, Genette." He brushed one side of her face with the scarf. "Things that would drive you mad with wanting," he whispered, his eyes dark with passion.

Cher Dieu! *He* does *know!* Genevieve thought wildly, overwhelmed by guilt and terrified, as well. *Somehow he knows in every detail what happened between Noir and me that night aboard the* Crimson Witch*!*

"*Non!*" she cried sharply. "*Non!* Let me go!"

Desperately she tried to wrench away from him, but still, he held her fast.

"You see?" He lifted one eyebrow demoniacally and laughed at her mockingly, the sound low and animalistic, reminding her crazily of a devil. "You cannot escape from me."

His eyes ravaged her mercilessly, taking in the way in which her hair billowed down about her like a sail in the wind, how the lashes she had closed to avoid his gaze were like two crescent smudges of soot upon her cheeks, the manner in which her lips had parted slightly with her rapid, shallow breathing, how the small pulse at the hollow of her throat beat erratically, and how her ripe, round breasts heaved beneath the translucent fabric of her nightgown.

She was afraid, he realized, but why? Then suddenly he knew the answer. Of course. She was no longer a virgin, and she feared he would discover that fact if he made love with her. A smile quirked at the corners of his lips, and for an instant, he was sorely tempted to tell her that seldom was proof of a woman's innocence as obvious as hers had been, that rarely could a man physically discern the difference between a maiden and a whore. But then he recognized that in pointing out this fact, he would be forced to confront her with the whole of his suppositions, as well, for how else would he know she was not a virgin? She would deny his suspicions, he knew, and he had no tangible evidence with which to make her to admit the truth. He would only give himself away and, by doing so, would lose her in the process, for it was as he had reasoned previously. If he could not compel her to reveal her duplicity, she would dwell on the affair in silence, come to believe he had played her for a fool, and withdraw from him on both fronts. Then he would never learn for certain if she were the smuggler he loved. No, he must be absolutely sure, beyond a shadow of a doubt, that Geneviève and Rouge were one and the same before he accused her of such, and he must have proof of it so she could not fob him off with a lie, but would be forced to acknowledge her love for him.

But in the meantime, he would have a taste of his deceitful bride, the damned elusive, enchanting witch!

Abruptly Justin tossed his neckerchief onto the floor, caught Geneviève's hair with one hand, and ground his mouth down on hers hard. Ah, yes. Yes! Surely these soft, vulnerable lips that trembled beneath his were the lips he had kissed so many times before, the lips that had been so bruised and swollen from his lovemaking that night aboard the *Crimson Witch*. Lingeringly he traced their outline with his tongue, then savagely compelled them to part so he might taste of the honey within. His tongue probed her mouth, seeking out every warm, damp, secret place he knew, with certainty, that he had explored before.

"Sweet . . . sweet," he muttered thickly against her lips.

Geneviève's head spun dizzily, and frantically she struggled against him, filled with shock and disbelief. She had heard those words before, in another time, another world, whispered throatily in French as Noir had kissed her, had claimed her as his own. She loved him! How was it possible, then, that her traitorous body was beginning to respond to her husband? That, even as her fists beat helplessly against his chest, the strength was draining from her limbs, leaving her weak and faint?

Justin's powerful arms slid down her back, crushing her to him and bending her over backward so she would have fallen, she knew, had he not held her so tightly. And still, his mouth went on kissing hers demandingly, forcing her tremulous lips to give way to his violent onslaught upon her senses. She could feel his teeth nibbling her tender mouth, the rough edges of his tongue grazing hers as they met and intertwined, his tongue constraining hers to surrender.

Without her even realizing they did so, her hands at last stilled their futile attack against him; her fists uncurled, and slowly, shaking a little, her fingers crept up to tunnel through his shaggy black hair. Justin's mouth slanted hotly across her cheek to her temples. She could feel his breath, warm and smelling of claret and tobacco, against her face. He blew gently in her ear, murmured words of passion into the small, curved shell, words that made her heart leap with foreboding and a burgeoning feeling of anticipation and excitement, as well.

Non. This wasn't real; this simply could not be happening to her, she thought frenziedly, enveloped by the sense that she had lived through this before.

But still, the heat of his lips scorched her throat and then seared the hollow between her breasts. Before she could become aware of what he intended, he suddenly caught her up in his arms, lifting her easily, as though she were as light as the fairy queen she resembled. Then, striding across the room, he laid her on the bed, the spreading ripples of her hair like a pool of shimmering fire and snow-powdered ice beneath them both as he knelt over her.

Her moss-green eyes locked with his silvery ones, now dark and grey and fathomless, like a misty midnight eve, chilling yet intoxicating. For a swift, pulsating moment, something so strong and electric hovered in the air between them that it was like a tangible thing, igniting them with its intensity. Like an animal that knows it is but a heartbeat from death, her eyes pleaded mutely with him for mercy. But with a low, exultant snarl of triumph, he sprang upon her, his blood singing in his ears, his loins taut with the sweet, agonizing rush of desire.

"*Non*, Justin. Please," Geneviève whimpered, trying once more to fend him off. "*Non*."

But he paid no heed to her soft, pitiful cries as he yanked impatiently at the buttons on his shirt, then reached out and caught the bodice of her negligee, ruthlessly ripping it down to bare her breasts to his all-encompassing gaze. With a keen sigh of pleasure, deliberately he appraised her, noting how of their own accord her rosy nipples puckered and stiffened beneath his ravishing eyes, as though touched by the cold autumn wind that whispered like a ghost against the window, moaning to be let inside.

Inexorably his hands fastened on her breasts, cupping the twin spheres and kneading them lightly with his palms. His fingers tightened on the luscious mounds of flesh until she felt they would burst from the passion that swelled within them. Sensuously his hands glided over them, moving in a wide, languid, circular pattern that gradually focused on the flushed crests at their centers. The feel of his callused palms against the smooth peaks teased them to even greater heights and sent quivers of rapture racing through Geneviève's body as, against her will, she found herself writhing beneath him, straining against his fondling fingers, her blood burning.

Desperately she tried to still her beating heart, the response of her flesh to his expert caresses. But she was young and alive, and Noir had wakened her to the ways of love. Justin was too strong, too relentless in his pursuit of her. She could not fight him, could not rid herself of his presence. Nor could she prevent the budding blossom of desire within her from unfurling its petals beneath his assault upon her.

Groaning, he caught the tip of one breast between his teeth and began to manipulate the little button with his tongue, causing Geneviève's maternal instincts to rise, then to deepen into a feeling even more primitive as he went on sucking her nipple, rolling it between his lips and teeth, laving it with his tongue. Slowly his mouth trailed a path across the valley of her chest, then steadily climbed the other soft mound that beckoned to him so enticingly. While his thumb flicked its mate, his lips closed over the rigid peak, conquering it as easily as he had its twin.

She cried out, tried once more to escape from him, but he only laughed, the harsh, mocking sound grating in her ears. Brutally he tugged down her torn nightgown to a tangle between her legs. Then his hands swept down, pulling the remains of the material away and tossing it aside, so that except for her open wrapper, she lay naked beneath him.

"And now, *ma chère*, I will show you what it means to be a bride," Justin uttered fiercely as he bent over her once again, his eyes hooded so she could not tell what he was thinking.

Geneviève set her teeth into her bottom lip to silence her moans of shame and passion as implacably, after casting away his garments, his knees nudged her shrinking thighs apart, and one hand found the hot, wet chasm of her womanhood nestled between her flanks. Rhythmically he stroked her, his fingers sliding in and out of the enveloping crevice, his thumb teasing the hidden place that was the key to her desire. Geneviève trembled uncontrollably as he explored her, intimately trespassing where only Noir had dared to touch her.

Oh, Noir. Noir!

The words were torn from her throat, only to be muffled and lost as Justin's mouth claimed hers again rapaciously, smothering her sobs. Her head twisted beneath his; her lips sought their freedom, but there was none to be had. His hands tangled themselves roughly in her hair, imprisoning her; for a fleeting eternity, his eyes bored down into hers victoriously. Then he growled low in his throat with triumph, and at last the tip of his maleness found her.

Geneviève gasped sharply as she felt him slide into her, then just as swiftly withdraw, only to thrust into her again and then again. And then all sense of reality spun away, and there was nothing for her but the feel of Justin spiraling down into her savagely, driving from her mind all thoughts but those of him. His fingers gripped her buttocks, compelling her hips to meet his, forcing her to arch against him wantonly.

Outside, the wind rose, howling with a ferocity that equaled his own as he took her, branding himself upon her like a white-hot flame. Horrified, she felt her passion soaring to match his, as though he had unleashed some raging storm within her, and at last her climax came, utterly shattering her. Her nails dug into his back, spurring him on as his own release shook him and his body stiffened, then shuddered violently.

After a time, he withdrew, cradling her in his arms and kissing the salty tears from her cheeks. Petrified now, she waited for him to speak, to accuse her of having betrayed him with another man. But he said nothing, and finally, filled with overwhelming relief, she decided he must not have guessed she had not been a virgin.

At last Justin spoke.

"You see," he told her quietly, "there was naught to fear. You are mine now, *chérie,* in every way."

"*Non.* Not in every way, monsieur," she whispered, once more closing her eyes so she would not have to face him. "For you'll never have my heart, I promise you! What you have done to me this night has ended whatever there might have been between us."

"I do not think so, *amoureuse,*" he breathed. "Indeed, I believe, for us, 'tis only the beginning."

Then, laughing softly at the stricken expression on her countenance, he rolled over on top of her and, pressing her down among the pillows, took possession of her again and then yet a third time until, finally sated, he slept.

Chapter Thirty

When Geneviève awakened the following morning, only the slight indentation upon the pillow beside her remained to tell her that last night had not been a horrible dream, but reality. For a moment, as her eyelids fluttered open, she lay very still, not quite sure why she should have such a sense of impending doom. Then suddenly everything came flooding back, and she wanted to die of shame as she remembered how her husband had made love with her, and how in the end, the third time he had taken her, she had so wantonly surrendered to him, had even begged him to make her his. *Jésus!* The things he had done to her! The things he had forced her to say, to do to him in return! She blushed scarlet with mortification at just the thought of them. She had never dreamed such an—an *animal!* lay beneath Justin's cool, arrogant exterior, a man who had savagely, sensuously, bullied and broken her and bent her to his carnal will. She would never be able to face him again!

Fortunately Geneviève discovered, from a note that lay upon the breakfast tray Emeline brought up, that she would not have to see her husband—at least not this morning anyway. On the single page of the missive, in his bold, flourishing hand, Justin had written that he had been called away on urgent business and would be gone for several weeks.

Despite her vast relief upon learning this, Geneviève could not help but feel a tiny twinge of pique and anger, too, for there was nothing in the letter about last night or anything to indicate his feelings toward her had changed. It was as though, for Justin, the interlude had never occurred, she thought. But then, what had she expected? That he would fall at her feet and declare his love for her? How could she have been such a fool as that? Of course Justin would make no mention of what, to him, had been merely an amusing evening. No doubt he had spent just as many pleasurable nights with one of his whores! That Geneviève was his wife had meant nothing to him. He had gratified his physical desire for her and then had gone on about his affairs.

Well, two could play that game, she decided determinedly. Quickly she rose and dressed, then rang for Ives-Pierre. Once her trusted servant had arrived, she told him to get in touch with Vachel immediately, that she intended to sail the *Crimson Witch* on another foray into France and that they must make further plans. Then resolutely she thrust Justin from her mind, dwelling instead on Noir and wondering if he still loved her, as she did him—now more than ever.

* * *

Like a woman possessed, Geneviève threw herself into her work, hastily making arrangements for another venture into France, despite her brother's protests and his once more suggesting that he take command of the *Crimson Witch*.

"*Non*," she said resolutely. "We've been over this before. You're to handle the financial matters, Vachel. Have you even been down to Papa Nick's theater here in London yet? Have you opened any of those crates he's shipped over here?"

"*Non*," he reported, flushing guiltily. "I've—I've been . . . busy."

"Busy? Doing what?" Geneviève inquired, exasperated.

"Well, I—I met a girl . . . in the country," he confessed at last, "and she's come up to London to see me. I've been meeting her at a teahouse near Covent Garden. 'Tis called the China Cat."

"A girl! Oh, Vachel! Is it serious this time?"

"Well, of course it is. I would scarcely have mentioned her otherwise, Genette." Vachel glanced at his twin with disgust. "One doesn't discuss one's casual affairs with one's sister, after all. But the thing is, Genette . . . well . . . I'm afraid there's going to be the devil of a row, for she's only a common servant—a—a maid. Still, I love her all the same, and I don't intend to give her up—any more than you appear to be inclined to part with that damned spy of yours!"

"He's not a damned spy! He's—he's . . . well, he is a spy, but don't you dare curse him, Vachel! I love him! Oh, *Sainte Marie*, what a mess, what a mess! I'm sure I don't know what Papa and Maman are going to say to either of us, *mon frère*, when they find out what has been going on in their absence," Geneviève declared ruefully. "We don't seem to have managed anything properly."

"*Non,* we don't," Vachel admitted glumly, "which is all the more reason for us to get everything taken care of before they get here. If they're presented with a fait accompli, they'll just have to accept it and make the best of it!"

"*Oui,* that is so," Geneviève agreed.

But in her heart, she knew that, while Vachel might be able to wed a common servant and thumb his nose at society, there was no way she herself could avoid a dreadful scandal if she ran away with a married man. The world into which she had been born would shut its doors firmly in her face and never open them to her again.

But now she no longer cared, for she knew she could not continue to live with Justin after he had taken her and conquered her so thoroughly, seeking only to amuse himself. If he had come to her lovingly, as Noir had done, things might have been different. But Geneviève would be no man's plaything—to do with as he pleased. She had been totally devastated by their lovemaking, while her husband seemed not even to have been moved by it. His abrupt departure without a spoken word had wounded her deeply, and she was certain she hated him.

Lifting her chin proudly, she kissed her brother farewell, then climbed into the phaeton Justin had ordered from Haverill's for her shortly after they'd arrived in London. At her signal, Ives-Pierre clucked to the matched set of showy chestnut horses that had come from Tattersall's, and they started off at a brisk trot toward Brighton, where the *Crimson Witch* would be waiting.

*   *   *

The unfurled sails of the *Black Mephisto* flogged gently as the wind caught and lifted them, sending them billowing like silver clouds against the night sky. Justin Trevelyan, alias Capitaine Diabolique, listened content-edly to the sound as he drew the woman whose head he cradled against his shoulder more closely into the circle of his embrace. Though he called her Rouge, he now knew without a doubt that she was his bride, Geneviève, and for a moment, it was all he could do to keep from blurting out the truth. But still, with difficulty, he held his tongue, for the time was not yet right. He still needed some tangible proof that would compel her to admit to her dual role, and this he would have, he vowed, before returning to England. In the meantime, he comforted himself with the thought that the play they acted, which he had once believed would end as a tragedy, would yet reveal itself as a farce.

He smiled to himself at the notion, then glanced down at Rouge—he simply *must* remember to call her that—in his arms. She looked like a cat, Justin reflected, who had just finished a saucer of cream. Her skin still glowed from their lovemaking, and he trailed one hand idly down her body, enjoying the smooth, satiny feel of her flesh. No, he could not be mistaken. This was indeed the same woman he had taken so savagely two nights ago. He wished he had not had to be so rough with her then, though he had not physically hurt her, of course. But his violent possession of her had been necessary so she would be so frightened she would not connect him with Noir, who had taken her with such tender fury. He had been clever, Justin thought, to play on her guilty conscience by threatening to tie her to the bed, as he had done the first time he'd made love with her. The shocked, culpable expression on her scared countenance at the suggestion alone had assured him she *was* Rouge. Otherwise, he would never have given in to his desire for her.

The morning after officially consummating his marriage, Justin had reluctantly risen and returned to his own room to dress. He'd been descending the stairs when a footman had appeared in the hallway below, bearing a message for him on a silver tray. The viscount had scanned it quickly, then sworn violently under his breath. His friend Parker, after several long weeks of investigation, had finally located Edouard and Lis-Marie. They were being held captive in La Conciergerie by Claude Rambouillet. So far, for reasons unknown, Claude had kept them in isolation instead of having them tried and sentenced to Madame Guillotine. But, Parker had warned, their time was undoubtedly running out.

Justin had immediately sent word to his crew and had driven his curricle posthaste to Brighton, where he'd rendezvoused with the *Black Mephisto* and set sail for France. He'd weighed anchor off the coast of Dieppe and, shortly thereafter, had—not unexpectedly— spied the *Crimson Witch* in the distance, making her way toward France's shore. He'd signaled the sloop with his flag, and after the ship had drawn near and dropped anchor, Rouge's cabin boy had rowed her across to the schooner.

Their reunion had been so joyful and passionate that it had left them both breathless. Now Justin sighed, knowing they dare not linger together any longer this close to shore, where they might be sighted and fired upon by a French patrol boat.

"Rouge, as much as I hate to part with you, 'tis time you returned to your own ship," he stated firmly, kissing the top of her head, "for there is much I must accomplish these next few days. Some . . . relatives of . . . Le Renard are being held prisoner in La Conciergerie." He told her as much of the truth as he dared, for he loved her, and he wanted her to know he had located her parents and would get them safely out of France. "I must make arrangements to rescue them."

Geneviève inhaled sharply at his words, her heart leaping suddenly with hope and fear as she stared at him in the lantern light.

"Who—who are these people?" she asked hesitantly, dreading his answer but knowing she must have it all the same.

"Monsieur le Comte de Château-sur-Mer and his wife," the viscount replied quietly, his heart aching for her as he saw her blanch. "They were attempting to flee the country when a note they had written to Le Renard, begging for his assistance, was somehow intercepted by Claude Rambouillet, a member of the Assembly with whom you yourself are well acquainted," he added dryly, recalling all the hateful letters she had sent to the man. "They were arrested immediately, of course. I do not know why, but Rambouillet has kept them in an isolated cell in La Conciergerie and has yet to bring them to trial. But I will find a way to free them. I swear I shall not let y—Le Renard down."

To hide her churning emotions, Geneviève clenched her trembling hands and fought the sick feeling at the pit of her stomach. *She* knew why Claude had not yet executed her parents. He was still searching for her and meant, if he found her, to demand she share his bed to save their lives.

"Please"—she looked up at Noir's masked face—"let me go with you. Let me help you. I—I would like very much to do something for . . . Le Renard, who has aided me so often in the past."

"*Non.*" Justin shook his head. "I'm sorry, Rouge, but I cannot allow it. 'Twill be too dangerous, and I dare not risk your falling into Rambouillet's clutches. You have taunted him terribly with those mocking poems of yours and made him a laughingstock. *That*, he will never forget or forgive. Even now, there is a price on your head in France, and a fairly accurate sketch of you has been circulated to all the *gardes* and *gendarmes* in Paris."

"How do you know these things?" Geneviève questioned. Then she smiled wryly. "But of course. You are a spy. 'Tis your business to know them, is it not?"

"*Oui.* Trust me, Rouge. This is one time you simply *must* listen to me. I want you to stay here, off the coast of Dieppe. Take the *Crimson Witch* out into La Manche, and wait there with the *Black Mephisto* until I return. Trust me," he repeated insistently. "I love you."

"And I love you," she whispered fervently.

"Then do not venture into France," Justin reiterated urgently. "Stay here and wait for me. Promise me you will!"

"*Oui,* I promise," Geneviève murmured—but she knew it was a vow she would not keep.

Chapter Thirty-one

With the palm-sized stones Edouard and Lis-Marie Saint-Georges held concealed in their hands, they sawed awkwardly but unobtrusively at the ropes that secured their wrists tightly behind them. It had taken them many long weeks to work out the details of their plan and to acquire the necessary implements to carry it out. But now, this late evening, they would see their plot brought to fruition—or they would die trying.

During the endless days of their captivity, they had huddled together for comfort in their solitary cell located near the infamous Rue de Paris in La Conciergerie, and they'd discussed in muted whispers the steps they must take to regain their freedom. It was impossible, they'd thought at first, their hearts sinking, for though they'd searched every crack and cranny of the dark, crumbling cubicle that had contained them, they'd found no means of escape. The two men who'd served as their guards had proved brutal and taciturn and could not be bribed, and at last Edouard and Lis-Marie had clung to each other desperately, knowing that soon they would make that all-too-short journey to the Place de Grève, where they would be executed.

But weeks had passed, and still they'd remained in isolation, had not been brought to trial. They'd been curious to know the reason why. Then finally they'd been enlightened. One afternoon, a man had come to their cell; their iron chains had been removed; their wrists had been bound behind them with thick hemp, and they'd been escorted to the office of Claude Rambouillet, who'd interrogated them unmercifully about their daughter, Geneviève. And so they'd learned of their child's successful escape from France and why their own lives were not yet forfeit.

Hope again had surged within them. After one of their meager meals of thin gruel, they'd confiscated a spoon and hidden it. Fortunately—for such would surely have earned them another vicious beating—its disappearance had not been noticed. Painstakingly, at night, when they'd thought no one would hear, they'd sharpened it against the blocks that formed their rat-infested cell. Then, little by little, they'd gouged two small, sturdy rocks from the decaying walls of the cubicle and honed them with other stones until their edges were as keen as a knife. Then they'd concealed their tools and waited.

Again they'd been summoned before Claude Rambouillet, and, relieved, they'd observed that the same procedure as before was followed. Once in Claude's office, they'd taken careful note of their surroundings and the entrances and exits of the sentries and hirelings who reported to him. Then they'd returned to their cell, certain Claude was not yet done with them.

Now they sat silently in his office, their fingers deftly manipulating the razorlike rocks they'd prepared for this occasion. Claude was so busy shouting at them that he never even noticed their machinations, and there was no one else in the room to point out to him their secretive maneuvers. For this, Edouard and Lis-Marie were very grateful, for they had counted on being alone with their interrogator. Their scheme, in fact, depended on it.

At last they were free. But still, they sat, waiting until Claude had turned his back on them. Then, together, they sprang from their chairs, Edouard tackling Claude and wrestling him to the floor before he could cry out for aid, and Lis-Marie picking up a large heavy bust from his desk and bashing him in the head with it. Ascertaining that Claude was now unconscious— and likely to be so for some time—they dragged him across the floor and stuffed him into the kneehole under his desk so he was hidden from view. Then they tiptoed to the main door of his office and, their hearts pounding violently in their throats, listened quietly to be sure the brief scuffle had not been overheard. Satisfied that it had not, they took up their positions and waited.

Presently a guard knocked on the door and, at Edouard's muffled "Come," entered the room. Quickly, again employing the statue, the comte dispatched the startled man with a blow to the head. Then Lis-Marie hurriedly stripped off his cap and uniform and began to dress herself in his garments. Thirty excruciating minutes later, another sentry appeared, only to meet the same painful fate as his fellow. Luckily he was bigger than the other guard, and his clothes fit Edouard to perfection.

After that, the enterprising Saint-Georgeses calmly walked out the rear entrance of Claude's office to freedom.

Groaning with agony, Claude Rambouillet poured himself another large snifter of brandy, then lay back on the sofa in his apartment. His head was aching horribly, and gingerly he rubbed the sensitive place where he had been struck by the bust the comtesse had wielded so expertly. He had a gash there and a lump so huge he considered himself fortunate he had not been killed. Who would have thought Citoyenne Saint-Georges, weak from her ordeal in prison, would be capable of delivering such a crack? Truly it was a wonder his skull had not split open!

Well, he thought grimly, she would pay for it—and soon, for even now, his men were combing the city, searching for her and her husband, and Claude would make certain they did not escape from him again!

So thinking, he closed his eyes and slept, never even hearing the sound of a window in his bedroom being prised open.

From the rope hanging from the roof of the Hôtel de Ville, Geneviève carefully swung herself into Claude's apartment, entering through his bedroom window, whose sash she had quietly forced open some moments ago with her knife. With a light thud, she landed like a cat upon the floor, where she crouched motionless for an instant, holding her breath as she gazed about the chamber warily, gradually accustoming her eyes to the darkness within and listening intently to be certain her unorthodox ingress had not been heard. At last, sure Claude was unaware of her presence, she crossed the room on tiptoe, the silver moonbeams streaming in through the window lighting her path. Then slowly she opened the door a crack and, after peeping out anxiously, sneaked soundlessly down the hall to the drawing room, where she discovered Claude asleep on the sofa.

Quickly Geneviève checked the rest of the apartment; upon finding it was empty, she realized with relief that Claude had dismissed his servants for the night. She was alone with him.

Methodically she made sure the door to the apartment was bolted, then quietly she dragged a small chest that sat in the foyer over to barricade the entrance. Now, even if Claude shouted for help, it would take the sentries who guarded the *hôtel* some time to break into the apartment.

Then she returned to the drawing room, where, wielding her dagger, she crept deliberately toward Claude's snoring figure.

At the painful prick of the sharp blade against his throat, Claude started violently wide-awake, his arms flailing wildly as he attempted to rise.

"What—what the devil—"

"If you value your life, be silent!" Geneviève hissed, jerking his head back roughly by the hair and reinforcing her warning by jabbing him in the throat with her steel. "And don't make another move, or I swear I'll slit your scurvy throat, you worthless piece of *merde*!"

Though the vulgar, threatening words were more

suited to a man, Claude knew they had been uttered by a woman.

"Who—who are you?" he stammered nervously, for his assailant knelt behind him so he could not see her over the padded arm of the sofa. "What—what do you want?"

"Why, I'm shocked, Claude," Geneviève replied with false dismay, "that you have forgotten me so soon—and when I thought 'twas your most ardent wish to make me your mistress. Do you not know me? 'Twas I who sent you all those witty little poems."

"The Crimson Witch!" Claude gasped grimly. "*Oui,* I thought as much! I even know your true identity, so you needn't think you have been so clever after all . . . Citoyenne Saint-Georges!"

"Ah, so you *did* guess! What a pity, monsieur, for I had hoped to surprise you. But 'tis of little consequence, after all." Geneviève shrugged. "I am Madame la Vicomtesse Blackheath now, you know, for I married *mon cousin,* to whom I was betrothed, you will recall, when you attempted to blackmail me into becoming your paramour. I'm going to kill you, Claude," she uttered softly, "but first, I want to know what you have done with *mes pères.*"

"I'm sure you won't believe me," he began sourly, seeing no point in withholding the information, "but although 'tis true I did have them prisoner in La Conciergerie, they escaped this very evening!"

"You're right," Geneviève announced frostily. "I *don't* believe you! What have you done with them, you filthy *canaille?*" she questioned angrily, yanking his head back savagely again and pricking him with her knife.

"I told you! They escaped! For Christ's sake! I'm

telling you the truth, citoyenne! They managed somehow
to fashion some crude tools out of some stones chipped
from the walls of their cell, and earlier this very night,
while I was interrogating them in my office, they cut
the ropes that bound them and attacked me, knocking
me unconscious with a large bust of Colonel Bonaparte
that I keep on my desk. Then they assaulted two of my
guards, stole their uniforms, and fled. 'Tis the truth, I
tell you! Why, you can feel for yourself the huge lump
upon the back of my head, where your mother hit
me.''

Tentatively Geneviève groped for the spot Claude
had mentioned. Then, upon locating it without difficulty, she started softly to laugh.

"Oh, Claude. Truly you are a fool!" she exclaimed.
"For 'tis not I alone who have bested you, but my
whole family!"

Unfortunately her triumphant mirth proved her
undoing, for, sensing she had relaxed her guard, Claude
suddenly grabbed her wrists, and, twisting them brutally
so she was unable to use her blade against him, he
hauled her over his head onto the sofa. Viciously he
struck her, sending her reeling against the cushions.
Then he sprang upon her ferociously. Frantically she
tried to stab him, but during the ensuing conflict, she
lost her grip on her steel, and the dagger tumbled with a
dull, ominous thud to the Turkish carpet that covered
the floor. Fully aware of her now-desperate circumstances, Geneviève struggled furiously against him,
but Claude was surprisingly strong for a man of his
emaciated build, and presently he managed to subdue
her.

"Now, you conceited little whore," he spat, panting
for breath as he stared evilly at her masked face, "I'm

going to teach you a lesson you shan't soon forget, and since you're so smart, you shouldn't have any trouble learning it!''

Cruelly wrapping one hand in her long hair, which had come loose from its queue during their fight, he ripped open her domino and shirt, tearing madly at the fabric that bound her breasts. When he had finally managed to free the full, ripe mounds, he pressed his mouth to one nipple hotly. He was so excited that Geneviève could actually feel him slobbering on her flesh. She thought she would die as she pummeled his back mercilessly with her fists, but to no avail. He would not be budged. At last, recognizing the futility of her actions, she let her arms fall lamely to her sides, biting her lip with anguish as Claude squeezed her breasts, grazing their tender, cringing peaks with his teeth.

Geneviève writhed in torment beneath him, her body shrinking from his touch, her hands spread wide, her fingers clawing at the rug as she struggled to wriggle out from under him. Suddenly her fingertips touched something hard and sharp. *Sacrebleu!* Was that her knife?

Oh, Sainte Marie, *please let it be so,* she prayed fervently.

Compelling herself to concentrate solely on the blade, she reached down and out as far as she could with her left hand, and finally her fingers just closed around the hilt of her weapon. Her palms damp with sweat, she then forced herself to wait, to suffer Claude's advances in torturous silence as she watched eagerly for her chance.

At last he half rose, drawing back to unfasten her breeches and tug them down about her knees. He was so aroused by his desire for her and so engrossed in trying to strip off her pantaloons that he never even noticed the glittering length of silver steel Geneviève brought up and drove deeply into the side of his neck.

Blood gushed from his jugular vein, spraying warm and wet and sticky upon Geneviève's flesh as, with an expression of shock and horror, Claude stared at her, then slowly toppled to the floor, his beady black eyes glaring up at her accusingly in death.

"Papa Nick! Papa Nick!" Justin's voice echoed in the stillness as he glanced warily about the large, dark theater. But there was no response, and, frowning with puzzlement, he threaded his way slowly across the disordered stage to his grandfather's office. "Papa Nick!" he called again, rapping urgently on the door, but still, there was no reply, and finally the viscount turned the knob and went in.

The office, too, was empty and in complete disarray, as though its contents had been hurriedly rifled and then abandoned. Books and manuscripts and other assorted papers lay scattered about on the desk and floor, and boxes of files had been opened and their contents dumped out haphazardly. A single oil lamp was burning brightly, as though someone, in his haste, had forgotten to extinguish it.

What on earth had happened here? Justin wondered anxiously. Had Papa Nick's furtive activities been discovered by the authorities? Had they come to take him captive, or had he managed somehow to flee? The viscount didn't know. Still, it was obvious that something untoward had occurred, and he knew he must find out what it had been—and soon, if he were to save his relatives from Madame Guillotine.

Well, there was plainly nothing here that would be of help to him. He would go to Papa Nick's apartment and see what he could learn.

So thinking, Justin crossed the room and bent to blow out the lamp that sat upon his grandfather's desk. It was then that he observed the small envelope propped against the light's glass base. It was addressed simply to Capitaine La Folle, but the viscount paid no heed to this as he hurriedly ripped it open and scanned the missive within, which read:

> *Dear Capitaine La Folle:*
>
> *I have gone to England to visit my ENTIRE family. I quite strongly suggest you do the same.*
>
> > *All my love,*
> > *Le Renard*
>
> *P.S.   In case you haven't figured it out yet, you dear child, your husband, Justin, and your lover, Noir, are one and the same. I simply couldn't go on letting you think otherwise!*
>
> *P.P.S. Capitaine Diabolique, what do you mean by reading other people's mail?*

Upon reading this last line, Justin threw back his head and howled with amusement. He laughed until the tears ran down his cheeks. Then finally he sobered and reread the letter thoughtfully. Obviously Papa Nick had employed great care in writing it so as not to reveal Geneviève's identity or their relationship to each other, should the note, by some mishap, have fallen into the hands of the French authorities. Also, the fact that the word *entire* had been printed in capital letters gave the viscount pause. What could his grandfather possibly have been attempting to relay to Geneviève and him? Justin wondered, for it was obvious the missive had been intended for his own eyes, as well. Suddenly he had it.

Of course! Somehow Uncle Edouard and Aunt Lis-Marie had managed to escape and were even now on their way to England with Papa Nick—and doubtless Vachel, too! It was probably they who had torn up Papa Nick's office in their haste to collect various documents vital to their business affairs. Naturally they'd not dared to leave the valuable papers behind, and Papa Nick had had them stored here in the theater, the viscount knew. There had been time to write only one letter, he surmised, and so his grandfather had addressed it to Geneviève, knowing full well that his grandson eventually would read it, too.

Justin tucked the missive into the breastpocket of his domino, then blew out the lamp. He must get back to the *Black Mephisto* as quickly as possible.

He was halfway across the stage, headed toward the door, when, without warning, it was suddenly flung open wide. To his horror, his wife staggered in, sobbing and gasping for breath, her clothes torn and bloody, her face white with shock.

"Noir!" she whispered, then nearly collapsed.

"Rouge!" he cried, running to assist her as, weakly, she clutched the doorjamb for support. "*Mon Dieu!* What has happened? What are you doing here? *Jésus Christ!* You've been hurt!"

"*Non.*" She shook her head, stumbling blindly

toward his outstretched arms. " 'Tis Claude's blood. I've—I've *murdered* him! We must get out of here—and now! My—Renard's relatives have escaped and fled, so you need not rescue them, after all. I'm sure they are even now on their way to England—as we must be, too, if we do not wish to be taken captive. The *gardes* from the Hôtel de Ville are hot on my trail!"

"Then come!" Justin said, grasping her hand tightly and pulling her out into the darkness.

Chapter Thirty-two

Slowly Geneviève stepped out of the bathtub in Noir's cabin aboard the *Black Mephisto* and, sighing with pleasure, made no attempt to stir from his arms as gently he drew her into the circle of his embrace and began to towel her dry, his hands lingering on her breasts and thighs.

"You are a fool, Rouge," he breathed as he caressed her trembling form, realizing how close he had come to losing her forever. "I told you to stay behind, and you promised me you would!"

"I know," she replied, biting her lip, "but I—I just couldn't. Oh, Noir! I want you so! Hold me! Make love with me! I love you, you know."

"*Oui*, I know."

Wordlessly he led her to his bed, his heart beating with joy and yearning as he gazed down at her lying there, waiting for him, her arms outstretched to him in passionate invitation. Slowly he undressed, loving the way her moss-green eyes watched him from behind her mask, roaming over his now-naked body with obvious delight and admiration.

How she loved him! Geneviève thought, studying the crisp black curls that matted his dark chest and tapered down his firm, flat belly to his hardening manhood below. Blushing a little as she recognized where her gaze had strayed, she lifted her eyes once more to his masked face and smiled as he sank down beside her and gathered her into his arms.

His kiss was all she could have wished—and more. His mouth moved gently on hers, his tongue following tenderly the outline of her lips before parting them to caress the sweetness within. Eagerly her tongue intertwined with his as she strained against his hands that fondled her breasts, arousing her in all the ways that pleased her best. His kiss deepened, became more demanding as wantonly she undulated beneath him, seeking to draw him even nearer. Her hands intertwined with the strands of his glossy black hair, stroking the wings of silver at his temples, then creeping down his neck to his broad back. Her fingers dug into his skin; she loved the feel of his muscles as they bunched and rippled beneath her palms, making her breathlessly aware of his strength and her own weakness in comparison.

The powerful arms that clutched her to him could easily have crushed the very life from her instead of molding her to fit his shape, filling her with a desire that intensified unbearably as he took one rosy nipple into his mouth and began to tantalize it with his tongue. Circles of pleasure radiated through her being, making her feel like quicksilver in his warm embrace.

Deep in her throat, she moaned her surrender as one of his hands swept down to part her flanks, finding the dark, moist core of her, turning her to molten lava as, sensing her suddenly urgent readiness to receive him, he poured himself into her, carrying them both on a sea of passion to the edge of the world—and beyond. Then there was nothing for her but the furious thrumming of their hearts sounding now like breakers crashing upon a beach, then gently slowing like waves turning with the tide to drift back out into the ocean.

After a time, he kissed her and withdrew, turning over and pressing her head against his shoulder.

"Come away with me, Rouge," he entreated earnestly in the stillness, some small demon of doubt making him yearn to discover just how much she truly loved him. "I will make you happy, I swear!"

"Oh, Noir, you don't know how much I long to do just that!" she cried softly. "But there are so many things that stand in my way—and yours—so many people who will be hurt—"

"*Non,* there are only the two of us," he insisted. "Now and forever. You know that is all that matters! Come away with me, Rouge, I beg of you."

But though her heart was in her eyes, she did not answer, and at last they slept. But Geneviève's slumber was troubled, and finally she awoke to gaze quietly at the man resting so peacefully by her side. She loved him! How could she not do as he asked?

As though he sensed her distress, his eyelids fluttered open, and once more he made love with her in the moonlit cabin, urgently, as though he feared perhaps it were the last time. Melodiously the song of him played on her heartstrings, echoing sweetly through her being, and she knew then that she could not part from him, though she damned her soul to hell for all eternity for loving him.

"Well, Rouge," he muttered against her lips, "will you come away with me or not?"

"*Oui*," she responded fiercely. "*Oui, mon cher*. I will come."

"Then meet me off the coast of Brighton in two days' time—just before midnight," he urged, knowing neither one of them would keep the appointment, that he would tell her the truth about them both, once they'd reached the townhouse in London. But he would warn his men of the proposed meeting, nevertheless, just in case his wife decided not to return to the city before joining him aboard the *Black Mephisto*. "That should give you and your crew enough time to deliver the stolen goods you smuggle into England," he explained. He paused for a moment, then he continued. "I love you, Rouge. I have always loved you, only you. No matter what happens, never forget that, *ma chère*."

Then, before she could respond to these cryptic words, he sealed her lips with a kiss that drove from her mind all thoughts but her love for him.

BOOK FIVE

Curtain Call

Chapter Thirty-three

London, England, 1792

"I'm—I'm leaving you, Justin," Geneviève said quietly to her startled husband as she descended the stairs to the hallway of their townhouse, her portmanteau in hand. "I—I know 'tis very sudden and 'twill doubtless cause a terrible scandal, but I—I just can't help it. I've been . . . very unhappy ever since our wedding day, and there's—there's . . . someone else in my life, besides. I love him! And I can no longer live without him."

"I see," the viscount drawled slowly, his eyes hooded so she could not read his thoughts. "Well, I must admit this is . . . quite a surprise," he lied, stifling, with effort, the smile of triumph and admiration that threatened to curve his lips as his glance raked her hungrily, taking in her unbound, unpowdered hair and her face devoid of paint and patches.

Mentally he imposed a mask over her beautiful, aristocratic features, fully revealed to him for the first

441

time since their marriage. He inhaled keenly with appreciation, realizing at last how much she resembled his lovely mother and his striking aunt. Then silently Justin cursed her soundly for the wicked trick she had played on him. If he had seen her looking like this to begin with, the entire misunderstanding between them would never have happened, for he would have loved her from the start, he knew. Once more he veiled his eyes.

"Why don't we go into the drawing room, Genette," he suggested, "where we can discuss your leaving in privacy. After all, at this juncture, I am *still* your husband, and I think I'm entitled to a better explanation than the one you have just given me. There are some things, as well, that I feel I must tell you before you embark on this . . . impetuous course you have chosen."

She shook her head.

"There's no use in trying to dissuade me, Justin," she insisted, "for my mind is quite made up. Now, if you'll kindly move aside, I'll be on my way."

"Genette, if you think I'm simply going to stand here while you walk out of my life, you're mistaken," the viscount growled. "As I mentioned to you previously, I've got some extremely important things to say to you, and 'twould be in your best interests to hear them. Now, will you come into the drawing room? Or must I embarrass you before the entire household by forcibly dragging you inside?"

Geneviève's green eyes flashed at him dangerously for a moment, reminding him so hauntingly of the way she had looked as Rouge that it was all he could do to keep from ravishing her right there in the hallway. With difficulty, Justin restrained himself, opening the doors for his bride as, recognizing that he did indeed mean to carry out his threat if she didn't comply with his demand, she lifted her chin haughtily and wordlessly preceded him into the drawing room.

He had no sooner closed the doors, however, than the butler, Chilton, knocked and entered, interrupting them.

"I'm sorry to disturb you, my lord," Chilton intoned to the viscount, "but an urgent message has arrived for you from Lady Northchurch, and it requires an immediate reply."

Hastily Justin read the letter, than sat down at a nearby secretary to dash off a response. Once he had finished, he sealed the note and handed it to Chilton for prompt delivery to the Trevelyans' London townhouse. Then he turned to address Geneviève, a wide smile on his face as he thought of how happy the news he had just learned was going to make her.

To his dismay, the far doors leading to his study stood open, and the drawing room was empty. Damn! While his back had been turned, his enchanting, errant wife had fled!

The grand reunion of the Trevelyans and the Saint-Georgeses, who had escaped safely to England, along with Papa Nick, had been in progress for well over an hour when Justin arrived at his parents' townhouse. He was admitted to the drawing room by Danesfield, the butler, and after the doors had closed behind him, the viscount immediately crossed the room to greet his tired relatives.

"Oncle Edouard! Tante Lis-Marie!" He hugged them both close. "How very happy I am to find you both here and well!"

"And what about me, Justin?" Nicolas Dupre asked, grinning. "Aren't you glad to see your poor grandfather, too?"

"I have some reservations about you, Papa Nick, you old rascal!" Justin retorted tartly, but he embraced the elder man tightly all the same.

"But . . . where is Genette?" Lis-Marie inquired anxiously, once all the amenities were out of the way and the story of the Saint-Georgeses' flight from France had been recounted at some length. "Was she not at home when Dominique's message arrived?"

"*Oui*, she was there," Justin replied, "but I fear I had no opportunity to tell her you had reached London. 'Tis a long story, so, please . . . make yourselves comfortable, and give me a chance to explain. It all started with some rather harsh words of mine, which Genette inadvertently overheard—"

At that point, Danesfield knocked upon the drawing-room doors, interrupting the tale the viscount had barely begun.

"I'm sorry, my lord." Danesfield spoke to Lord Northchurch. "But a message has arrived for her ladyship . . . the countess, I mean . . . Lady Northchurch, that is, not Madame la Comtesse de Château-sur-Mer," he elucidated with some confusion as he gazed at the two women. "It is marked urgent, so I thought her ladyship would want to read it at once."

"*Oui*, of course," Dominique stated, then broke the seal to scan the contents of the missive. "*Bon Dieu!*" she cried, leaping to her feet. "Oh, my poor son! My poor, poor son! I simply cannot credit it. 'Tis from Genette. I fear—I fear she has—she has *run away* with that notorious spy they call the Black Mephisto!"

"Jesus Christ!" Justin expostulated. "Why must females always leave a damned note behind?"

Before he had a chance to apologize and to explain this rather odd statement that was not at all the response his agitated mother had expected, the drawing-room doors were suddenly flung open again, and this time, the abigail Rose burst into the room.

"Oh, my lady!" she shrieked, drawing up short and panting for breath. "Oh, my lady, I'm—I'm so sorry to interrupt, but—but—Lud, save us!" She held out a visibly shaking hand that contained a rather lengthy letter. "Miss Mannering has eloped!"

"Kitty! Eloped!" Dominique exclaimed disbelievingly. *"Non!* It cannot be!"

"There! What did I tell you!" the viscount uttered triumphantly. "They always leave a note! 'Tis like some damned conspiracy or something!"

This churlish lack of consideration for her overwrought nerves proved too much for Lady Northchurch, and, quite overcome, she promptly swooned. It was some time before her sister, Lis-Marie, managed to arouse her with a vial of smelling salts, and even then, Dominique declared she did not think she was going to survive much longer, that her heart had received too many shocks all at once.

"Nonsense, my dear," Lord Northchurch dismissed this news gruffly. "I'm sure we shall get matters all straightened out in a trice."

"Oh, William, I do not see how," the countess insisted, dabbing with her handkerchief at her tearstained eyes. "For here is our precious Genette run off with a spy and our darling Kitty eloped with a common criminal. This spy at least I have heard of, you understand."

Dominique sniffed disdainfully. "But this—this *cow* person I do not know at all."

"*Cow* person?" the earl inquired, confused.

"Well, *oui*. That is what the letter says, William," the countess asserted. "See here. Read it for yourself if you do not believe me. Kitty, my darling Kitty, has absconded with a disreputable man known only as the French Cow, and she claims we need not worry that he is only after her money, for *he* thinks *she* is Prinda, the parlormaid, whoever that may be. I just do not understand any of it all! *Sainte Marie!* The French Cow!" Dominique wailed, bursting into tears again and once more collapsing on the sofa.

"Good Lord!" Justin swore, clapping one hand to his forehead in sudden enlightenment. "*Vachel! That* was how Genette managed to be in two places at once. How could I have been such a fool as not to have figured it out. My God! *Vachel!* Oh! Just wait until I get my hands on that deceptive little witch!"

"Yes, I certainly think you should have been a trifle more astute, Justin," Lord Northchurch pointed out dryly, "for I told you, did I not, that Vachel, the incorrigible scamp, was bound to show up sooner or later—and in disguise, too!"

"Oh, *oui*. He has been here for months," Nicolas put in, causing everyone to glare at him censuringly for not volunteering this information sooner.

"There now, my dear." The earl patted his wife's hand soothingly. "Dry your tears. I told you we would straighten everything out, did I not? And so we have. Genette has not left Justin, for Justin is the Black Mephisto, only Genette does not know that—that he's Justin, I mean. She thinks the Black Mephisto is Capitaine Diabolique, a man she calls Noir. And Kitty has not run off with a crook, but with your nephew, Vachel, for Vachel—which means 'little cow' in French, as well you know—is no doubt the highwayman who held up the coach that night in Devon when Kitty pretended she was only a maid. It all seems quite plain to me."

"William," Dominique began, a martial light now glinting in her eye. "Lean down here, please, for I would like very much to box your ears!"

"And so you shall, my dear, just as soon as I have fetched Kitty and Vachel home, for I have no doubt they are currently en route to Gretna Green, and I must stop them so they can return to London for a proper wedding." He looked at his son impatiently. "Well, what are you just standing there for, Justin? I would suggest you go after your wife immediately. And for heaven's sake!—this time, tell the dear girl the truth!"

"Well!" the countess remarked indignantly, once her husband and her son had departed without another word of explanation. "It seems 'tis not only those idiots in France who have run mad, but the entire world, as well! I have no proof, of course"—she paused, leaned forward conspiratorially toward the three remaining occupants of the room, then went on adamantly—"but, depend upon it! There is something in the water!"

Chapter Thirty-four

Geneviève sat, waiting somewhat anxiously, in Noir's cabin aboard the *Black Mephisto*. The ship lay at anchor in the English Channel, just off the coast of Brighton, not half a league from the *Crimson Witch*, which Geneviève intended should follow her and Noir wherever they chose to travel. They would doubtless never return to England or to France, she thought, but what did that matter when there was a whole world out there waiting for them?

She bit her lip and glanced nervously at the little ormolu clock ticking on Noir's desk. He was late, she realized, for it was nearly two o'clock in the morning; and she wondered if perhaps he'd changed his mind, if he was not coming, after all. Still, his crew had been expecting her, and they had not demurred when, after being rowed over by Ives-Pierre in one of the dinghies from her sloop to the schooner, she had demanded to be taken aboard. *Non*. Noir would come. He must, for there was no way she could ever go back to Justin now, not after the things she had told him. Thank God she had managed to get away while his back had been turned, before he could interrogate her and learn the whole! No doubt he would have been so angry he would have handed Noir over to the French authorities and beaten her black and blue. She shivered at the thought. *Non*. She was not sorry she had left him. Her one and only regret, Geneviève knew, was that she had not been able to make certain her parents had reached England safely, that she had not been given a chance to bid them goodbye. But Vachel would send word to her, for Ives-Pierre would serve as their liaison, and if her parents had not escaped from France, she would continue her efforts to locate them.

A sound in the passageway interrupted her musings, informing her that Noir had arrived at last, and joyfully she rushed to greet him as he entered the cabin.

"You came!" she cried. "Oh, *mon cher, mon amoureux!* You came!"

"But of course," he said, enveloping her in his arms and kissing her passionately. "Did you think I would not, sweetheart? Stand back. Take off that damned mask and let me look at you. There's no need to hide your identity from me any longer, for I know who you are now—Madame la Vicomtesse Blackheath, Geneviève Angèle Saint-Georges Trevelyan," he announced. When, slightly startled, she made no reply, he continued coaxingly. "That *is* who you are, isn't it? Or are you denying it, Rouge?"

"*Oui. Non.* I—I mean . . . how do you know 'tis so?" she questioned lamely.

"I found this at Le Renard's theater in Paris," he explained, withdrawing Papa Nick's letter to her from his breastpocket. " 'Twas addressed to you, but I read it nevertheless, for I feared some ill had befallen him.''

"Let me see it," she demanded, a little frightened that Noir had learned her real name, for she had wanted to keep her secret a little longer, at least until they were well away from England and he could not send her back to Justin.

"*Non*. Not so fast, Madame la Vicomtesse," Noir told her, snatching the note from her outstretched fingers and replacing it in his pocket. "Now that I know who you are, I want you to remove your mask and let me see your face.''

Hesitantly, seeing no further reason to protest, since it seemed he had incontrovertible proof of her identity, Geneviève untied the crimson silk device, feeling almost naked in his presence without it. Then defiantly she tossed it aside.

"Now you," she urged softly.

"In a moment, *ma chère*," Noir told her. "I want to look at you; you are beautiful, you know," he said, remembering how gorgeous she had appeared standing in the hallway of their townhouse in London. "I love you very much, Rouge. Remember that when you see my own face. But, first, there are some things I must do before revealing myself to you."

So saying, he stepped behind his washstand, the back of whose huge mirror blocked him from Geneviève's view.

"What are you doing?" she queried anxiously, curious and feeling a little twinge of sick apprehension at his cryptic words. Was he about to show her his true self, only to inform her that he could not run away with her, after all? " 'Tis not fair of you to ask me to take off my mask, then refuse to remove your own!"

"*Oui,* I know, but I have to get rid of my disguise, as well," he elucidated, to her surprise, peeling off his false mustache and throwing it on the bed.

Geneviève stared at the fake bristles, stunned and growing faintly excited as she recognized that she had never seen Noir as he really was. He had fooled her as cleverly as she had Justin! There then came the sounds of water splashing in the basin, and presently a cloth streaked with grey dye followed the mustache. Then finally a black silk loo mask lay upon the bed.

"Are you ready?" Noir inquired teasingly.

"*Oui!* Hurry up!" Geneviève replied eagerly.

"All right. I am ready to unveil my true identity," he confessed. "But, first, you must promise me one thing, Rouge-Genette! You must absolutely swear that you will never again wear anything upon your head but a very small, plain hat!"

"Justin!" she shrieked disbelievingly as he came around the washstand. "Justin! You—*you* are Noir!"

"Yes, my dear," he announced coolly in his most English manner. "I'm afraid I am." Then passionately he declared in flawless French, the language of love, "And, oh, *ma chère, mon amoureuse!* How I thank God that I am!"

EPILOGUE

The Encore

Chapter Thirty-five

The High Seas, 1792

Justin had at last exlained to Geneviève the whole truth
of their tangled affair, informed her that her parents
were safely in London, and told her about Vachel and
Kitty.

Now the two masquers, whose roles had finally
ended, lay in each other's arms, their hearts soaring
with joy and filled to overflowing with their deep,
abiding love for each other.

Outside, the cold, winter-tinged wind whispered to
the sails of the *Black Mephisto* and the *Crimson Witch*,
sending them billowing like silver clouds across the
starry night sky. The sea slapped gently against the
hulls of the vessels as, like twins—or lovers—they
sliced through the water, rising and falling magnificently
upon the whitecapped waves.

"I think I must have loved you from the very
beginning," Geneviève admitted softly to her husband.
"I think I have always loved you, from the time I was a
child, and you were so beastly to me."

"Well, I had to be, Genette," he teased, smiling down at her lovingly. "For i' faith, you were a shrew! But I have tamed you at last, my sweet Katherine, have I not?" he asked a trifle suspiciously.

"*Oui!* But of course, *mon cher* Petruchio! You have!" she lied, wanting to allay his doubts, for there must always be a part of her that remained unconquered to intrigue him and to keep him interested. It was a secret as old as time and known to every woman who had ever loved a man. "Now, what will you do with me, monsieur, I wonder?" she asked, her eyes veiled and a small smile lurking upon her mouth.

"Why, make love to you, of course," he murmured, bending his head to kiss her.

She grinned mischievously at that. Then, deftly eluding his lips, she slid from his warm embrace and slipped off the bed they shared.

"You'll have to catch me first, you know," she said, darting away.

"Genette! *Genette!*" Justin cried, astonished. "Just what do you think you are doing? Come back here, you minx! *Par Dieu!* Just you wait until I get my hands on you!" he exclaimed. "I'll tie you to the bed again, and this time, I'll keep you there for days, you witch!"

"Oh, Justin, you devil," she called back laughingly over her shoulder, "do hurry up and catch me, for this time, my love, I can hardly wait!"

Author's Note

The reader who is acquainted with modern Paris is bound to be curious about some of the locations in that city as described in this novel, for many are today much changed.

La Conciergerie currently serves as a wing of the Palais de Justice; and the small cell for important prisoners, where Queen Marie Antoinette, after being removed from the Temple, was incarcerated until her death, was, in 1816, converted by the royal couple's only remaining daughter, the Duchess of Angoulême, into a chapel and may be visited today.

The Place Dauphine, built in 1607, formerly contained a continuous triangular building of red brick houses ornamented with white stone, around which were various of the ancient trees that one may see everywhere in Paris. In 1871, the row of houses and trees along the side of La Conciergerie was demolished to expose the remodeling that had been completed on the Palais de Justice, but both did exist when Justin used one of the trees to gain access to the roof of La Conciergerie.

The Place de Grève, as it was known during Justin and Geneviève's time, is the square in which one can still today find the Hôtel de Ville (now City Hall); it was not until 1830 that the square's name was changed to the Place de L'Hôtel de Ville. It was here that the hideous instrument known as Madame Guillotine was first erected and that many of the executions during the French Revolution took place. For the beheading of King Louis XVI, however, the guillotine was moved. Some accounts give the Place de la Concorde (then known as the Place Louis Quinze) as his place of execution (near the current statue of Brest). Others give the Place de la Republique, just north of Le Marais, as his place of execution. These accounts also state that four months after his death, the guillotine, which had been moved back to the Place de Grève, was returned to the Place de la Concorde and erected near the gates of the Jardin des Tuileries. Approximately 1,343 beheadings are said to have taken place at this spot, with a like number of deaths occurring in various other parts of Paris.

Of the beautiful, Gothic church Saint Jacques la Boucherie, built between the years 1508 and 1522, all that remains is the original tower, known as La Tour Saint Jacques. Sadly, the rest was destroyed in 1797.

The Place des Victoires, where the *hôtel* of Geneviève's parents was located (fictionally, of course) still exists, and one may still view numbers 4 through 12 of these lovely old townhouses, which are now primarily small shops. Unfortunately the appearance of the others has been so altered over the centuries that they no longer resemble the rest.

During Justin and Geneviève's time, the Rue Saint Honoré was the main street along the north shore of the River Seine. Construction of the Rue de Rivoli did not begin until Napoleon was created emperor of France.

Château-sur-Mer, Port-d'Or, Le Théâtre Dupré, and, in England, Northchurch Abbey and Blackheath Hall, all exist solely in the author's imagination.

Marie Grosholtz, who made the death masks of many of the victims of Madame Guillotine, is doubtless better known to the reader as Madame Tussaud. Her mentor, Dr. Curtius, died in 1794, leaving her sole heir to his famous wax exhibition. In 1795, she married François Tussaud, and in 1802, she moved to England, taking thirty wax figures with her. There, in London, at the Lyceum Theatre, Madame Tussaud set up her exhibition. In 1835, at the age of seventy-four, after endless touring, she established her exhibition permanently in London at The Bazaar in Baker Street. After her death and the death of her eldest son, Joseph, her grandson, Joseph Randall Tussaud, moved the exhibition to its current location on Marylebone Road. Now known as Madame Tussaud's Wax Museum, it is still open to the public, and in the infamous Chamber of Horrors, one may still view, along with that of Robespierre, the death masks of King Louis XVI and Queen Marie Antoinette, as well as the actual guillotine blade that beheaded the royal couple. The author has seen this exhibition, and she assures her readers that it is, indeed, quite gruesome. Although the Tussaud name has been adopted by various other wax exhibitions, today the only two genuine Madame Tussaud's Wax Museums are located in London and Amsterdam.

The words *joli rouge*—pretty red—that Geneviève used to describe the flag on Justin's schooner was an expression ironically employed by the French for the bloodred banner flown by many earlier pirates. It is from this term, it is sometimes claimed, that our own expression "Jolly Roger" was derived.

The author would like to thank her dear friend Patricia Maxwell, better known as author Jennifer Blake, for providing her with the original name of the Place de la Concorde.

The author would also like to thank her friend and fan Prinda Taylor, of Springfield, Missouri, for the use of her lovely, unusual first name.

Rebecca Brandewyne

About the Author

Rebecca Brandewyne was born in Tennessee, but she has lived most of her life in Kansas. She has a Bachelor's Degree in journalism, Minors in music and history, and a Master's Degree in communications. Before becoming a writer, she taught interpersonal communication at the university level. She still resides in the Midwest, with her husband, vocalist/musician Gary Brock (with whom she composes songs), and their son, Shane Alexander Brock. Her favorite pastimes are reading, playing the guitar, belly dancing, and horseback riding.

Dear Reader,

I wanted to take this opportunity to thank you for buying my book. I hope you had as much fun reading this lighthearted change of pace from my usual style as I had writing it.

I deeply appreciate the fact that you, the reader, have given all my novels such a wonderful reception, and I always love hearing from you. You can write to me in care of Warner Books, Inc., 666 Fifth Avenue, New York, N.Y. 10103. Your letters will be forwarded to me, and I will respond as soon as I can.

I hope I will continue to bring you many hours of enjoyable reading in the future. I am currently working on a trilogy for Warner Books, Inc., that will detail the lives and loves of three strong, passionate women. The first book, the story of Maggie Chandler, will be released in 1988.

Till then, happy reading!

Rebecca Brandewyne